THE STARS AMID THE STORM

AMBER D. LEWIS

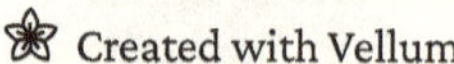 Created with Vellum

To ________________, thank you for sticking with me on this journey. We did it. We fucking did it.

ALSO BY AMBER D. LEWIS
RECOMMENDED READING ORDER

CONTINENT MAP

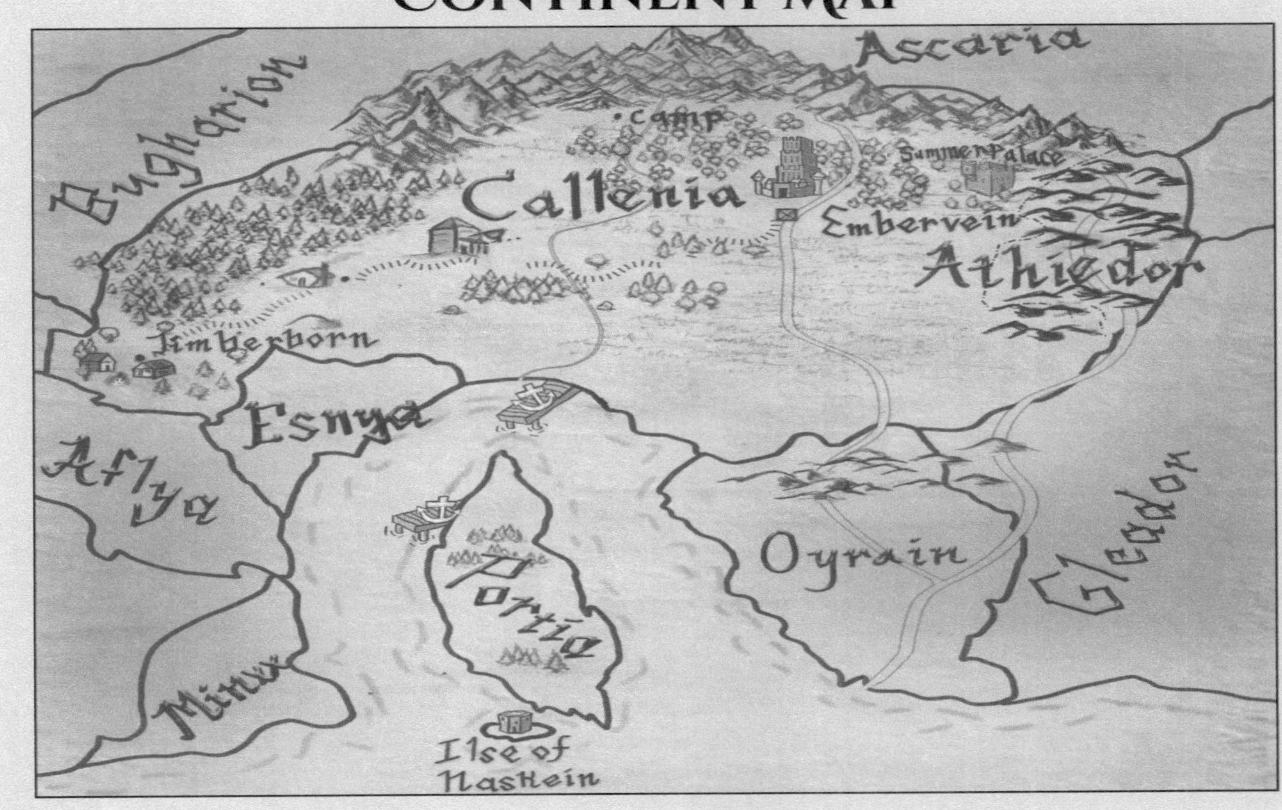

MAP OF ATHIEDOR

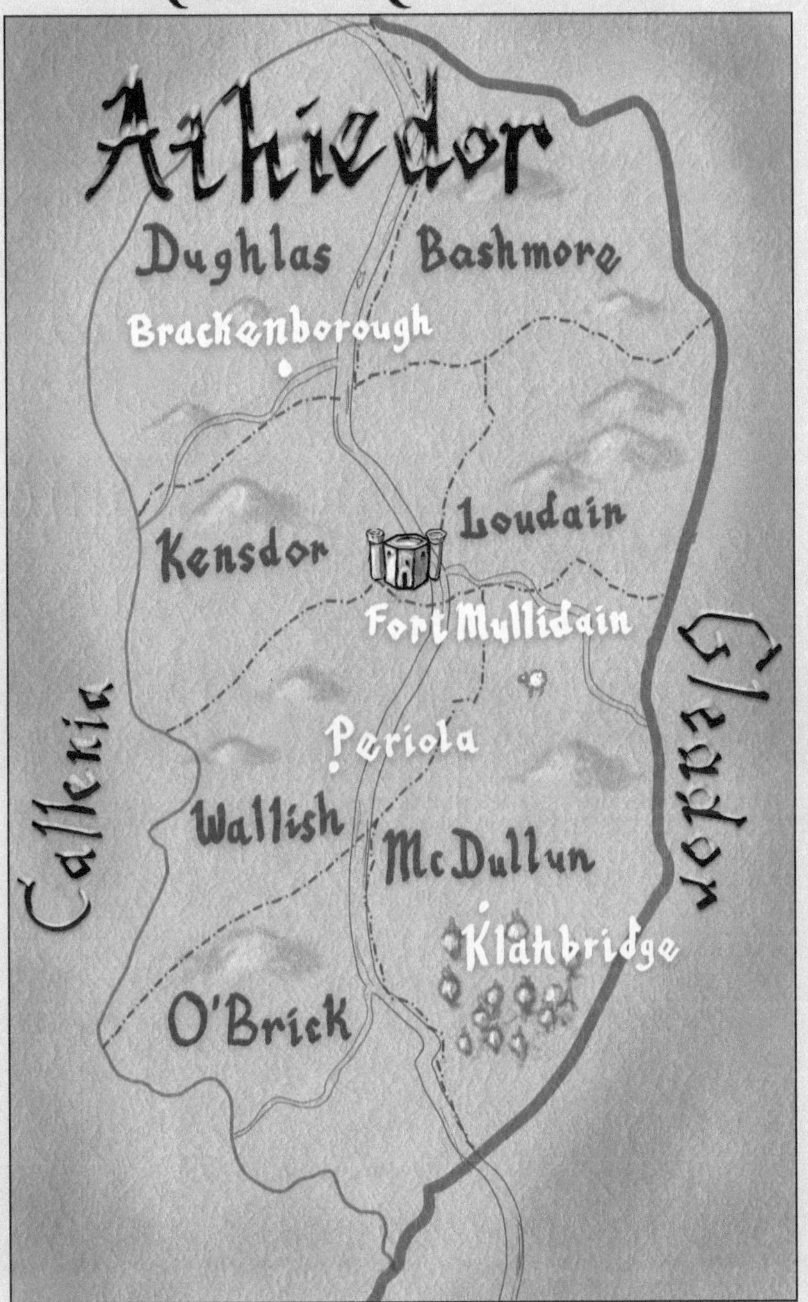

THE EDGE OF THE WORLD

Character Pronunciation Guide

Aine:	än-yā (Awn-yay)
Alak:	æl-ik (Al-ick)
Arcanis:	ar-kā-nis (Ar-kay-nis)
Astra:	æs-truh (Ash-truh)
Bram:	bræm (Bram)
Cadewynn:	kad-u-win (Kad-uh-win)
Caitlyn:	kāt-lin (Kate-lin)
Cal:	kæl (Kal)
Ehren:	eh-ruhn (Air-un)
Eleni:	ē-län-ē (Ee-law-nee)
Felixe:	fē-liks (Fee-licks)
Hycis:	hī-cis (High-cis)
Iefyr:	īf-er (Ief-ur)
Ievis	īv-is (Iev-iss)
Jessalynn:	jes-u-lin (Jes-uh-lin)
Kaeya:	kī-uh (Kie-uh)
Kai:	kī (Kie)
Kato:	kā-tō (Kay-toe)
Kayleigh:	kā-lē (Kay-lee)
Luc:	luk (Lewk)
Mara:	mär-uh (Mar-uh)
Niall:	nī-el (Nile)
Nova:	Nō-vu (Noe-vuh)
Nyco:	nē-kō (Nee-koe)
Pax:	pæks (Paks)
Ronan:	rō-nin (Roe-nin)
Sama:	sam-u (Sam-uh)

AUTHOR NOTE

This story contains some material that may be upsetting to some readers, including talk of infertility, reference to past suicides and suicide attempts, grief and mourning, PTSD, brief suicidal thoughts, brief consideration of self-harm, and bouts of depression and anxiety.

This book also includes depictions of war which includes general violence, references to torture, beheading, and unexpected amputation in battle.

For more detailed information visit amberdlewis.com/content-warnings or view the extended author note following the acknowledgments.

"THE STARDUST IN THE ASHES" RECAP & KEY PEOPLE

KEY PLOT POINTS

Part One: Fallen

- Astra, Ehren, and crew have fled to safety at the Summer Palace while Cadewynn has gone with her mother, Sama, and Nyco to Gleador.
- Ehren is struggling with the loss of Makin and his father and is in the deep throes of depression. Only Astra is able to get through to him.
- After some effort, Ehren joins Astra, Alak, and others in a meeting and decides to start working on a plan to salvage what remains of his kingdom. He sets up in the library and starts going over letters from allies, spies, and his Guard and discovers that there may be an army of magic and non-magic assembling. He additionally discovers a letter from the kingdom of Ascaria that seems promising. With

Cal by his side, Ehren constructs a plan to find the army and create allies.

- After receiving a letter, Alak heads into the nearby village of Oxwatch and escorts Ronan to the Summer Place. Ronan brings them their horses and shares word from Athiedor. Ehren makes Ronan his official liaison with Athiedor.
- Ehren shares his plan to mixed reactions. Bram is furious that he is to be sent away with Alak to recruit the army while Ehren will take a small group into Ascaria to hopefully bring back allies. Astra agrees to stay behind with Kai and Ronan to look for a way to contact the Fae.
- The night before they are set to leave, Alak and Bram clear the air. Alak shares his story of what really happened with Isabella, and Bram agrees to try to mend their broken friendship.
- Meanwhile, Cadewynn travels to the Hundan Valley with Sama and Nyco to beg Jessalynn for her help in recruiting the provinces of Gleador.

Part Two: Rising (Astra's Events)

- With Alak gone, Astra researches a new way to sustain the warding around the Summer Palace. She quickly becomes frustrated by the lack of magical texts. Ronan comes to her rescue, sharing some of his own books, and they find a spell that only needs to be refreshed twice a day.

- Once the warding is secure, Ronan and Astra work together to search the library for information regarding ways to contact the Fae about the poisonous Bellyon berries. Ronan requests additional texts from the other Clan Lords.
- While talking with Healer Heora about a sleeping aid, Astra inquires about her missing cycles and discovers that her magic likely made her unable to bear children. She is upset and is comforted by Ronan and Kai.
- Once more books arrive, Astra and Ronan discover a children's nursery rhyme containing clues to a Faerie ring. With help from Hanna, they are able to identify the flower mentioned in the rhyme and narrow down the location for the Faerie ring to an area in Athiedor.
- Queen Khristianna of Paravlia arrives and offers an army in exchange for Kai's help to take down a rogue shifter. Astra is sad to see Kai go, but knows it's for the best.
- Astra and Ronan reach a frustrating end in their research, but Ehren contacts Astra through dream walking and suggests that she try to contact the dead on an upcoming holiday. Astra finds a spell in a book filled with relatively dark magic and reaches into the realm of the dead. Makin appears and helps her obtain the information she was seeking. Before he fades back into the darkness, he gives Cal and Ehren his blessing.
- Astra is with Ronan in the library when a frantic Felixe appears. Astra realizes Bram and Alak are in trouble, and she rushes to their aid.

Part Two: Rising (Alak's Events)

- Bram and Alak's journey starts off rocky, but the two manage to get along, making strides in their efforts to restore their friendship.

- A group of siblings raid their camp one night, and Alak and Bram are able to get some information from them regarding the refugee camp recruiting soldiers. Using the new information, they head to a nearby village to get more specific directions.

- The residents of the village are hostile at first, not willing to trust strangers looking for information about refugees, but after a boy with truth seeking magic verifies their intent, the villagers share the location of the camp. With renewed hope, Bram and Alak set out.

- When they reach the location shown to them by the villagers, they follow a trail of magic clues and physical clues. When a young woman holds Alak at arrow point, Bram comes to his rescue, only for them to discover that Mara, Astra's childhood best friend, is the one in charge of the camp. After a quick tour, Alak sends for Astra so she can visit with Mara. Bram and Mara seem to have a connection.

- The next morning, Pax arrives and leads Bram, Alak, and a fresh group of recruits to where he's training the magical army in a mountain pass. Bram and Alak stay a while, helping to train the soldiers while weeding out the top recruits to take back for Ehren's army.

- Once the final army has been selected, Bram and Alak take them through the mountains, heading toward a fortress near the Summer palace. They're leaving the mountains when they're attacked by an overwhelming amount of magic users and Dragkonians. In an act of desperation, Alak calls out to Astra.

- Astra wisps to their location, but there's nothing she can do to help besides wisp the entire army to the fortress, draining her magic to a fatal level. Desperate to save her life, Alak transfers most of his magic to her, willing to risk his life to save hers.

Part Two: Rising (Ehren's Events)

- Ehren, Cal, Pascal, and Lorrell head into the mountains on their way to Ascaria. Ehren continues to struggle with his depression and feelings of worthlessness. When Pascal allows him to sleep though most of one of his night guard shifts, Ehren becomes frustrated and furious, lashing out. Cal is able to calm him down, promising Ehren that no matter how many times he falls apart, he will always be there to help him.
- One night they make camp next to a lake with murky water. After Lorrell and Pascal are unsuccessful in catching many fish, Cal and Ehren take over, bringing in a better haul. When Cal heads up the bank to take the fish to be prepared for dinner, a large creature rises from the water and attempts to attack Ehren. Cal rushes forward and slays the beast. Needing to wash away the guts and gore from the attack, Cal and Ehren go off to a more secluded area to wash and they have a moment.

- As they continue their trek through the mountains, Ehren and Cal grow closer. On one particularly cold night after a day of freezing rain, Cal finds Ehren in their shared tent nearly naked after having shed his frozen clothes. Cal wraps him in a blanket and helps him change into warm, dry clothes. In order to stay warm through the night, they share the blankets and end up holding hands as they sleep.

- Shortly after they arrive on Ascarian soil, they are greeted by Prince Luc and Princesse Nicolette traveling with a group of Ascarian soldiers meant to escort them to Château des Chamans. Since it is late in the day, they go back to a camp instead of traveling all the way to Château des Chamans.

- Princesse Nicolette insinuates that perhaps Cal is more than a friend and a solider to Ehren. Due to her speculation, Cal is colder to Ehren than usual, sending Ehren into a spiral. When Ehren discovers Cal standing guard outside his tend, he convinces Cal to come inside his royal tent so he doesn't have to be alone with thoughts. Cal begrudgingly agrees, not wanting to harm Ehren's reputation on such an important mission. Ehren wakes, disappointed to find Cal already gone.

- After arriving at Château des Chamans, Prince Luc tells Ehren at dinner that he would be fine and accepting if Ehren and Cal's relationship is more than Guard and Prince, even going as far as to encourage him to pursue a relationship of love that would make him a stronger king.

- The next day, Ehren meets with Prince Luc and Princesse Nicolette as well as some of Ascarian's significant figures. After a brief history detailing how Luc and Nicolette came to the decision that they would rule Ascaria together in lieu of their aging father, talks of peace and becoming allies are brought forward. Ehren makes his case and Prince Luc promises them an official decision in a couple days, encouraging them to enjoy the celebration of the Festival of Visc in the meantime. Luc takes a marriage alliance with either him or Nicolete off the table, but tells Ehren he can pursue a marriage alliance through members of the Ascarian Court.

- In order to secure the allies needed for the alliance, Ehren meets with significant members of the Ascarian Court. Realizing his Ascarian is rusty, he begs Cal to help him sharpen his language skills. Cal complies, and they spend time locked away from everyone else. When Cal suggests Ehren go back to meeting the Ascairan court, Ehren tells him that he would rather spend time with him. Cal tells Ehren that he won't be the reason the alliance falls apart and leaves the room.

- During a tea with Duc Dubois and his daughter Gabrielle, the duc makes it clear he would like a match between his daughter and Ehren. Ehren politely declines, but agrees to dance with Gabrielle later at the ball. Back in their room, Cal scolds Ehren for throwing away the opportunity to court Gabrielle, and the two argue. Cal tells Ehren he will likely feel differently after the ball, and he leaves. Ehren spirals.

- During the ball, Ehren makes an effort to be the perfect prince, but decides to follow his heart. He convinces Cal to join him on the dance floor, but as soon as the dance ends, Cal excuses himself and heads outside. Ehren is afraid he blew his chance and goes after Cal. They end up confessing their feelings and affection for each other and kiss passionately for several minutes before rejoining the dance together.

- Cal is hesitant to follow Ehren to his room after the ball, but Ehren convinces him. The next morning the two talk everything out, and Ehren makes it clear that he is choosing Cal. They spend the morning together before heading to a religious service that's part of the ongoing festival.

- Despite being bored during the ceremony, Ehren finds the part about the nécromacromanciens— magic wielders that could raise and talk to the dead —interesting. After discussing it in more detail after the service with Prince Luc, Ehren stores the information away to share later with Astra. Ehren, Cal, Lorrell, and Pascal head out into the city to celebrate the festival.

- Ehren and Cal enjoy time together, trying food and browsing the booths. They purchase candles for a ceremony that night and have a moment of honesty and connection, before heading back to their suite to spend time just being together. At the candle ceremony, they hold hands and say goodbye to their ghosts.

- The next day, Ehren has his final meeting with Luc and Nicolette. They seal an alliance and Ascaria promises to send armies to aid Callenia. Luc will join Ehren in Callenia shortly with his armies, while Nicolette will stay behind in Ascaria. Ehren and Cal celebrate their victory.

- The next morning, Ehren and Cal wake up happy in bed together and have a brief discussion of the future of their relationship. Ehren assures Cal that he is all in. When Noah, one of Ehren's spies and Guard members currently positioned in Ascaria, unexpectedly drops by to give his report, the mood is temporarily derailed when Cal confesses some of the details surrounding his falling out with Noah.

- Luc sends Ehren and crew—which now includes Noah—with an escort to the mountains to ensure their safety. As they travel, Ehren encourages Cal to make up with Noah, and Cal takes that advice.

- A couple days into their mountain trek, the group is attacked by a Dragkonian. In the heat of battle, Ehren leaps in to protect Cal, and Cal is furious at Ehren for sending him to safety when it's Cal's job to protect Ehren.

- To shield the group from further attacks, Ehren takes a piece of jewelry from each member and uses them to hold a spell that will mask them from Dragkonians. Ehren insists Cal take his signet ring and Cal is hesitant. Ehren confesses that he cannot stand the thought of Cal getting hurt, and the two agree to do everything together from then on. Ehren asks Cal to marry him and Cal accepts.

- They return to the Summer Palace in the middle of the night to discover Astra is missing. Ehren starts to panic, but Cal holds him steady. The next morning they get the details from Ronan, and Cal and Ehren rush to Astra and Alak's unconscious sides.

- When Bram realizes Ehren and Cal are together, he reacts poorly, accusing Ehren of making a rash decision. Ehren is clearly hurt and Bram excuses himself to go rest in his room. Ehren begs Astra to wake up, while Cal confront Bram. When Bram digs his heels in, Cal punches Bram. Bram goes to react, but stops when he sees the ring on Cal's finger, everything suddenly shifting.

Part Two: Rising (Jess's Events)

- Jess is surprised by the number of people willing to join the army to fight for Callenia. She reluctantly agrees to help Princess Cadewynn gather support, and even more reluctantly agrees to leave Deven in charge of the Valley in her absence. She sends out letters to the farther provinces requesting aid, asking that they send their willing soldiers to Koshima.

- Jess, Kaeya, Cadewynn, Nyco, and Sama head out for the city of Forduna in the Jakuma Province. Cadewynn expresses frustration at how long the journey is taking, and Jess and Cadewynn sit down and learn a little about each other's pasts and desires. They discover that maybe they're not as different as they first thought.

- Once in Forduna, they meet with Sobek, the leader of the Jakuma Province. Cadewynn shows that she has a fierce side perfect for negotiation and Jess is left impressed. Cadewynn secures aid from Sobek, and they make plans to continue their journey as soon as possible.

- Cadewynn keeps them pushing forward, and they arrive at the city of Hyati late at night. Jess has a special connection with Tola, the leader of the Luma Province, and she seeks her out despite the late hour. The two chat over tea, and Tola comforts and reassures Jess, telling her that she supports the decisions and actions Jess is taking.

- The next morning, the group meets with Tola together. Since Luma is a peaceful province, Tola can't provide many soldiers, but she does offer to provide supplies. With that settled, Tola offers the use of a portal so they can go directly to Heldonia. Tola promises to write to the leader of Muldainah to encourage support since they will be skipping over that province by using a portal.

- Despite Jess's general dislike for Kiera, the leader of the Heldonian Province, the group is accepted with relatively open arms once they step through the portal. Kiera takes them on a quick tour of the magic silver mines before showing them weapons made with the silver. Among the weapons are some specifically ordained by the gods for particular people. Jess receives a special dagger.

- Cadewynn orders a large number of magical weapons, agreeing to the high prices, but Jess later discovers that Cadewynn may have spent a little more than she had. She recruits Kaeya's help and they haggle the prices to a more reasonable level. Cadewynn is extremely grateful.

- On their way to the capital city of Koshima, they visit Yoon in the wealthy province of Yomori. They have a less than pleasant meeting with Yoon, and Jess gets very angry, defending Cadewynn against him and calling Cadewynn her sister for the first time. Despite the negative results from the meeting, Yoon's assistant agrees to help them out anyways.

- Jess is reunited with Brock in Koshima, and she is blown away by the positive response shown by the gathering forces. When she is called before the king, she defends her position and receives his blessing to move the armies to Callenia to fight in the war.

- Jess finds Sama after her discussion with the king, and Sama confesses that she has no intention to return to the Valley after the war since she is now in a happy relationship with both Nyco and Princess Cadewynn. Jess gives Sama her blessing.

- During dinner one night, Jess starts to feel poorly and goes outside for some fresh air. There she is approached by a Seer who insists that she needs to get to Callenia sooner rather than later or everything will fall apart. Despite feeling manipulated by the Seer, Jess decides to heed her advice and move out a little earlier than planned.

- When Jess returns to the dining hall, she discovers that Princess Elaine, former princess of Gleador and current wife of an Oyrain prince, has returned. When Elaine finds her after dinner, the princess confides that her and her husband have brought a small force of their own to support the war effort.

She also confides in Jess that she is pregnant but wishes to remain by her husband's side because she a strong Healer and feels that remaining behind would be the wrong choice. Jess agrees to keep her secret.

KEY PEOPLE

- **Astra**: twin with starlight magic; Prince Ehren's Court Sorceress
- **Kato**: twin with fire magic; dubbed the "Fire King" due to his rebellion against Ehren and murder of the Callenian king
- **Mara**: Astra's best friend; leader of the refugee camp
- **Pax**: Kato's best friend and former lover; captain of the refugee army
- **Bram/Captain Bramfield**: Prince Ehren's Captain of the Guard
- **Ehren**: Crown Prince and rightful king of Callenia
- **Healer Heora**: Healer who helped Kato and Astra
- **Hanna**: Healer Heora's granddaughter; Healer in training
- **Pip**: Seer who joins Hanna and Healer Heora
- **Alak**: Syphon with illusion magic; Astra's bondmate
- **Felixe**: an adorable Fae Fox who can wisp at will and turn invisible; Alak's familiar
- **Cadewynn/Winnie**: Princess of Callenia; Ehren's sister

- **Ronan**: Liaison/Ambassador to Athiedor; Lord of Clan McDullun; has warding magic
- **Luc**: ruling prince of Ascaria
- **Cal**: in a relationship with Ehren; member of Ehren's Guard
- **Nyco**: talks to insects and spiders; spy for Ehren and part of his Guard; in a relationship with Winnie and Sama
- **Kai**: wolf-shifter who grows protective of Astra; from the Valley
- **Sama**: gentle Syphon from the Valley
- **Niall**: Alak's cousin; has shadow magic; dangerously pro-magic
- **Kayleigh**: Alak's cousin; has telekinesis; seamstress
- **Saran**: Alak's cousin; eight years old; talks to shadows
- **Cillian**: Son and heir to Lord Bashmore of Clan Bashmore (Sister is Eire)
- **Caitlyn**: Niall's fiancé; an empath who can see auras
- **Ian**: Niall's friend; strong in spellwork
- **Aine**: Niall's friend/ Ian's sister; has metal attack magic
- **Akaash**: Leader of the Dragkonians; can create wounds with dark magic and black fire that can't be Healed
- **Master Arcanis**: Head of the Order of Naskein
- **Aoibhinn**: the goddess of magic; speaks to Astra in dreams
- **Caedios**: Evil counterpart to Aoibhinn; inside Kato's mind

- **Hycis**: Fae woman who promised to help defeat the Dragkonians
- **Rynia**: Fae woman; Hycis's bondmate
- **Elaine**: former Princess of Gleador; married to a prince from Oyrain; strong Healer
- **Jessalynn:** Ehren's half-sister; leader of the Hundan Valley
- **Kaeya**: Jessalynn's Captain and life partner
- **Brock**: Jessalynn's Lieutenant and life partner

View character profiles and art, maps, and more on my website: https://www.amberdlewis.com/storytelling

My Dearest Mother,

I hope all is well with you and father. I know it is the off-season, but a farm is never quiet. I regret that I was not able to spend as much time with you as I would have liked during my last visit. I am hoping the war will be settled soon, and I will be able to take some time to visit you all again.

As I am sure you can understand, I am unable to share many details surrounding my current circumstances, but I feel the need to fill you in at least a little. I am currently safe in a training fortress in Northern Callenia that sits about half a day's travel from the Summer Palace. I am working with Alak—I am sure you remember the young man with the Athiedor accent—and Prince Luc of Ascaria to prepare our troops for the inevitable battles in our near future.

It is Ehren's intent to fight every battle using both soldier's skills and magic. I admit I was a bit wary at first, but our efforts at combining the two have proven successful overall. We were lucky to find a large group of soldiers training with magic and skill in a mountain pass under the care of a soldier by the name of Pax Greystone. With the additional training regimen created by myself and Alak, we have taken the army the extra steps required and now have a decent force.

I love you dearly and cannot wait to see you all again. Please pass on my endearments to Diana as well as my brothers.

Until we meet again,

Your Son,

Alexander Bramfield

Part One: Overcast

CHAPTER ONE

ASTRA

"You can't keep me locked in this fortress forever, Ehren," I argue for the millionth time this week.

"I know," Ehren says with a sigh as he rakes his hand through his hair. It's getting long again. "But you've only been up and about for a week now. You haven't had time—"

"I've had plenty of time and you know it," I cut him off. "It's been a full month since the attack. I'm fine. Even Healer Heora agreed I can get back to normal activities."

Ehren turns and looks out the window overlooking one of the training fields where soldiers run drills. He clasps his hands behind him as he stares down.

"Normal activities include walking to and from the library, having tea and dinner with the rest of us, and general everyday things. It does not include being on the front lines of a war."

I sigh and cross the room, placing my hand on Ehren's shoulder. "I know you're worried, but I'm not even asking to go to the front lines. I just need to go to Athiedor to contact the Fae."

Ehren turns his head to look down at me. "What if something goes wrong?"

"Then I'll handle it," I reply. "I can't stay here, Ehren. I just can't. You can come with me, you know."

A ghost of a smile plays on the corner of Ehren's lips. "Oh, can I?"

"Of course. I need someone to carry my bags."

Ehren's rich laugh fills the room as his eyes shine. "All right fine. We can go to Athiedor. I need to check in on a few things here and set everything up for my departure, but we can leave in the morning."

"Thank you, Ehren!" I cry, throwing my arms around his neck as I press a kiss to his cheek.

Ehren chuckles as red tinges his cheeks. "Careful, Cal gets jealous easily."

"I do what?" Cal says from the doorway.

Ehren turns toward Cal and his grin grows, his eyes shining with pure and utter joy.

"Astra was trying to ravage me. It's understandable as I am incredibly irresistible. I was reminding her how jealous you get," Ehren teases and I roll my eyes.

"Yes, that's exactly what I was doing."

Cal smiles, shaking his head as he approaches. "Have you finally decided to let her leave the fortress grounds without an escort?"

"Well," Ehren says, closing the distance between them to wrap his arms around Cal's waist, "she is going to Athiedor, but we're going with her."

"Both of us?" Cal asks, arching an eyebrow.

Ehren nods. "Unless you have a specific reason not to go?"

Cal shakes his head. "No. Not really."

"You swore to stay by my side always, remember? How can you do that if you stay behind?"

Cal rolls his eyes and looks over Ehren's shoulder to me. "I suppose you're on board with us coming along?"

I grin. "The more the merrier. Besides, while I don't expect anything to go wrong, I may need some help or backup."

"I can gather a crew," Cal offers. "Just a few soldiers."

Ehren nods. "That wouldn't be a bad idea. Not too many, though. We don't want to draw attention, but a few for protection would be good. Magic and non-magic."

"I'll talk to Bram and see who he can spare."

Ehren tenses slightly. Something happened between Ehren and Bram while I was unconscious, but I haven't been able to get the full details. All I know is Ehren and Bram try to act like nothing is wrong, though it's very obvious that something is off. I also know that Bram had a mysterious bruise on his left cheek when I woke up. According to him, he "fell," but when I asked how he accidentally fell on someone's fist, he clammed up. I know Ehren didn't punch him, but from the way Cal avoids looking at me whenever I mention it, I'm almost sure he's behind it.

"I can talk to Bram—" Ehren starts but Cal cuts him off with a kiss.

"I can handle Bram," Cal insists.

"You've made that much obvious," Ehren mumbles under his breath and Cal grins. "I'll also check with Prince Luc and see if he wants to join us or if he'd rather stay here."

Prince Luc was another recent development. By the time I awoke, Prince Luc and a small band of soldiers had arrived from Ascaria with more on the way. Princesse Nicolette, his sister and co-ruler, stayed behind in Ascaria to take care of things there.

In addition to the Ascarian armies, Bram worked with Pax to bring another few hundred refugees, giving us a small army of nearly 500 trained with magic and non-magic soldiers working together. Ehren somehow also managed to rally any other remaining soldiers from the corners of Callenia. Most of the army, however, isn't stationed here, but divided up with the top generals Ehren has available under his command, fighting what battles they can find. Often times, they arrive too late and can only pick up the pieces left behind by Kato's evil allies. Sometimes, however, they do engage in bloody battles that result in the occasional victory, typically when Dragkonians aren't present.

"I'll send word to Ronan," I offer. "I don't know if he'll want to join us in Athiedor or remain at the Summer Palace. I'll tell him to meet us there if he wants."

"Either option is fine with me," Ehren says. "We'll be in Athiedor for the Winter Solstice. He might enjoy being home, or close to it, for the holiday. Where exactly did you say this Faerie ring is supposed to be?"

"It's along the Brighrock River along the edge of Clan Dughlas's land," I reply. "Ronan managed to get a positive confirmation from Lord Dughlas himself. Apparently his main place of residence is nearby due to high levels of magic in the area."

"Well, that checks since that land contains a magical healing river and a Faerie ring."

I nod. "Apparently the creek near where we stayed while in Athiedor is a small offshoot of that river."

"I'll send word on ahead to Lord Dughlas then. Or," Ehren says, pausing thoughtfully, "maybe Ronan should do it? I did appoint him Ambassador with Athiedor."

"I'll mention it to him," I reply. "I'm sure he won't mind."

"All right," Ehren says with an affirmative nod. "You go write Ronan, I'll go talk with Prince Luc, and Cal, you go talk to Bram."

"As you wish, my prince," Cal murmurs, pressing a quick kiss to Ehren's cheek before pulling from his arms and striding from the room.

Ehren watches him go with longing. When he turns back to me and finds me watching him with a grin, his cheeks tinge red as his lips turn up in a smile.

"What?" he challenges, but there's no heat in his demand.

"Nothing," I say, shaking my head. "I love seeing you happy. You deserve it."

"Not sure about deserving it," Ehren says with a crooked grin, "but I am very happy."

"Good." I give his shoulder a playful shove. "Now, go off and do princely things so I can leave this gods-forsaken fortress."

Ehren mock bows from his waist. "As you command."

I laugh as he grins, sauntering from the room. I exit not long after him, weaving my way toward the little corner study I've been using in place of a decent library. Along the way, I pause at one of the courtyards, leaning against the stone archway that leads outdoors to watch the soldiers training with magic. Alak leads them dressed in a special version of Ehren's Guard uniform that marks him as a captain. I grin with pride as his voice echoes across the training yard, giving orders. I know he can sense I'm near through our bond as much as I can sense him. Though he never looks my way directly, he can't hold back his smile.

After a moment I continue on my way. My little study is tiny and overflowing with books, most of which were sent by Ronan while I was regaining consciousness. I was completely out for nearly two weeks. Sometimes I was able to hear and even react slightly to Ehren, but I never fully woke up. Even after I woke, I spent a week recovering my full strength. Alak recovered a little quicker, resuming normal activities days before me. At least I could read.

I clear a spot on the desk and pull out parchment. It doesn't take long to write my letter to Ronan. I half-hope he'll come with us. I miss him. On the other hand, I want him to stay safely stored in the Summer Palace so I don't have to worry about losing anyone else I hold dear.

I sign and seal my note and go in search of a messenger. I find one near the kitchens, and I'm handing off the letter when I feel the surge of familiar magic behind me. I thank the servant and turn to face Alak, who leans casually against the wall.

"You were spying on me again, weren't you, love?" He grins, pushing away from the wall to gather me in his arms.

"It's hardly spying when you know I'm there. Besides," I say, taking a step closer, running my hands along the buttons that line the front of his uniform, "I like seeing you in this uniform. You only wear it when you're leading the training sessions, so if I don't sneak a peek I never get to see you in it."

Alak groans. "I hate this bloody thing. It's not who I am at all."

"I disagree. You deserve the honor it suggests."

Alak shakes his head, glancing off. "If you say so, love."

"Well, I say so. Also, I was looking for you to tell you something. Ehren is finally letting me go to Athiedor."

Alak grins down at me and cocks his head. "Let me guess—you want me to join you?"

I shrug. "I suppose. I've grown rather attached to you."

Alak laughs and bends down to kiss me. I lean into his

warmth.

"I can think of plenty of ways to make myself useful," he purrs, running a gentle finger down my cheek.

My face heats and I kiss him again. "Is that a promise?"

"Always."

Someone clears their throat and we pull away. Alak glances over his shoulder with annoyance as Bram strides closer.

"Sorry to interrupt," Bram says, not sounding sorry in the slightest as he glances from me to Alak, "but I am looking for Ehren."

"I saw him not too long ago, but no idea where he's at now," I reply. "Sorry."

Bram sighs and looks past us down the hall. "It is fine. He is still avoiding me, I guess."

"What the hell happened between the two of you?" I demand, crossing my arms.

"Nothing," Bram says, shaking his head. "I was an idiot and said things I didn't think through or mean and . . . Nothing."

"And Cal punched you?" Alak jumps in, barely containing his grin.

"No," Bram snaps. "I already had that injury from the battle."

"Mate, you most certainly did not," Alak scoffs.

"Whatever. It doesn't matter. That is the past. In the present I need to ask Ehren if I can accompany you on your trip to Athiedor."

I raise my eyebrows. "You want to come with us? What about the army here?"

"The army will be more than fine for a couple weeks under the care of Pax. Prince Luc will also be here if needed. I don't like the idea of Ehren leaving without me, even if he does have Cal by his side all the time."

I nod. "I can understand that, especially considering the lake monster incident."

Bram's eyes shoot to mine. "The what?"

Alak elbows me, swallowing a laugh.

"Um, nothing."

"Astra Elisabeth Downs," Bram says, taking a step toward me, "what lake monster incident?"

"When did you learn my middle name?"

Bram arches an eyebrow. "What lake monster incident, Astra Elisabeth Downs?"

I grin. "You'll have to ask Ehren."

Bram opens his mouth to ask again, but I wisp both Alak and I away before he can. As soon as we reappear in our room, Alak bursts out laughing.

"Stepped into that one, love."

I laugh, flopping down on the bed. "How was I supposed to know no one told him?"

"It's like you don't know Ehren at all sometimes." Alak chuckles, taking a seat beside me. He pauses, glancing around. "Since we're in our room, maybe we should—"

"Pack?" I jump in, popping up onto my elbows. "Excellent idea."

Alak leans down, pressing a quick kiss to my lips. "I had another idea."

"We really do need to pack."

Alak groans. "Fine, but maybe when we're done, can we try my idea?"

I tilt my head, pretending to consider his offer, although we both know I've already decided. "I suppose I could be convinced."

Alak grins, stealing another kiss. "I figured as much." He bounces off the bed. "Let's get started, then. The sooner we're done the sooner we can move on to more intimate things."

He waggles his eyebrows and offers me his hand. I laugh and allow him to help me up. After all, I'm just as eager to get packed and on to other things as he is.

DINNER at the fortress is loud and chaotic. The room is large, meant to feed all the soldiers and staff at once, with tables crammed so close together I don't know how anyone can move enough to enjoy their food. As a member of the royal court, I sit at a table on a slight platform at the head of the room with Ehren, Cal, Alak, and Prince Luc—Bram opts to eat down with the others. We have more room to move around than the other tables on the main floor, but even we don't have nearly as much space as I'm used to.

"Oh, another dinner of soup," Ehren grumbles, staring dismally into his bowl.

The corners of Cal's lips twitch, holding back a smile as he lifts his spoon to his mouth. "It's good."

"I'm sure it is. As was the soup last night and the night before that and the night before that . . ." Ehren's voice trails off as he ladles his soup absentmindedly.

"You're lucky to have it," Cal scolds. "Rations are low in many places."

"I know, but I don't have to like it," Ehren mumbles, finally eating a spoonful.

"Hey, did Bram ever find you earlier?" I ask.

Ehren continues staring down into his bowl as he answers. "Yes."

"So, is he coming with us then?"

Ehren refuses to meet my eyes as Cal shoots him a sharp look. "He didn't mention that to me."

Ehren releases a long breath that's bordering on a dramatic sigh as he finally looks up to where Bram sits at the cluttered table across the room. "I told him it was fine."

Cal smiles gently, taking Ehren's hand in his. "Good."

Ehren shifts his gaze to Cal, "You're sure?"

"Of course, Ehren. You are two are friends and Bram is trying."

"All right, mates," Alak says, leaning forward on his elbows so he can talk past me. "What the hell happened while we were taking our little magic nap? You three have been—"

Alak's words are cut short as the doors to the dining hall are thrown open and a soldier covered in blood stumbles in. All eyes turn to him as Ehren and Bram rise from their seats. The man's eyes dart around until they fall on Ehren. He pushes his way through the crowded room and drops to his knees in front of our table.

"My king," the soldier says, bowing his head in respect as he places a fist over his heart.

Ehren tenses but shows no other reaction to being called a king as he says, "Rise, soldier."

"I bring news from the battles," the soldier continues as he stands. "We managed to intercept an army headed to the city of Dankerell."

"That's where we've been getting our weapons since the capital was taken," Bram says, elbowing his way to stand at the man's side.

"Yes," the soldier says with a nod. "A group of us managed to ambush them, setting them off course and taking out a good number of their soldiers. Most of my troop adjusted to further delay their path, while messengers went directly to the city to warn the citizens of the impending attack so they could take necessary precautions. I came here to see if you could provide assistance for the city."

Bram turns and looks at Ehren, who's face is scrunched in concentration, already calculating a plan.

"How long will it take to get to Dankerell?" Ehren asks, meeting Bram's gaze.

"It's not far, but moving with an army would take several hours. If we leave now, we could possibly be there by dawn."

Ehren nods. "Very well. Prepare the troops. We'll move out as soon as possible." He turns and looks down at Cal. "Chart a route for us to travel."

"Right away," Cal agrees, pushing up from his seat.

Ehren looks back to the man. "Were there any Dragkonians with them?"

The man shakes his head. "Not that we saw. If there had been, I'd likely not be standing here."

Ehren nods and commands the soldiers to assemble in the east training yard to be selected for duty. The room erupts into chaos as soldiers pour from the room. I stand with the intention of following Ehren, but he moves too quickly for me to stay by his side.

"I will send some of my men as well," Prince Luc says to Ehren as they're swallowed by the crowd.

"I know what you're thinking, love," Alak mumbles in my ear. "Ehren isn't going to let you go with them."

I spin to face Alak. "He has to. If Kato or the Dragkonians show up they could die without my magic."

"You heard the soldier. No Dragkonians were present."

I shake my head. "Just because they weren't present during the initial ambush doesn't mean they won't have some come as reinforcements."

Alak takes a deep breath, releasing it slowly as his eyes drift over the chaotic crowd. "You're right, love. You go find Ehren and I'll repack our bags to be better suited for this rather than our previously planned trip to Athiedor."

Alak kisses me quickly before disappearing into the crowd himself. I wait a moment for the hall to empty out a bit more before I dash through the fortress in search of Ehren. I check the training field first, but only find Bram dividing out the soldiers. I race down another corridor, dodging and weaving the hurried movements of servants and soldiers. Cal is in Ehren's study, but he's alone. I'm about to give up when I finally spot Ehren on the second floor, staring out over the training yard from a balcony. I take a deep, rallying breath and approach slowly, turning over words in my head.

"I know what you're going to ask," Ehren says, still staring down at the assembling soldiers. I pause at the entrance to the balcony.

"What's your answer?" I ask, my voice barely audible over the rumble below.

Ehren shakes his head, his hands gripping the balustrade so tightly his knuckles are white. "I can't lose you."

I take a hurried step toward him. "You won't lose me."

He spins to face me, his eyes welling with tears. "You can't know that. You'll be safer here."

"Are you going?"

"Of course I'm going."

"Then I'm going, too."

Ehren shakes his head. "No. You need to stay here. I need you safe."

"Ehren Andrewe Daniel Montavillier, you are the crown prince and rightful king of Callenia. If anyone needs to stay safely stored away, it's you, but you're going into battle. You don't reserve the right to worry about the safety of those you love while the rest of us are forced to stay behind worrying about you." I take another step toward Ehren and look up into his shining sea-green eyes. "If you think you can leave me behind to wait for answers, you've got another thing coming. I want to be by your side, fighting and making sure you make it out alive. I can't stand the thought of losing you any more than you can stand the thought of losing me."

Ehren makes a sound somewhere between a sob and a laugh. "You're too stubborn, Ash. You know that?"

I cock my head and grin. "So I've been told. I think it's why you and I get along so well."

Ehren laughs, shaking his head. "I fear you're right." He sobers as he takes my hands into his. "If you come along, you have to promise me that you won't kill yourself again. Not for me."

I sigh and glance away. "I didn't kill myself."

"You nearly did," Ehren counters, tightening his grip on my hands. "Please, Ash, promise me."

I look back up into Ehren's eyes and nod. "I promise."

Ehren releases a long sigh of relief, pressing a kiss to my forehead. "All right. You better get ready to go."

I pull back and grin up at Ehren. "Alak is already on it."

Ehren gives a shaky laugh and runs a hand through his hair. "Of course he is."

I turn and start to walk away, but Ehren calls my name.

I glance at him over my shoulder. "I mean it. If it gets to be too much, you leave. Don't worry about saving everybody. You get out."

I offer Ehren a tight smile. "I will."

Ehren nods but we both know I'm lying.

CHAPTER TWO
EHREN

We ride under the mask of darkness, the chill of the night biting through our cloaks like we're not even wearing them. My hands are numb inside my gloves as I grip the reins, but we don't stop. We ride fast and hard, desperate to get our army to Dankerell before Kato's soldiers. The first glimpse of the city silhouettes against the setting sun, casting an illusion of fire, and it's as beautiful as it is unsettling. So far, the city appears to be unscathed, but I don't allow myself to relax. I know from experience everything could go wrong in a heartbeat, and I will not allow myself to be caught off-guard again.

We wait outside the city gates, sending in a couple scouts to assess our situation. They return with good news: Kato's men have not yet arrived, and many of the citizens not trained for fighting have already been moved to a safer location.

We position our army along the hillside bordering the town, waiting and watching for the enemy. We take shifts, allowing the weary soldiers to get a little sleep after a night of traveling. My stomach is twisted into too many knots to even consider sleeping, but Cal ensures I at least get a chance to rest.

Midmorning, soldiers appear like ink blots against the clear sky in far more magnitude than expected. They must have called in recruits. Not only are their numbers more than the amount the soldier gave to Bram, but at least four Dragkonians stalk the sky above them. I suck in a breath and glance over at Cal. He meets my eyes and draws a slow breath.

"Together," he says, his voice steady and firm. "We stay together."

"Together," I confirm.

We quickly mount our horses as the army shifts into their battle positions.

Bram rides up next to me, his attention fixed on the approaching army. "We charge on your order."

"Wait until they're a little closer," I reply. "Our army is tired—there's no need to exhaust them further."

Bram nods, his eyes still trained on the enemy. "Agreed. I have those with magical shielding ability around the edges to help ward off as much magic as possible and attack magic users are spread throughout."

"Good," I reply, allowing my eyes to trail over our small army. "Are Alak and Astra with them?"

Bram nods. "Alak is leading his soldiers with Astra at his side."

I swallow, managing a nod. "Have your soldiers attack the wings of the Dragkonians if they can. Take away their ability to fly. We may not be able to kill the bastards with our weapons, but we can at least take them from the sky."

Bram finally glances to me. "I have already set that order."

I offer Bram a tight smile. He's good at what he does.

"Any further orders?"

"Don't die?" I offer with a half-shrug.

Despite the seriousness of the moment, the corner of Bram's mouth almost turns into a smile as he replies, "I will do my best."

I shift my attention back to Cal as Bram rejoins his soldiers, ready to lead the charge.

"You're not allowed to die either," I say, trying to make my voice light, but I fail miserably.

Cal meets my eyes. "Same goes for you. No heroics. Got it?"

I smile, ducking my head. "Fine."

I look away to my far left where Astra is stationed. Her eyes are fixed ahead on the approaching army as well, already calculating, magic swirling at her fingertips. As promised, Alak isn't far away. We're ready for battle whenever it reaches us, and when it does, I only pray we're prepared.

"Onward!" I yell, my voice echoing across the landscape.

Our army lurches forward, horses galloping, feet pounding. Magic pulses around me as the shields go up. The other army responds, plunging forward, magic and weapons drawn. This is going to be quite bloody. It's a good thing we brought Healers.

Cal and I ride side-by-side into the fray. On our horses, we swoop ahead, striking down soldier after soldier. A concentrated blow of magic strikes me hard, and I tumble from Dauntless. Cal leaps from Gallant so quickly I don't even realize he's left horseback until he pulls me to my feet, sword drawn.

"Are you okay?" he asks, his eyes darting over me.

"I'm fine," I reply, looking past him to the battle. I glance back at him and grin. "Let's go."

Cal matches my grin as we plunge back in, fighting amongst the clash of swords. I reach into my pocket and pull out one of my prepared spells, throwing it into the face of an attacking soldier. The spell explodes, knocking the man and several others around him back. Cal jumps in and cuts them down before they can regain their footing, their hot blood spraying across our skin. Together we're almost invincible. At least, I feel invincible until another blast of magic strikes my face, searing pain rippling from my cheek and down my spine. I scream, stumbling back as I claw at my throat, the action pointless against the magic.

"Ehren!" Cal yells, catching me in his arms.

I wince, trying to stand on my own, but I can't. I feel like I'm on fire from the inside out. I clutch Cal, struggling to think.

"I have a spell," I gasp. "In my pocket."

Cal nods, his fingers fumbling to find the spell. "This one?" he asks, lifting a small blue vial.

I manage a nod. "Yes. Throw it down. Hard," I say through clenched teeth, fighting the culminating pain the best I can.

Cal obliges, a blue cloud surrounding us as the vial shatters.

"What is this?" Cal asks, looking around as the spell curves into a dome around us.

"It's a barrier of protection," I grit out. "It won't last long, but it should shield us for a moment."

Outside the smoky blue of the spell, the battle rages on.

"What can I do?" Cal asks, easing me down to the ground.

I shake my head, pushing up into a sitting position, my arm looped around Cal's neck. "I don't think there's anything you can do but wait with me."

The effects of whatever spell struck me are fading away. Thank the gods whatever hit me wasn't meant to last long. After a few moments, I'm able to stand, the pain subsiding to a dull ache.

I take a deep breath and look at Cal. "I'm ready."

Without another moment of hesitation, we charge back into battle. I call forward a couple attack spells I have stored in my Syphon ring, taking down a few more soldiers, but the enemy isn't backing down. And why should they? The Dragkonians screech above us, swooping down, breathing black fire, but it can't touch us thanks to the magical shield. The Dragkonians know as well as we do that the shield is only a temporary solution, and they're willing to wait it out. Thankfully, our army isn't going to go as easily as I'm sure the enemy hopes.

An archer in the center of our army lands a flawless strike on a Dragkonian's wing. Another strike to the Dragkonian's remaining wing has it staggering off to recover. A magical burst of light blinds another, and it flies off as well. Meanwhile, the soldiers on the ground push the invading army back.

When Astra crafts a prison of starlight, trapping the two remains Dragkonians in bubbles of silver, the battle turns in our favor. We can't kill them, but we can wound them, and without them we have a chance.

"Concentrate your magic on the beasts!" Alak yells from atop Fawn. "Bring them down!"

His voice carries as much authority as his presence. He argued profusely when I offered him a version of Bram's captain uniform, but he wears it well. He wears it with honor.

The soldiers listen to Alak's words, streams of magic pelting the trapped beasts. They roar in pain and fury, but the magic doesn't let up, not until the creatures are rendered mostly helpless. As Astra's hold on them fades, they retreat into the skyline.

Without the Dragkonians, our attackers falter. Bram raises his sword and leads the final charge. Blood soaks the hillside, but we drive the enemy to retreat, taking several prisoners. As the clamor of battle fades into victory, I look at Cal and grin.

"We did it," he whispers, matching my grin despite the clear exhaustion in his eyes.

I throw my arms around him pull him into a kiss. "We did it."

THE BATTLE MAY HAVE BEEN WON, but many men were lost. The hours following the battle are grim. Out of the 600 men we brought, at least 250 were lost, with many more among the Healers. But we saved the village and managed to renew some level of hope.

Although I have a desire to get back to the fortress as soon as possible, we agree to stay the night. Not only will it give our army a chance to recover and rest but also make sure the attackers don't return with more reinforcements. I take a seat next to a crackling fire off the to the side so I can be alone with my thoughts as Cal goes off in search of dinner. Bram finds me first, though.

"Mind if I take a seat?" he asks, gesturing to the empty space on my left. "If you want me to find somewhere else, I can."

I shake my head and motion to the spot. "Sit."

Bram eases down on the ground with a soft groan. It's only then I notice the blood-soaked fabric on his side.

"You're wounded? Why aren't you with a Healer?" I ask, the words rushing out.

Bram tilts his head, offering me a weak smile. "I am fine. It is a small cut." I open my mouth to argue but he holds up a hand. "I have already seen a Healer and had my wound bandaged. They can save their magic for those that truly need it."

I relinquish with a nod and stare into the fire. "You did well today. I don't think the title of Captain fits you anymore." I look back over at Bram and smile. "How do you like the sound of 'General Bramfield'?"

Bram's eyes widen as his mouth drops open. "General?"

"You've been a great Captain of my personal Guard, but you've outgrown that title. You're leading my army. 'Captain' just doesn't fit anymore."

"I won't say no if your offer is sincere," Bram says, his voice tight, "but I am not sure if I am the best for the job."

I release an amused scoff. "You clearly are. You're not only an outstanding soldier, but one of my oldest and dearest friends. There's no one I trust more to oversee my army."

Bram nods, glancing away. "So we are still friends?"

I wince and glance down at my blood-splattered boots. "Of course."

"Ehren, I know I have apologized at least a dozen times for the way I acted, but I need to say it again. I am sorry. I thought you were acting rashly, but . . ." He trails off, running a hand through his hair. "Do you remember the summer you turned sixteen, and we snuck off to the abandoned ruins roughly a day out from Embervein?"

A smile curls on my lips as I lean back on my palms and glance over at Bram. "Of course I do. That's the only time I've ever seen you get completely wasted. And on summer wine of all things."

Bram's smile is tight as he nods. "I had a good reason."

I take a deep breath and nod, all hints of a smile fading. "It was the first anniversary of Isabella's death."

Bram pauses, looking down at his hands. "But that is not what I remember the most about that day."

"With as much as you drank, I'm surprised you remember anything."

Bram meets my eyes and smiles. "Some parts are admittedly a bit . . . fuzzy, but there's one conversation I remember quite clearly. You were a little drunk yourself. You sang the entire Ballad of Ramsy, do you remember?"

I laugh and look up at the stars. "I finally learned all the dirty parts of that love ballad. I was quite proud."

Bram chuckles. "Yes, I recall. Do you remember what you said when you finished?"

My heart leaps as I turn my gaze to Bram. "I said, 'I want love like that.'"

Bram nods and smiles, meeting my eyes. "That is exactly what you said. You then went on a whole tirade about how ridiculous it was that you would never have a love like that because you would always be held back by your princely duties."

"I can't believe you remember this," I mumble, shaking my head.

"I asked you if you thought you could ever find someone to love like that if you were given the chance, and you said something like, 'Maybe I already have.'" Bram pauses and looks down at my finger where my signet ring would normally sit. "You then went on a long rambling argument with yourself over your feelings for someone, though you never said a name. You finished and looked me directly in my eyes and said, 'If I ever decide to live for love, I'll give them my ring. You see that ring on their finger and you'll know.'"

I smile and duck my head. "I did say that. Gods, I really can't believe you can remember that."

"It was Cal then as much as it is Cal today, wasn't it?"

I look back over at Bram, my smile softening at the memory. "It was, though I think that night was the only time I ever let myself admit it out loud. Well, until recently."

"I saw your ring on Cal's finger and I knew. I am sorry I doubted you. I hope you can forgive me."

I laugh, shaking my head. "Bram, I've already forgiven you. You just have to forgive yourself."

Bram smiles and nods. "Good. Because our friendship means the world to me and to think I messed it up because of something stupid I said—"

"All is forgiven," I cut in.

Footsteps behind us have both of us twisting to look behind us. Cal stands behind us smiling, the flames reflecting in his eyes.

"I don't mean to interrupt," he says. "I found some food."

"Not interrupting at all," Bram says, standing and brushing bits of dirt and dried grass from his uniform. "I was just about to leave and find some dinner of my own."

"You can share with us," Cal offers, easing down on my free side.

"Like hell he can," I mumble, reaching for a piece of dried meat. "Maybe from your share, but I'm starving and have no plans to share."

Cal shakes his head, but his eyes are shining as he scolds me. "You're horrible."

"It is fine," Bram insists, waving his hand. "I need to check on a few things. I will catch up with you two later."

Bram offers us one final nod before striding away. Once he's gone, I turn to Cal.

"How long were you standing behind us?"

The tips of Cal's ears flush crimson as he stares down at the plate of food, his fingers absentmindedly tearing at a piece of bread. "Not long."

"Cal," I whisper, taking his hands in mine and tracing my thumb across my signet ring. "How much did you hear?"

Tears shine in eyes as he raises his face to mine. "You were sixteen when you chose me?"

I nod, tears reflecting in my own eyes. "Yes, though, I think I knew before then. You've always drawn my attention as long as I can remember."

"Why?" His voice is so quiet against the night I barely hear him.

"Why?" I laugh, taking his other hand in mine. "Because you were brave and strong and determined. Not to mention you were by far one of the most handsome among the soldiers."

Cal scoffs. "I was not."

"I beg to differ. It was very hard to concentrate on my training anytime you were near," I mumble, leaning in for a kiss.

When I pull back, a tear is sliding down Cal's cheek. I quickly kiss it away.

"I love you, Cal, and I'm a fool for waiting so long to tell you. At first, I told myself you would never love me anyway, that you'd wait for a lovely young woman from Embervein to catch your eye, and you'd live happily with her, making beautiful little babies."

Cal laughs, shaking his head. "*That* was never going to happen."

I grin. "I know that now. That night when you admitted that you loved men and not women, I almost confessed my feelings."

Cal freezes, searching my face. "What? Why didn't you?"

I smile and glance away. "Makin showed up, remember?"

"Oh. And you thought . . ."

I look back at Cal, squeezing his hand. "I thought it would be best not to get in your way. So, I stepped back."

Cal leans across the food and presses his lips to mine. The kiss quickly escalates, and I wish very fervently that we had a private tent to go back to. But we don't, so I eventually pull back. I shift and rest my head on Cal's shoulder. He wraps his arm behind me, pulling me closer. For a while, we sit, staring into the fire as our hearts beat as one. After a while, Astra and Alak join us, Bram returning a bit later. Together we laugh, and, for a few brief moments, it's almost like there's not a war.

But nothing good lasts forever.

CHAPTER THREE

ASTRA

"So, from here we'll go straight on to Athiedor?" I clarify, glancing down at the map Ehren spread out between us. "It does seem like the most direct route, saving us some time, but what about the army?"

"That's up to General Bramfield," Ehren grins, glancing over at Bram.

General. The new title fits him well, and he wears it proudly, even if he shifts awkwardly every time Ehren uses it.

"I will remain here for another day to get everything settled, but then I will gather a small group and follow after you. So be careful and don't do anything foolish."

"What makes you think I would do something foolish?" Ehren says, feigning shock.

Bram narrows his eyes. "I heard about the lake monster."

Ehren spins to face Cal. "You swore you wouldn't tell him!"

Cal bites back a grin as he holds up his hands. "I didn't say a word."

Ehren spins to me. "Astra!"

"Sorry. It slipped out." I grimace.

"I have never felt more betrayed." Ehren sighs, dramatically clasping his heart.

I narrow my eyes at him. "Whatever. You know Bram's concerns are valid, nonetheless." I turn to Bram. "Cal and I will keep him in check."

"What about me?" Alak asks, kissing my cheek. "Don't forget about me, love."

"The chance you'll be adding to the trouble is more likely than you stopping the trouble," I tease.

"Hey, now, love," Alak protests. "I'm a respected captain now. Look at my new uniform."

"Trust me, I'm well aware of the uniform change," I murmur, pressing my lips to his.

Bram clears his throat louder than necessary. "Anyway, you will head on to Athiedor, and my men and I will be a day or so behind."

Ehren nods, crossing his arms. "It's a solid plan. It will put us all in Athiedor together for the solstice." He looks up at Bram. "Any plans for your birthday?"

"It's your birthday?" I ask with a smile.

Bram shakes his head, rolling up the map. "You know I don't celebrate my birthday. Why bring it up?"

"Because I like cake," Ehren replies with a shrug. He turns to me. "Bram's birthday is the day after the solstice."

"You better not make any plans to celebrate," Bram growls.

Ehren sighs dramatically. "Every year I try and every year I fail."

I grin and loop my arm through Ehren's. "Maybe this year we can come up with something together."

Bram sighs and closes his eyes. "Please don't."

"I'll keep them in check," Cal promises.

"Thank you," Bram says with a nod. "You should all get on the road if you want to make good time."

Ehren nods. "We have everything ready to go, so I guess there's no reason to delay."

Bram meets Ehren's eyes. "Be careful."

I expect Ehren to play off another joke, but his face is serious as he replies, "You too."

According to Ehren, it will take roughly four to five days to reach our destination. We make good time the first day, stopping to camp after night falls. We left the fortress so quickly we didn't pack good tents, but Alak and I form a bubble of protection around our party and the fire, encasing the warmth and protecting us from the elements.

The second day we make even better time, stopping in a village for the night. We agree to hide our identities, Alak casting an illusion charm around us to change our appearances.

The third day we cross the border into Athiedor around midmorning, progressing toward our destination. Heavy gray clouds loom over us, turning into icy rain and snow by dusk. With no villages nearby, we leave the path, venturing toward a farmhouse we spot sitting a decent hike off the main road.

"Anyone home?" Ehren calls, knocking on the door. When no one answers he tries again. "We're just looking to get out of the snow."

Cal walks around from the back of the house. "I don't think anyone is here. Even the barn is empty."

I try the door and find it unlocked. I glance up at Ehren. "I think it's abandoned."

"I'll get the horses set up in the barn," Alak offers as Ehren and I step inside.

"I don't think anyone has been here in a while," I say, looking around as I let my magic trace the edges of the room.

"Someone clearly lived here," Ehren replies, nodding to a small stuffed bear leaning against one of the walls.

I frown and scoop up the bear. What child left this behind and why? A fire roars to life behind me, making me jump.

"Sorry," Cal grins from his position kneeling near the fire. "I thought to warm us up a bit."

Ehren grins as he saunters over to Cal. "I have other ideas of how you can warm me up."

Cal stands and wraps his arms around Ehren as he smiles. "And how is that, my prince?"

Ehren inhales sharply and presses his lips aggressively to Cal's.

"If you two are going to be doing that, go to the barn with the horses," I groan, but don't bother hiding my smile.

"I don't think the horses want to have any part of that, either," Alak adds, pausing in the doorway to kick snow from his boots.

Ehren rolls his eyes as he glances at me over his shoulder. "As if you two are any better."

Cal chuckles as Alak grins.

"We have an excuse," Alak drawls, sauntering toward me and drawing me into his arms. "We have to constantly consummate to keep the soul bond intact."

"That is a bald-faced lie, Alak Dunne," I chide with a grin as I place my hands on Alak's chest, pushing him back. "Take off your cloak. You're getting snow everywhere."

Within a few minutes, we're all snuggled in around the fire, wrapped in knitted blankets the former residents left behind as we munch on rations.

"I wonder who lived here and why they left," Alak says, his eyes trailing over the bare room.

"My brother's soldiers had to come from somewhere," I mutter, staring into the fire.

Ehren scowls, tearing a piece of bread and popping it in his mouth. "You think that's what this is? A house abandoned so they could fight in Kato's army?"

I shrug, pulling my blanket tighter around my shoulders. "It's possible, isn't it? A lot of Athiedor supported Kato, and that support didn't dissolve with the treaty."

"I suppose you're right." Ehren sighs.

Cal reaches out and takes Ehren's hand. "Don't blame yourself. It's not your fault if anyone chooses to betray the treaty."

I nod. "He's right, Ehren. You can't control everyone."

"I know. I know," Ehren mumbles. "How about we do something to keep our minds off the war. Maybe play cards?"

We agree and are soon caught up in a lively game. We play late into the night, eventually curling up in front of the fire to sleep. At least, that's the plan. I'm pretty sure Ehren and Cal do *something* else before sleeping, but Alak and I are courteous enough to pretend not to notice.

The next morning, we wake to find a blanketed landscape of slippery ice and snow, though, thankfully, the precipitation has ceased for now. As the sun rises, the snow turns to slush and mud. By the time we reach the residence of Lord Dughlas, most of the snow has melted completely.

Lord Dughlas's residence sits comfortably between the look of a fort and a castle but has a regal air that makes "castle" the more fitting term. Servants rush forward to greet us, taking our horses to the stables while others gather our bags to be delivered to our rooms. Another servant directs us to a study to meet Lord Dughlas. The pompous old man sits in a chair that's just shy of a throne and makes no move to rise to greet us when we enter the room.

"Ah, my weary travelers. Welcome to the land of Clan Dughlas. Please, make yourselves comfortable," he booms, gesturing to nearby seats.

"If you'll pardon our rudeness, we would very much like to get on with our reason for coming," I say, inclining my head. "How close is the location?"

Lord Dughlas scowls. "It's about an hour on horseback, but surely you'd rather rest and go in the morning?"

I shake my head. "There's still enough daylight for us to start today. I'm not sure how long it will take for the spell to work, so I'd rather not waste any more time."

Lord Dughlas sighs. "I suppose it can't be helped. I'll arrange for a guide. Surely, though, you'd at least like to visit your rooms for a minute to rest and refresh? Have a cup of tea or a glass of ale?"

I exchange a quick look with Ehren before he steps forward. "Of course, but only a minute or two."

"Excellent!" Lord Dughlas declares, clapping his hands together once. "And then when you return, we can discuss the upcoming ball."

I frown. "What ball?"

Lord Dughlas rears back like I slapped him, clutching his heart.

"The solstice ball, of course! It is a revered tradition to honor the goddess Flaik and her brother Flurris—both born on the solstice, albeit years apart. Flaik is the goddess over the ice and storms and Flurris the god over snow and winter warmth.

Gods forbid we not honor them properly and the balance is thrown off."

I clench my teeth as I bow my head. "Of course. Only we did not prepare the correct accommodations for a ball."

"It is no matter," Lord Dughlas says with a wave of his hand. "I have the top tailors and seamstresses on standby to assist with any of your needs."

"Thank you," Ehren says, inclining his head. "Your generous hospitality is appreciated."

Lord Dughlas nods like a giddy schoolboy as he motions for a servant to come forward. The servant, a young woman with curly red hair, guides us through maze-like hallways to our room.

"Please, if ya need anything, don't hesitate to ring," she mumbles before scurrying away.

Our room is decorated to remind us that we are in Clan Dughlas territory, almost every inch of the available wall space draped in banners displaying the Fae Fox crest. Even the furniture has the crest stitched or carved into the design. Off the main room we find two small bedrooms sitting side by side, with a shared washroom between them.

"I suppose we'll set up a bathing schedule," Ehren mumbles, looking over the washroom.

"At least the doors lock," I reply with a shrug.

A few minutes after being led to our room, someone knocks on our door. Cal answers, his hand casually resting on the hilt of his sword.

"I'm ta show ya the way," a young woman with frizzy red hair and freckles says, stepping into the room. "Name's Saoirse," she adds, pronouncing her name like "Ser-sha."

"I'm Astra," I say, stepping forward. "And that's—"

"Don't matter none," Saoirse interrupts, her voice sharp. "We stand around wagging tongues for no good cause, and we'll be traveling back in the dark."

"Well, she's lovely," Ehren mutters in my ear as we follow Saoirse out the door.

I choke on a laugh as I shush him. If Saoirse overhears, she doesn't react.

Our horses are already prepared and ready to go, so we're on the road quickly. None of us bother speaking as we ride, our eyes fixed on the road ahead. After roughly an hour of travel, we reach a thick wood. At Saoirse's insistence, we leave our horses tied at the edge of the trees before we hike deeper inside, though she never gives a clear reason why.

"I can feel the ring," Alak whispers as we crunch through the forest toward the trickling river.

"We can take it from here," I call out to Saoirse.

She turns and furrows her eyebrows. "Are ya sure? I'm meant to lead ya the whole way."

"We'll wait here with you while Astra and Alak go on ahead and do what needs to be done," Ehren insists, stepping forward and offering the woman his most charming smile. Her frown only deepens.

"Your wiles are failing," Cal whispers with a grin.

"If they are, it's your fault," Ehren whispers back. "You've stolen my ability to flirt."

I shake my head and march forward. "We'll be back shortly. Don't go far, and we'll find our way back."

Saoirse glares but doesn't stop us as we brush past. Alak takes the lead, pulling me along behind him. He holds a branch out of my way, and we step into a small clearing at the edge of the river. I gasp as my eyes fall on the small ring of blue flowers trembling in the evening air.

"There it is," I whisper in awe, approaching the ring with care.

"It's smaller than I thought it would be," Alak muses.

I nod in agreement. The ring is only a few feet wide, but it will do. I step over the edge of the ring into the center and warmth swells around me despite the chill of the day. I kneel, pulling a piece of paper from my pocket. I take a deep breath and study the runes and spell written on the paper. Carefully, I start at the top of the circle and make my way around, whispering the spell as I trace the runes into the dirt. When I finish I stand, repeating the spell again, my heart beating wildly in my chest. I don't even dare to breathe as I wait.

I'm about to try the summoning again when a beam of light shoots up from the edge of the circle opposite me. I stumble back, but make sure I remain inside the Faerie ring. After a moment a shadowy figure appears against the light, stepping forward into the ring as the beam fades. For a moment I'm lost in the beauty of the figure, a sharp-eyed female with long pink hair and willowy limbs. Somehow, I'd forgotten the startling elegance of the Fae, though it seems all the more pronounced in the human realm as opposed to the Fae realm which gleams with opulence.

She speaks, but it takes a moment for the musical tone of her language to translate to my ears.

"Why have you summoned me, human?" I blink back at her for a moment, my words refusing to come. "Well?"

I shake my head, clearing my thoughts. "I apologize," I say, bowing my head. "Thank you for answering my call. My name is Astra Downs. I seek an audience with the Fae to discuss the possibility of getting some of the Bellyon berries so we stand a chance against defeating the Dragkonians that plague our kingdom."

The Fae stares at me, betraying no emotion. "A plague you set upon yourselves by human greed."

"The greed of one human led to their release, yes," I concede, refusing to back down. "I do not want his greed to destroy us all. I have already spoken with a few Fae by the names of Fenian, Hycis, and Elidyr and they have agreed to help."

I pause, wondering if Fae have last names. Surely they have some way to differentiate between those with the same name? Maybe I should have done more research.

"I know of your plight and of your conversation with the Fae of the North. Our realm is not so vast that we do not communicate when it comes to matters of such great importance as this."

I relax, not even realizing how much I had tensed up.

"However," she adds sharply, causing my anxiety to spike again, "it will be a few days before they could speak with you. Their section of our realm is the only to still grow the berries, most of us having enough sense to raze the fields so they cannot be used against us."

"Should I contact you again? If so, when?"

The Fae woman sighs as if talking to me is the most bothersome thing she's ever had to do in her life. Her eyes wander around, taking in the forest.

"It is nearly the Winter Solstice in your realm, is it not?"

I nod. "Yes. In two days' time."

"Good. Return in four days," the Fae replies. "Our realms are more closely aligned now than they were before, and the solstice should help lock them in place. Return in four days, and I will either have your Fae allies or their refusal to give further aid."

I open my mouth to protest but instead give way to agreement. "Of course."

The Fae looks me over with disdain before waving her hand in the air and reanimating the beam of light. She steps into the light and varnishes. The beam disappears and suddenly the forest seems very quiet and dull. After taking a moment to let it all sink in, I turn to Alak.

"You did it, love," he whispers, stepping closer.

I cautiously step over the edge of the ring and look up into his eyes. "We still don't have the berries. What if they've changed their minds?"

"They won't," Alak whispers, drawing me into his arms. "They want the Dragkonians gone as much as we do."

I sigh and lean into his chest as his grip tightens. "Do you really think so?"

He kisses the top of my head. "I know so. Now, let's go rejoin the others before Saoirse kills them and hides their bodies."

I chuckle and take Alak's hand as we weave back though the forest. Ehren doesn't say anything as we approach, but he's watching me, fear in his eyes.

"It worked," I answer his unasked question.

"Oh, thank the gods," Ehren declares, collapsing against Cal's shoulder in relief.

Cal loops an arm around Ehren, keeping him upright as he asks, "Are the berries coming along then?"

"I'm to contact them again in four days to finalize everything," I add.

Ehren nods but then groans, burying his face in Cal's neck. "So there's no way to avoid the ball?"

"Like you mind a ball," Cal mutters with a shake of his head.

Ehren grins, straightening and pressing a kiss to Cal's cheek. "Well, I guess dancing with you wouldn't be the worst thing in the world." He links his fingers with Cal's. "I only feel a bit guilty celebrating when most of my kingdom is in shatters."

"Most of Callenia will still celebrate solstice," I say. "Even in Timberborn when things were the most difficult, we always looked for a reason to celebrate."

"Enough chatter," Saoirse cuts in, glaring up at the sky though the trees. "We need to leave."

I look up, taking in the bright colors already painting the sky. She's right. Without another word, we cross through the forest back to our horses. Night falls before we reach the castle, but we still make it in time for dinner.

We are given places of honor at the table with Lord Dughlas, which, after listening to story after story of the clan leader bragging about himself, I'm thinking it may actually be a form of torture. Judging by the exasperated looks Ehren keeps exchanging with me, he agrees.

"Oh, I've arranged fittings for all of you so you can have the finest gowns," Lord Dughlas proclaims, his voice somewhat muffled by his mouthful of food. "The theme is, of course, ice and snow, so you will all be decked in silvers, creams, and whites."

"So glad he gave us a choice," Ehren grumbles under his breath so only Cal and I can hear him.

"Ehren," Cal chides, struggling to hold back a smile.

"Thank you, Lord Dughlas," Ehren says, raising his voice so Lord Dughlas hears. "We are honored."

Cal smiles, shaking his head as he takes Ehren's hand under the table.

"It is my pleasure." Lord Dughlas grins. "You will soon see

that Clan Dughlas is the finest Clan, and we hold nothing back."

Ehren offers Lord Dughlas another charming smile, and I grin at him. Honestly, the idea of a ball sounds like fun, but I'm not sure I would admit it to Ehren right now. Judging by the way he glances over at Cal, though, I think he may be looking forward to it a little himself. I think we all are.

CHAPTER FOUR

EHREN

Bram arrives with fifteen men the morning of the ball. He seems truly affronted by the idea of the festivities, which honestly makes it a little more appealing to me.

"I will station guards around the castle grounds to ensure everything remains safe," Bram insists.

"Oh, please, let them attend," Astra protests. "They could use some fun."

Bram glances over at Astra and his resolve falters. I bite back a grin. I relish the control Astra has over him sometimes.

"I will allow those that wish to attend to take shifts," Bram relents as Astra grins.

"Good man," I say, clapping a hand to Bram's shoulder.

Bram ducks out from under my grip, shaking his head. "Don't make me regret this."

We spend most of our day doing nothing until it's time to prepare for the ball. I may have had some doubts about allowing Lord Dughlas to dress us all like little dolls for his pleasure, but when I see Cal in his striking deep silver tunic, I'm willing to forgive Lord Dughlas his every transgression.

"It's not fair that you look better than me," I murmur, drawing Cal into my arms. "I'm the prince."

He grins and brushes his lips against mine. His teeth purposefully catch my bottom lip as he pulls back, his eyes gleaming his own glorious brand of mischief.

"I think you look quite nice in your white tunic."

I pull back from Cal and examine myself in the nearby mirror. I turn, assessing the way the white fabric sewn with silver thread fits, brushing my hands over it.

"It's not a bad look, is it?" I muse.

"You look irresistible," Cal says, his voice low.

I laugh and look over at him. "You can't keep looking at me like that, or we won't make it to the ball. I don't even want to imagine what missing the ball could do to our relations in Athiedor."

Cal grins and brushes a quick kiss on my cheek. "Well then, perhaps we should be on our way."

I sigh and run a hand through my hair, glaring at my reflection in the mirror. "Fine."

"You know," Cal says as we exit the room and stroll through the sitting room. "I rather like your hair a little longer."

"Really? Because it's driving me crazy," I mutter.

"I can tell," Cal grins, reaching to twirl his fingers in my hair as we walk. "You keep messing with it. But I like it."

I'm tempted to pull Cal back into our room and call it a night, but I take a rallying breath and power on.

I'm impressed by the ballroom. It easily rivals the one in Embervein, complete with floor-to-ceiling stained glass windows depicting dancers in traditional Athiedor formal dress. Everything in the room glitters and shimmers in near-royal elegance. Lord Dughlas has managed to create a bright bubble of happiness in the center of a dark time. Guilt still wells in my chest at the thought of my people suffering while I celebrate, but Cal slides his arm around my waist and my thoughts switch drastically elsewhere.

"Dance with me?" Cal asks, his lips brushing my ear.

A shiver of pleasure runs down my spine as I turn my face toward him. "Of course."

Cal keeps his arm looped around me as he guides me to the dance floor. I lead the first dance, but Cal leads the second. I can't help but marvel with pride at Cal's newfound confidence. He's so focused on me, I don't think he notices a single glance sent our way. I'm happy to spend the entire night with my arms wrapped around Cal, but when Astra makes her entrance, I feel compelled to greet her.

She sweeps into the room with a beauty and grace most mortals envy. Hell, most gods would envy her. Everything about her is magical, from her gleaming cream and silver gown to the diamond tiara atop her head. Somehow, she's managed to portray both power and peace. Alak escorts her into the ball-room, a pleased smirk on his lips. Hand-in-hand, Cal and I wend through the growing crowd to Astra's side.

"I don't suppose I can steal you away for a dance?" I grin, bowing from the waist.

Astra smiles, her entire face glowing. "I suppose so."

I look past Astra to Alak. "You don't mind if I take her first dance, do you?"

Alak laughs, shaking his head. "As if I would ever try to control Astra in any way. You can have the first dance, and I'll take as many as she'll give me the rest of the night."

Astra rolls her eyes, placing her hand in mine. "I don't

really care who I dance with. You're all the same to me. Just don't step on my feet."

"I think I feel slightly offended at the insinuation," I mutter as she drags me toward the dance floor.

"Oh, you know I love you," she says, pressing a quick kiss to my cheek.

I laugh and lead her in a fast-paced dance. She's light on her feet and practically floats the entire time. Dancing with Astra is very different than dancing with Cal, but I love it nearly as much. When the dance ends, she's breathless with bright pink cheeks and sparkling eyes. I've barely escorted her from the floor before Cal swoops in to ask her for the next dance.

"I don't know. Perhaps I should ask Ehren's permission first," Astra says with a pointed look.

I throw my hands up in surrender. "While I am insanely jealous of anyone who dances with Cal, I'll allow it."

Cal shakes his head, grinning. "Allow it? Please. You know you want to admire me from a distance."

I throw my head back and laugh. "Too true."

With a wink, Cal leads Astra onto the dance floor and, as promised, my eyes are locked on him almost the entire time. Alak stands next to me, watching Astra with the same level of admiration.

"How did we manage it, do you think?" I ask, leaning toward Alak, my eyes still on Cal as he spins Astra.

"Manage what?"

I gesture toward Cal and Astra. "Manage getting two such wonderful people to love us."

Alak chuckles. "Well, you're a handsome prince, so I think you had a bit of an advantage."

I shake my head. "I might be a prince, but that doesn't buy

genuine affection any more than your soul bond guarantees a match." Cal smiles at something Astra says and my heart skips a beat. "I wonder every day how I got so lucky."

"You're right. I have no idea, either." He glances over at me, grinning wickedly. "Maybe Fate isn't the bitch I always imagined her to be."

I laugh and shake my head. "Perhaps not. I feel like I should apologize to her."

Alak chuckles, shifting his gaze back to the dancing couple as the music slows and stops. They're not even off the dance floor completely before Alak dashes forward and asks Cal to dance. Cal's eyes widen and he shoots me a questioning look. I only laugh as Cal accepts. I sweep in and escort Astra onto the dance floor. Side-by-side we dance, lost in the bliss of the ball.

The night creeps on and we manage to find other dance partners occasionally, but we seem to keep circling back to each other. I even find myself dancing with Alak twice. We're finally taking a break, toasting to the solstice with glasses of sparkling wine, when chaos erupts at the far end of the ballroom.

"Please, I have to talk to Alak and Astra!" It's a young woman's voice with a thick Athiedor accent. "I need to warn them!"

I scowl and exchange a quick look with Astra, but she seems as perplexed as I am. The music fades as the dancing stutters to a halt, curious glances shifting toward the entrance, whispers filling the air. I straighten and march across the ballroom, Astra close on my heels. Just outside the door is a disheveled young woman with red hair struggling to get past the guards stationed at the door. When she lifts her eyes to us, I recognize her immediately, my hand going to the hilt of my sword, though I don't draw.

"Kayleigh?" Astra gasps.

"What are you doing here?" I demand.

"I came to warn you," Kayleigh says. "Please . . . I have to warn you."

"Let's take this further into the hall," I suggest, stepping forward.

Two of the guards nod, each grasping one of Kayleigh's wrists as they drag her out of the view of the ball guests. Behind us, the music resumes, though low whispers still carry across the room.

"What do you need to tell us? Better yet, what makes you think we'll trust you?" Astra asks once we're far enough away, her voice hard.

Kayleigh straightens, her eyes looking around wildly. "They're coming," she whispers. "They'll be here soon. You have to go."

"Who—?" I start but she cuts me off, her manic eyes meeting mine.

"They're coming. They want you disabled. Dead."

"They can't find us. We're warded," I counter, though even as I say the words, I realize Kayleigh found us well enough.

"The shadows know where you are," she whispers, her eyes darting around again. "The shadows are everywhere. You can't keep them away with simple wards. No one can. They know you're here, and they can hear you—he can hear you."

Astra steps forward, genuine concern replacing her former fury. "What shadows, Kayleigh? Who can hear us?"

Kayleigh's eyes snap to Astra's, wild and wide. "Saran can hear the shadows, and he shares information with Kato. The shadows know you're here."

A loud shattering crash echoes from the ballroom behind us, followed by screams. My breath catches in my throat and I meet Cal's eyes briefly before we take off rushing toward the ballroom.

"They're here," Kayleigh whispers ominously as we run away.

"Lock her up," Astra orders, following behind me. "We'll need her later."

Chaos doesn't even begin to describe the scene that greets us. Every single window is broken, shards of glass scattered across the floor. Guests scream and run, but there is no escape. Dozens of Dragkonians sweep in through the broken windows. More people wisp in with them, attacking everyone nearby with different forms of magic. Most of them are strangers, but I recognize Niall and Aine among the attackers. I unsheathe my sword.

"Fight to kill," I order as I charge into the fray. "We don't need prisoners."

Every single guard joins the fight as well as anyone with magic, but it's not enough. Our blades simply don't penetrate the scales of the Dragkonians, and the attackers with magic are cleverly warded so we can't land a strike. The only person with any luck seems to be Astra. Her eyes glow silver as her magic manifests in silver lightning that strikes and brings down some of the magic users and intimidates the Dragkonians enough that they back away from her.

Bodies fall around me. Innocents. People who were never meant for war, their gowns and fine tunics stained with blood. Astra screams and a rush of magic courses over the ballroom. The magic users among our attackers seem startled and I realize that she's managed to bring down their wards. With renewed hope I strike again, cutting down one of the attackers closest to me, his blood spraying my face. We still can't fight off the Dragkonians, but at least we stand somewhat of chance against the humans.

I take down two more magic users and charge toward Niall. He meets my gaze with a wicked grin, his dark shadow magic surrounding me. I can't see him though his shadows, but I can sense his movements. When he uses a sword to strike me, I'm able block him.

"You'll have to do better than that," I snarl, swinging somewhat wildly, but my sword clashes against his.

"Oh, I can," Niall laughs, striking again.

I block him twice more, but a third attempt sinks into my side. I gasp and stagger back, my hand instinctively going to the wound. It's deep. Too deep. Blood is already soaking my tunic. He knows he struck me, but I can't let him know how bad the wound is. I lunge forward but only stumble, my head feeling light. Niall easily blocks my blow, letting out a low laugh.

"To think I will take down a prince, my fa—"

He doesn't get to finish. I thrust my sword forward, following his voice, and meet resistance. I force my sword in deeper, and the shadows slink away to reveal Niall inches away, my sword sticking directly through his heart. I jerk my sword back and his body falls to the ground with a wet thud. I glance down at my side, soaked crimson.

"Shit," I mutter, my head swimming. The wound is even deeper than I initially thought. It's likely a killing blow. I know it is.

I lift my gaze across the ballroom turned battlefield and find Cal. He's up against two magic users at once, and while he seems to be holding his own, he's covered in blood. I can't tell if it's his own or blood from those he's struck down. We're too far apart. We're supposed to stay together. Always. I have to help him. I have to make sure he's okay. I summon every bit of strength I can, which honestly isn't much, and stumble forward, but the room won't stop spinning. Cal takes down one of his opponents as I fall to my knees, struggling to breathe, the pain prickling across my skin like sharp needles.

"No!" Cal screams, but I can't focus on him. Everything is getting dark. "No!"

I feel a trickle of magic pass over me. A shield. At least no one else can strike me. Not that it matters. I know I'm done for.

Arms lift me and I force my eyes open. Cal's blurry face peers down at me. He has a cut. I lift a shaky hand to his cheek, brushing it gently.

"You're hurt," I rasp.

"Shh," he whispers, pulling me to his chest with one hand while the other presses firmly against the wound at my side. "Save your strength."

I close my eyes and draw a shaky breath. "Thank you for loving me."

"No, none of that. No," Cal says, his voice quavering. "You're going to be fine. You're—"

His voice breaks off into a sob and tears well in my own eyes. Not for me. No, I don't care if I die, but I don't want Cal to hurt. I try to open my eyes. I want to see his face one last time. But I can't. I . . .

"Ehren, hang on. Just—please! I need you." He chokes on a sob, his grip tightening. "I need you."

The pain is subsiding. Everything is fading to a vague numbness. The only thing tethering me to this world is Cal's pleading voice, but even that's growing distant, echoing against the darkness.

"You can't leave me. You can't! Don't die on me, Ehren." His voice breaks. "Please. Stay with me."

I want to comfort him. I want to hold him. I want one last kiss. One last moment of happiness for us both. But I can't manage any of it before the world disappears entirely. The last thing I hear is a whispered, "I love you," and I can't even say it back.

CHAPTER FIVE

ASTRA

Broken and crumbled bodies drown in a sea of crimson, the marble of the dance floor almost entirely hidden from view beneath the carnage. I use every bit of magic I can to force the Dragkonians back. If I can just push them back enough, I can cast a shield to protect those who haven't been struck down. It takes some work, but I manage to disable the wards around the magic users. That helps. Ehren charges forward, disappearing into a cloud of twisting shadows. I feel a tug on the bond and know Alak is already pushing his magic, but he's crafting some sort of illusion, allowing a few of the trained soldiers to take down several of those attacking us.

Someone strikes me from behind, a sliver of metal barely missing my neck but catching the skin on my shoulder. I spin and come face-to-face with Aine.

"You missed," I spit.

"Did I?" Her lips curl into a cruel smile. "Maybe I want to see your face when I kill you."

I summon a sword of starlight, matching her grin. "Good luck with that."

I charge forward, but she swerves out of the way. I spin, my sword nearly striking her. She shoots more metal shards, but my magic senses them and I dodge them with little effort. My second blow lands, slicing her left hand off. She screams and thrusts more metal my way. I block most of them, but one shard imbeds in my right arm. I scream and she grins, despite her own injuries. She charges again, but I'm done playing. Silver lightning crackles over my skin and reaches for her. She doesn't stand a chance. Her back arches in pain as her scream rips through the air. Her body crashes to the floor, charred and broken, never to rise again.

"No!" Cal's voice carries across the room.

My head shoots up, heart racing with panic as I search for him. Cal seems fine, save for a cut on his cheek, but he's running toward Ehren. Oh gods. Ehren is on his knees covered in blood. I charge forward, but I'm cut off by a snarling Dragkonian. I throw magic toward the creature, but it barely reacts. I look past the beast to Ehren and Cal. Ehren is dying. I can taste his death in the air. I do what I can, casting a shield over him and Cal.

The Dragkonian in front of me lunges, and I dive away, drawing my sword and striking as hard as I can. It does nothing but anger the creature, and he swoops back toward me. I feel panic down the bond, but I don't know if it's for me or if Alak's in trouble. I can't lose focus. I have to take down this creature. I have to save Ehren.

The Dragkonian shoots black fire my way, and I dodge, slamming to the ground. The creature leers down at me and hopelessness fills my chest. I can't beat this. I'm ready to accept death when suddenly the creature rears back in pain, a stick poking from its eyes. No, not a stick—an arrow made from a branch.

I jump to my feet and look around. More people are swarming into the ballroom, magic swirling around them, but they're fighting for us. More arrows whistle through the air. Some bounce off the natural scaled armor of the Dragkonians, but others strike eyes and fly into the open mouths of the creatures. Sensing the stakes, the creatures begin their retreat, the remaining magic users fleeing as well. With their departure I can concentrate on . . .

Ehren.

I race toward Cal and Ehren. Cal is screaming at him, pressing his hands to Ehren's side in an attempt to slow the blood, but it's still flowing too thick and fast, oozing between his fingers. I slide on the slick blood-coated marble and crash to the ground. I jump back up and stumble to Cal's side. He looks up at me, desperate.

"Save him," Cal begs, his eyes swollen with tears. "You have to save him."

I nod, tears stinging my eyes as I reach out my magic. Ehren is almost gone. His life-force is a whisper. I grab it and hold on tightly as my magic begins working, but it's not enough. My magic is weak. Even when Alak kneels next to me, his hand gripping my shoulder, sharing his magic, it isn't enough. I can't do it. Even if I empty every spark of magic I possess, I can't save him. I take a shuddering breath and meet Cal's eyes.

"No," he whispers, shaking his head. "No. I can't lose anyone else. I can't lose *him*. Please. Astra, *please*."

"Cal," I say as a hot tear snakes down my cheek. "I . . . I'm sorry."

"No," Cal sobs, cradling Ehren's body against his. "Please, no. No."

I feel so helpless as I squeeze my eyes shut, my body shaking with sobs of my own. What is the point of all my magic if I can't save those I love? Will I just be forced to watch them fade off one by one until I have no one left?

Another figure kneels next to me, placing delicate hands over mine. I jerk my face up to meet a young woman around my age with soft copper skin and silky black hair.

"May I?" she asks, her Gleador accent strong but her Callenian crisp.

I swallow and nod. What choice do I have? The young woman takes a deep breath and closes her eyes as she reaches forward. A soft yellow glow stretches from her to Ehren as healing magic warms the air. The seconds drag at a terrifyingly slow pace until the girl settles back on her heels with a nod.

"Is he okay?" I ask, scanning the girl's face.

"He'll need more healing, both magical and non, before he is back to normal, and he will likely have some scarring."

"But he'll live? He's going to live?" Cal presses, his voice trembling with equal parts terror and hope.

"He'll live," a voice says from behind me. I spin around and look up at Sama, her face drawn.

The woman nods her agreement. "As I said, his wound is severe and still needs tending to. He'll need bandages and ointments and additional care, but the worst has passed. He will live."

I nod, releasing a long sigh of relief. "We can handle that." I look back at Cal. "Can you carry him to the healing rooms?"

Cal nods, his breath shaky, but he also looks relieved. I look back up at Sama before letting my eyes drift over our rescuers for the first time. Jessalynn stands at the far end of the ballroom next to Kaeya, assessing the damage. My heart leaps. Jessalynn came through.

"Your magic is very weak," Sama says softly, drawing my attention back to her. "You aren't of any use to us here. Go rest with Ehren."

I shake my head as I stand. "If Ehren is out, someone needs to be in charge."

"Not you, love," Alak says, his voice soft in my ear. "She's right. You're weak."

I turn to face Alak. "You're weak, too."

He forces a smile but it doesn't go to his eyes. "Aye, love, I am, but you need to recover more than I do."

"I will take over here," Bram says, making me jump. I didn't realize he was nearby. I wonder at what point he joined the battle. He's covered in enough blood to indicate he was here for most of it. "I will fill Jessalynn in and work with her. You go take care of Ehren."

I finally concede and allow Alak to lead me away. We head to the normal healing room already overflowing with wounded. I make sure Ehren is set up, a healing assistant binding his wounds, before I allow them to check and bandage my own injuries. I lie down next to Alak on a cot in the corner of the room. As much as I long to stay awake and make sure we can turn everything right again, sleep claims me almost immediately.

I wake in a groggy haze, memories tumbling back into my mind. I sit up too quickly, the blood rushing to my head, making me dizzy. I steady myself on my makeshift cot and realize Alak is gone.

"You should be careful," a sharp voice with a thick accent commands. I look over to find the Healer from earlier approaching, her sleeves rolled up to her elbows. "You used a good bit of magic from what I hear."

"How long was I asleep?" I ask, shaking my head.

"I guess it's been about three hours now."

"That's long enough," I reply, pushing up from the cot. I nearly stagger but manage to keep myself upright enough to look competent. The woman still eyes me warily.

"Be careful," she insists. "I don't want you back in here for an injury that can be prevented."

"I understand, but I really need to check on things, on people." I need to see and count the dead. I need to know how many friends are lost. I need to do something besides lie here and be useless.

The woman watches me with an expression of deep understanding. I open my mouth to ask her how many are dead, how many are alive, how many are somewhere in between, but can't find the words. She offers me a sympathetic smile, seemingly reading my thoughts.

"I don't know that they have a final death count, but it is high." She glances over her shoulder where wounded are stretched, their moans and cries filling the halls. "Many more may join that count soon." She looks back at me. "I am truly sorry we were not able to get here sooner. My father should have helped with armies the first time you asked."

I start to nod but freeze, my eyes meeting hers. "Your father?"

She smiles and dips her head. "Yes. I suppose you and I haven't been formally introduced. I am Princess Elaine of Gleador, now the consort and wife to Prince Benito of Oyrain."

She extends her hand to me and I accept, giving a gentle shake as I wrap my head around what her words mean.

"Are you here on behalf of Gleador or Oyrain?"

Elaine lifts her shoulder in a small shrug. "Both, I suppose? My husband only has a small army to offer, but he offers it nonetheless."

"And you're a Healer?"

She nods, her eyes brightening. "A powerful one, I'm told."

"Thank you for everything, but especially for helping Ehren." I pause and glance around, trying not to seem too frantic. "Is he—?"

"He's healing well and resting in a private area as we speak."

I loose a long breath. "Good." I meet her eyes. "Thank you."

She tilts her head. "He means a good deal to you, doesn't he?"

"Yes. Ehren means so much to me in a way I can't even begin to describe."

"You love him?"

A small laugh escapes. "Yes, I do. I love him very much, but probably not in the way you mean."

Elaine nods. "I understand. However, the young man that brought you here, he you do love in that way?"

I feel like I'm glowing as I reply, "Yes. That's Alak. He's my bondmate."

"Ah, that explains the magic I sensed. What you have together is powerful."

"Do you happen to know where he went?"

Elaine shakes her head. "I'm afraid I don't. He was in here resting by your side for about an hour or so. I'm not entirely sure where he went, but I believe he said something about a prisoner."

I nod, my stomach sinking. Kayleigh. He must have gone to Kayleigh.

"Thank you, Princess Elaine."

She waves her hand. "Please, call me Elaine. The 'Princess' feels a bit unnecessary given our circumstances."

I return her smile. "You and Ehren have that in common."

"Hmm," she muses. "I haven't had much of a chance to chat with your prince, but the more I hear about him the more I think I like him. Now, go find your bondmate, but don't strain yourself."

I offer her a parting nod and leave the healing area. I come to a halt when I round the corner and see that the ballroom is being used to lay out the dead. My heart clenches as I step into the room, drawn by some unknown thread. I walk between the lines of bodies, my eyes trailing over their faces, taking them in. I don't know most of these people, and yet they were in the same room as me when they died. These are people I couldn't save. These are people I failed.

My eyes fall on a familiar face, his eyes staring unseeing at the ceiling, his brother clutching his hand as he sobs. Lorrell is dead but Pascal lives. How is that fair? Why would the gods allow it? My chest clenches with an almost unbearable pain. I struggle to breathe. Unable to bear it any longer, I turn and practically run from the room, nearly crashing into Kaeya.

"You are awake," Kaeya says, surveying me from head to toe with a scowl. "Should you be awake?"

I straighten, trying not to appear as shaken as I am. "Well, I am, regardless. Can you tell me where I can find Jessalynn?"

Kaeya eyes me a moment longer before nodding. "Follow me."

She turns and strides away, leaving me to trip after her. She turns each corner sharply, and I wonder how many times she's traveled this path. She stops abruptly outside of Lord Dughlas's study.

"She's in there," Kaeya says with a sharp nod toward the door. "Now, if you'll excuse me."

Without another word, she sweeps away. I gather what little strength I have and enter the study. Jessalynn sits on top of Lord Dughlas's desk, one leg hanging down and the other propped up on the desktop. Brock sits in the chair behind the desk. When I enter, Jessalynn's eyes dart to me.

"Ah, the Court Sorceress," Jessalynn grins. "Welcome to our war rally."

I frown as I cross the room. "This doesn't seem like the right time to be so cheerful."

Jessalynn's grin fades and she nods. "Trust me, I know. You're lucky we got here when we did. If we had arrived even a few minutes later, you'd likely all be dead."

"Yes, thank you," I say, inclining my head. "How did you know to come?"

Jessalynn sighs and pulls a dagger from a sheath on her thigh, using it to pick her nails. "It's a long story, but to sum it up, we were headed your way and stopped to camp for the night a little ways out. We saw the Dragkonians flying through the air in formation and decided to follow. They weakened the wards protecting . . . wherever we are, and we fought our way through as well. You also might want to throw some thanks to a random Seer in Gleador who forced us to leave when we did."

"Why are you here at all, though?" I press, taking another step forward. "Where did the army come from? How did you know to come?"

Jessalynn's eyebrows shoot up and she tilts her head, eying me curiously. "Cadewynn."

I still, my mouth dropping open. Jessalynn drops her leg and leans forward, watching me closely.

"You . . . didn't know?"

I shake my head. "I knew she was going to try and rally some support from King Naimon, and I knew Princess Elaine must have come for a reason but—"

Jessalynn laughs, shaking her head. "But you had no idea she was recruiting a whole army. Multiple armies, actually. Well, girl,"—she hops off the desk—"you're in for a surprise. The little princess has provided you not only with an army three thousand strong, but with supplies galore."

I stagger back, leaning against a nearby armchair for support. "Three thousand?"

"Yep. Possibly more. I got bored counting. And magical armor and weapons . . ." She trails off, narrowing her eyes at me. "You really had no idea?"

"None. Neither did Ehren, I can assure you." I pause, glancing around the study. "Where are the rest of the soldiers?"

Jessalynn shrugs. "On their way. It takes a while to move an army that big. Many are stationed a little ways out where we were when we saw the Dragkonians approaching. Cadewynn is with them. The rest are a day or so behind."

Color drains from my face as I lean more heavily on the chair. "Cadewynn returned to Callenia? She was supposed to stay in Gleador."

Jessalynn throws her head back and laughs. "I don't know how any of you thought you could tell that girl *anything* and expect her to comply."

I shake my head, trying to make sense of everything.

"Either way, she'll probably be here tomorrow if you want

to yell at her. It's a miracle I convinced her stay behind with Nyco in the first place."

I'm still processing everything Jessalynn has told me when suddenly I remember Kayleigh. I push away from the chair, standing straight.

"What is it?" Jessalynn pries, pointing her dagger toward me. "You just had a thought."

I pause, debating whether to not to share, but Jessalynn did save our lives.

"Right before the attack, someone came to warn us. Alak's cousin. I need to find her and see what else she knows."

"Who's Alak?" Jessalynn asks. "Oh, wait. He's your little bondmate, right?"

"Yes, he's my bondmate."

"Yeah, I think he already talked to the prisoner, being her cousin and all. Maybe you two could chat and see what he already knows."

I frown. It's not a bad suggestion, but part of me wants to talk to Kayleigh myself.

"Are you going to talk to the prisoner or find your lover?" Jessalynn cuts into my thoughts. "If it's the latter, I think he finally went to bed at the bequest of my dear brother's general. If it's the former, I'd love to come along."

I pause, my hand on the doorframe. If Alak really is resting, I should let him be. I close my eyes and travel down the bond. He's at peace which can only mean sleep given our circumstances. I turn back to Jessalynn.

"Fine, you can come with me, but follow my lead. I know Kayleigh and don't need you messing everything up."

Jessalynn practically bounces with glee as she bounds to my side, offering me a false salute. "Aye, aye, Captain."

I sigh and step into the hall. I'm not familiar enough with

the castle to know where the dungeon might be, but luckily I manage to find a servant who directs us. As we enter the dungeon I hear a familiar voice echo behind me.

"Why are you here? You are supposed to be resting."

I turn and offer Bram a weak smile. "I already rested."

Bram sighs, shaking his head. "You need more rest. I finally got Alak to go to bed and now you are here. You two are impossible."

"I need to talk to Kayleigh," I press. Jessalynn coughs pointedly and I amend, "*We* need to talk to Kayleigh."

"I doubt she'll make any more sense now than before," Bram mumbles, but he turns and motions for us to follow anyway. "She keeps rambling about shadows and dark magic."

He stops a few cells down from where Kayleigh lies in a crumpled heap, whispering to herself as she traces her finger in the dirt, drawing random swirls. Seeing her like this makes my heart ache.

"Don't go getting emotional," Jessalynn hisses in my ear.

"I'm not," I mutter. "It's just—"

"She's the enemy here," Jessalynn says, her voice hard. "Remember that."

I turn and glare at Jessalynn. "It doesn't mean we have to treat her poorly."

Jessalynn shrugs. "It doesn't mean we have to feel sorry for her and offer her cakes and biscuits either."

I grit my teeth and approach the cell. Kayleigh lifts her eyes to me and leaps to her feet, grasping the bars of her cell.

"Astra! Good, you came. I knew you would come. Alak came, too, but he didn't understand."

"Understand what, Kayleigh?" I say softly, stopping directly in front of her.

"The shadows," Kayleigh whispers, her eyes darting around wildly.

"I told you," Bram mutters under his breath.

I wave my hand to shush him and meet Kayleigh's eyes. "You mentioned the shadows before. You said Saran can speak to them?"

Kayleigh's head bobs up and down. "Yes. That's his magic. It's like Niall's but different. He doesn't control them. He speaks to them. He can talk to shadows, and they can tell him everything they've witnessed. They like to talk to him. The shadows are lonely."

"I think she's lost beyond help," Jessalynn whispers in my ear.

But I don't listen. My mind is whirring, thinking. The pieces are beginning to fit together. Suddenly, things make sense.

"Kayleigh, are you saying that the shadows are spying on us and reporting to Saran?"

Kayleigh nods vigorously. "Yes! Exactly! All he has to do is ask the right question and the shadows answer."

"That's how Kato knew we left Naskein," I muse, the rest of the pieces clicking into place. "That's how he knew we were here. And how he knew to attack Bram and Alak with their army as well as Ehren and Cal in the mountains. He finally asked the right questions."

I turn to Bram to find him staring at me in wide-eyed horror. "We need to get Saran," he says.

"No!" Kayleigh screams, throwing her body against the bars. "You can't hurt Saran! He's just a boy. He doesn't even want to help Kato. He's being manipulated."

"We won't hurt him," Bram says gently, taking a step toward Kayleigh.

"We want to rescue him," I add. "Do you know where he is?"

Kayleigh gnaws on her lip, looking from me to Bram. "You swear you won't hurt him?"

"On my life," Bram says, placing his hand over his heart.

Kayleigh hesitates and nods to Jessalynn over my shoulder. "What about her? She might hurt him."

"Me?" Jessalynn says, taking a step back. "I don't even know who he is enough to hurt him."

I turn to Jessalynn. "Saran is a young boy."

"He's eight. Only eight. You have to help him, not hurt him," Kayleigh pleads.

"Shit," Jessalynn says, holding up her hands in surrender. "Even I wouldn't hurt a kid."

I turn back to Kayleigh. "See? We want to help. Now, can you tell us where Saran is?"

"Kato hardly ever lets him leave his side anymore. He's obsessive about keeping Saran close."

"Well, that's just dandy," Jessalynn mutters. I glare at her.

"Is Kato in Embervein?"

Kayleigh studies me for a moment, chewing her lip so hard it starts to bleed. I step forward and place my hands over Kayleigh's on the bars.

"I can't help him if I can't get to him."

"He's in a village to the south. Hillbourough. He—he wants me dead, so he'll likely stay there until he can get to me. He's not happy I went against his plans. He'll be furious I got away."

I glance over at Bram and he nods. "I can find a map, but I think I know where the village is."

"You have the whole kingdom memorized, don't you? You seem like the type," Jess says, her head cocked as she studies Bram.

I roll my eyes, choosing to ignore Jess and the glare Bram sends her way, opting to turn my attention to Kayleigh. "We'll get your brother and keep him safe."

I release her hands and turn to walk away.

"But remember the shadows!" she calls after me. "Don't let the shadows hear your plan."

I look back at her and offer her what I hope is a reassuring smile, though I don't really feel confident at the moment. "Don't worry. We won't."

Bram, Jessalynn, and I leave the cells and head back to the study. We light every sconce and candle we can, driving as many shadows from the room as possible. Once we have plenty of light, we clear the room of people, save for Brock and Kaeya.

"How soon can you get to Hillbourough?" I ask Bram as he stares down at a map.

"Within a few hours, I think," he says without lifting his eyes. "It should be quick and relatively easy to get there."

"How many men do you need?" Jessalynn asks. "I have some I can spare while yours recover from the attack."

Bram lifts his eyes to mine. "I just need Alak."

I scowl and cock my head. "Just Alak?"

Bram nods. "The more people I take with me the more likely we are to be detected. We need stealth. Alak can help with illusion and warding. Plus, Saran may recognize him and be more inclined to trust us. He may be wary of a small army, and we need to make it as easy as possible to get him to come with us willingly."

"What if something goes wrong? What if . . ." My voice trails off, and Bram quickly crosses to me, placing his hands on my shoulders. Tears burn my eyes as I look up at him.

"I told you before, I will protect Alak. Trust me. I will do everything in my power to make sure he comes home to you."

I swallow and nod as I stare into the intensity in his eyes. "When will you leave?"

"First thing in the morning," Bram replies, dropping his hands from my shoulders and turning to look out the window. "We have a couple hours before dawn. We should all get some rest before it arrives."

I'm too tired to argue, so I nod. "Fine."

"Do you—would you like me to walk you to your room?" Bram asks, glancing to the side as red tinges his cheeks.

A small laugh escapes and I shake my head. "Thank you for the offer, but I'll manage. I might check on Ehren first though."

"Last I checked he was still resting, Cal by his side."

I sigh. "Then I guess I'll head to bed." I close the distance between Bram and place a quick kiss on his cheek.

Bram flushes, blinking down at me. "What was that for?"

I smile softly. "It's a thank you for being there when I need you. Goodnight, Bram."

I leave the study and manage to find my room, although I feel like I'm sleep walking. Alak is sprawled across the bed on top of the covers, still fully dressed, boots and all. I chuckle and climb into bed next him. He shifts and blinks over at me, his gaze blurred by sleep.

"Astra?"

I smile, snuggling up against him. "I missed you."

He adjusts, pulling me closer and angling his body toward me.

"I'll argue with you later about leaving the healing room," he mumbles, his voice groggy, "but for now, I'm happy you're here."

I take a deep breath and close my eyes. Slowly, we drift off to sleep, neither of us ready for what will greet us soon.

CHAPTER SIX

ALAK

"So let me get this straight. You decided to interrogate a prisoner without me and then made a rescue plan all on your own?" Ehren says, scowling at Astra and Bram from where he's propped up on a healing cot, leaning against Cal.

"It needed to be done," Bram says firmly, standing at his full height.

"You're not the only one who can make plans," Astra adds quickly.

Ehren looks over at me. "Were you also involved in this?"

I shake my head. "Nope. I was sleeping like a good boy while they were planning their coup."

"It's not a coup," Astra protests, rolling her eyes. "Besides, the only reason you weren't there was because you had already checked on Kayleigh and left."

"True enough," I reply with a small shrug.

She turns her attention back to Ehren. "Last time I checked, I was your Court Sorceress and Bram was your general. You would think we could have a modicum of control over these choices."

"You two, sure, but why is she involved?" Ehren asks, gesturing dramatically to Jessalynn standing along the back wall picking her nails with a dagger.

"My involvement was more . . . proximity." Jessalynn grins. "Besides, I'd think you'd be a bit more grateful, dearest brother, seeing as how I saved your life and all."

"We are very grateful," Cal cuts in, pressing a kiss to Ehren's cheek.

Ehren sighs and takes Cal's hand, weaving their fingers together. "Yes, I'm grateful. I just hate being confined to this damn bed."

"According to Elaine, you can get out of bed this afternoon as long as you're stable," Astra says. "So stop pouting."

"Good, because I have a birthday party to plan."

"Oh, whose birthday is it?" Jessalynn asks, her eyes bright with mischief as she pushes away from the wall.

"No one's," Bram says through gritted teeth.

Jessalynn's smile fades as she collapses back against the wall with a huff. "Oh. Yours. That would be the most boring birthday party ever. We can play a rousing round of 'pin the scowl on the general.' The kids will love it."

Astra bites back a smile as she turns back to Ehren. "Anyway, Alak and Bram should really get on the road soon if they want to reach Hillbourough before Kato leaves."

Ehren sighs dramatically. "Fine, but if anything goes wrong —"

"I'll wisp us out," I cut in. "At the first hint of trouble. Even if we don't have my cousin. I swear."

Ehren eyes me for a moment before switching his attention

to Bram. "I know you're lying but I guess I don't have a choice. Hurry back. Okay?"

Bram offers Ehren a half-smile and sharp nod. "We'll be back before you know it."

"For cake."

Bram sighs and strides from the room.

"You better come back for cake, Bram," Ehren calls after him. "That's an order."

I grin and follow Bram out of the castle and down into the courtyard where our horses are ready to go. The air is cold and the sky is full of heavy gray clouds, but any bad weather holds off. Around noon, the village comes into view. Even from this distance, it looks abandoned. I cast the strongest illusion around us I can and we push forward.

Hillbourough is a ghost town. I don't know the last time it was occupied, but my best guess is no one has been here in months. We leave our horses at the edge of town to walk through.

"Can you sense any magic?" Bram asks, his voice low as he scans the streets.

I shake my head. "Nothing yet."

Every step we take feels weighted, like we're marching to our doom. I can't shake the dark cloud surrounding me, but I can't sense anything directly that we should fear.

"We should split up," Bram suggests.

"I don't think that's a good idea," I mutter, shaking my head. "If something goes wrong, I can't wisp you away."

"It looks like everyone is gone, but they may have left behind some sort of clue. We can cover more ground and get back sooner if we split up."

I finally concede to his plan, but I still don't like it. There's something ominous here, even if I can't place what it is.

Roughly half an hour later, we're both still perfectly fine, and we're almost done searching the town. Thankfully it's pretty small. I'm headed back toward Bram when I feel it—something dark and powerful. I race down the street.

"We have to go!" I yell toward Bram as he exits a house at the opposite end of the street several yards away.

Bram knits his eyebrows. "Did you find something?"

"No, but I *feel* something. We need—"

My words are cut short as a pillar of fire roars to life in front of me, Kato stepping out, his lips curled into a cruel grin.

"Ah, Alak," he says, his voice not quite his own as the fire dissolves into smoke. "It's been a while since you betrayed me. We really should catch up."

I gather my magic to wisp to Bram so I can get him out, but Kato chuckles.

"No, I think not."

An invisible force grabs my magic, cutting off access. I fall to the ground with a gasp, and I try to fight off Kato's hold. Where the hell did he learn this trick?

Bram glances to me, keeping one eye trained on Kato. "Alak, are you okay?"

"My magic," I gasp, panic rising in my chest. "I can't . . . He's blocking my magic."

"Let him go," Bram demands, focusing entirely on Kato.

Kato laughs and turns to stare at Bram, who now stands only a few feet away.

"Who are you to tell me to do anything?"

Kato throws a blast of magic toward Bram and Bram dodges, the flame barely missing him.

"Fight fair," Bram yells through gritted teeth. "Use your sword."

Kato laughs again, and holds out his hand, his fire sword appearing in his palm. "This sword?"

He launches forward and Bram blocks his blow.

"Stop this, Kato," I cry as he and Bram spar, their swords flashing faster than my eyes can follow.

Kato ignores me as he concentrates on the battle. I stand by, watching in terror. Kato still has a hold on my magic so I'm useless. Gods, why did I never learn how to competently wield some sort of weapon?

"This is tiring," Kato growls before wisping a few feet away behind Bram.

"Behind you!" I scream.

Bram spins and manages to block Kato's blow just in time. Kato seems more than annoyed. He wisps again. This time, Bram isn't fast enough, Kato's sword plunging through his back.

"NO!" I scream, scrambling forward.

"There," Kato says, jerking his sword from Bram's body.

Bram falls onto his knees, his eyes wide, mouth gaping. I tumble down in front of him, catching his body as he falls forward.

"Well, I meant to kill you, Alak, but I guess Bram will do for now. It sends the same message."

"What message is that?" I manage between gritted teeth,

Kato's grin is feral as he says, "Tell Astra I said hello and I look forward to seeing her again soon."

Kato disappears in a flash of fire before I can reply. I turn my attention back to Bram. With Kato gone I can feel my magic retuning slowly. Bram gasps and I shift his body so he's stretched out looking up at me, the life quickly fading from his eyes.

"Hold on," I whisper. "I need you to hold on. I'll get you

back to Astra and Ehren and we'll get you a Healer. One of the really good Healers. Okay?"

I stare down into his gold-speckled brown eyes, barely able to breathe. Bram takes a strangled breath, his mouth moving like he wants to speak, but can't quite get the words to form. Tears burn my eyes, blurring my vision.

"You hear me? We'll get you home and you can have your birthday cake. I bet it's good. What's your favorite flavor? Mine's chocolate."

Bram coughs, blood dripping from his mouth.

"Alak, I need—" His voice breaks off as he coughs up more blood.

His eyes shutter closed, and I shake him.

"No, no, no. Hang on. Just hang on."

Why isn't my bloody magic returning to full force yet? I need to wisp us out of here. I need to save him.

"Alak," Bram tries again, forcing his eyes open part-way. "Tell Astra I kept my promise. Tell her—" He pauses for a breath that almost doesn't come. "Tell her I l-love her. M-make sure she knows."

"You can tell her yourself," I say, my own voice trembling as tears trail down my cheeks. "Okay? Give my magic a few more seconds and I'll take you back to her. I'll even let you kiss her. That's a promise."

A whisper of a smile crosses his lips. "Just . . . love her and g-guard her . . . with everything . . . you possess."

Every word is a struggle, and I can't find it in myself to interrupt.

"Alak, you've been . . . a good friend. Better than I . . . d-deserve. You—"

His voice drops off. I expect him to cough or try to take a

breath but nothing happens. He's just staring off at nothing. I shake him but nothing happens. He's gone.

"No," I scream shaking him as hard I can. "You can't die like this. Get up. P-please get up."

But he doesn't move. His eyes just stare up at me. Another pair of gold-speckled brown eyes that will never see again. I lose all control. Sobs rack my body as I gather Bram's limp body against my chest. I cry and cry, my tears soaking his hair as I cradle him.

It's not fair. Bram was a good man. He deserved the world and he got nothing. He should have died in the blaze of battle. No, he should have died of old age, long after the war, a retired war hero. He should have had a chance to find love and marry a good girl and have lots of little babies with gold-speckled brown eyes. He never even got a chance to really live.

I don't know how long I sit there, soaked in blood and tears before I manage to rally. I use my fingertips to pull his eyelids closed. Now he looks like he's sleeping. I manage to gather enough strength to carry his body back to the horses. Solomon steps forward and I lose it again. I'm tempted to wisp Bram and I back and come back for Fawn and Solomon. But, no. Bram needs one last ride atop his horse. The journey back to the castle is slow. I feel like I'm emptied of tears by the time I enter the courtyard. Ehren comes bounding out, a smile on his face.

"Good! You're back. I have—" His face falls when he meets my swollen eyes as I dismount. "What…?"

His eyes shoot to Solomon and his hand flies to his mouth. He stumbles back, shaking his head. Cal catches him, his eyes also fixed on Solomon's back. He takes an unsteady breath and turns Ehren around, drawing him against his chest, stroking his hair gently. Ehren doesn't fight it, burying his face in the crook of Cal's neck.

"It was a trap," I manage, my voice raw. "Kato showed up and stabbed him through with his sword. He did something to my magic so I couldn't fight him or get us out."

Ehren pulls away from Cal and looks at me. His gaze is heavy, and I feel a fresh stab of guilt.

"I tried. I really did."

"I believe you," Ehren says, his voice quiet.

"I need to tell Astra."

"No," Ehren says sharply. "I'll tell her."

"But I—"

"You need a moment to mourn," Ehren says, standing straighter. "You witnessed the m-murder of a friend. Take a few minutes to collect your thoughts. Astra is with Jess and Winnie, so your room is vacant. Take a moment for yourself."

I know I should protest. Ehren is more affected by Bram's death than I am, but he has Cal. Even though Cal looks like he could fall apart at any moment. But he's right. I need a moment. I need to figure out what I'll say to Astra. I thought about it for hours all the way back, but I still can't think straight.

"Go on, Alak," Ehren whispers, his voice cracking as a tear slides down his cheek. He places a hand on my shoulder. "I've got this. I need a moment to s-say goodbye on my own, anyway."

Without any more hesitation, I wisp directly to my room. I can't stand the thought of accidentally running into Astra or anyone else. I collapse on the bed and weep. Why can't I keep any of the Bramfields alive? Why am I always covered in their blood?

CHAPTER SEVEN

ASTRA

After Bram and Alak ride off, I distract myself helping Ehren plan Bram's party. Bram will protest every moment, but I know he'll still secretly love it. Jessalynn even joins in, claiming she has nothing better to do. It's lucky for me she agrees or it would have been ten times harder to get Lord Dughlas onboard. It seems he gets jittery around daggers and will readily agree to things when one is present.

We're heading from our discussion with Lord Dughlas when Cadewynn arrives with more of Jessalynn's soldiers.

"I missed you!" she cries, rushing into my arms so hard we topple to the ground.

I laugh. "I can see that."

Cadewynn rolls to the side, grinning. I stand and offer her my hand. She accepts and I pull her to her feet.

"Want to help me make a cake?" I grin.

"Absolutely!" Cadewynn says, clapping her hands in delight. She pauses, cocking her head. "Though, I've never made a cake before."

"Great," Jessalynn huffs. "Two people who can't bake are making the cake."

I stick out my tongue. "*I've* made a cake before."

Jessalynn waves us off. "Whatever. I'll help, but only because I want it to be edible."

Cadewynn rolls her eyes and loops her arm with Jessalynn's. Jessalynn scowls down at their linked arms but doesn't pull away.

"Well, let's go make a cake," she grumbles.

I don't think Lord Dughlas's cook is happy with us being in his kitchen, given the way he glares as we mix the batter. He storms out with a huff when we go to set the cake in the oven. We're in the middle of mixing icing when something feels off. I lean against the counter, and Cadewynn stops mid-laugh to tilt her head in concern.

"What's wrong?" she asks.

I place my hand to my head. "I'm not sure."

I pull on the bond. It's still there, but it feels weaker some-how. If something were truly wrong, I would know. I shake it off and force a smile.

"Let's finish this cake."

The final product ends up being a little lopsided with uneven icing, but it's not bad. Jessalynn insists on being the one to carry it into the dining hall.

"You two would drop it," she sneers.

"Whatever," I reply with a shrug. "If you want to haul the heavy cake all the way into the dining hall, I'm not going to stop you."

After she attempts to carry the cake a few times, Jessalynn concedes that the cake might be a bit heavy and awkward, so we end up having servants assist us. We spend the rest of the day making decorations. We even enlist help from some of the recovering wounded who are stuck in their beds. Once we have a good amount of various streamers and other decorations, we head to the dining hall to put them up. After Ehren is officially released by the Healers, he swings by multiple times to check on our progress. More than once, we have to chase him away from the cake.

"Stop sticking your fingers in the icing!" I chide, smacking his hand.

Ehren grins, licking a lump of icing off his finger. "I'm the prince. I get to taste the icing."

"No, you don't," Jessalynn snaps. She grabs his shoulders and steers him away, shoving him out the door. "Get out of here and go do something useful."

Ehren laughs, linking his hand with Cal's as he walks away, and we resume our preparations. About an hour later a servant enters, glancing around nervously.

"What is it?" Jessalynn demands.

"I'm here to take Mistress Astra to meet the prince."

My first thought is that Ehren has another ridiculous idea that Bram will hate, but my smile immediately fades at the girl's somber expression.

"What is it?" I ask, barely breathing as I wait for her reply.

The girl glances away. "I've only been instructed to take you to Prince Ehren."

I exchange a worried glance with the others.

"I'm sure everything is fine," Cadewynn offers with a weak smile that doesn't reach her eyes.

I nod, faking a smile. "I'm sure you're right."

As I follow the girl from the dining hall, I check the bond. It's still there, though I think something is wrong. I can't quite place what, though. It feels like maybe Alak has some sort of barrier up. He and Bram should be back soon, and I'll feel better being able to see them. The servant girl stops just short of a room I haven't been in yet, but I know it's meeting room of some sort.

"He's in there," the girl says, avoiding my eyes as she nods to the room.

I swallow, my mouth suddenly dry. "Thank you."

I rally my strength and walk into the room. Ehren stands at the far end and before he even turns to face me, I know something is wrong. Everything about this room is wrong. The air is heavy and thick with despair. About a dozen servants and soldiers stand around the room, but no one will look at me, save for Cal, whose arm is wrapped around Ehren's shoulders. The look he gives me through bloodshot eyes does nothing to calm my unease.

I check the bond one more time. It's still intact. Alak is alive but... My heart seizes.

"Ehren, what...?"

He turns to me and everything about him is broken. His eyes are red and swollen and tears stain his cheeks. His mouth opens but no words come out. He reaches toward me.

"Astra," he finally manages, his voice trembling and hoarse. He doesn't need to say more. The message is written on his face, in his broken posture.

I back away, shaking my head. "No. No."

He takes a shuddering breath and with it he takes the last oxygen in the room. There's no more air left for me. At least, that's how it seems as my lungs struggle to breathe.

"No," I manage again, my voice weak.

My heart feels like it's cracking, pain rippling through my core. Ehren takes another step toward me. He presses his lips together and squeezes his eyes shut. When he opens them again, another tear slides free and he focuses his gaze on me.

"Bram . . . ," he starts again.

"No," I whisper, shaking my head violently. "Don't you say it! Don't you dare say it!" My voice grows louder with each word until I'm yelling. My magic rises, led by the storm of emotions, the entire room trembling and shaking. "If you say the words, then it's true. So don't say it."

My entire body is shaking. Ehren reaches out and pulls me against his chest to steady me, resting his chin on my head. He holds me tightly as a sob escapes. I jerk back after a moment, shaking my head fiercely, refusing to surrender completely.

"No, you're wrong. You have to be," I say, my voice raw.

Ehren shakes his head. He sucks in a breath, trying to gain control over his own tears. "I wish I was." He motions to the table at the back of the room. The table where something lies still and unmoving under a red and gold cloth.

I back away further, my breath ragged. "No, that's not him. It's a mistake." It takes a second for my voice to break through my sobs. "It has to be a mistake."

"Astra," Ehren says again, his voice breaking. "It's not. I wish to the gods it were but it's not." He looks up toward the heavens, but if that red cloth is what he's claiming, there are no gods listening to us right now. They've abandoned us.

I stare at the table, at the lifeless form beneath the cloth. Slowly, on unsteady feet, I make my way forward. I stand at the edge of the table and look down. Ehren stands behind me and nods to a soldier standing watch. The soldier grabs the corner of the cloth and slowly pulls it back, revealing a cold, pale, lifeless face. I cover my face with my hands and sobs rack my body.

Ehren holds me tightly as I bury my face in his chest. After a moment, I pull back enough to glance at the table. This time I can't look away. Bram lies there, eyes closed. He must just be asleep. He has to be asleep. I watch closely, waiting for the smallest movement. A single breath. A blink. Anything. Nothing happens. No matter how long I look, no matter how much I long for it, he doesn't move and he never will again. I feel as if I have been shattered into a million pieces—pieces that can never be put together again, no matter how hard I try.

"My magic," I gulp. "Maybe I can . . ."

"No, Astra," Ehren weeps into my hair. "He's gone."

I surrender wholeheartedly to my sobs. Ehren holds me, sobbing right along with me. Eventually, I pull away. I stand over Bram's body and look down. I brush a lock of hair out of his face with a trembling hand.

"I would have fought with you," I whisper. "I would have saved you. I would died with you." I turn to Ehren and look into his swollen eyes. "What happened?"

Ehren doesn't answer. He glances down and his hands.

"Ehren," I say, my voice cold and lethal. "Did Kato do this?"

Ehren nods and looks me in the eye. He reaches over and pulls the cloth down a little further. In the middle of Bram's chest is a burn mark, one the exact size of Kato prefers for his fire sword. I look back up at Ehren.

"Yes. Apparently h-he—" Ehren's voice breaks.

Cal steps to Ehren's side, drawing him into his arms. Ehren collapses against him and Cal looks over Ehren's shoulder at me.

"Kato stabbed him from behind, according to Alak," Cal says, his voice low and barely controlled.

My heart stops as a new horror fills my mind. I struggle to breathe as the world closes in. Alak was there. Alak could be hurt, dying. But no. The bond is still strong enough that I know Alak is fine. I would know if he wasn't, wouldn't I?

Cal must read the fear on my face and quickly shakes his

head. "Alak survived. He brought . . ." His voice falters but he pushes through his grief. "He brought Bram back as well as both horses."

Ehren pulls away from Cal. Collecting himself the best he can. "I told him to take a moment to himself while I told you. He disappeared immediately."

I raise my chin, feeling slightly fortified knowing that Alak is alive. I look back at Bram and clench my teeth. "This was a personal strike."

Ehren nods once, his eyes unforgiving. "Yes."

I turn and stride across the room toward the door, a plan already forming in my mind. I may not have the gods-blessed sword Aoibhinn and the histories say I need, but I can sure as hell still find Kato and destroy him and the dark empire he's trying to build. I won't let him take anyone else from me.

"What are you going to do?" Ehren calls, chasing after me.

I don't even glance back as I answer, "First, I'm going to find Alak, make sure he's okay. Then, I'm going to go kill my brother."

"Astra, stop!" Ehren yells, catching my wrist.

I spin to face him, power coursing through me. He drops my wrist like it burns, and I feel a brief flash of regret that my magic may have hurt him. He recovers quickly, placing his hands on my shoulders and forcing me to meet his eyes.

"You need to stop and think before you do anything rash," he says, his voice bordering on a pleading tone.

"He cannot get away with this. I *will* kill him," I spit. "I will go out and find him and end this once and for all."

"He'll answer for this. I swear on the life Bram lived, Kato will answer for this." He releases me and takes my hands in his, holding them firmly yet gently. "But we will do it together. Do you understand? I can't lose you both in one day."

A harsh laugh escapes my lips and I shake my head. "I won't let my brother kill me."

Ehren's eyes lock with mine. "There's more than one way to lose a person, and I won't lose you, Astra. Not today or any day soon. I am not going to let you kill your brother without someone else there to catch you if you fall. We will do this *together*. Swear to me that you will wait. Swear you will let us develop a plan before you rush into action." He squeezes my hands. "Swear it."

I study his face, his desperation and fear palpable. Something in me sinks. Ehren is right. This is something I shouldn't do alone.

"Fine," I manage. Ehren raises an eyebrow and I add, "I swear I'll wait."

Ehren exhales and his posture loosens as he leans forward and presses his forehead to mine. "Thank you, Ash." He releases my hands and straightens. "I promise, he will not get away with any of this, Ash. I swear on Bram's life."

I swallow and manage a nod. I open my mouth to say something else, but the words don't come. I glance back toward the table where Cal stands, watching us—more Ehren than me. Looking at Bram just lying there twists my insides up again, and I'm overcome with the need to be anywhere else. I turn and stride away before I can fall apart again publicly.

I race through the halls toward my room, a literal shadow covering my body. My power ripples out from me, unwilling to be controlled. For the first time in ages I reach through an old, almost forgotten bond, its path cold and stiff.

I'm going to kill you.

A cruel laugh ripples through the bond, rife with wicked, dark amusement.

You can try.

I startle at the voice, Kato's and yet not. I'm still reeling from grief, anger, and confusion when I stumble into my room, ready to throw myself on my bed and weep for a while, but I stop short in the doorway. Alak sits on the edge of our bed, his head bowed into his hands. When he hears me enter, he lifts his head and my heart plummets at the sight of his swollen eyes and tear-streaked face.

"It's my fault," he chokes out as I rush to his side. "Kato was going to kill me. It was supposed to be *me*, but Bram got all heroic."

He chokes on a sob as I wrap my arms around him and pull him close. I let tears run silently down my cheeks as I rest my chin on his shoulder.

"I'm sure that's not true," I whisper, my voice uneven.

Alak pulls back and his eyes meet mine. "But it is. Kato was going to kill me. He had me down and cornered, but Bram jumped in, challenging Kato, drawing his attention away from me." His voice breaks and he puts his face in his hands. "Damn fool. Why would he do that?"

Bram's promise to keep Alak safe echoes through my mind and guilt washes over me. It's not Alak's fault. If anyone in this room is at fault, it's me. I place a finger under Alak's chin and raise his gaze to mine.

"Bram was a soldier. He knew what he was doing. Don't dishonor his memory by doubting his last actions, the last choice he made."

Alak attempts a smile but fails miserably. "He did it for you."

I jerk back. "What?"

Alak straightens and swallows as he nods. "After Kato withdrew his sword, Bram fell into my arms, still alive albeit barely. Kato had blocked my magic so I couldn't wisp or do anything useful. I couldn't get him back here. I begged him to hang on, to live. Bram looked up at me and said 'Just love her and guard her with everything you possess.' His last words and thoughts were of you, Astra. He literally loved you until his dying breath."

Any resolve I'd been holding onto up to this point shatters, and I fall into Alak's arms weeping. He wraps his arms around me, easily switching from being the comforted to the comforter. He gently strokes my head and back. I finally raise my eyes to his.

"I'm sorry," he whispers, his voice breaking. "I'm so sorry I couldn't save him."

I shake my head. "No more apologies." I brush away a tear from his cheek. "At least I still have you." He opens his mouth to speak, but I shake my head again and press a finger to his lips. "I would rather have you both alive, but if Kato had taken you from me or even worse, both of you, I do not know that I could go on living." I press my palm over Alak's heart. "You and I are soul-bound. I cannot survive without you."

Alak holds my gaze for several moments before he closes the gap and presses his lips to mine. He pulls back and whispers, "I love you so much. You know that? It's more than the bond. I love *you*."

I swallow and nod. "I know. I love you, too."

And then my lips are on his. Everything moves quickly, our movements born out of a need to be comforted rather than passion alone. Every heated kiss, every caressing touch means something more. As we shed our clothes and our bodies intertwine, we become one, our magic ebbing and surging, echoing our need, our pain. Together, we mourn the dead and celebrate those who survived.

CHAPTER EIGHT

RONAN

When I arrive at Clan Dughlas's fortress, everyone is clearly in mourning, dressed in layers of black. Dread pools in my gut as I navigate the shuffling crowd, terrified to discover if one of my friends died. It doesn't take me long to find out. Even though I was never close to Bram, his death affects me in a way I didn't expect.

What I expect even less is Astra silently slinking away from the castle toward the stables. I chase after her, calling her name.

"Ronan?" she asks, turning around and blinking.

"Aye, love," I reply, catching up to her. "I only arrived a little bit ago. Things seemed settled enough at the Summer Palace and I thought, as your representative to Athiedor, it made sense for me to join you here." I pause, glancing up at a black banner waving in the breeze. "I heard what happened."

Astra swallows hard, nodding, unable to find her words.

"I'm quite sorry for your loss. Even more sorry I wasn't here for you when it happened."

She looks up and meets my eyes, offering me a small, joyless smile. "Well, you're here now."

"Aye, love, I am, and I'll stay as long as you need me."

"Thank you."

"So," I start, glancing toward the stables, "where are you sneaking off to?"

"I have an appointment of sorts."

I cock an eyebrow. "An appointment?"

She nods, hesitating a moment before adding, "Would you like to come with me?"

"As long as my presence won't be an intrusion."

Her smile this time seems more genuine. "Your presence is never an intrusion."

"Well, then, how could I turn down such an offer?"

A few minutes later, I'm riding by her side away from the village and castle. For a long time, neither of us speak. I glance over at Astra occasionally. Her eyes are slightly bloodshot with dark circles underneath. I wonder how much sleep she's gotten. I wonder even more why she's leaving alone without Alak or Ehren, but if she wanted to share those details I know she would. She doesn't need me to pry.

"Where are we going exactly?" I ask when I realize that our destination isn't as close as I first suspected.

"Do you see that forest?" she asks, nodding to a line of trees still miles in the distance.

"Sure."

Astra stares straight ahead. "That's where the Faerie ring is."

My heart races at her words. "You're contacting them now?"

She turns to me with a wry smile. "Yes. Perhaps I should have mentioned that before we left?"

I laugh, shaking my head, my mind spinning. "Perhaps. I'm not sure I have time to prepare myself."

"Trust me, no amount of time is enough when you're dealing with the Fae. They're quite"—she pauses, searching for the right word—"cantankerous."

I laugh again and a little light returns to her eyes.

"Anything I should know about the Fae before I come face-to-face with one?"

"Don't piss them off," she replies, a smile twitching at the corner of her mouth.

"I know that much from my faerie stories."

Her smile takes hold as she looks over at me with something akin to affection. "I suppose out of everyone you'd be the most acquainted with the Fae through your stories."

We ride in silence for a bit longer before I decide to attempt conversation again.

"Is this the first time you've contacted them?"

She shakes her head. "I contacted them the day we arrived, but the particular Fae I need to speak to weren't available. I was told to come back today."

"Ah. Thus the reason we're heading out despite . . . everything."

"Yeah." She sniffs but keeps her tears in check. "Plus, I could really use the distraction."

I've been where she is now, mourning a loved one. At some point, you can't find any more tears to cry, no matter how much your heart still aches. Then grief comes back with renewed force when you least expect it. It's not even the big moments of emptiness. Those you can handle. It's the tiny moments, the simple thoughts that sneak up on you in the quiet. The reminders in the way someone says something. A favorite color. A favorite food. Each tiny little thing catching you unaware. I know how she's suffering, and some part of me wishes I could take that away. No one deserves to feel this brand of helplessness.

As we ride I relay idle chatter and share some basic Athiedor history. Astra nods along, staying mostly silent, happy to let me carry the weight of the conversation. When we reach the edge of the forest, Astra dismounts.

"Leave the horses here."

"May I inquire as to why?" I ask, following her lead without waiting for her reply.

Astra shrugs. "We had to leave them the first time. Our guide didn't really give a reason, but I'm sure she had one."

"So," I clarify with a grin, "I'm just supposed to abandon my horse and follow you into the trees?"

Astra looks up at me, a smile playing on the corner of her lips as her eyes shine. "You can do whatever you want. Of course, if you decide to stay here with your horse, you run the risk of never meeting a Fae."

I laugh, placing a hand on my chest. "Oh, you do know the way to my heart."

She glances to my cane before quickly looking back up to my eyes. "You can handle a little hike, I assume?"

"I'm sturdier than I look," I reply with a wink. I gesture toward the trees. "Lead the way."

Astra crunches through the forest until we reach a river. I inhale sharply, my eyes widening when I see the circle of flowers that hum with magic.

"So all that research was worth something. Faerie rings are real, legitimate things," I mumble in awe, eyeing the ring.

"Yes," Astra replies, stepping into the center of the ring and kneeling down.

Astra whispers the spell under her breath as she traces

symbols in the dirt. I want to step closer, but I don't dare disrupt the process. She stands up, repeating the spell louder this time.

"Shite!" I yell, stumbling back as a beam of light shoots up from the ground. Astra glances over her shoulder at me and grins before turning her attention back to the light.

My eyes go even wider, and I stumble back a step from the circle as a Fae steps from the light. She's tall and lean with long limbs and bright pink hair. I've imagined and dreamed of the Fae since my childhood, but I must admit seeing one this close is terrifying. When she flashes her sharp teeth in what I suppose is a smile, my chest constricts in fear. I tighten the grip on my cane. I've never used it as a weapon before—I doubt it would do anything against the Fae—but for once I'm glad I have the blasted thing handy.

Astra, however, doesn't seem to hold an ounce of fear.

"Hycis," she says, leaning into hug—*hug!*—the Fae woman as the beam of light dissolves.

"One of my favorite humans," the Fae says with a laugh. Her eyes turn to me and I freeze, my heart pounding so hard in my chest it's almost painful. "Oh, and you brought another little human along."

Astra glances over at me with a smile. "This is my friend, Ronan." She pauses before adding, her smile falling away, "I didn't feel like being alone today."

Hycis turns her attention back to Astra and studies her. "You are in mourning. I am sorry."

Astra barely manages to control her emotions as she nods. "Yes, my brother killed Bram."

The Fae's lips part in shock and she bows her head. "He was a good man for a human. I am sorry for your loss."

"Thank you," Astra whispers. "I don't want to lose anyone else. Can you help?"

Hycis nods, a smile curling on her lips. "I can."

She pulls a bag the size of a fat cat off her shoulder and hands it to Astra. Astra opens the bag and her eyes brighten.

"They're ripe," Astra breathes, reaching into the bag and withdrawing a handful of blushing red berries.

"Some are. The rest of the crop will be ripe within a week, maybe two. Then it will be another week or so for us to harvest them. The juice is strong, however, and is still fatal when diluted. You can mix the juice with water or other substances to make it stretch further while you wait for more."

Astra nods, dropping the berries back into the bag. "Thank you, Hycis. We may actually be able to survive this war now."

"I have more news for you," Hycis says. "I reached out— well, Fenian reached out since he is the one with connections —and we elicited the help of our Fae kin. We have no firm solution, but with their help, we are closer to finding a solution to take care of the Dragkonians once and for all."

"You can seal in the Dragkonians?" I blurt out before I can catch myself.

Hycis looks over at me, delight dancing over her features. "Yes, nosy human. How did you think the humans did it before? Luck and prayers? No. The Fae."

I straighten my shoulders and study the Fae woman. Her words sound harsh, but there's undeniable amusement in her voice. Hycis meets my eyes for a moment before breaking into a wide grin.

"You humans are so much more fun than the older Fae let on," Hycis says with a chuckle, placing a hand on her hip. "I think I rather like the idea of our realms finally aligning. Rynia disapproves, of course."

Astra smiles. "At least one of you has some sense."

Hycis laughs again and the sound sends shivers down my spine. I'm not sure how I feel about being in such close proximity to a Fae, and I'm even less comfortable seeing how at ease Astra is.

"We should probably head back," I say, clearing my throat.

Hycis narrows her eyes at me, and I fight every instinct I have not to shrink back.

"He's right, unfortunately," Astra sighs with a shrug. "As much as I want to hide away, I really need to get back. I didn't even tell anyone I was leaving."

I'm a little surprised by that. She probably has the entire fortress in a worried tizzy. I smile, shaking my head. Hycis studies me for a moment before turning her attention back to Astra. She slips a leather strap bearing a small blue stone from around her neck and extends it to Astra.

"This is a Fae Stone," Hycis explains as Astra turns it over in her hand. "It will help me find you if I step into your realm and you're not present."

"So you'll contact me?" Astra says to the Fae.

Hycis nods. "Our realms are not quite as aligned as I would like, but I will try. Whether it will be to replenish your berry supply or to bring the news that we've found a way to seal the Dragkonians away for good this time. If you don't hear from me within the estimated time frame, you know how to find me." The Fae grins, drawing Astra into a quick hug. "Farewell, friend. May we meet again soon and toast to better times."

The beam of light reappears as Hycis steps back. Astra offers Hycis a parting nod as the Fae turns to step into the beam.

"I am truly sorry you lost your friend," Hycis says, looking over her shoulder as she steps into the light.

Once the light vanishes, Astra steps from the circle, slipping the stone into her pocket and lifting the bag to her shoulder.

"So I guess I can check 'met a terrifying Fae' off my list of things I want to do before I die," I say, offering Astra a grin. "Now I just need to meet that handsome Fae warrior."

The corner of Astra's lips twitch, almost turning into a smile. "If you think Hycis is terrifying, you might want to avoid meeting her brother who, as it happens, isn't a warrior. Not that I know of at least."

I arch an eyebrow. "Exactly how many Fae do you know?"

Astra shrugs, marching past me through the forest. I follow along.

"Seriously, how many Fae?" I press. "And are you *sure* none of them are warriors?"

Astra laughs and starts telling me her story. She shared parts of it before while we were researching in the library, but now she's willing to give me more details. As we crunch through the trees, she tells me about her and Alak's first interactions with the Dragkonians and how that led to their meeting the Fae. I listen with rapt attention to every detail, marveling at everything she's gone through in the past year. I knew a bit of it, but somehow I'm left more impressed with the strength she's able to show every day.

We ride back to the castle in silence. Astra's brow is furrowed in concentration almost the entire time, and I don't want to interrupt her thoughts. We leave our horses in the care of the stable boy, heading toward the castle.

"Thank you for coming with me. I—I didn't really want to be alone, but I also didn't want to be a burden to everyone else mourning right now. I appreciated your company," Astra whispers as we enter the castle.

Something so earnest shines in her eyes it steals my breath. She's been through so much and yet her first instinct is to think of others.

"Of course, love. I'm always happy to help you out, however you need. If you need to wander off again, let me know. I often prefer the outdoors to people."

Astra laughs. "If I need to escape again, I'll let you know."

We round a corner and Alak barrels into us.

"There you are," he says, pulling Astra into his arms. "I was looking everywhere for you, and the bond wasn't any bloody help."

She melts into him, resting her head against his chest. "I had to contact the Fae."

"You didn't need to go alone, love," Alak whispers as she draws back.

She smiles and casts a glance my way. "Ronan joined me."

Alak starts, noticing me for the first time. His surprised expression shifts into a sheepish grin. "I didn't know you'd arrived."

"I was here for a grand total of about five minutes before I went off with Astra on her little adventure."

Alak smiles but there's something sad about it. "She put you right to work, huh?"

Astra rolls her eyes. "He volunteered."

"I'm sure. Anyway, while you were gone the rest of Jessalynn's army arrived with the weapons Cadewynn commissioned."

"Heldonian silver?"

Alak pauses before giving a nod quickly followed by a shrug. "I believe so."

Astra turns to me, bright eyed. "Want to come look at magical weapons with us?"

I'm tempted but end up shaking my head. "Naw. I should probably meet with Lord Dughlas and find which room my things were sent to."

Astra's eyes spark with something akin to mischief. "Have fun with that. He's a delight."

My laugh echoes down the hall. "Oh, believe me, I know."

"I'll see you later?"

I nod, brushing a quick kiss on her cheek. "Of course, love." I look to Alak. "We can catch up later. Perhaps over some mead?"

He inclines his head. "Sounds good."

With one last parting nod, I leave them be and go off in search of Lord Dughlas, or at least someone who can help me get sorted.

CHAPTER NINE

"Where the hell did you sneak off to?" Ehren asks as I join him and Cal in one of the side dining halls.

I smile, ready to make a joke, but he's too tense. He's genuinely worried. Guilt rises in my chest.

"I'm sorry," I murmur, taking a step closer. "I needed to take care of something."

Ehren swallows, studying me. "I was worried something happened to you."

I offer him a weak smile and step forward, taking his hand in mine as I meet his eyes. "I'm sorry, Ehren. I didn't mean to worry you. I needed some time away from the castle. It was starting to feel too heavy. When I realized it was the day I was supposed to contact the Fae, I didn't stop to think. I just acted."

Ehren returns my smile, but it doesn't even begin to reach his eyes. "I understand."

"So, weapons?" Jess says louder than necessary, her voice echoing through the hall.

For the first time since entering the room, I allow my gaze

to travel over the tables covered in weapons. As we're barely an hour out from dinner, I'm sure the staff is disgruntled we're taking their workspace, but this is the best way to handle them, I suppose.

"This is more than I expected," I confess.

Jess grins, placing her hands on her hips. "I wish I could take credit, but this is Cadewynn's doing."

The corners of Ehren's mouth turn up slightly as he steps forward, lifting one of the throwing stars. "Who would've guessed she'd have such an eye for this?"

"I won't pretend like I didn't help *some*," Jess grumbles, rolling her eyes. "She can be a bit hopeless."

"What are those?" Ehren asks, nodding to the nearest stash of weapons on his right.

"Those are the weapons apparently commissioned by the gods," Jess replies. "They're meant for specific people."

"Who?" Alak asks, stepping toward the table.

"No idea," she confesses with a shrug. "We were given vague descriptions, but no names or titles or anything remotely useful."

I join Alak, peering down at the weapons. They're all finely crafted and their magic intrigues me. I wonder if one of them is meant for me.

"Do you remember the descriptions?" I ask.

Jess opens her mouth to reply but only closes it a moment later, shaking her head. "Not really."

"That's why she has me," Kaeya's voice calls out as she approaches the table, shooting Jess a soft look that flickers between amusement and something warmer. "I knew better than to leave that up to Jess."

Jess glares at her but Kaeya only smiles and winks at her as she steps up to the table.

"These two swords are meant for a pair who share one heart on the battlefield and off." She looks over at me. "I assume, now that I've seen you two together and heard more of your power, that these are meant for you. One is promised to end the war."

Dread floods my heart and I find it hard to breathe. Is one of these the sword I'm supposed to use kill Kato, a copy of the sword Aoibhinn used to slay Caedios? I draw an unsteady breath, moving closer to the swords. I glance over my shoulder at Ehren and see my own fear reflected in his eyes. He knows what this sword could mean. I reach out, my fingers tracing the sapphire on the hilt.

"How will I know if one is meant for me?" I ask, my hand drifting to touch its twin.

"You'll just know," Jess offers unhelpfully with a shrug. I reach out a bit of my magic, but it doesn't connect to anything. I can tell the sword is magical, but that's it. There's no bond or calling. I'm not sure if I feel relieved or disappointed.

I pull my hand back. "I don't think either of these is meant for me."

"Then who—" Jess starts to ask, but she stops short, looking past me. I follow her gaze to Cal. His eyes are focused on one of the swords, his brow furrowed in confusion.

"I think one of them might be mine," he whispers, stepping forward hesitantly.

Ehren looks over at Cal, marveling as Cal reaches and allows his fingers to trail tenderly over the hilt of the sword. When he grips the sword, he inhales sharply, his eyes going wide as he stares at the sword in awe. There's no doubt—that sword was made for him. Even I can feel the hum of magic pulsing through the air.

"It feels like it was an appendage I had always been missing," he whispers, his voice filled with awe.

I look at Ehren. "I bet the other sword is for you, then."

He runs his tongue across his lips, eying the remaining sword with something akin to terror. "Do you really think so?"

"You'll only know if you pick it up," I say, gesturing to the sword.

Ehren swallows, nodding as he steps forward. His hand hovers over the hilt before he finally gives in and grasps it. It's immediately evident it was for him. He turns and faces Cal, a smile spreading across his lips.

"One heart," Cal whispers, meeting Ehren's eyes with a level of intensity that stills everyone in the room.

"On the battlefield and off," Ehren whispers in return, closing the distance between them to press a kiss to Cal's lips.

"All right," Jess mutters, waving her hand at them, though she doesn't seem truly annoyed. "No need to prove that bond here. We get it. You're meant for each other."

My eyes fall on the remaining weapons. "What about the rest of these?"

Alak strides to the table and plucks up the remaining sword.

"This one," he says, holding the sword up so it catches the light, "who is it for?"

"You, I'm guessing." Kaeya grins. "According to the crafter, it's for a man who knows what it's like to be lost and alone."

Alak lowers the sword slowly, his eyes filled with sadness. "Aye, that does sound a bit like me."

I reach out and take his free hand.

Kaeya inclines her head. "If I remember correctly, that sword has magic that can cleave more than physical objects."

I tilt my head, scowling at the sword. "What does that mean?"

"Who knows?" Jess cuts in. "Those crafters in Heldonia love speaking in damn riddles. We're lucky we understand anything they said."

"Now we just have to figure out who gets these daggers," Ehren muses, his eyes fixed on the weapons before he lets his gaze drift back over the remaining armor and supplies. "Who gets the rest of this?"

"That's up to you," Jess says with a shrug. She motions to a section of weapons close to us. "Those are meant for those with magic and those"—she turns and gestures at the rest—"can be used by anyone."

Ehren nods. "I'll have—"

He stops suddenly, gritting his teeth as his hands clench by his sides, the name catching in his throat. Grief shimmers in his eyes, and he struggles to push it aside. I'm about to cross to him when Cal quickly takes his hand, giving it a squeeze.

"I'll have someone distribute them shortly," Cal says, his voice heavy.

Jess nods. "Very well. As much as I think the kitchen staff might disapprove, I don't feel like hauling all this silver around anymore, so it will stay here for now."

"I'll have someone start organizing it right away," Cal replies with a nod.

"Don't care who does it or when, just make sure it gets done," Jess replies with a careless flick of her hand. "I'm going to go sort some other things. If you need me, find someone else."

Jess turns and strides form the room, Kaeya following after and giving us a somewhat apologetic glance. Ehren sighs and leans against Cal, placing his head on Cal's shoulder.

"I'm ready for this war to be over," Ehren mutters, closing his eyes.

Cal presses a gentle kiss to Ehren's head. "Me too."

"If you'd like, I can help you sort the weapons," I offer.

Cal smiles at me as Ehren straightens. "Thank you."

"I'm happy to help as well," Alak says with an agreeing nod. "And I can go fetch Ronan if you'd like."

Ehren seems to perk up a bit. "Lord Mc— Ronan is here?"

I nod. "He actually accompanied me when I left earlier. He said he had a couple things to sort, but I'm sure he'd be willing to help."

Ehren nods thoughtfully. "Good. I have a couple things I wanted to discuss with someone about funeral traditions in Athiedor and wasn't looking forward to discussing things with Lord Dughlas. As my official liaison with Athiedor, maybe Ronan will be willing to help."

Cal narrows his eyes at Ehren. "You merely want to pass on conversing with Lord Dughlas to someone else."

A smile twitches at the corner of Ehren's lips. "Can you blame me?"

"I can't," I cut in. "That man is borderline insufferable." Cal shoots me an admonishing look and I shrug. "What? It's true."

Cal looks up at the ceiling, a smile playing on his own lips. "Gods help us all with you two in charge."

Alak chuckles and pulls me in for a kiss. "I think it just proves they're both sensible people."

"See," Ehren says, his eyes twinkling. "Alak gets it."

Cal rolls his eyes and loops an arm around Ehren's waist, pressing a quick kiss to his lips.

"So, should I go find Ronan?" I ask.

Ehren starts to nod, but Alak cuts in first. "Actually, I'll go find him. I can seek out his magic easier than you lot. Besides"

—he lifts his new sword—"I want to put this somewhere safe."

"I can have a sheath made for you," Ehren offers, lifting his own sword. "I'll have ones made for all of us."

Cal looks down at his sword. "I wonder if they need some sort of magical sheath?"

I shrug, feeling a little left out not having my own new weapon, though I'm still relieved no one handed me the sword meant to slay my twin. "I doubt it, but I don't know much about magical weapons. I bet one of the soldiers here will know."

Cal nods knowingly and glances toward the door. "I'll ask around." He takes a step back from Ehren and extends his hand. "Give me your sword, and I'll make sure it's kept safe until you have your sheath."

Ehren smiles softly, passing his sword to Cal. "Thank you."

Cal presses a quick kiss to Ehren's lips before stepping back and clearing his throat. "I'll go take care of these"—he lifts the swords—"and recruit some more hands. I'll be back momentarily."

While Cal is gone, Ehren comes up with a plan to sort and organize the weapons. We start in on the work, joined shortly by Ronan and Alak. Ronan and Ehren step into the corner for a bit, their expressions somber. A few minutes later, Cal returns with soldiers. He oversees the distribution of the supplies with a sense of authority I haven't seen him display often. He's made for leadership, but the air around him is heavy. This isn't Cal's job. Not really. Bram should be here.

A warm hand lands on my forearm, and I look up into a pair of concerned green eyes.

"You okay, love?"

I open my mouth to assure Alak I'm fine, but I shake my head instead. "No, and I don't know if I'll ever really be okay."

Alak nods with a sad understanding. "If you need me, love, I'm right here. I'll always be here for you."

I stand on my tiptoes and brush a quick kiss across his lips. "And I'm here for you."

He smiles softly down at me for a moment before we turn back to the weapons. It's nice to have a task to keep us busy.

CHAPTER TEN

EHREN

I hate how I look in black. It doesn't suit me at all. This tunic, while finely made and sewn with silver thread, is no exception. I fiddle with the top button, my shaking hands finally forcing it through the hole as I stare into the mirror. I hate this.

"How are you doing?" Cal asks, appearing behind my reflection.

He's watching me like he expects me to fall apart at any moment, and I very well might. I take a deep breath, exhaling slowly as I turn to face him.

"Right now I'm okay. I'm not sure what's holding me together, but I'm managing." I reach out and take Cal's hands in mine, tugging him a little closer. "Just stay by my side, okay?"

The corner of Cal's mouth turns up slightly as he leans forward and presses a quick kiss to my cheek. "I'm here for you, Ehren. Always and forever. You don't have to ask. I'm not going anywhere."

I pull him close, burying my face in the crook of his neck.

He immediately wraps his arms around me, holding me close, keeping me together. For moment, neither of us speak or move. We just grip each other tightly, craving the comfort only the other can provide. When I pull back, tears shine in my eyes, but I still manage to keep them at bay.

"You know, you don't have to do this," Cal whispers, fighting back his own tears. "I'm sure someone else can step in. I can do it, if you need me to. I didn't know Bram quite as well as you did, but I think I can still do the ceremony justice. Just say the word."

I shake my head, glancing away. "No, I'm not only the prince but also the person who knew him best. It's my responsibility. I owe it to him." I look back up into Cal's eyes as a tear breaks free. "Besides, I think I need to do it for a sense of closure."

Cal nods as he brushes the tear from my cheek with his thumb then replaces his touch with a gentle kiss. "I understand."

I take a rallying breath and look toward the door. "We should go."

Cal offers me a tight smile and slips his hand into mine. "Together."

Hand-in-hand, we navigate the strange halls, and it feels so wrong. We shouldn't be here. We should be in Embervein. Bram deserves more than a hurried funeral in a foreign castle. He should be given full honors. Every single Guard and soldier should line the streets as a procession takes his body into a holy temple for consecration. His family at the very least should be present, but the best we could do as far as attendees was to reach out to the guards and soldiers nearest so they could attend. His body is preserved with magic, but even that wouldn't hold long enough for his family to arrive. It's already been a week.

His family wasn't at Isabella's burial, either.

A sob catches in my throat and I stumble back. I catch my myself, pressing my palm to a cold stone wall to steady myself. I gasp, the air suddenly thin as more tears burn my eyes. My chest feels tight, too tight. I pull my hand from Cal's and undo the top button of my tunic but it doesn't make it easier to breathe. I squeeze my eyes shut as the world caves in around me, a sharp needle piercing my heart.

"I'm here," Cal whispers, gripping my shoulders and turning my body to face his. "Look at me."

I open my eyes, forcing myself to focus on Cal's face through the blur of tears. His eyes are filled with concern but his gaze is steady, comforting.

"Take a deep breath."

I comply, though it's still a struggle. Cal nods encouragingly.

"Now, do it again."

He breathes with me, and I match my breaths to his. A few breaths later, I feel steady. "I'm all right, now."

"Are you sure? We can wait a few more minutes," Cal says, lifting his hand to trace comforting circles on my cheek.

I lean into his touch, offering him a tight smile as I nod. "I'm sure."

Cal studies me for a moment but doesn't argue. He steps back and extends his hand. I place mine in his and grasp it tightly. Without another word, we finish our trek through the castle to the room that serves as a chapel.

The small chapel room doesn't seem sufficient, but it's all we have. People are already crowding in. At the far end of the chapel is a raised platform with a podium and a table bearing

Bram's body on a slat of wood with handles designed to transport the dead. He's wrapped tightly in a blue silk cloth conforming to his shape, his sword lying on top of his body, waiting to be entombed with him.

Astra and Alak are already present, standing near the front row of seats—our seats. Next to Astra is Ronan. He's hardly left Astra's side since arriving yesterday, partially out of guilt for not being here before and partially out of whatever affection he holds for her. But that's why he's here, really. For Astra. He barely knew Bram, although he walked me through some of the funeral traditions common in Athiedor. I'm glad Astra has someone else to lean on.

I catch Ronan's eye as Cal and I enter. He looks over at me and inclines his head. I offer him a tight smile as we walk toward them. Astra turns, following Ronan's gaze and my heart stops. She's not actively crying, but her eyes are bloodshot and swollen again. I inhale slowly, attempting to keep myself from falling apart again. Cal squeezes my hand, and I focus on crossing to Astra, one step at a time.

"Hey," Astra whispers as I stop at her side.

She doesn't ask how I'm doing. She knows because she feels the same. I reach out my free hand and take hers. Her eyes meet mine and her resolve falters, tears sliding down her cheeks.

I pull my hand from Cal's and wrap Astra in my arms, trembling as I hold her. I'm not strong enough to comfort anyone, but I'm sure as hell going to try. When I pull back, she brushes a quick kiss on my cheek, her eyes shifting past me. I turn and find Winnie entering with Nyco and Sama. Winnie floats in, her chin high. Jess enters a moment later, Kaeya and Brock following behind. They take seats in the front row on the right side of the chapel across the aisle from where we stand. Winnie meets my eyes for a brief moment before sitting.

"Maybe we should begin?" Alak suggests, his voice so quiet I almost don't hear him.

I look around. The chapel is full, every seat filled, save the ones reserved for us. Additional soldiers line the walls, among them Pascal, a firm reminder that Bram isn't the only life that's been lost to this war. Nyco meets my eyes from his seat next to Winnie and offers me a slight nod of sympathy.

"All right," I say, turning back to Astra and Cal. "It's time."

Cal squeezes my hand reassuringly before taking his seat. Astra, Alak, and Ronan follow his lead. I take a rallying breath and walk up onto the platform. I avoid looking at Bram's body as I step behind the podium, my hands resting on the edges. I look out over the crowd as everyone falls silent, taking their seats. It's too quiet. No one is moving. They're watching me.

The air closes in on me, my chest constricting as the darkness pushes in. I take a breath, but it's shaky. I grip the edges of the podium tighter, my knuckles turning white. I can't breathe. I can't think. My heart races faster than it ever has before.

A small sniff from the front row draws my attention. My eyes snap Astra as she leans into Alak, wiping her eyes with a handkerchief. I shift my gaze to her left, my eyes locking with Cal's. He nods once, letting me know he's with me. I know he'd join me if I needed, and that gives me strength. I take a deep breath and straighten, holding his eyes the entire time. He is my light in the dark. With him, I can navigate.

"Today," I say, my voice ringing out over the crowd as I pull my eyes away and look over those assembled, "we gather to honor to a great man. No, 'great' doesn't do him justice. General Alexander Bramfield was one of the best men I've ever had the privilege to meet. He was not only the Captain of my

Guard for three years, but also my best friend for many more. Without him, I wouldn't be who I am today. And not just because he kept me alive whenever I decided to do stupid things."

I manage a small smile as a few in the know chuckle. I meet Cal's eyes and he smiles.

"Bram and I were separated by rank. He was born a farmer and I a prince, but somehow Fate saw fit to push us together. We hated each other at first. I'm not exactly sure when that flipped and we became friends, but I thank the gods every day for the years we had together.

"Many of you knew him as Captain Bramfield and you served under him or by his side. You know he was skilled more than any soldier who has ever served. You studied under him, learned from him. I can assure you, every single one of you meant something to him. He was very proud of all his soldiers. He—"

My voice breaks, and I take a moment to collect my thoughts before continuing. I look at Astra as the tears flow down her cheeks, Alak holding her tightly, tears brimming in his own eyes.

"He was a man worthy of love and affection. Some of you loved him as much I did, perhaps even more. You've seen first-hand the compassion and affection he can show. He once told me that as long as he was remembered fondly by those he loved, it would be enough. How we will continue through life without him, I don't know, but I'm sure he wouldn't want his death to hold us back."

Astra sobs, burying her face in Alak's shoulder. He buries his face in her hair, hiding the tears now streaking his own cheeks. I look back at Cal.

"Bram lived his last moments as he lived his life—in

service of those he loved. His instinct was always to protect, and he died doing just that. He saved the life of another dear friend, sacrificing his own."

Alak looks up at me and meets my eyes. It takes everything I have to hold it together as I look into his tear-filled eyes. I get the sense he's also on the verge of losing it completely.

"Bram wouldn't want us to live in the past, though, dwelling on what could have been different. He'd want us to move forward. So, that's what we'll do. We move on, fighting for justice. We've all lost people in this war, and we will lose many more before it's over."

My eyes drift along the back wall and fall on Pascal.

"We have lost brothers."

I meet Cal's eyes.

"We've lost best friends."

Cal squeezes his eyes shut, nodding as he clenches his fists in his lap. Astra pulls away from Alak and takes Cal's hand. He meets her eyes and she leans in, placing her head on shoulder. He rests his head on hers as they cry softly.

"We've lost so many people and, while we are gathered here to mourn General Bramfield, we mourn them all. That's how Bram would've wanted it. He wouldn't have wanted all the attention."

I pause, taking a deep breath as I rally, but a tear still slides free.

"Today we honor Bram and all the fallen. We ask the gods to carry them home, to find their places among the stars. They deserve it."

I pull away from the podium and walk over to Bram's body and look at him, my back to the crowd. Tears tumble from my eyes as I reach out and run my fingers along the hilt of Bram's sword. I gave him this sword when he became my captain. I had it commissioned just for him.

"Thank you for your service, General Bramfield. I hereby relieve you of your duties with honor."

My voice is quiet, barely above a whisper, but my voice still carries across the silence of the room. With effort I turn and look at Cal, giving him a nod. He takes a deep breath, standing to his feet, Alak following. Nyco also rises from his place in the crowd, joining us on the platform. I move down to Bram's head and grab one of the handles of the slat Bram's body lies on. Cal takes the one across from me while Nyco and Alak take the ones at his feet. I nod to them and together we lift.

As we leave the chapel, people rise and follow us. Astra and Winnie are directly behind us, Ronan, Jess, and others falling into rank behind them. We step outside and I almost freeze. The entire village has gathered, hundreds of people lining the street. As we walk between the rows of people, they drop to their knees, placing a fist over their hearts as they bow their heads. I breathe slowly in and out as we inch forward.

When we reach the mausoleum of Clan Dughlas, I halt, suddenly paralyzed and overwhelmed by the wrongness of leaving Bram here. He doesn't belong here in Athiedor. He deserves a proper burial with full honors back in the city he called home for the last several years. The world starts closing in around me, but Cal's voice snaps me back.

"It's only temporary," he whispers. "We'll bring him home as soon as we can."

I look over at Cal and nod, allowing his steady hand to guide me inside the mausoleum. Lord Dughlas waits inside, greeting us with a low bow.

"We are honored to house your general."

For the first time, he doesn't sound pompous. He sounds

sincere, though he has no reason to honor Bram in any way. I suppose a man of his age knows the sharp dagger of loss. He steps to the side, motioning to the spot that's meant to entomb Bram until we can get him home. My breaths are shaky and uneven as we slide him inside, Astra sealing the tomb with magic. I step back, taking Cal's hand.

"I'll allow you a moment," Lord Dughlas says, offering us a parting nod before he leaves. Ronan and Nyco duck out with him, leaving me, Astra, Cal, and Alak.

Astra takes my other hand and I hold it as tightly as I can without hurting her. Side-by-side, hand-in-hand we give way to our grief as we say goodbye. I'm not sure how long we stand there, but by the time we leave the crowd outside has dispersed, allowing us a semblance of privacy as we make our way back to the castle, our cheeks still wet with tears.

Part of Athiedor tradition includes a banquet in celebration of the life the person lived. According to Ronan, it's not only supposed to help those left behind heal and focus on something other than sorrow, but also supposed to help the spirit of the deceased move on, knowing that those they left behind will be okay.

For a while, we push our sorrow aside, sitting in a circle and exchanging memories as we enjoy the decadent food provided. As his closest friend, I have plenty to share. Cal laughs and smiles, sharing tidbits from training and various missions. Astra shares stories of her own, her cheeks tinging pink as she whispers of stolen kisses. Even Alak jumps in with a tale or two.

As we sit and talk, Winnie pops by as do other soldiers and Guards, all happy to share their stories. Bram was loved and respected, and it becomes more and more evident every moment. All the stories almost make it seem like he's still here. Almost.

Slowly the joy fades into exhaustion, the heaviness returning. I stare down into my goblet of wine, swirling the liquid. It looks too much like blood. I squeeze my eyes closed a moment before setting the goblet on the ground next to me with a loud clunk.

"I think I'm going to head to bed," I say, standing in one smooth motion.

Cal stands to follow me but hesitates as if considering whether or not I need to be alone. I extend my hand to him and he accepts with a small smile. Astra rises and kisses my cheek.

"I know you have Cal," she whispers, "but if you need me, I'm here."

I nod and offer her a tight smile. "I know. And while I might barely be holding myself together, I'm here for you, too. You need only ask."

She nods. "I know."

I take a deep breath and glance over at Cal. He squeezes my hand and we turn and leave. I walk in a haze all the way to our room. I manage to find the energy to remove my boots and shirt, but that's all. Cal is half undressed as well, but he stops when he sees me standing frozen in the center of the room.

He crosses to me and loops his arms around may waist. He meets my eyes, lips parting, studying my face. I lose myself in his eyes and I lean into him, pressing my lips to his. I can sense his need and sorrow as through we really are of one heart. I pull him toward the bed, but we don't do more than kiss. After a while, we lie there, foreheads pressed together and arms wrapped around each other, slowly drifting to sleep.

I wake in the middle of the night, disoriented for a moment before reality crashes back in. My head aches from all the tears shed. I slip from Cal's arms, doing my best not to wake him, and walk over to the desk in the corner of the room. I smooth my palm over the maps stacked on the desk and mull over them in the moonlight. I'm so focused I don't realize Cal has woken until he speaks.

"What are you doing?"

I start and spin to face him. He's sitting on the edge of the bed watching me, his eyes still clouded with sleep.

"I just . . ." I turn back to the maps, looking down. "I needed a distraction."

The bed creaks as Cal rises and joins me. He glances down at the maps then back up at me, arching an eyebrow.

"Maps?"

I nod, moving one map aside to view the one beneath it. "We've been here for too long. The war hasn't stopped. We need to—"

"Ehren," Cal says gently but firmly, as he takes my hands in his, turning me away from the maps. "We can figure all this out later. There's no need to rush back into things this exact moment."

I look directly into his eyes. "I *need* to do this. I need something to focus on besides death. I need a plan to put into motion. I need . . ." I break off, looking away. "I just need this."

Cal exhales slowly. "I understand." He releases my hands and angles the top map so he can see it better. "So what are you thinking?"

I place a hand on Cal's arm and he lifts his eyes to mine.

"You can go back to sleep. You don't have to stay up with me in my madness."

Cal smiles softly. "I can't sleep well knowing you're up stressing. I'm here for you. We do this together."

I probably should protest, but I can't given the earnest love in his eyes. Instead, I offer him a grateful smile. "Thank you."

Cal nods once and looks back at the maps. "So what are you thinking?" he repeats.

I clear my throat and shift so I'm facing the maps. "I figure we should utilize the soldiers from Gleador as much as possible. Prince Luc has most of his troops stationed in the south and along the Callenia-Ascaria border, our troops are more heavily in the middle and along the coast, so that leaves the North unguarded aside from the small army provided by Athiedor."

Cal nods, tracing his finger along a portion of the map. "It would make sense to station some of them here." I study Cal's face in the silver of the moonlight as he studies the map. "Additional troops could be sent here to defend these cities."

He glances over at me and his brows knit in confusion. "What?"

I smile and lift a hand to his cheek. "I love you, Cal."

Cal relaxes, turning his head to kiss my palm. "I love you, too, Ehren."

"You know, I need a new Captain of my Guard. Perhaps even a new general."

Cal holds my eyes for a moment before he realizes what I'm saying. He looks away, shaking his head.

"I'm not qualified."

"You're as qualified as any other of my Guard," I argue. "And I trust you more than any of them. Plus, you and Alak work well together."

When he looks back at me, there's something cold and hard in his eyes I don't quite understand. "People will think you promoted me because I'm warming your bed."

His words sting and I drop my hand from his cheek, stumbling back a step.

"I . . . ," I begin, but I hesitate, the words I need escaping me. "I didn't think of that. If you'd rather not . . . I mean, I don't want anyone to think less of you. I only need someone to fill . . . to fill his shoes and I trust you and—"

"Ehren," Cal whispers, his expression softening as he draws me into his arms. "I would be honored to be your Captain or your General."

"I don't want to force you into a position you're not comfortable with. I don't want people to think less of you when you mean the world to me. I don't want to do something that can harm your reputation, but I swear to you if you accept the position, I'll do everything in my power to protect you from ridicule. I love you, Cal, and I know that you are more suited for this title than anyone."

Cal presses his lips to mine. When he draws back, his eyes are shining.

"Ehren, I trust you and your judgment. Honestly, I'll never feel worthy of any position above a foot soldier. I'll never feel worthy of you. But I'll *always* trust you."

I scoff, a smile rising on my lips. I reach up and trace the tips of my fingers along Cal's cheek.

"If one of us falls short of being worthy, it's me not you. I don't deserve you, Cal. I'm broken and you'll forever be picking up my pieces."

Cal pulls me closer. "I'm happy to put those pieces back together as many times as it takes."

Our next kisses are slow but deep. Little by little they consume us, and we find ourselves back in bed. We can finish the maps in the morning. Tonight, Cal is all I need to fill the empty hole of sorrow in my chest. We can get through this. Together.

Part Two: Thunder

CHAPTER ELEVEN

ALAK

"Why exactly are we leaving already?" I ask, sitting on the edge of our bed, tugging on my boot.

"Ehren really wants to get things back to normal," Astra replies as she weaves her hair into a braid in front of the mirror.

I grumble under my breath as I pull on my second boot. It's not that I don't get it—I do. I understand the need to have a project to focus on. That doesn't mean I appreciated Ehren bounding into our room at dawn to make his announcement. A sharp knock on the door pulls me from my thoughts.

"Come in," Astra calls out, turning from the mirror.

The door creaks open and Ronan steps into the room.

"Ah," he says, his eyes falling on the packed bags sitting at the foot of our bed. "I see you also got the message."

"Yep," I reply, pushing up from the bed. "Are you joining us?"

Ronan sighs, glancing away as he leans forward on his cane. "I'm conflicted, to be honest. Being back in Athiedor has reminded me I do have a duty to my Clan, but I also want to make myself useful." He looks up at Astra and meets her eyes. "I feel guilty I wasn't here for you when—I don't want that to happen again."

Astra smiles softly and crosses to him, placing a hand on his shoulder. "I already told you I don't blame you."

"She's right, mate," I cut in. "It's not your fault at all." Guilt rises in my chest, but I force it down. It's not my fault either, but it sure feels like it.

Ronan nods. "My most recent correspondence with the Clans seems to have everything in order, but I may make a slight detour and catch back up with you later. I'd like to check in with a few of the more dodgy lords firsthand. I'm pretty sure a few of them are hedging about because I'm not yet thirty and they refuse to acknowledge my credentials."

"That sounds good," Astra replies, dropping her hand before turning to me. "We should—"

"Wait a second," I cut in. "What do you mean you're not thirty?"

Ronan looks surprised for a moment before he laughs. "How old do you think I am?"

I shrug, heat rising in my cheeks. "At least thirty."

Ronan grins, shooting me a wink. "I'm only twenty-six." He pauses, tilting his head. "Well, nearly twenty-seven, but I have a couple more months before I have to claim that."

"I really assumed you were older," I confess.

Ronan sobers slightly, but his eyes still twinkle. "I guess it's part of the curse of being a Clan Lord earlier in life than expect-ed." He lifts his cane. "I'm sure this doesn't age me down at all."

"The cane makes you more distinguished, but plenty of young men need aids," Astra says with a gentle smile before turning to me. "We should probably head down. We don't want to keep Ehren waiting."

Ronan inclines his head. "Safe travels. May we meet again soon."

We each offer Ronan one last parting nod and head out. We find Ehren with Jess and her army, sorting through the remaining weapons in a side courtyard.

"We're almost ready," Ehren says as we approach. "Just loading up these last few things."

"We can help," Astra offers with a smile. She elbows me. "Right, Alak?"

I grunt. "Yes, of course."

A few minutes later, nearly everything is packed when Hanna skips through the crowd, Pip trailing behind her.

"You can wait for us in front of the castle," Ehren says with a gentle smile. "We'll be out in another minute or two."

"I was waiting there," Hanna says, her eyes scanning the remaining weapons behind Ehren, "but Pip said there's something here for me. Right Pip?" Pip nods.

Hanna's eyes fall on the dagger with the pink hilt, one of the few weapons not already packed away, and her eyes go wide. She pushes past Ehren and plucks up the dagger with a sharp gasp. She turns back to Pip, her face glowing with wonder.

"You were right, Pip," she whispers, turning the dagger over in her hands.

Pip nods and takes a hesitant step forward, his eyes falling on the dagger with an obsidian hilt. Astra picks it up and offers it to him.

"This is for you, isn't it?" Pip looks up and meets Astra's eyes with a sharp nod. Astra extends the dagger. "Take it."

The dagger falls into Pip's hand and his lips part as he stares at the weapon in wide-eyed wonder.

"Now that we know the owners of the daggers, all is well," Ehren says with a heavy voice.

Hanna and Pip are children, and yet apparently they have a destiny that requires them to be armed with weapons from the gods. Damn this war. Damn this fecking war.

Within the next hour, we're on the road. We split into three main groups. My group consists of me, Astra, Ehren, Cal, Nyco, Sama, Cadewynn, Hanna, Pip, and Jessalyn. Kaeya and Brock follow behind with one army, and another Gleador army follows behind under the leadership of a general I haven't had the privilege to meet and the small army from Oyrain led by Prince Benito and Princess Elaine. As our group is the smallest, we move the quickest, driven forward by Ehren's focused determination.

Toward the end of our first day, snowflakes start drifting from the gray sky. By morning, the ground is covered in a blanket of white. It makes travel slower and Ehren's frustration is palpable. However, as we exit Athiedor, we leave the snow behind. When we arrive at the fortress, Prince Luc greets us at the gate, bearing mostly good news.

"We've managed to secure several more villages," he says, striding in step with Ehren as we walk inside. "Pax also brought the last of the army, ready to fight. They're well trained. He's done an excellent job."

"Good," Ehren mumbles nodding, calculating.

"We have discovered, however, that Kato managed to recruit armies from Esnya."

"What?" Ehren freezes, his eyes snapping to Luc.

Luc nods grimly. "Yes, it appears that he has leverage over them in some way. He also has recruits from other countries, though they are individuals and not sent by the countries as a whole."

My heart sinks. This is not good news. I step forward. "What do we do?"

Ehren turns to me. "I'm not sure." He glances back to Luc. "Do you have their locations marked on the maps?"

"Of course," Luc says, inclining his head. "Allow me to show you."

"Ehren," Astra says softly, stepping forward to place a hand on his arm. "Let us come with you. We can work together."

Ehren licks his lips, scanning our small party. Even Hanna and Pip have trailed along with us. Finally, he shakes his head.

"Alak, you come with me, and Cal. You're my captains, so I need your input." Ehren shifts his gaze back to Astra. "I'll keep you informed, I swear, but I need to think, and the more people around me, the harder that is."

Astra nods, though I can tell she's a little hurt. "Very well."

"I'll see you later," I whisper, pressing a quick kiss to her cheek before following Ehren down the hall.

The war room, as it's come to be called, has a large table down the middle with a large map of Callenia spread in the center. Different figures representing the armies are positioned across the map with more figures standing in for suspected places where Kato's armies are positioned. Ehren scowls down at the map, his hands on his hips as he studies it from several angles.

"Those are the new troops from Esnya?" he asks, nodding to small cluster of figures in the south of Callenia.

Luc nods. "Yes, and these"—he points to a few more armies spread out across the southern portion—"are the armies made mostly of new recruits."

I step forward, staring down at the map. There's something off, but I can't quite place what it is. I press my palms to the table as I lean forward, brow furrowed in concentration.

"What do you see?" Ehren asks, stepping to my side.

I shake my head. "I'm not sure. Something is—Wait."

I straighten and rush around the table, tilting my head as I look down at the top corner of Callenia where it meets Ascaria and Paravlia above Athiedor.

I thrust my finger at the map. "Look here. What do you see?"

Ehren frowns, shaking his head. "Nothing."

"Exactly," I reply, watching Ehren. "Nothing. We have evidence of Kato's activities all over Callenia." I make a wide sweeping motion with my hands to indicate the full map. "And yet, nothing in this area. Doesn't that seem odd?"

Ehren's mouth drops open as his eyes brighten. "It is odd. It's almost like something is being masked. But what?"

I shake my head, crossing my arms. "No idea, mate, but you might want to send an army or group of spies in to check it out."

"An army would be too easily detected," Cal counters. "A small scouting party would be better."

Ehren rubs his chin as he nods, studying the map. "Yes, a scouting party is what we need." He raises his eyes to Cal's. "I'll head it up."

"No," Cal says, shaking his head. "You can't."

"I have to," Ehren insists. "I need to do this, Cal, and I won't debate it. If I stay here in the fortress or if I'm forced back to the Summer Palace, I won't be able to stay afloat."

A shadow crosses Cal's face but he nods. "Very well."

"I'll go with you," I jump in. "I know I failed with Bram, but I'm your best chance at escaping in a moment's notice."

Ehren meets my eyes. "You didn't fail with Bram. Your magic was inaccessible."

I shake my head, glancing away. "Either way, I can help. The only other option is Astra."

"Maybe you should give Astra the option," Cal suggests.

"No," I say firmly, meeting Cal's eyes. "I'm volunteering right here right now, and it works best if we're not together. Besides, I don't want her to see what Kato has become if he's there. He's not the same person."

Cal's eyes soften as he nods. "I don't know that I agree, but I understand."

"Fine. You and me," Ehren cuts in.

Ehren turns to Cal, but before he can speak Cal says, "Just try and leave me behind. See what happens."

Ehren grins, his eyes shining. Cal glances off, trying to hide a smile of his own.

"I can accompany you if needed," Luc offers, stepping forward. "I've been feeling a little cooped up in this fortress. I would love to serve, especially considering this location is so close to my own kingdom."

"The four of us, then. No more," Ehren says with a sharp nod. His eyes drift to the window, taking in the setting sun. "It's too late to leave today, but we can head out first thing in the morning."

We quickly make our plans before Ehren dismisses us. My thoughts swirl as I follow the bond to where Astra stands along an outer wall, watching the troops train.

"What are you hiding?" she asks without even bothering to turn to face me.

I grimace as I take a step forward. "I'm leaving with Ehren tomorrow on a scouting mission."

"I suppose it will be dangerous?" She glances at me over

her shoulder. "I can feel your anxiety through the bond. You're worried."

I take a deep breath, stepping to her side and leaning on the wall to look down at the soldiers. "It could be. We really don't know. There's a quiet spot in the corner of Callenia. Ehren wants to check it out."

Astra nods, her eyes focused on those below. "I see. So there's a chance I could lose you both."

I reach over and grab her hand, drawing her eyes to mine. "I'll come back to you." Her chin wobbles as she struggles to hold back tears. "I promise, Astra. I didn't wait my entire life to meet you only to throw it away. I will come back, and I'm bringing Ehren, Cal, and Luc back with me."

She raises her eyebrows. "Prince Luc is going, too?"

"Yes. The area is along the border of Ascaria, so he's linked to this as well."

"And how long will you be gone?"

I shrug, glancing away. "Not sure. Ehren says it shouldn't take much more than two days to reach the area."

"So, four, maybe five days deepening on what you find?"

I offer Astra a weak smile, giving her hand a slight squeeze. "We've survived longer apart."

She laughs softly, shaking her head. "Doesn't mean I like it."

She scoots closer, resting her head against my arm. I release her hand and wrap my arm around her, pulling her closer.

"Don't forget I have my new shiny sword," I mumble, pressing a quick kiss to the top of her head.

"Since when did you learn how to use a sword?" she mutters, smiling.

"Hey!" I cry, pulling away from her. "I can use a sword."

She chuckles and looks up at me, her eyes shining. "Oh?"

"I—I can use a sword," I insist, but even I don't believe my words.

She laughs and I find myself grinning.

"Okay, fine," I concede. "The sword may not be my weapon of choice, but I'm not as hopeless as I once was."

Astra grins as she settles back against my arm. "Just be careful. And remember the pointy end is for your enemy."

"Got it, love." I laugh. "I'll do my best to remember."

THE NEXT MORNING I'm seriously doubting my life choices. I've spent most of my life traveling, but Ehren and his crew always seem to want to be leaving places at the crack of dawn. Astra escorts me down to meet Ehren, pressing kisses to both our cheeks. I feel the bond tug as we ride away. I hate leaving her. I glance over my shoulder as we ride through the gate and nearly charge back to her. She's all alone. Until Jess steps out, accompanied by Cadewynn and Sama. I smile softly. No, Astra will never be alone. Even if something happens to me, she'll be taken care of.

Our journey is cold, but we have fair enough weather and make decent time, arriving near the location toward the evening of the second day.

"We should head into the mountains," Prince Luc suggests, nodding to the low mountains that edge down into the suspect territory. "We'll be less likely to be spotted should there be enemy forces here."

Ehren follows Luc's gaze. "Good idea."

Ehren takes the lead while I cast an illusion charm around us to be on the safe side. The sun is already setting by the time we reach the rocky edges. Our horses follow the provided path for a while, until it twists into a steep incline.

"We have to leave the horses," Luc says, his eyes shadowed.

Ehren and Cal exchange a quick glance while my hands tighten on Fawn's reigns. Last time we had to leave our horses, we didn't get them back for months.

"They have grass and shelter here," Luc says, motioning around. "They'll be safe. We can climb and see what the terrain is like, maybe get a better view, and return for them in an hour or two."

At length, Ehren nods. "You're right. It's nearly dark, so if we want any daylight to climb, we should do it now or we'll have to wait until morning."

I dismount Fawn and secure her between Dauntless and Galant. We get in a little less than an hour of climbing before darkness creeps up on us, bringing with it freezing cold winds. We finally make it to a level ledge, but we can't see anything but more rocks. I'm about to ask if we should go back when Ehren freezes, throwing his arm back to stop me.

"Oof," I grunt as I slam into his arm. "Wha—?"

Ehren turns back to me, his forefinger held up to his lips. That's when I hear the low voices. Ehren glances at Cal, who already has his hand on the hilt of his sword. Luc sidles up next to me, his eyes watching the path ahead with trained precision as footsteps approach.

"It's always like that," a voice is saying, growing closer by the second. "I doubt he'll ever change."

"I know, but given the circumstances, you'd think he would take things into consideration," a second voice answers as two figures round the bend.

We're hidden enough in the crevices of the surrounding rocks they don't see us, but I still hold my breath, willing them away. Luc catches my eye and nods back toward the path we followed up. I nod and look to Ehren who also nods his agreement. We turn and inch our way back down the path but stop abruptly when six dark figures step out of the shadows.

"Well, what do we have here?" a large man booms.

"Looks like we've got us some spies," a gangly man says, stepping up next to the first, his sword extended.

"Nonsense," Cal says. "We've come to join you."

"Now, why don't I believe that?" The first man grins.

"Oy," a voice says behind us. I spin and discover the two men from before have caught up with us. "What we have here, Cap?"

"Intruders, likely spies," the other man answers. He flashes us a grin that makes my skin crawl. "Prisoners."

We shuffle closer together, our bodies touching. Ehren's eyes dart around as he formulates a plan, and gods, I hope he has good one.

"Alak," Cal mutters under his breath. "Can you get us out of here?"

I nod, almost imperceptibly. I pull on my magic, but nothing happens. I try again. The man in front of us laughs, the sound echoing off the rocks surrounding us making it far more ominous than it should be.

"Trying to wisp away, eh? Won't work. You're on our territory now. You can't just wisp out. You see, my magic stops others' magic from working when it suits my will, and right now, I definitely don't want you accessing it." The man's feral grin grows as he gestures to us. "Get them."

Ehren, Luc, and Cal react on soldier's instinct, swords in their hands before I can even register to pull mine. But it's pointless. These men all have magic, clearly not affected by the man holding mine captive. The largest of our captors has a concentrated attack power that knocks us off our feet. The others have us trapped within minutes, one of them taking our weapons while another ties our hands.

"Get moving," the largest man says gruffly, shoving Ehren forward.

Ehren grits his teeth but complies. I can tell his mind is still racing, his eyes taking in everything with a calculating intensity as the men force us down a narrow path. I gasp when their camp comes into sight, Ehren inhaling sharply beside me as he exchanges a pointed look with Cal. An army stands ready to march, filling the majority of the low valley before us.

This is no small operation. There are hundreds, possibly thousands of soldiers here, but their threat pales in comparison to the dozens of Dragkonians scattered around. We're so fucked.

The man leads us through camp to a small inlet cave at one end. A few curious people look our way, a woman stepping toward us with a leer.

After mercilessly shoving us inside one by one, the man turns to the woman and grins. "Seal 'em in, Freya."

The woman steps closer, grinning as she rubs her hands together. "With pleasure."

She holds her hands up, palms out, and a barrier of buzzing red magic shimmers across the entrance of our prison. With the ward in place, I'm cut even further off from my magic to the point it's painful.

"Done," the woman says as she steps back, smacking her lips. "They won't be getting out. Not unless they wanna melt all their flesh off."

I shiver. I definitely do not like the sound of that.

"Good," our first captor replies. "Send for Master Kato. I have a feeling these four are important."

My heart plummets. Kato? I glance over at Ehren to find him pale. He's terrified.

"Right away," a third voice echoes.

They walk away and silence surrounds us. None of us speak, not yet. There's no telling what they can hear. I concentrate on working the ropes on my wrists, managing to free myself after a couple minutes. I grin as I shake the rope from my hands. Sleight of hand for the win.

Ehren mouths *How?* I motion for him turn and I quickly untie his ropes. He then works on Cal's while I help Luc. As soon as Cal's hands are free, he weaves his fingers with Ehren's and Ehren relaxes, leaning against Cal.

"Can you use your magic at all?" Luc asks, his voice so quiet I have to read his lips to understand him.

I shake my head. Ehren gnaws on his lip as he looks around our prison. There's not much here, definitely no weapons of any kind and nothing that can easily become one.

"I can try Felixe," I whisper.

Ehren's eyes drop to mine. "Will that work?"

I shrug. "Maybe. His magic isn't so easily tied."

I close my eyes and concentrate. It's difficult, but I manage to reach him. A few moments later, he appears on the cave floor, looking frustrated and disgruntled. I grin, reaching out to him, and he leaps into my lap.

"Anyone have any parchment and ink?" I ask, scanning the group.

"I have parchment," Luc replies, pulling a folded piece of paper from his pocket. "But no ink."

Not surprisingly, no one has ink. It's almost like we didn't plan properly to be captured and imprisoned. I sigh. I don't want to reach down the bond without being able to explain everything. Last time I did that, Astra rushed in and we both almost died. The stakes are even higher this time. I look around the cave and find a small twig, but nothing I can write with. I hear a sharp inhale and jerk my eyes to Cal. He's sliced his hand on a rock. He winces, offering his hand to me. I meet his eyes as understanding strikes. I nod and dip the twig in his blood and write my message. When I'm done, I send it off with Felixe.

"Now, we wait," I whisper.

And wait we do. For two days without food or water. We're weak and drawn when someone finally comes to get us and throws us at Kato's feet.

CHAPTER TWELVE

ASTRA

The entire mood of the fortress shifts after Ehren, Alak, Cal, and Luc leave. We all know this means something. Dread and anticipation fill the air. I can't keep from pacing around the fortress, struggling to keep my attention focused on anything except worry. It doesn't help that Jess keeps eyeing me like I could explode at any moment.

Jess disappears to spend time among the ranks of her armies, only returning to share news that any remaining soldiers should arrive within the next week or so. At least it gives us something hopeful to look forward to.

I decide the best way to spend my anxious energy is by working with Cadewynn to figure out a way to best implement the poison in battle. It doesn't take us long to figure out that my small "office" isn't nearly enough room for our work, and we relocate to one of the smaller underground storage rooms. I'm leaning over a group of bowls filled with berry juice when a voice startles me.

"Is that the poison?"

I glance up at Jess for a moment before looking down at my notes.

"Yes. We've diluted it a bit, but it should still be effective."

"Wait, is this all we have?"

I bite my lip and look up at her a bit guiltily. "Yes, and while Hycis said it can be diluted, I don't want to do more than we have."

"Wasn't she supposed to get back in contact with you? Where are the rest of our berries?" she demands. "Do you even have that stupid stone?"

I glare at her and touch a small blue stone tied around my neck. "I'm not an idiot. Of course I have the stone. How do you even know about it?"

Jess starts and then her expression sinks into a scowl. "I have sources."

I sigh, knowing there's no use pursuing more information. "I don't know why she hasn't contacted us. Maybe there was a problem or the worlds aren't as aligned as she thought. All I know is that this is all we have, and we need to maximize the damage we can do until we have more."

Jess huffs and crosses her arms, glancing at the weapons. "All right. Let's see how the berry juice works with arrows first, since they're likely our best option."

Cadewynn hands Jess an arrow and she dips the tip into the poisonous juice. When she lifts the arrow, the point is died with the juice, almost as if it absorbed it.

"That's interesting," I mutter leaning in to examine it.

Jess reaches out and brushes the poison covered area. It's sticky, but none of it comes off on her finger.

"Careful," Cadewynn hisses, her brows furrowed.

"Don't worry. I'm not a Dragkonian. I'm safe." Jess hesitates, shooting me a look of concern. "Right?"

I nod, barely masking my amusement that she didn't even bother to check *before* touching the poison. "It only harms Fae and Dragkonians. I've touched it several times and I'm still alive."

"The poison stays on the arrow without coming off, but I'm assuming it would still be lethal if we manage to penetrate the Dragkonian skin. Or rather, eyes," Jess says, passing the arrow to Cadewynn for further examination. "From what we've seen from our previous attack, the eyes and wings are the most vulnerable parts of their bodies. We strike those areas, and we might have a chance at killing the bastards."

I nod in agreement. "Basically, we need to get even trace amounts of the poison on as many weapons as possible."

"I can have my army come in a little at a time and coat their weapons. A little should go a long way. I'll start with the archers," Jess replies, turning toward the door.

"Don't forget the darts," Cadewynn cuts in. "I know they're meant for a closer range than arrows, but they also hold poison and would be easy for an army to carry."

"Good idea, princess." Jess grins. "Who knew you'd turn out to have so much knowledge about battles?"

Cadewynn ducks her head, but I can tell she's proud. She likes feeling useful. I'm familiar with that feeling.

Cadewynn and I spread out the bowls of poison so when Jess's army starts tramping through, they have plenty of room to maneuver without causing too much chaos. They form crooked lines, dipping their weapons in the juice. By some miracle we have enough to coat almost all the arrows and a few smaller weapons like the darts, daggers, and some throwing stars.

We're bottling up a couple small vials of the remaining

poison, making sure every drop counts, when Felixe pops up in the middle of the table. Jess jumps and swears under her breath.

"Hey, Felixe!" I grin, reaching toward the fox. "Do you have a message?"

He yips, his eyes wide, dropping a scrap of paper on the table. I scoop it up, all the blood draining from my face.

Captured. Kato's army here. Possibly 1000s. All magic. Very orga-nized. Ton of Drag. Kato not here. Coming. Trapped. No magic. No weapons. Warded. Have escape plan or we all die.

Love you.

-A

"Is that blood?" Jess asks, peering over my shoulder.

"I—I think so," I mumble, my eyes rapidly skimming the page, rereading Alak's words.

"Well," Jess presses. "What is it and who is it from?"

"Alak and Astra are connected through a soul bond," Cadewynn explains softly. "They share Felixe as a familiar and he often helps them communicate when they're apart."

Felixe barks his agreement.

"Oh," Jess mumbles, the pieces clicking into place. "So that letter is from Alak, and if it's written in blood . . ."

Her voice trails off as I finish reading the letter a third time. I set the paper on the table with trembling hands. "They stumbled into enemy territory and have been taken captive."

Cadewynn inhales sharply, her hands flying to cover her mouth as tears rise in her eyes.

"There's apparently a large army of magic wielders and Dragkonians stationed in the area they went to investigate." I pause, trying to keep my voice even but it breaks anyway when I speak again. "Kato is on his way there."

"No," Cadewynn gasps. "Kato will kill them."

I take a shaky breath and meet her eyes. "I have no doubt."

"Well, that's it then," Jess says, standing straighter. "Time for a rescue mission."

"It sounds like they're warded and their magic is blocked. We'll have to travel on foot, and getting in and out won't be easy."

"Let's take my army," Jess says. "They're ready to fight and have weapons that can kill the Dragkonians. If this is one of Kato's main armies, we need to take them out anyway."

"Do we have time for that?" Cadewynn asks. "It takes time to mobilize an army."

I chew on my lip as I weigh it over. "I think it has to work. It's our best option. But we should move out tonight."

"Whoa," Jess cuts in. "Tonight? It's already nearly dark. We can't move an army out at night."

Power surges in me and my attention snaps to Jess as a ripple of raw magic courses over the room. She stumbles back a step, holding up her hands up in surrender.

"Look, I know time is precious, but moving an army takes time. And moving over unknown terrain at night has risks of its own."

My eyes flash. "Then I'll go on ahead. You and your army can catch up."

I brush past Jess, marching toward the door, but she grabs my arm. I spin to face her, yanking my arm away.

"If you think you can stop me—"

"I'll come with you," Jess cuts me off.

I blink, a strange calm washing over me. "You will?"

"Sure." Jess shrugs and forces a smile. "Why the hell not?

Give me a few minutes to set up the army to move out in the morning. You can even come with me if you want while I talk to Kaeya and Brock."

"I'm coming, too," Cadewynn says, stepping toward us.

"Like hell you are," Jess growls. "You need to stay here."

Cadewynn crosses her arms defiantly. "I want to help."

"Winnie," I say softly, placing a hand on her arm, "If something happens to your brother, gods forbid, you're the heir."

Cadewynn's mouth drops open as my words register, her eyes wide. She's clearly never considered this before.

"Don't worry, though. We'll bring Ehren back," Jess adds quickly. "I swear on my life."

Cadewynn sighs and studies Jess for a moment before nodding meekly. "All right."

Jess leads the way and I follow a step behind. We find Kaeya and Brock, and Jess quickly relays our plan.

"I don't like the idea of you being so far ahead," Kaeya says, crossing her arms as she glares at me over Jess's shoulder.

"Me neither," Brock grunts. "That distance would make it difficult for scouts to communicate between us. How will we know what you've found or if you get in trouble?"

"Pax," I jump in. "Pax Greystone. He was the one recruiting and training the soldiers in the mountain pass. He's a Whisperer."

Kaeya's eyes widen as Brock swears.

"A Whisperer?" Jess says, just as shocked as her paramours. "I thought they were a myth."

I shake my head. "No myth, merely rare, and Pax is one. If he rides with the army, he can Whisper ahead to us."

"You still wouldn't be able to communicate back unless there's another Whisperer you can take with you," Brock points out with a scowl.

I pause, glancing off. "I'll borrow some of his magic and store it in my Syphon Stone. I've never used Whispering before, so I can't guarantee how well it'll work, but it's better than nothing."

"Fine," Kaeya says at length. "We'll leave at dawn. Don't do anything foolish."

Jess flashes her teeth in a grin. "Oh, but what fun would that be?"

Jess continues hashing out the details while I go off to find Pax. It doesn't take me long. His face brightens as I approach.

"Astra!"

I smile, guilt swirling in my gut. "Hey, Pax. Sorry we haven't had much time to really talk since you arrived."

Pax shrugs, grinning. "I know you've been busy. You're basically helping to run the kingdom."

I shake my head. "Ehren's the one running everything. I just support him."

"Either way, everything you're accomplishing is truly amazing." He pauses, narrowing his eyes playfully. "I have a feeling you didn't come here to catch up."

I blush. Pax always could see right through me.

"No, I didn't, though I wish that could be why I'm here." I pause, trying to find the right words. "I need to borrow some of your magic."

Pax's grin fades as he scrunches his face in confusion. "My magic? You know I'm just a Whisperer, right? I don't have anything powerful."

"And your Whisper magic is exactly what we need."

I quickly fill Pax in on the recent developments, and he nods along. When I finish, he nods and carefully pours a little of his magic in my Syphon Stone.

"Is—is that good?" Pax asks, drawing his hand back as his worried eyes meet mine.

I nod, focusing on the swirling addition of his magic among the magic already stored in the stone. It's warm and familiar. Somehow knowing Pax's magic is so close makes me feel a little safer and a little less alone.

CHAPTER THIRTEEN

ASTRA

"Pip said I have to go with you."

I turn to face the stable door. Hanna's small figure is silhouetted by the orange blaze of the setting sun, a packed bag at her feet.

"Sorry, Hanna, but this mission is a bit too dangerous for you to tag along."

Hanna frowns, gesturing to Sama who's attaching a bag to her horse. "She gets to go with you and she doesn't even have magic."

"I have magic," Sama says with a smile, stepping to my side. "It's just borrowed. I also have Ares who can act as a scout."

Ares screeches his agreement from Sama's shoulder.

"What are we talking about?" Jess asks, pushing past Hanna, her bag slung over her shoulder as she saunters toward her horse.

"Hanna seems to think she's coming with us," I answer.

Jess cocks an eyebrow. "Oh, and why is that?"

"Pip said I need to come. He had a vision."

Jess shrugs. "Pip can't See everything. You're not coming on his word alone."

Hanna frowns, crossing her arms defiantly. "You need to take a Healer with you. I'm a Healer."

"There are other Healers we could take," Jess says, attaching her pack to her horse. "And there'll be Healers following behind us with the army. Hopefully, we won't need a Healer before they arrive." Jess glances at Hanna over her shoulder. "Have you even finished training?"

Something close to panic flashes in Hanna's eyes as she says, "That doesn't matter! You *have* to take me with you. I don't know the exact reason, but if I don't go with you, something bad will happen."

"What will happen?" I ask, meeting the girl's eyes.

She shakes her head. "I don't know, Pip couldn't See that part clearly, but I know someone will die if I'm not there."

Jess exchanges quick glance with me. I think we're on the same page until she shrugs and says, "Let's bring her along."

My mouth drops open. "You can't be serious."

"I have my dagger," Hanna offers, her whole face brightening. "I've been practicing with it and I'm quite good."

"See, she has a dagger," Jess says, barely containing her smile. "What if she's right and someone dies because we didn't take her?"

"What if *she* dies?" I argue.

Jess opens her mouth to answer, but Sama jumps in first.

"If I sense anything too dark, we'll have her hang back. We can keep her away from the worst of it."

I look to Hanna's hopeful face and sigh in resignation. "Fine. We don't have time to argue."

Hanna bounces on the balls of her feet, lunging forward to hug me. "Thank you! You won't regret it!"

I fight a smile as she pulls away. "I better not. Now, hurry up and get your stuff on a horse."

A few minutes later, we're racing through the dark toward our sure doom. We take a break a few hours later to rest, but we're back on the trail shortly before dawn. Our second day of travel is hard, freezing rain covering us like a curtain. I hesitate to use my magic, knowing very well I might need it at full capacity. We end up taking shelter in an abounded barn, forced to wait out the storm.

By the time we get back on the road, several hours have passed. I try to focus on the road, but I can't keep myself from continually checking our bond. Whatever wards Kato has in place dampen it, but it's still there. Alak is still alive.

We're nearing our destination when a familiar voice whispers in my ear, sending shivers down my spine.

Half a day away.

My companions sit straighter on their horses, so I know they heard it too. I hope to the gods we don't find immediate trouble. We're arriving any minute and our army is too far behind to be of assistance.

We edge toward the suspected territory, and I craft a shield around us to help us avoid detection. Sama sends Ares ahead and he returns with a screech a few minutes later. He lands on her arm and Sama leans toward her Shadow Hawk, listening to him.

"They're right over that ledge," she whispers, nodding ahead. "Kato is there, I think."

I inhale sharply, but words are unnecessary. We all know how bad this could be without my brother there, but if he's indeed present, things could be so much worse. We inch forward toward the ledge and peer over. The sight below instantly stops my heart. There are thousands of soldiers here with probably a hundred Dragkonians. We always assumed Kato was keeping most of his force in Embervein, but that is obviously not the case.

"Shit," I whisper, my eyes traveling over the assembled hoard.

"What do we do?" Hanna asks, a slight tremble in her voice.

"*You* stay up here, hidden away," I say firmly, fixing her with a hard gaze.

"And us?" Sama asks, looking over at Jess and back. "What do we do?"

I take a deep breath, staring down at the army below. "We stay hidden until our own army arrives. There's no immediate dang—"

I swallow my words as the crowd shifts and four figures with bags over their heads are herded toward the center of the camp where four poles have been erected in the center of piles of sticks and straw covered in what looks like tar. They're going to burn them alive.

"No." My voice catches as I look desperately over at Jess. "What do we do?"

She casts a hurried but calculated gaze over the crowd below. "The army is too far away to wait for them. We are so outnumbered it's not even funny. If we go down there, there's a good chance we won't come back up."

One of the prisoners, Ehren I think, fights back against the man pulling him toward the pyres. The soldier slams his fist into Ehren's stomach and Ehren stumbles, doubling over.

"I'm going down there," I say, clenching my fists at my side. "I can follow the bond past their wards."

"You go in, you're stuck," Sama whispers, placing a firm but gentle hand on my arm. "I can feel the shield. You might be able to get in using your bond connection, but you can't wisp back out. You'll be trapped with them, good as dead."

I look down at the pyres, my eyes wide and manic. "I can't let them die. I—"

"I suppose I should go with you, then," Jess says, my attention snapping to her. She says it casually like it's an offhand comment, but her tense body language proves she knows there's nothing casual about this situation. "Maybe we'll have a better chance together. If I'm going to die, might as well go out in the blaze of glory."

"I'll come too," Sama says, setting her jaw.

"I—" Hanna starts.

"No," I snap, spinning to Hanna before she can volunteer to join us. "You stay here." She opens her mouth to argue but I wave her off. "If we don't come back, find the army. Someone needs to stay behind so they know what happened. Given you're the least trained for battle, it makes sense for you to be that survivor."

Hanna holds my eyes for a moment before she relents with a nod. I look back into the camp below. They're tying them to the pyre.

"Can you get us directly to the center?" Jess asks.

"I don't know with these wards, but I'll get us as close as I can."

"Good enough for me. At least it's a beautiful day to die," Jess says, attempting to force a grin.

I take a deep breath and wrap my magic around the three

of us, pulling us into a wisp. The warding fights against us, and it feels like we're being pushed through a tiny hole where every limb is on fire. I can barely breathe as I drown in the darkness, but I cling to our bond and find a way to the other side. Suddenly, my feet are on solid ground and my vision is clearing.

Shit. We're not quite in the center of camp, but we are very much surrounded by soldiers. They blink back at us in confusion, which gives us the slight upper hand for a moment. I summon my magic, crafting my twin blades, and slash into the crowd, bringing down two soldiers before the rest can react. Jess storms along beside me, her own sword easily taking out her opponents.

The soldiers scramble into a formation, attacking us from every angle. Sama grabs the wrist of a man and he screams as her eyes glow a bright red. I've never seen her steal power before, but I'm positive that's what she's doing. The man crumbles to the ground as Sama charges into the crowd, clearing the way with explosions of attack magic.

"Kill the captives!" a voice commands. "Light the pyres!"

"No!" I scream, my swords disappearing, replaced by silver lightning stretching from my fingertips. I wrap the magic around the throats of at least a dozen men, dragging the life from them.

Behind me, Jess sheathes her sword, grabbing an arrow from her quiver. She sends it sailing toward the man approaching the pyre with a torch. The arrow stabs through his throat and he collapses like a rag doll. Another man steps toward the pyres, fire swirling at his fingers. An arrow through his hand gives him pause, but he still has one hand left. Before she can load another arrow, a Dragkonian swoops our way, catching her shoulder with one of its talons. She leaps to the side and grabs a poison arrow. In one smooth motion she shoots, using her magic to direct the arrow into his eye. He roars first in anger then in fear. I hold my breath as the poison takes hold, watching in near-relief when the Dragkonian crashes to the ground, dead.

Swearing swarms around us and the Dragkonians circle us like prey. We're no longer three intruders; we're a viable threat.

I throw myself into battle, switching between using my lightning magic and my swords as Jess continues to fire poison arrows at the Dragkonians. Darkness covers us as Sama draws from Ares, casting shadows around Ehren, Alak, Luc, and Cal as well in an attempt to keep the pyres from being lit. I create a shield around us, blocking the now furious Dragkonians from attacking.

A spell slips through a weakened point in my shield. It misses me but judging by Jess's swearing it didn't miss her. I glance over my shoulder as she pushes up her sleeve, revealing a black starburst where she was hit, black tendrils slowly spreading from the center like veins. Death magic. She raises her eyes to meet mine. We both know what this means. If this is the type of death magic I suspect, she only has until it reaches her heart before she dies.

"Jess," I whisper, not sure what else to say.

She shakes her head, letting her sleeve fall back into place. "If I die today, I'm at least taking a few more of these bastards with me."

I nod and we charge into the swarm, swords in hand. Hot blood sprays across my face as we inch forward. I slice at attackers with my right hand while unleashing more magic with my left. Soldiers scream as my magic wraps around them. Sama steals more magic and sends a blast of ice daggers, clearing a path for me to get to the center. Jess races behind me as we dive into Sama's shadows. I balance an orb of silver light in my palm, clearing away enough of the shadows so we can see. Soldiers charge in behind us, but Jess summons her earth magic, sending a spray of dirt and rocks into their faces, blinding them before they can reach us.

Sama's shadows weaken as I reach Ehren's side. I summon a small dagger and saw at the ropes binding his hands. He jerks at the contact.

"It's me," I whisper, sawing faster.

Ehren relaxes. "Astra?"

"Who else would show up to rescue your sorry ass?"

The rope falls free and Ehren shakes out his wrists. I move to free his feet as he removes the sack from his head.

"I knew I kept you around for a reason," he says, attempting a joke, but his voice quivers slightly, betraying his fear.

"Stop chitchatting!" Jess yells, fighting off another soldier who has braved the thinning shadows.

I'm tempted to bite back but choose to keep silent and focus on freeing Ehren. As soon as Ehren's feet are free, he moves on to Cal while I work to free Alak and Luc. Luc nods to a pile of weapons to the side and I recognize the sapphire hilts. Ehren reaches them first, tossing one sword to Cal who snatches it from the air. Alak and Luc are armed moments later. All four men are weak, barely able to stumble forward, but that doesn't keep them from joining the battle.

We take down soldier after soldier but it's not enough. I can feel the Dragkonians pressing in above us. When the shield breaks, we're dead. We're probably dead even if it holds. I don't have to be a Syphon to know all our magic is fading while our attackers still have plenty to spare.

Ares screeches and arches up into the air, soaring away. Sama scowls after him in confusion. The crowd of soldiers forces the seven of us together. We stand back-to-back as they inch forward. I pull in my shield tighter to encase our little circle. We're all breathing hard, tired from fighting.

"It was nice knowing you, love," Alak whispers, taking my hand.

Cal and Ehren exchange a look as they also grab hands. I glance over at Sama, but her eyes are on the sky, a smile curling on her lips. I raise my eyes and gasp. The sky is filled with birds of every shape and size. They dive down, most transforming midair to human forms before landing amongst the enemy, weapons drawn.

But it's not just birds. A howl draws my attention to our left. A large gray wolf stands on the edge of a mountain cliff, hundreds of other animals and a few dozen humans marching behind him. With another howl, he leaps from the mountain and the army of shifters plunge into the crowd. I grin and meet Alak's eyes.

"Kai came through," I whisper in disbelief. "Kai came through."

Once again we charge into battle, but this time the odds are in our favor. Some of the shifters stay in animal form, tearing out the throats of soldiers, stinging them, or using whatever gifts their animal forms provide. Others shift into their human forms and strike with weapons made of steel and bone.

Dragkonians press down, but even they are wary of the shifters after a few Dragkonians stumble back with torn wings. Jess's wounded arm is weak, but she still manages to fire off a few poison arrows.

The enemy soldiers start wisping away. They're retreating.

Even the Dragkonians are slowing their attack and disappearing from the sky. We won. By some miracle, some twist of fate, we won. Ehren meets my eyes, grinning. I manage a small smile as Alak's hand slips into mine. I turn to Jess just in time to see her collapse.

CHAPTER FOURTEEN

I'm looking at Jessalynn when she collapses. I rush to her side, searching for an injury that I might be able to help with, but I don't see any blood that belongs to her. When I lift the sleeve of her right arm, I fall back with a gasp.

"What?" Alak asks, dropping to my side. His eyes fall on her arm. "Shite. That's death magic."

"I don't think I can heal this," Astra whispers, kneeling next to me, her fingers tracing over the black veins on Jess's arm.

"Likely not, love," Alak whispers, his voice heavy. "It takes a special kind of Healing magic only select Healers can manage."

My breath catches in my throat. I've only just gotten to know Jess again. It's not fair that she be ripped away so soon. Astra glances off into the distance, something close to hope or understanding shining in her eyes.

"Maybe this is why she had us bring her along."

"Who?" I ask, desperation lining my voice.

Astra looks at me, brow furrowed. "Hanna."

I blink at her. "You brought a child into battle?"

"There was a prophecy," Sama cuts in before Astra can answer. "She insisted we needed her and someone would die if she didn't come. Maybe she's meant to save Jess."

I take in our surroundings. The enemy is retreating, but there are still too many people for us to make it safely to the area where Astra was looking. Judging by how Astra's shoulders are drooping I doubt she has enough magic to wisp Jess there, either. My eyes dart around the shifters until I find Kai. He's still in his wolf form, but I recognize him well enough by now. His gray eyes meet mine and he charges toward us, shifting when he's a few feet away.

"Hey, Kai," Astra whispers, tears shining in her eyes, suddenly at a loss for words.

The corner of his mouth turns up into something that could almost be considered a smile. "I promised I'd bring you an army."

"Just in time, too," I reply. I glance back down at Jess. Her breathing is too shallow.

"Can you help us get Jess to Hanna? She's hidden over there," Astra says, motioning past me.

Kai replies with a sharp nod. He calls out to someone behind him and a tall man with dark brown skin steps forward.

"Can you shift and get this girl to a Healer hidden through there?" Kai asks, pointing.

The man follows Kai's finger before replying in a language I don't know. Whatever he said must have been agreement because a moment later the man shifts into a large elk. I'm still processing the sudden shift as Kai helps lift Jess onto his back.

"Can I go with her?" I ask, stepping forward. The elk blinks at me so I add, "She's my sister."

The elk inclines his head and allows me to climb on behind her. Once I'm situated, I pull her against me, holding her firmly.

"Be careful," Cal whispers, placing a hand on my knee.

I force a smile. "I'll be right back."

The elk lurches forward and we drive through the crowd with ease. Jess's breathing is uneven and she lays against me like dead weight. She's fading quickly and my heart races with each hoofbeat. As we round a corner, I leap from the elk's back.

"Hanna!" I yell, my voice echoing. "Hanna!"

Hanna slinks out from behind a rock, her eyes going wide when she sees the elk.

"I need you to heal Jess," I rush, easing Jessalyn's limp body off the elk, who immediately transforms back into a human.

Hanna inches forward, her lips parting when she sees Jess's arm. "Is that death magic?"

I nod. "Can you heal her?"

Hanna meets my eyes, her fear evident.

"I've never done it before," she whispers, "but I can try."

She reaches out her hands, closing her eyes. Soft yellow magic flows around Jess's arm and neck. I barely dare to breathe as I watch, but nothing happens. Hanna stops looking down in confusion.

"My magic isn't working. I think I need something. . ." She trails off, glancing around.

She gasps, her eyes widening, and reaches down into her boot, pulling out her dagger. The blade gleams as she turns it in her hand. Hanna takes a deep breath and presses the tip against Jess's arm where the black marks seem to center.

"Pray to your gods that this works," Hanna mumbles as she pushes the blade harder, slicing into Jess's skin.

I inhale sharply as the blood oozes out, but I'm even more startled when I see it's black, not red. Hanna doesn't seem affected or shocked. She drags the dagger, lengthening the cut and increasing the blood flow. Hanna reaches for her magic again, the glow absorbing the blackness from the blood. At first I don't think it's having any effect, but little by little the black veins trailing up Jess's arm retreat toward the wound. As the last bits of black disappear, the wound seals itself into a fine line. With a soft grunt, Hanna falls back, drained, but her eyes are locked on Jess. I don't even dare to breathe as I stare at my sister, praying silently to any gods willing to listen. Jess's eyes shoot open and she gulps air.

"You're alive," I breathe.

Jess blinks at me in confusion. "What happened to the battle?" she asks, her voice rougher than usual. "I guess we did okay since you're here." Her eyes fall on the shifter. "And who is that?"

"My name is Makal," the man replies in a heavy accent, inclining his head.

"You were hit with death magic," I explain.

Jess licks her lips and glances away. "Oh, that." Her eyebrows knit together as she grabs her arm with her left hand and stares down, baffled. "How . . . ?"

"Hanna healed you," I reply. "And Makal helped me get you to her in time."

"Good thing I let you come along, huh?" Jess says, turning toward Hanna and attempting a grin that looks more like a wince.

"Careful," I say, frowning. "I think that death magic took a good bit out of you."

Jess looks at me and rolls her eyes. "You think? It's almost like it was meant to kill me."

"We should rejoin the others," Makal says, his eyes scanning the sky. "There is no guarantee our enemies will not return."

I swallow, nodding my agreement. Hanna joins us this time as we head back down to the camp. Sama, Alak, and Cal are searching through the supplies left behind while Luc hovers nearby with Astra. Kai and a woman I don't know stand off to the side, heads bowed together in deep discussion. As we approach, Astra notices us first, her shoulders relaxing when she spots Jess beside me, tired but alive.

"You're okay," Astra says as we come to a stop a few feet away.

Jess shrugs like she wasn't on her deathbed moments ago. "I guess I'm not dying today after all."

Astra opens her mouth to say something else but stops short when Kai approaches, the strange woman by his side.

"You came back," she whispers, her voice hoarse.

"I told you I would," he says, pulling Astra into a hug.

"So," the woman drawls in a thick Paravlian accent as she crosses her arms, surveying our group. "You must be Astra, you're Ehren, and over there must be Cal, Sama, and Alak." She nods at us each in turn, pausing when she gets to Luc. "I have no idea who you are."

Luc grins, not put off by the woman's abrupt manner in the slightest. "You may call me Luc."

She cocks an eyebrow. "Oh, can I? Is that supposed to be a privilege?"

Luc's eyebrows knit together and he tilts his head. I wonder if he's trying to find a polite response, or if he's trying to figure out if he's missing something in translation.

"Luc is a prince of Ascaria," I offer. "A *ruling* prince."

She blinks as if bored of our conversation. "From the way Kai talked of you, I expected . . . more."

Kai growls, sounding more wolf than human. "Eleni."

The woman, Eleni, waves her hand as she flashes me a grin. "I joke."

"Found it!" Alak cries behind me. I turn to see him digging through a crate of apples, one already in his mouth.

"Thank the gods," I mutter, kneeling next to Alak and tossing an apple back to Cal. He catches it in one hand and my chest fills with pride at the simple movement.

Luc looks over at us and I see the hunger flash in his eyes as he says, "We have not eaten since we were taken captive."

"We should all eat," Sama jumps in. "I can feel how drained everyone's magic is."

We settle in a circle and pass around the food, sending more through the crowd of shifters.

"So, what exactly happened? You said in your letter that Kato was coming," Astra asks, taking a bite of an apple.

Alak nods, swallowing his food. "Aye, love, and he came this morning. Took one look at us and laughed, congratulating the men that captured us."

She frowns but Jessalyn voices any concerns before Astra gets the chance.

"Why didn't he kill you?"

I shrug. I've been wondering the same thing myself. "He left us for a while and returned a bit later and told us we were going to be burned alive."

"I felt his magic disappear shortly before you arrived," Alak says, nodding to Astra.

Astra's expression darkens. "He knew I would come for you. He used you as bait. He was probably hoping to kill all of you and have me taken captive when I showed up to rescue you."

"Joke's on him, then," Jess says. "We not only rescued his bait without anyone getting caught, but also took out a good portion of his army in the process."

I nod, thinking it over. Kato may have known we had reserves coming, but he didn't know everything. He underestimated Astra yet again—something I learned long ago never to do.

"He must still have Saran with him," I muse. "Didn't Alak's cousin say something about asking the right questions? He clearly asked if you were on the way, but he didn't know about Kai's army or the poison."

"He'll know about the poison now, though," Alak says, gesturing to a dead Dragkonian lying a few yards away. "No way that will stay a secret."

"True," Cal says, reaching over and taking my hand. "He knows we're an even greater threat."

"We shouldn't stay here long," I agree, glancing around as I weave my fingers with Cal's. "He knows we're weak and he could retaliate."

Astra stands, brushing dirt off her dress. "Ehren's right. We should move out soon. We can meet up with our army for extra protection."

"You have an army?" Eleni asks, staring up at Astra in disbelief. "And you charged in without them?"

Astra sets her jaw. "Not that I owe you any explanation, but lives were on the line."

Eleni mumbles something under her breath in what I assume is one of the Paravlian dialects. Kai glares at her.

"How close is the army?" I cut in before Eleni can say

anything else negative or Astra does something she'll regret later.

Astra glances down at the Syphon Stone on her wrist. "I don't know but I still have some Whisper magic. I can ask."

I watch as Astra closes her eyes and brushes her fingers across the stone. The stone brightens in response as she draws the magic out. When she opens her eyes, they're glowing softly.

We ran into some complications and need to meet you. How close are you?

Her voice curls around me, sending shivers down my spine, but not in an unpleasant way.

Pax's reply comes a few minutes later, his voice a quiet echo. *According to Kaeya, we are a couple hours out.*

We are on our way with an army of shifters. Keep heading our way and we will meet in the middle.

Pax sends back a few messages asking for more information, but Astra's eyes have dimmed, the Whisper magic used up. Unable to reply, we make quick work of scavenging the camp and finding our horses to be on our way. Night is starting to creep up on us by the time we spot our army approaching in the distance. I don't have the energy to explain anything, but thankfully, Kai seems fine taking over while the rest of us crash in the first available tent.

It's still dark when I wake with a jolt. I'm piled on bedrolls between Astra and Cal but manage to shift away from them and slip outside without waking them. I gasp as the freezing air strikes me with full force.

"You're supposed to be sleeping," a voice says behind me.

I spin around and come face-to-face with Kai. "Sleep doesn't always come easily these days."

Kai nods knowingly.

"I'm not disturbing you, am I?"

"No," Kai says, staring off across the camp, his eyes unfocused. "I was making the rounds before heading into my own tent."

An awkward silence washes over us and I'm debating going back into my tent just to avoid it when Kai speaks up again.

"Thank you."

My eyebrows shoot up as I study Kai in confusion. "Shouldn't I be thanking you? Without you and your army I'd be a dead man."

Kai meets my eyes. "Thank you for taking care of Astra."

A laugh bubbles out before I can stop. "She's been doing more to take care of me than I've been doing to take care of her."

Kai hums softly and nods. "She does tend to take care of those who need it. She's good at it. Sometimes it makes it easy to forget she needs to be taken care of, too."

Guilt swirls in my chest and I force the sensation away. I know I've been there for her and I'll be there for her again. And she always has Alak. I shake my head, trying to force the dark thoughts away before they have a chance to take hold.

"So, are these shifters your new pack?" I ask, eager for a change in conversation.

"I suppose," Kai replies, sighing. "That's how it works, I guess. I took out Hammon and took his place as their leader. Even those who weren't locked into loyalty through his godsdamned blood oaths still swore their allegiance to me. To be honest, I don't know exactly how to handle it, but that's where Eleni comes in. She's better at this sort of thing."

"She seems . . . nice," I mutter.

Kai chuckles. "She can be. You just have to get to know her.

She doesn't trust easily, but she's a good person. She saved my life."

We fall into silence again. When I shiver as a cold breeze passes over us, I suddenly crave the warmth of my bed. I bid Kai good night and head back to my tent. I wedge in between Astra and Cal and manage to drift off to sleep.

CHAPTER FIFTEEN

RONAN

I almost feel guilty watching Astra and her crew go off one way while I go my own, but I have a duty to fulfill. I've been able to keep decent contact with most of the Athiedor Lords, but Lord Loudain has been particularly tricky when it comes to open communication. I figure the best way to keep up to date with all the developments is to pop by.

I've been to Clan Loudain often enough that I could wisp, but if I'm honest I don't care much for wisping. It's draining and I don't have the focus for it. Plus, it always seems to make my leg ache more than normal. A ride, even days long, on the back of Pixie is relaxing, even in the bitter winter.

When I arrive at the fortress of Lord Loudain, a servant girl greets me with a low bow, while a couple other servants rush to take my bags.

"The lord is currently in a meeting," the girl apologizes as she leads me down a hall. "He shouldn't be much longer."

"Ah, well, I did come somewhat unannounced, though he shouldn't be surprised to see me."

"I do not think he will be," the girl agrees as we come to a stop outside a large set of double doors. "I'll let him know you're here."

I nod as the girl slips inside the room. When she returns, she leaves the door cracked behind her.

"Lord Loudain said to send you in."

I open my mouth to protest and tell the girl I don't mind waiting when a loud voice booms from inside the room.

"Don't keep me waiting, Ronan, my boy!"

I barely hold back my wince at being addressed so informally. I know I've told others such as Alak, Astra, and even Ehren to address me casually, but when done by Lord Loudain, it's a slight. He's known me my whole life and has no problem reminding me that he has many more years of experience under his belt. I bury my frustrations and push into the room, a wide smile on my face.

"I do hope I'm not interrupting anything," I say, letting my eyes slide from Lord Loudain to his guest.

I was half-expecting someone I might recognize, but the man standing next to the lord is a stranger. He looks a fair bit older than Lord Loudain with a long gray beard. He's dressed in strange ivory robes decorated with ancient symbols sewn with shimmering golden thread.

"Ach, naw!" Lord Loudain says with a forced laugh, waving his hand. "Master Arcanis has just come to blather away and try to convince me to let Naskein have foothold on my land."

The man—Master Arcanis—smiles tightly, but speaks in a calm, almost soothing tone. "The Order wishes no such thing. We only wish to establish a healthy relationship with all the Clans that would be mutually beneficial."

Lord Loudain shakes his head. "And I've told you that I don't care if my brethren bend to your will and allow portals to be set up on their land, I have no such desire."

"Portals?" I ask, taking step toward Master Arcanis. "Like the ones Astra and Ehren were activating?"

He meets my eyes and his smile turns more genuine. "Yes. Exactly those type of portals."

Lord Loudain scoffs but I ignore him. "Perhaps, when I'm done discussing things with Lord Loudain, you and I could discuss the possibility of portals on McDullun Clan land?"

"I would very much like that," he says with a sharp nod. "It is my intent to discuss them with all the Clan leaders, and if we can—"

"You can talk later," Lord Loudain cuts in, his voice tinged with ardent displeasure. "I assume the young lord didn't come here to chat with you, Master, and you're now wasting both my time and his."

"I do apologize," Master Arcanis says with a slight bow, though nothing in his voice sounds apologetic. "I will leave you be to discuss whatever matter has brought Lord McDullun to your residence."

"Thank you," I say, inclining my head to show the man the respect he deserves. "I will find you when I'm done with Lord Loudain, if that suits you."

Master Arcanis nods. "I look forward to our discussion."

Once the door closes behind Master Arcanis I turn my attention to Lord Loudain, but he speaks before I can.

"I suppose you're here to lecture me on the lack of men and supplies I've sent to aid the war in Callenia?"

"I wasn't intending on lecturing you. I only mean to keep communication open and see what more you might be willing to send."

Lord Loudain sighs and marches over to a drink cart, pouring a heavy amount of amber liquid into a glass tumbler.

"Whisky?" he asks, glancing at me over his shoulder. "I find it's always better to drink when discussing matters of war, and after dealing with that tiring man all morning, I more than need this."

I hesitate. While I've never been much a fan of whiskey, I'm even less a fan of Lord Loudain, especially here lately. A tumbler of whiskey might make the man—and this conversation—more tolerable.

"Whiskey would be nice, thank you."

He nods and pours a tumbler for me. I take it and follow him over to a set of armchairs in the corner of his office. He takes a hearty swig of his whiskey and smacks his lips contentedly. I take a small sip, barely containing my wince at the burn.

"I take it the war must be going poorly if your new masters have sent you back to me to beg."

I bristle, but I refuse to let him know his words have the desired effect.

"You don't need me to tell you how the war is going. You have plenty of spies doing that work themselves."

"Aye, that I do. That's how I know it's not going well. It's a losing battle." He takes another gulp of whiskey. "Which is why I won't be sending any more of anything."

I sit up straighter. "Ehren needs the help of the Clans."

"Look, Ronan—"

"Lord McDullun," I say curtly, barely managing to maintain a sense of decorum.

Lord Loudain arches an eyebrow. "Pardon me?"

"I would prefer if you would refer to me by my title as we are in a formal discussion. I am both a Clan Lord and an Ambassador to Callenia. I would prefer that you treat me as such."

Lord Loudain narrows his eyes. "Very well, *Lord McDullun*," he sneers, dragging out my title with distaste. "When I signed the treaty with the little prince, it was made clear that Athiedor would be made free with or without my Clan aiding in the war effort. I have done nothing to hold my people back from joining the cause."

"You haven't done much to encourage it either."

Lord Loudain laughs. "And you've done so much more? I'm sure your little sheep farms are going to be what turns the tide in this war."

I clench my jaw to keep from snapping at him, tightening my grip on my cane.

"My Clan sent supplies to feed and clothe the army," I manage through gritted teeth. "In addition, many of my people have joined the prince's cause in whatever way they can. I've seen firsthand how we're helping the war effort."

"You act all high and mighty, Lord McDullun, sitting in the palace by the prince and his sorceress, but you're no better than the rest of us." He lets out a long sigh and leans back in his chair. "We're all trying to get through this war in one piece. I may not be parading through my territory singing the praises of the prince and his war, but I'm not stopping anyone from helping him, even though I think it's a lost cause. I've left it to free will."

"Do you truly understand the risk? If Kato wins, there will be no second chances. Athiedor will likely be destroyed, and free will or anything close to it will be a thing of the past." I pause, narrowing my eyes at him. "Unless you know something I don't."

Lord Loudain raises his palms and shakes his head. "I swear I don't." He pauses, tilting his head in consideration. "Well, I know that many citizens of Athiedor—not just my Clan, but people from all over—opted to join Kato despite the treaty we have with his sister. I don't have any exact numbers, so don't bother asking. Perhaps Kato will see fit to spare those families and extend that grace to more of Athiedor."

I shake my head. "There's no chance of that, I can promise you. Kato's not the one truly in control. He's working with the Dragkonians, and they will show no mercy. They'll make no alliance with Athiedor."

"Maybe, maybe not. Only time will tell."

I open my mouth to argue further, but Lord Loudain cuts me off with a wave of his hand.

"No more, Ronan," he says, his voice tired. "I've had enough of negotiations for today. Nothing you can say will change my mind, so there's no point in wasting our time. You are, of course, welcome to stay here as long as you like, providing you don't meddle. I'm sure your room is ready, so why don't you go relax?"

It's a clear dismissal. I sigh and rise, my heart heavy as I leave. I want so badly to help, to turn the tide of this war. I'm numb as I follow a servant through the halls to my room. I sink down into an armchair, staring off at nothing. I tap mindlessly with my cane, hoping that some sort of solution will appear before me. I want to prove my worth as a Clan Lord. It hasn't been easy being decades younger than the other lords.

I don't know how long I've been sulking when I'm startled by a soft knock. I ease up and make my way over to the door, opening it slowly. Master Arcanis smiles at me on the other side.

"I do hope I'm not intruding."

I manage a sincere smile and step back, opening the door wider and motioning the man inside. "Not in the slightest. Please, do come in."

Master Arcanis enters and I lead him over to the armchairs. I resume my seat while he settles across from me.

"How did your meeting with the lord go?" he asks, offering me a small smile. "Hopefully better than my own."

I shake my head. "Unfortunately I did not fare so well."

"Pity. Let us hope that in the end we will all be all right."

I hum and nod my head absentmindedly. It'd be a lot easier to have hope for the future if people would stop being so stubborn.

"Anyhow, if now is an acceptable time, perhaps we could discuss the portals?" Master Arcanis breaks into my thoughts.

I blink as if waking from a dream and manage a nod. "Yes, of course." A wry smile makes its way onto my lips. "I don't really have any other plans for my day."

"You said you spoke with Mistress Astra already regarding the portals?"

I shrug, shifting in my chair so I'm sitting straighter. "We never really discussed any details, but they came up in conversation."

"But you know their purpose? You know how the portals work?"

"They use magic stored in stones, if I recall correctly, and the portals link back to one main portal located on your isle."

Master Arcanis nods. "Yes, that is the gist of it. My purpose in talking to the Lords of Athiedor is to arrange placement of a few more of portals in your territory. Your land is more heavily imbued with magic than many other areas. As you may already know, active portals already existed in parts of Athiedor before magic was restored. We hope to add to that number."

I tap the head of my cane as I consider his words. "How many portals are you wanting to add?"

"We would like two or three per Clan."

"And they pose no risk?"

"None to you and none to us. Using a portal would require both parties to be on board."

I nod again, but my mind is already drifting. It's hard to focus on something as simple as portals when people are dying at the hands of a madman. I don't want to sit here and chat idly with an old man about magic portals. I want to help end this war. I want to prove that I'm worthy of my title. I want to live up to my father's legacy and not be a disappointment. If the portals had something to do with the war, then maybe . . .

I bolt upright, eyes wide, my thoughts spinning. Master Arcanis watches me curiously.

"Do the portals have to connect directly to Naskein?" I ask carefully.

Master Arcanis considers me a moment before answering. "The portal stones we are currently using only connect to the source in Naskein, but it is possible to create portals that link elsewhere."

"And it's easy and quick to close a portal?"

"Yes, it takes only a word to close it. Why? What are you thinking?"

"I'm thinking," I say slowly, rising from my chair and wandering toward a window, "that we could create temporary portals behind the lines of battle to help innocents and wounded escape." I look down into a bustling courtyard below. "It could allow people to return home to their families who would not be able to otherwise."

"Hmm," Master Arcanis muses. "So you would send the wounded to a second location where they could recover while also allowing refugees to escape?"

I glance at him over my shoulder. "Is it possible?"

He sits quietly for a moment before nodding. "Yes." He looks up, his eyes meeting mine. "I think it would be. It would take some arranging and some willing participants, but yes. It might even allow you to have access to additional Healers. The Healers on the Isle are highly trained, more so than other Healers, and may be able to heal wounds beyond that of those readily available at the edge the battlefield." He pauses briefly before adding, "You know, when you were born, I offered your mother Healing for you."

My breath catches in my throat and I turn to face him, my brow furrowed. When I was born my leg was twisted around in a mangled mess, nearly backwards. The midwife had claimed I was cursed by the gods and refused to touch me. A more level-headed healer was called in and assured my parents that I wasn't cursed and that the issue could be righted so no one else would judge me so harshly. It had taken months to correct, my bone being broken and allowed to heal, the process repeated over and over until it appeared "normal." In the end, it looked like everyone else's leg, the tiny scars from breaks gone wrong hidden beneath the fabric of my pants. With practice, I learned to walk with the assistance of my cane and only a bit of a limp.

"What? You offered her magic to heal my leg?" I ask, breathless.

He lifts a shoulder in half-shrug. "I did not tell her it was magic. It is unlikely she would have believed me. I merely reached out and offered her the assistance of our highly trained Healers."

I swallow and nod. "Would it . . . would it have made a difference? The magic?"

"We likely would have had to go through similar procedures, but the healing would have been faster and more efficient."

"Would I still have my limp?" My voice is barely above a

whisper, but in the silence of the room, Master Arcanis hears me clearly.

"I cannot say for sure. Even magical Healing has its limits, but it is possible."

I take an uneven breath, my heart racing. Life with my limp is all I have ever known. So many times as a young boy I watched with envy as the other children raced about without effort, without pain, without frustration.

"If you would like, you can visit us in Naskein and have our Healers examine your leg. I make no promises, of course, but Master Janza is especially skilled when it comes to bone Healing and can—"

"No." The word startles me as it escapes my lips. I swallow and start again.

"Thank you, but I don't think I want that. Had you approached me a few years ago, my answer might have been different, but as it is, I am fine. I have found contentment and acceptance."

If Master Arcanis is surprised by my reply, he doesn't show it. He merely nods, offering me a kind smile. "Very well. If you change your mind, the offer stands." He pushes up from the chair. "It was a pleasure chatting with you, Lord McDullun, but if you do not mind, I will take my leave."

"Of course," I reply, escorting him to the door.

"I will touch base with the Order and get back to you soon with details for portals," he says as we reach the door. "We obviously cannot set them up for every battle, but if the prophecies ring true, a larger battle is coming soon."

"I look forward to our correspondence," I say, opening the door.

He meets my eyes one last time before giving me a parting nod and slipping out of sight.

CHAPTER SIXTEEN

EHREN

The morning after Astra's daring rescue, we meet around a campfire to decide our next move.

"We have to strike hard and fast," Jess says, punching her palm with her fist. "Kato knows we can kill the Dragkonians, and we need to make our move before he can come up with a way to protect them."

"But we don't have enough of the poison," I counter, shaking my head. "We don't even have enough to survive another battle like that one."

"But he doesn't know that," Jess insists. "If we take down a few with what we have, maybe the rest will flee."

"Flee?" Luc cuts in, sending a sharp look Jess's way. "To where? Ascaria?"

Jess shrugs. "Maybe Gleador."

"No," I cut in, glancing between the two. "It's too risky for us to attack them until we have the poison. Until then we should remain on the defensive."

Jess looks over at Astra. "When are your Fae friends going to deliver the rest of the berries?"

"I don't know. I could try to summon Hycis again, but it would mean going back to Athiedor."

"No," I jump in, the words tumbling out before I can stop them, but I can't stand the idea of Astra being separated from me again so soon. Not with Kato likely growing more aggressive after our escape. Not when we know that he's willing to do whatever he can to get at her. "No going back. You don't even know if that would help."

"She did say she would contact me," Astra says with a sigh. "But—"

"Exactly. And I'm sure she will."

Jess narrows her eyes at me. "Do you even know this Fae?"

"I don't have to know her to know it's best to make a plan that moves us forward not backward."

"Okay! Okay!" Astra says, waving her arms. "I won't go back to Athiedor, but that means waiting. We have some weapons ready to go, so we're not entirely without help. Now that we have the shifters on our side, we stand even more of a chance."

"So, what's our next move?" Alak asks, shifting his eyes from me to me to Jess. "We obviously can't hang around here waiting for the shadows or whatever to talk."

We all fall silent for a moment as we think. There are no glaringly obvious choices. It's all guesswork. This is where I need to come up with a plan. Cal reaches over and squeezes my hand. I look over and meet his eyes. It's calming. It helps me think. It . . .

"We need to rescue Saran."

All eyes turn to me, most along with expressions of shock. Cal cocks his head curiously.

"What?" Jess yells, blinking at me in disbelief. "Isn't that the kid that's deep, *deep* in Kato's pocket? It's not a quick snatch."

Cal studies me a moment longer before speaking. "It would undeniably put us at an advantage if we could get him, but it's risky. Can we make it work?"

Alak's jaw tightens as he shakes his head. "Saran is my cousin—I want him out of Kato's reach more than anyone—but I don't think it's possible."

"I don't know. I like it," Astra says with a grin. "I say we rescue the boy."

Alak jerks around to look at Astra. "You can't be serious, love."

"Oh, I'm dead serious."

"You do this you'll just be dead," Jess counters, shaking her head.

"Look, Kato would never expect us to rescue Saran at this point," Astra insists.

"Because it's stupid," Jess says, looking over at me pointedly.

"But what if we used rescuing Saran as a decoy," I pose, my thoughts turning.

Astra's grin grows as her eyes light up. "If Saran goes missing, Kato will go after him. We can use that distraction to draw his attention away from our army while we surround Embervein."

"Is Kato even in Embervein?" Kai asks, speaking for the first time.

"We don't know for sure, but based on the conversations we overheard while we were being held captive, it's more than likely," I insist. "His full army may not be there, but he's there along with the head Dragkonian."

Luc frowns, shifting his gaze to me. "It sounds very risky.

What if we mobilize our armies and move directly into a trap? Such a move would not be wise until this Saran is in our possession. Besides, even if we manage to draw Kato away, that does not guarantee the Dragkonians will follow. Without the poison, we die."

"The prince is right," Kai says with a nod. "If we want to take the boy back, then we need to do it without the armies on the line. Having the boy would take away some of Kato's power and give us a chance, though."

I pause, chewing on my lip as I think. I meet Astra's eyes and I can tell she's weighing our options just as carefully. Kai and Luc are both correct. Saran is a key player and he needs to be removed from Kato's grasp, but we can't risk losing our soldiers.

"What if," I say, "we do the exact opposite and move fake armies? As a distraction?"

"I don't understand," Luc murmurs with a scowl.

"You want us to create an illusion?" Alak asks slowly.

I nod, a grin spreading across my face. "Exactly. Make it look it as realistic as possible. We can even include a small group of real soldiers that have the ability to wisp out at a moment's notice. Give them a rendezvous location nearby. We send in our fake army and draw Kato's attention while a second, much smaller group goes in to extract Saran."

Luc nods as he mulls over my plan. "That could work if such an illusion could be maintained."

"I think I could do it," Alak offers. He glances over at Astra. "As long we're in the same basic location and we don't have to maintain it for too long."

Astra smiles softly, looking at Alak. "We can make it work."

"Okay, so Alak creates the army with Astra's help, but who

will lead the army? An illusion or a real person?" Kai asks, crossing his arms.

"I will do it," Luc volunteers without hesitation. "I will take some of my soldiers. I have stationed armies in that area anyway, so it would be a logical move for my army to be the one to attack. Though I am not sure how many can actually wisp."

"I'll send Kaeya with soldiers from our army," Jess says with a sigh of resignation. "Wisping out additional soldiers is an easy enough task as long as they don't have to go too far. Most of my army has been wisping since they were toddlers. It's practically like breathing at this point."

"That leaves Cal and I to lead those going in to rescue Saran," I confirm with a nod.

"You need someone with magic," Astra counters.

"I can join you with some of my shifters," Kai offers.

Astra meets my eyes and takes a step toward me. "I want to join you."

I shake my head. "You need to be with Alak to create the illusion."

"We don't have to be within reach to share magic through our bond, just in the same general area," she argues. "I'll give his magic the boost it needs and help him maintain it while we're in the castle."

"I can handle it on my own for a short time anyways—long enough for you to get in and out," Alak says.

"You all seem to be forgetting a major part of this rescue plot," Jess cuts in, crossing her arms with a scowl. "We don't know where Saran is being held. It's been a while since I've been inside the palace, but from what I remember, it's pretty big with lots of places to stash a kid. And that's assuming he's in the palace and not somewhere hidden in the city."

And like that the plan crumbles. My shoulders drop while my stomach twists, failure thick in my throat. Jess is right. Even if Alak can make a believable illusion and hold it, it won't be too long before Kato realizes it's a ruse. We won't have time to search everywhere. Cal notices my change in demeanor and moves closer, his arm pressing against mine. When he leans in, I'm expecting him to brush a kiss on my cheek, but instead he whispers a single name—a name that changes everything. My eyes widen as my mouth drops open.

"What did he say?" Astra says as Jess demands, "Speak up so we can all hear."

I take a rallying breath, a new plan forming. "Kayleigh. She would likely know."

Alak takes a deep breath and releases it slowly as he nods. "She's still in Clan Dughlas's dungeon."

"Wait," Jess cuts in with a glare. "You can't possibly be talking about the girl you took prisoner during the raid?"

I nod grimly as Cal says, "Saran is her brother and she wants him safe. The fact she came to warn us makes me believe she'll be willing to help."

Jess scoffs, shaking her head. "Fat lot of good her warning did before."

I clear my throat. "Either way, she's been in Kato's inner circle for a while. She may have important information, not only in how to rescue Saran, but maybe tips of ways to undermine Kato's power."

Alak nods. "Even when I was by Kato's side, he relied on Kayleigh a lot."

"I guess we're going back to Athiedor after all," Astra says with a weak smile.

I nod reluctantly, my stomach dropping. Cal shifts, slipping his hand around my waist.

"It would appear so. Though," I add, my eyes trailing around the group, "it wouldn't make sense for us all to go to Athiedor. Honestly, I don't like the idea of us splitting up quite yet, but I don't see another option."

"What about Ronan? He told Alak and I he had business to finish up in Athiedor. We can have him secure Kayleigh and bring her to the fortress," Astra says.

"How will we contact him?" I ask, shaking my head. "I know the general path he's traveling and which Clans he was planning to visit, but no real idea where he is on that path. I don't know that we have the time to find him."

"We could use one of my bird shifters," Kai volunteers. "They can travel faster and more efficiently, searching from the air."

"Ronan might be wary of a complete stranger, and I think I need to go back to Athiedor," Astra insists.

I open my mouth to protest but she cuts me off.

"I'll be careful, but I think it needs to be me. I can retrieve Kayleigh and contact the Fae, perhaps even locating Ronan along the way."

"I'll go with you," Kai volunteers. "I'll see if a couple shifters want to come with us. Eleni can handle the rest of them."

I'm going to lose this fight. I know am. Not just because Astra's determined, but because she's right. This is what needs to be done. I pull away from Cal and take Astra's hands into mine. She looks up at me with her shining amethyst eyes.

"Please, be careful."

She smiles and squeezes my hands. "I will. After all, between the two of us, I'm not the one that charged headfirst into enemy territory and got myself captured."

I laugh, shaking my head. "I didn't exactly charge in head-first. Things just didn't go as planned."

"If you say so." She grins, giving my hands another squeeze. "Don't worry. I'll even leave Alak with you so we can communicate at any moment."

"Whoa, love," Alak cuts in. "Don't you think I should be consulted first?"

"Like you consulted me before you volunteered for your suicide mission?"

Alak winces slightly. "Point taken."

"Okay, so we go back to the fortress and, what, wait?" Jess asks with a scowl.

I glance toward her with a shrug. "We can't safely make a move until we have Saran. With his shadow spies, Kato has too many tools at his disposal. And we need Kayleigh's knowledge to get Saran. So, until Astra returns with Kayleigh, we have little choice. We'll continue the campaigns we already have going, but we can't risk talking about our plan lest Kato find out."

Jess crosses her arms, her mouth a tight line. "Fine. We'll wait until we have the boy. Then, we take back our kingdom."

The corners of my mouth quirk up as I arch an eyebrow, my heart soaring at her words. "'Our' kingdom?"

Jess's cheeks flush as she purposefully looks away. "Well, I *was* born here . . ."

"No, Jess," I say, placing a hand on her shoulder. "I want it to be our kingdom."

Jess jerks her gaze to meet mine, her eyes wide with shock. Slowly, the surprise fades as a smile spreads across her face. "All right, brother. Then let's save *our* kingdom."

CHAPTER SEVENTEEN

RONAN

I remain with Clan Loudain for a couple days, waiting out a snowstorm. Master Arcanis waits as well, and we spend a fair amount of our time hidden away in the library discussing the possibilities for the portals. In the end, we manage to create a comprehensible plan. On the third day, he takes his leave to head back to his isle. I briefly debate heading back to my land but decide to go north and visit with Lord Bashmore.

The estate of Lord Bashmore sits only a day-and-a-half from the border of Clan Loudain's land. I'm not surprised when I'm greeted by a grinning servant the moment I pass through the gate. Lord Bashmore is not one that can be snuck up on.

"Good evenin', my lord," the servant says with a low bow as I dismount. "Welcome to Clan Bashmore. Shall I take ye to yer room?"

Another servant steps forward, taking Pixie's reins as I free my bag.

"Is Lord Bashmore available to chat?" I ask as my horse is led away.

"The old lord, unfortunately, is not available. He's been called away on business. However, the young lord is in residence and is ready to speak with ye when ye will."

"Cillian?" I ask, arching an eyebrow.

"Aye," the servant says with a sharp nod.

I pause, considering my options. "I suppose I would like a moment to rest from my journey. Perhaps you could show me to my room but let Lord Cillian know I've arrived?"

The servant smiles and offers me a nod before leading the way through the winding estate. Everything about Clan Bashmore is grand and opulent. Since they trade not only with the whole of Callenia but also Gleador and Paravlia, they're the wealthiest of the Clans and they have no problem displaying that wealth. When we come to a stop outside a large carved door, the servant parts with a bow, leaving me on my own. Inside I discover a massive room lined with bookshelves and filled with comfortable chairs and couches. The bedroom off to the side is no less grand, featuring a large, curtained bed piled high with pillows. Even the washroom puts my own at home to shame. I'm inspecting the balcony when there's an echoing knock at the door.

"Come in," I call out, stepping back inside and latching the balcony door behind me.

A grinning Cillian saunters inside, his green eyes bright.

"Do you like your room? I made sure to give you one with lots of books."

I laugh and meet him in the middle of the room, pulling him into a backslapping hug.

"You know me well."

Cillian pulls back, his grin widening as mischief sparks in

his eyes. "That I do." He pauses, his expression growing more somber. "From what I hear, you're not here on a casual visit, are you?"

I sigh, shaking my head. "I'm afraid not." I nod to a pair of armchairs a few feet away. "Shall we sit?"

Cillian agrees and we sink into the chairs, our knees practically brushing with how close we are. I grip the head of my cane to ground myself. We sit in silence for a moment while I try to figure out where to start. Thankfully, Cillian speaks first.

"The war in Callenia isn't going well."

It's a statement, not a question.

"No, it is not. Well," I amend quickly, "it's not going horribly, there is still hope, but things could be better. The prince has managed to secure some valuable allies, and his new army is quite talented. We have a chance."

Cillian nods thoughtfully and leans back in his chair. "The Court Sorceress, she is faring much better?"

I nod, not bothering to ask how he knew she was ever not doing well to start with. "She is."

"Though," Cillian continues, "it can't be easy moving forward after losing such a close and trusted member of the prince's guard. It was the captain of his guard, was it not?"

"His general, actually. He had been recently promoted."

"Hmm. Yes, I think I heard that, now that you mention it."

I force a smile, but I know it doesn't go to my eyes. "Your father's men are the best at collecting information."

Cillian's smile is more genuine. "That they are, though they aren't only my father's men. Not anymore."

"I'll admit I was a bit surprised when your servant mentioned you would be here and insinuated that you were helping with the business side of things."

"I can imagine that came as a bit of a shock." Cillian chuckles, crossing his legs. "But my father thought it was time for me to finally step into my place and learn how everything worked should he . . ." A shadow crosses his face but he recovers quickly. "Wars and all." He waves his hand. "You never know the outcome."

"I know better than most how quickly things can shift."

Cillian's face softens and he uncrosses his legs, leaning toward me.

"How are you doing, Ronan?"

"I'm fine."

"You can be honest with me, Ro. You know that."

He reaches forward and places his hand over mine where it rests on the head of my cane. I inhale sharply at the familiar feel of his skin on mine and for a moment I forget how to breathe. Part of me wants to react on instinct and link my fingers with his and draw him closer, basking in his warmth. Another part of me seeks to jerk my hand away and put more distance between us. I take a deep breath and force myself to meet his eyes. The intensity in his gaze has heat pooling in my stomach. I swallow hard.

"Cillian—"

I'm cut off as he leans in, moving into my space. He braces his hands on the armrests of my chair as he looms over me, his mouth a mere breath from my own. All thoughts flee my mind. He hesitates only a moment, giving me a chance to pull away, and when I don't, he closes the distance. His lips are a warm and welcome distraction. I arch up into the kiss, allowing the familiar feeling to consume me.

Before I can even register what I'm doing, my hands are tangled in his hair and I'm pulling him into the chair with me. He obliges, never breaking the kiss, straddling my lap as his hands cradle my head. When he slowly moves his mouth to press hot kisses along my neck I let out a breathy moan that manages to shake me from my stupor.

"Cillian," I manage, my voice trembling.

"It's okay, Ro," he whispers, his breath hot against my skin. "It's okay."

I groan and lean my head back against the chair as he shifts closer, pressing his body against mine.

"We should stop," I try again.

This time he pulls back enough to look down at me, his swollen lips curving into a smile. "When have we ever done what we should?"

I huff out a small laugh as he presses his lips to mine in another kiss, but I place my palm on his chest and push him back a bit. He frowns down at me.

"What's wrong?" He trails a hand down my cheek and my eyes flutter shut for a moment.

I sigh and shift, giving him another gentle push. He takes the hint, shoving up from the chair and standing over me, his brow scrunched in confusion.

"We can't do this, Cillian."

He shakes his head. "Why not? Give me one good reason."

I laugh, but there's no humor in it. "You know why. You made it quite clear to me when you broke things off that it would never work between us."

"That was years ago, Ro. Things have changed."

I stand, hands trembling at my side, my cane clattering to the floor.

"What exactly has changed, Cillian? Do you still intend to provide an heir for your father?"

Cillian at least has the decency to look guilty as he glances to the side. "I have to. It's my duty." He snaps his gaze back to me as he hurries to add, "But I also decided that some things are worth fighting for." He steps closer, taking my hands in his. "*You* are worth fighting for."

A sardonic laugh bubbles out as I yank my hands from his and storm away. My leg aches with the sudden movement and my limp is far more pronounced without my cane, but I don't care. I come to a stop at a large window to the right of the balcony and stare out the frosted glass at the bustling court-yard below.

"You always know what to say in the moment, but you never follow through. I won't be left behind again, waiting for you to fulfill a promise you never had any intention to keep."

Cillian's heavy footsteps cross the room, stopping a few inches behind me, but I don't turn around.

"I mean it this time, Ronan." His hand settles on my shoul-der. "My father is arranging a good marriage with a woman in my Clan who doesn't mind if our marriage is open."

I scoff and shake my head. "I won't be your mistress, Cillian."

"No, it wouldn't be like that!"

I spin to face him, nearly losing my balance, but I catch myself before he can reach out a hand to help me.

"What would it be like, then? Do enlighten me."

He licks his lips and takes a deep breath before answering. "She and I would be married and would produce an heir. The Bashmore line would pass on, but you and I could still have each other. She doesn't mind. She's like me, interested in both men and women. She has a lover of her own, you see, a young woman in her village. Some nights her and I would spend together and the others we would spend with our lovers." His eyes soften as he offers me a half-smile. "With you."

"And would people know of our arrangement?"

Cillian's smile fades and he clenches his jaw. "You know for the sake of the Clan it would be best if we were seen more as close friends."

I nod sharply, his words a dagger through my heart. "Ah, I see."

"I love you, Ronan, and I—"

"No," I whisper, taking a step back, fighting away the tears that burn my eyes. "No, I won't go through this again. I *can't* go through this again." I force myself to meet his eyes and it nearly breaks me. "I have my own Clan and line to worry about. I can't be your hidden secret, rushing to your bed and abandoning my own responsibilities as it suits you. I didn't mind when we were boys still figuring things out, still living on dreams, but now we're men. We're lords. We have duties and responsibilities."

"Come on, Ronan," Cillian says, his voice hard and his eyes suddenly cold. "What other option do you have? You'll never marry a woman. You'll never produce an heir. At least this way, you can be in a relationship where you're loved. When you die, we can combine our land, uniting our Clans as one."

I take another step away from him. My back hits the icy window, though it has nothing to do with the chill running through my core. "You just want my land and title."

He shakes his head firmly, stepping toward me and reaching to brush my face. "No, it's more than that."

I smack his hand away. "But it's part of it, isn't it?"

His mouth opens and closes as he struggles to find the right words. When he finally speaks, his voice his flat. "My father wouldn't support our relationship otherwise."

I huff out a small laugh of disgust and slide around him, heading for the door. He rushes to cut me off, an easy feat given I don't have my cane.

"Stop, Ronan. Let's talk about this. Really talk."

I shake my head and try to brush past him, but he puts out his arm to block me.

"There's nothing to talk about," I snap.

He grabs my shoulders and forces me to meet his eyes.

"I love you. I've loved you since before I even knew what love was."

My heart stutters in my chest and for a brief moment I want to throw away all my own standards and kiss him.

"I love you, too, Cillian . . ."

"But?"

I sigh and a tear slips free.

"But I can't do it this way. I don't know how exactly my line will pass on or how I'll choose my heir, but I can't just throw it all away to be your little secret. Even if I could, I couldn't share you. I know that works for some people, but it's simply not who I am. I could never be truly happy with that arrangement."

Cillian swallows hard, looking away as his hands drop to his sides. "I understand."

"I wish it could be different, but it is what it is."

He looks back at me and nods. "In case you ever change your mind—"

"I won't."

"—I'll keep the option open." He clears his throat and steps toward the door. "In the meantime, how about we get back to business. I assume you're here to look over our contributions to the war and see what else we intend to provide?"

I blink at the rapid shift in our conversation. "Um, yes, actually."

"Very well, then. I have all that organized. I'll, uh, arrange to have it sent up. You can look over everything and send any questions my way."

"That sounds good."

Cillian opens the door but pauses halfway through the doorway, tuning to look at me. "I do hope you'll make time to join me for dinner. Eire will be there. She's out spending the day in the village, but I know she'd like to see you."

I manage a tight smile. "I'd like to see her, too."

"Good. And maybe you'll stay a day or two before heading on to wherever you're headed next?"

I hesitate. "I'm off to Lord Dughlas next to see if he can fill in some of the spaces left by Lord Loudain, but I suppose I could maybe stay here a day or so as long as I'm welcome."

Cillian smiles, but there's there's something sad in it. "You're always welcome here, Ro. You always have been and you always will be." He runs a hand through his hair and straightens his shoulders. "Well, I'll leave you to resting and have those files sent up shortly."

The door closes with a click. I barely make it to the nearest couch before I collapse into it and let my tears consume me.

CHAPTER EIGHTEEN

ALAK

The idea of being separated from Astra is less than ideal, but I tell myself we'll back together soon. Eleni seems to be even less thrilled about the arrangement.

"What do you mean you're leaving?" she snaps, her eyes locked on Kai with a lethal focus. "This"—she motions wide—"is *your* pack and therefore your responsibility. Like hell you're passing it off to me."

Kai tightens his jaw, stepping forward so his face is inches from hers. "As you love to remind me, I am in charge and you will obey my orders."

Eleni clenches her hands by her side, letting out a growl that doesn't sound human. I take a step back, glancing over my shoulder at Ehren, who's watching with cautious amusement, his hand on his sword.

"I can't believe you're pulling rank," Eleni sneers. "That title is a technicality based on dark magic you claim you want nothing to do with. Maybe I'll take that title from you."

"You'd have to kill me, and you don't want the burden even if you could."

Eleni growls again, whipping away from Kai in frustration, turning her back to him as she crosses her arms. "Fine. You go off on your little adventure while I do your job."

Kai releases a long breath and takes a step closer. "I'm not abandoning you," Kai says, his voice barely above a whisper. "I didn't bring you all the way to Callenia to just up and leave. I will come back."

I suddenly feel like I'm intruding on a very intimate conversation and I glance away, eager for any distraction.

Eleni turns back to Kai. "Promise?"

"Promise."

"Fine. I'll go get Ega and Djimon to accompany you."

Kai steps closer to Eleni to say something else, but I step away. I've intruded enough. I wander away to seek Astra and find her securing her bag on Luna.

"Ready to go, love?"

She turns to me, tears shining in her eyes. I inhale sharply and rush to her, pulling her into my arms.

"I don't want to leave you again," she confesses, burying her face in my chest.

I tighten my grip around her and kiss the top of her head. "I don't want to leave you either. Let me go with you."

She pulls back and looks into my eyes. "But I need to be able to communicate with Ehren."

I brush a stray lock of hair from her face and shake my head. "There are other ways, other spells, other possibilities. Please, love, let me come with you. Don't leave me behind."

She glances away, chewing her lip as she thinks. "Okay."

My heart leaps into my throat. "Okay?"

She laughs and brushes her lips across mine. "Yes, I want you with me. We're stronger together."

A laugh bubbles out as I clutch her closer. "Yes, love, I believe we are."

No one seems particularly surprised that Astra and I changed our plans. Ehren even seems a touch relieved.

"We'll be as quick as possible," Astra promises Ehren with a firm nod. "We'll collect Kayleigh and bring her back to the fortress."

"Wait until you return before questioning her," Ehren warns. "We can't risk Kato finding out our plan or he'll be able to guard against it."

"Don't worry, mate," I grin, clapping a hand to Ehren's shoulder. "We'll take my cousin from one dungeon to the next without anyone being any the wiser about our actual intentions."

Ehren nods, but he seems a little uneasy. Cal steps forward and takes Ehren's hand, intertwining their fingers.

"Be quick and careful," Cal says. "We'll see you back at the fortress."

We say our last parting words and we ride off one way, while Ehren and the others lead the army back to the fortress. Our traveling party is made of me, Astra, Kai, and two shifters who look uneasy on the horses they've been riding. They talk to each other in thick, accented Paravlian. After a few hours, they shift into large birds and take to the sky, swooping above us in broad strokes.

By the end of the day we're crossing into Athiedor, though we're still a little ways out from the path Ehren said Ronan should be traveling. The wind is bitter and biting and the fire we build does little to guard against it. The shifters, used to the cold of Paravalia, seem less affected but still huddle close. Astra and I work together to create a bit of a barrier, but we're all piled inside our shared tent before long.

The second day we travel beneath heavy gray clouds that threaten snow and ice. Astra and I ride together on Fawn, Felixe curled up in her lap, and I wrap my arms around her, happy to share our warmth. The shifters seem to prefer the sky while Kai stays in his wolf form. As we near the end of the day, the shifters land ahead of us, bearing good news.

"A man fitting your description is a little ways to the east," Djimon informs us.

"If we adjust our course, we should meet up with him shortly after dark," Ega adds.

"Good," Astra says with a nod. "We'll adjust our course then."

"What if it's not Ronan?" Kai asks, making me jump. I didn't realize he shifted back into his human form. Normally I can sense the magic. The cold must be affecting me.

Astra shrugs. "Then we say hello, hope they're friendly, and move along in the morning."

Kai seems less than happy with the suggestion but doesn't argue. We start moving east as the sun sinks into the horizon. Astra starts shivering almost uncontrollably, and I'm about to suggest we call it a night when we spot a campfire not far in the distance.

"Kai," Astra says, her teeth clattering so much from the cold I can barely understand her. The huge gray wolf looks up at her. "G-go on a-ahead and s-see . . ."

Kai nods once and leaps off into the night before Astra finishes. I wrap my arms tighter around her and she sinks into me.

"You okay, love?"

"Mm-hm. I'm j-just c-cold."

I press a quick kiss to her temple. I hate that I can't do much more for her.

A few minutes later Kai returns, shifting into his human form.

"It is Ronan," he says.

With the affirmation, we plow on, eager to be near the fire. By the time we reach Ronan's camp, Astra's lips are practically blue and she's shivering even harder. Ronan approaches us, grinning, but his face falls into concern as he takes in Astra's condition.

"Is she . . . ?"

"She'll be fine. Help me get her warm," I say, my heart racing.

Ronan nods and helps Astra from Fawn.

"Hey," Astra whispers, looking up at Ronan.

Ronan forces a small smile. "Hey there, love. Let's get you to the fire."

Astra nods while I secure Fawn. By the time I join her by the fire, Ronan has her wrapped in a blanket with a cup of something with curling steam in her hands, Felixe snuggled in her lap. His warding magic buzzes around us, helping to trap the heat while releasing the smoke.

"Bit 'o broth?" he asks, offering me my own steaming cup.

I nod and accept as I settle next to Astra. "Thanks."

Kai remains in his wolf form, settling behind Astra. She leans against him without a thought and he rests his head on his paws. The shifters make quick work setting up our tent and disappear inside.

We sit in silence for a while, watching Astra, but after a few minutes, she starts to warm up, her cheeks tinging pink with the heat of the fire.

"So, what's the plan?" Ronan asks.

"Can't say much, really," I reply as Astra shakes her head.

Ronan scowls. "Why not?"

Astra's eyes flick around the edges of the camp before she whispers, "The shadows are listening."

Ronan looks confused, but he nods anyway. We promise to tell him a little more in the morning before we retreat to our tent.

The next morning Astra takes a scrap of parchment and scribbles down the plan, sharing it with Ronan. He reads quietly for a moment before nodding. We travel most of the day in silence. Ronan uses his magic to craft a shield similar to his warding the night before that protects us from the cold, Astra supporting his magic with her own. Heavy clouds loom above us, so when we enter a small town with a tavern inn shortly before nightfall, we agree that spending a night indoors would be our best option. After a quick dinner, I secure us some rooms.

"They had two rooms available," I say, dangling the keys for everyone to see as they finish up their ale. "Shall we go figure out how we're splitting up for the night?"

"Let's go," Ronan says with a grin, rising from the table.

The others follow suit, Astra slipping her hand into mine, and we head up the stairs in the back corner. Once upstairs we find our rooms are across the hall from each other. The room on the left is slightly smaller with only two beds and the other room boasts three.

"Astra and I will take this room," Ega says sharply, nodding to the room with two beds.

Astra scowls and glances at me. I frown and shake my head.

"We typically prefer to stay together," I counter, giving Astra's hand a quick squeeze.

Ega and Djimon exchange a scowl and mutter something in a language I don't understand. After a moment, Djimon takes a step forward.

"My sister is correct. It is not good for men and women to share a room when it is possible to . . . be proper."

Kai growls, his gray eyes flashing. "None of that."

Djimon ignores Kai's clear warning and continues. "Ega and Astra should take this room."

Astra's grip on my hand tightens and she moves closer to me so our arms brush.

"I would rather stay with Alak."

"But you are not married."

Ega's words sting like a slap to the face. Astra stumbles to the side half a step, clearly taken aback. Pink rises in her cheeks and I feel discomfort and shame surge down the bond. Hell no. No one gets make Astra feel like that.

"We are soul-bonded," I say, harsher than I intend, but I don't regret my tone.

Ega shakes her head. "It is not the same."

"We shared our cots and blankets so far on our journey with no issue. What's your problem tonight?" I demand.

"We had little choice," Ega says, her voice unwavering as she meets my eyes with a firm gaze. "Tonight, there is a choice."

"Ega," Kai says, his voice lethal, "this is not the time or the place. Stand down."

Djimon meets Kai's eyes. "I am surprised you allow them to share a bed, knowing how protective you are of her."

"They are bonded," Kai replies through clenched teeth. "And she is not mine or anyone else's to control."

Ega shakes her head. "She is an unmarried woman. Bond or no, Menos and Dwelle would not approve."

"Who are—" Ronan starts but Kai cuts him off with a growl.

"Your gods and goddesses have no place to dictate their lives."

A rush of understanding pulses through the bond as Astra steps forward. I glance at her, puzzled.

"Menos and Dwelle are your gods?" she asks, her voice far softer than the situation calls for.

Ega nods once, firmly. "Menos is the god of sanctified marriage and Dwelle the goddess of fertility. Their blessings are holy and their wrath is not to be tested."

As soon as Ega mentions Dwelle, Astra reacts. It's not obvious —a slight tightening of her jaw and a glimmer of sadness down the bond. I'm not sure why the words strike Astra in such a way but she feels wounded, hurt. I study her with concern, tracing my thumb over her knuckles, but she won't meet my eyes.

"Your gods are not—"

Astra holds up a hand, bringing Kai to a halt. "I understand. I can share the room with Ega."

"What? No!" The words tumble from my mouth, earning me a sharp glare from Djimon.

"Perhaps you should let her choose. Or do you, as her bondmate, control her every whim?"

I clench my teeth and grit out, "No, I don't control her."

Astra turns to me, her eyes heavy, "Alak, it's not a big deal."

I take her other hand in mine, turning her so we're facing each other. "If you truly want to be apart from me, I won't stop you." She looks down, no doubt unable to look at the hurt I'm sure is shining in my eyes. "But *I* don't want to be parted from you." I press a kiss to her forehead and she lifts her gaze to me. "What do you really want?"

"I . . ." She glances to Ega and Djimon before shaking her head slowly and looking back to me. "I don't want to be separated but—"

"Then that is that," Kai says, his voice flush with authority. "Astra and Alak will remain together and you two"—he nods sharply to Ega and Djimon—"will have no further say."

Djimon and Ega say nothing more as they move stiffly into the room. We cross the hall into the other room. Kai turns to Astra as soon as the door is closed.

"Are you okay?"

Astra forces a smile and manages a nod, but I can tell she's still affected. Kai sighs, shaking his head.

"Many of the shifters come from small tribes called *ortas*. They are very loyal to the gods and goddesses of their individual *ortas*. Djimon and Ega, I would assume, are no exception."

"So a woman's place in their tribe is to marry and produce offspring?" Ronan asks, genuine curiosity ringing in his question.

Kai huffs a laugh. "Hardly. From what I know and saw during my time in Paravlia, family is very important to them, and one of the best ways to make sure their lineage is tracked and everyone is taken care of is through marriage and tracking of their children. Add in their devotion to their gods and you get very opinionated beliefs coming out of some of the *ortas*. Though, I can assure you, not every *orta* would react in a similar fashion."

Ronan makes a "hmmm" sound and nods as he eases down onto one of the beds. "I suppose that makes sense." He shifts his gaze to Astra, concern in his eyes as he asks softly, "Are you sure you're okay?"

Astra starts, lifting her head. I was so focused on Kai's explanation I hadn't even noticed she's gone quiet and sullen.

"*Are* you okay, love?" I ask, taking her hand.

She glances from Ronan to me and nods. "I'm fine."

I frown and watch Ronan as he studies Astra with concern. I glance to Kai and discover he's also weighing every movement of Astra's more carefully than usual. When my gaze returns to Astra she meets my eyes and offers a subtle shake of her head. Something is wrong. I can feel it in every fiber of my being. I can sense it in the bond. I can see it in the disquiet of her eyes.

"So," Ronan drawls, breaking the tension. "How will we make three beds fit four people?"

"I can shift and sleep on the floor," Kai suggests with a shrug.

"Or Alak and I can share a bed," Astra says, offering me a weak smile.

I manage a smile of my own as I look over at the beds. "Aye, love, I think we could make that work."

"Excellent," Ronan says, toeing off his boots and stretching his legs. "I suppose no one would mind if I head off to sleep right now?"

Kai huffs a laugh, striding toward the center bed. "Not at all. I plan on sleeping as soon as possible."

Astra and I nod our agreement as we shuffle to the far bed. She settles down first and I rest behind her. Ronan and Kai take care of dousing the flickering lanterns that light the room as I wrap my arms around Astra, drawing her close. She sinks into me, her back against my chest. The minutes stretch in the darkness and Ronan and Kai drift off, their breathing evening out quickly. Astra, however, remains awake. I can practically feel her thoughts spinning.

"Love?" I whisper, my voice low in her ear. "Are you all right?"

She shifts, turning in my arms so she's facing me, her nose practically touching mine. Even in the dark I can see the anguish brimming in her eyes.

"I'm fine," she whispers, though we both know it's a lie.

I press a quick kiss to her forehead. "No, love, you're not." I run a tentative hand down her cheek. "I can't help if I don't know how." I pause, adding, "Is it because we're not married? Or at least engaged? Because—"

"Alak, no," she whispers, pressing a quick kiss to my lips. "That's not it."

"I'll marry you, tomorrow. Hell, we can leave this bed right now and I'll find someone to perform a ceremony tonight. I love you, Astra, and if marriage is what you want, it's yours."

Astra smiles softly and shakes her head. "I won't lie and say I don't like the idea of being married to you, but I want a proper proposal."

I laugh and she grins. The smile falters quickly, however.

"Astra . . . Please."

She snuggles closer, pressing flush against me. I'm afraid she's not going to answer until she mumbles into my chest, so quietly I barely hear her, "I can't have children."

"What?"

She pulls her head back to look at me, tears shining in her eyes. My heart shatters.

"I can't have children. My magic messed it all up and I . . . If you can't be with me—"

"None of that," I demand gently, tightening my hold on her. "I will always want to be with you. If you can't conceive a child, so be it. It doesn't make me love you any less." She makes a shuddering sound somewhere between a sigh and a sob. "I love you, Astra Downs, and nothing in this world or the next can change that."

Her chin trembles. "Are you sure?"

"Have I ever given you any reason to doubt?"

She gives a small laugh, shaking her head.

"Good." I kiss her forehead. "Now, get some sleep, love. I'll hold you all night and help you bear your burdens. You're not alone, love. Not as long as I breathe air."

With a sigh of contentment she snuggles against me. "I love you, Alak."

After a few minutes her breathing evens out and I know she's asleep. I wish to join her but my thoughts keep me up. Kai and Ronan knew something was wrong. They must have known. In a way it hurts that she hadn't told me, but I can understand why. Just like the bond, this isn't something that could be said through a letter, though I wish she'd told me sooner so she didn't have to bear it alone.

CHAPTER NINETEEN

ASTRA

It rains overnight, but by the time we're on the road, it's clear, leaving behind frozen ground. The cruel wind bites at any exposed skin until it's red and raw. I clutch my cloak tightly around me and call upon my magic for warmth, but even that seems to have its limits. I can feel Alak's concern through the bond and the heaviness of his gaze.

We can just make out the outline of Lord Dughlas's castle fortress when the sun begins its decent into the horizon. When Ega rides up alongside me, I barely spare her a glance, even when she speaks.

"I would like to clear the air between us before we arrive," she says, her voice low so Alak, who rides on my right, can't hear.

I keep my gaze fixed ahead. "Consider it cleared."

Ega shakes her head with a sigh. "No, my sorceress. I truly want it cleared. I was in the wrong. I was raised to believe certain things. Before this journey into your kingdom, I had barely left my home. I still struggle to understand the ways of the world, as does my brother. It is . . . difficult to meld the beliefs of others with my own and in turn accept those beliefs and choices. It is even more difficult to admit when I have made a mistake. Can you forgive me?"

I turn my head and offer Ega a small smile. "I forgive you."

Ega's smile is tight but there nonetheless. She inclines her head. "Thank you."

I glance over my shoulder where Djimon rides between Kai and Ronan. "What about your brother? "

"He is sorry as well but too proud to confess his mistake." Ega tilts her head, studying me. "Perhaps you can forgive his pride along with his words?"

"I can. After all, if we were to all hold grudges and never forgive people their past mistakes, what motivation is there for any of us to change?"

Ega smiles. "Indeed."

She falls back, her brother riding up by her side, and Alak pulls a little closer to me, eyeing me cautiously as concern pulses down the bond.

"What was that, love?"

"I know you caught some of it."

He smiles sheepishly, ducking his head. "Aye, a bit, but not all. I mostly felt your emotions." He glances back at Djimon and Ega as they converse in low whispers. "She apologized?"

"She did."

"And you're okay?"

I meet his worried gaze and smile. "Yes, Alak. I'm okay."

I send a rush of reassurance down our bond and he smiles, a blush rising on his cheeks.

A few minutes later we ride into the city surrounding the fortress and are met with a rush of servants and soldiers. Our horses are taken to the stables and our bags taken inside as we're ushered before Lord Dughlas who is apparently eating dinner. His eyes widen as we march into his bustling dining hall. He quickly controls his features and raises a glass of wine to us in a toast. The room falls into whispers as we stop before his table.

"Ah! My friends! To what do I owe this visit?"

"We have come to escort our prisoner back to Callenia," I say, my voice ringing through the room.

Lord Dughlas arches an eyebrow. "Surely you don't doubt that I have kept my word in caring for her?"

I shake my head. "Of course not. Prince Ehren merely has need of her."

Lord Dughlas studies me, picking a bit of food from his teeth with his tongue. I fight to keep the disgust from my face and maintain a look of dignity.

"Very well," he mutters with a shrug. "What does it matter to me what the prince does with his prisoners of war? We'll make the appropriate arrangements." He takes a swig of his wine, then gestures with his goblet to the dining tables. "In the meantime, please help yourself to some food. I'm sure you're hungry after your travels."

I incline my head. "Thank you for your hospitality."

A couple servants hurry forward and escort us to some free seats at a nearby table, providing plates and goblets of wine. Ega and Djimon stay on high alert, wearing fierce expressions that have people leaving space around them. Kai also remains alert, but appears to be brooding more than anything. Alak, however, jumps directly into conversation with those seated nearby. I join in when addressed but am content to remain quiet. When dinner finishes, servants reappear to take us to our rooms, where we are divided into pairs.

"Did you get the idea that Lord Dughlas feels we're stepping on his toes?" I ask Alak as the door closes behind us.

Alak shrugs, sinking down on the bed to kick off his boots. "Perhaps. I don't think it takes much to make him feel affronted." He looks up at me and grins. "His ego is terribly fragile."

I laugh and shake my head. "You better not let him hear you say that."

Alak hums and stands, sauntering over to me and looping an arm around my waist. "And what sort of things *should* we let him hear?"

Heat rises in my cheeks. "I have a few ideas."

Alak's eyes spark with interest as desire pulses down the bond. "Oh, tell me more."

I smile and we fall into a kiss that quickly becomes much more.

WE RISE EARLY the next morning before most of the castle is awake and moving. Alak and Kai take the lead on securing Kayleigh and making sure she's ready to go, but I need to talk to the Fae. I'm mounting Luna when a cheerful voice cuts through the morning air.

"Would you like some company, love?"

I smile down at Ronan. "I'll never turn down your company."

He grins, his eyes bright. "Excellent. Give me a moment to prepare Pixie, and I'll accompany you on your little adventure."

I chuckle as Ronan strolls to the stable and readies his horse. A few minutes later we're crossing the frost-covered landscape. For a while we ride in silence, taking in the view around us, but after a few minutes we fall into easy conversation. When we reach the woods, we tie our horses and trek the rest of the way on foot. When we reach the Faerie ring, Ronan lets out a low whistle.

"So I didn't dream that whole experience last time. I was starting to wonder."

I grin. "No, it was very much real."

I kneel down to trace the symbols. The ground around the ring is frozen, but somehow the ring itself remains warm, the grass in the center a bright green, the flowers flourishing. When I whisper the spell, I hear Ronan muttering along with me and I bite back a smile. With a whoosh of magic the glowing doorway appears. I wait with bated breath to see who steps through, and my heart surges with delight when it's Hycis.

"Of course it would be you who would come knocking so early in the morning," Hycis says with a sharp grin, her hands on her hips. "Do you humans not require sleep?"

I laugh. "Sleep? Who needs sleep?"

Hycis's grin grows as she takes me in. "Well, I suppose sleep is over for the day. I assume you've come for the berries?"

I nod. "Yes. I apologize if I've come too early yet again, but —"

Hycis waves me off. "No. I've been trying to contact you, but it seems the worlds are not as in tune as they should be." She glances past me and notices Ronan for the first time, her eyes narrowing. "Ah, you brought your human friend with you again." Her eyes spark with mischief. "Is he a new lover perhaps?"

"If only I could be so lucky, but alas her heart is quite taken and mine is not so easily given," he says with a grin.

"Hmm," Hycis muses, tilting her head. "I think I like you."

I roll my eyes and turn my attention back to Hycis. "What

of the berries? Are they ready? Or do you need more time to prepare them?"

"We have several batches ready to go. It will take a bit of time for us to prep them for travel, but not terribly long. As long as one of us remains within this circle, the door should remain open. When we are packed, we can travel together to your prince."

"I will wait here, then."

Hycis assesses me for a moment before nodding. "I won't be long."

She disappears through the door and I glance over at Ronan, who has started to shiver.

"Join me in the circle," I say, motioning Ronan over. "It's warmer."

Ronan approaches slowly, but pauses at the edge of the ring. "It won't mess with the magic?"

"It shouldn't, not while the door is open. If it does I'll just perform the spell again."

He takes a tentative step to my side and only relaxes after several seconds have passed. He leans forward on his cane and attempts to peer into the door but it's pretty pointless. It doesn't keep him from grinning down at me. It takes probably half an hour before Hycis reappears, a large, lumpy bag slung over her shoulder.

"Are those the berries?" I ask, nodding to the bag.

"Some of them." She glances over her shoulder. "More are on the way."

She steps to the side, cautiously stepping from the circle and Ronan follows suit. A second later, Rynia steps through the door, leading a black horse with a black mane and a silver horse with an iridescent mane. I start, realizing it's not a horse.

"Is that a Unicorn?" I ask, my mouth gaping open as I blink at the creature Rynia is leading from the circle.

Hycis flashes me a grin and steps forward, accepting the reins for the Unicorn and rubbing its nose. "Meet Vaeschia, my beloved Unicorn."

I'm so lost in the awe of meeting a true, real live Unicorn that I don't even notice the other two Fae that have stepped through the portal door until one of them clears their throat. I spin around and take them in.

They're clearly siblings, sharing many of the same features, including high cheek bones, hair such a deep blue it's almost black, and sharp golden eyes. The one on the left has broad, strong shoulders and his gaze is set in a fierce, hateful glare. The other is slightly shorter and wears a lopsided smirk, their bright eyes wandering around taking everything in.

"Ah, yes," Hycis says, stepping closer, linking her fingers with Rynia's. "You remember Rynia, my bondmate?"

I smile. "Of course. Good to see you again, Rynia."

Rynia smiles softly. "Likewise."

"And these two idiots are Iefyr and Ievis," Hycis adds, pointing to each sibling in turn as they step further into the human world, each leading a horse—just horses, no more Unicorns, sadly enough—of their own.

Ronan and I incline our heads in greeting.

"Welcome to the human realm," I say. "I assume you are brother and . . . " I hesitate, suddenly not very sure at all what their exact relationship may be.

Ievis, the taller of the two, eyes me with disdain but Iefyr answers with a wide grin. "We are siblings, yes. Ievis prefers more masculine terms. I don't really find that I fit into such categories and prefer neutral terms." They tilt their head. "I hope that's acceptable?"

"Oh, yes! Of course," I say quickly, my cheeks warming.

Ievis sighs and jumps in before I can say anything further. "Twins may not have existed in your realm for centuries, but they occur occasionally in ours."

"You're twins?" I ask, my mouth gaping.

Iefyr's smile grows. "Indeed we are." They turn to Hycis. "I can see why you enjoy these humans. They are a delight."

Ievis sneers. "If you find their moronic nature endearing, yes, quite delightful."

"Moronic but not deaf," Ronan says through a tight grin, his voice edged slightly.

Ievis straightens, his glare nearly lethal. Ronan visibly stiffens when Ievis fixes his eyes on Ronan's weaker leg and cane.

"My leg may not work well, but my ears work perfectly, I can assure you."

"I see humans love to jump to conclusions and assume the worst of others," Ievis snarls.

"Do you have the berries?" I ask, stepping between Ronan and Ievis, nodding to the bags attached to their horses—and Unicorn—before they can rip out each other's throats.

Rynia steps forward and makes a motion with a nod. "Hopefully this will be enough until we can close the Isle."

I raise my eyes to meet hers as my heart stills. "We can close the Isle?"

"Why do you think I brought these two along?" Hycis grins, thrusting her thumb toward the twins. "It wasn't because I was lacking in company."

Ievis glares at Hycis, but Iefyr only grins.

"Twins have special magic even among the Fae," Iefyr offers. "It is one of the few things Fae and humans have in common—twins mean power. Ievis and I possess more than the magic typically provided by nature. I can create unique portals that span great distances and break through otherwise impenetrable barriers, and Ievis can create new spells from old magic and twist known magic into something new unlike has been seen among even our kind."

I frown, glancing between all four Fae. "I'm afraid I don't follow."

"As expected," Ievis scoffs.

Iefyr shoots their brother a disapproving look before answering. "We believe that by combining spells and magics, Ievis should be able to close the Isle permanently, making it even stronger than before. He is quite close, I believe, to being able to craft the spell. A little more research and perhaps experimenting in your world to see how his magic works here, and your Dragkonians should be sealed away."

My heart races. We can seal them and kill them. This is more than I ever hoped for. I need to talk to Ehren. Now. I spin to face Ronan, but I can tell by the expression on his face he's thinking the same thing.

"If we hurry back we can set out in less than two hours. If the weather holds, we'll be back to the fortress in a matter of days."

I nod, running my own set of calculations and cursing myself for not bringing along my sleepwalking feather.

"Well, then," Hycis jumps in. "Let's not dawdle."

We make good time and get back to the fortress in under an hour. Kai and Alak have all the arrangements made and we're soon ready to be back on the road, though they do both take time to properly gawk at the Unicorn. When Ega and Djimon escort Kayleigh up from her cell, I gasp. The girl is a whisper of the one I remember, her face gaunt and colorless.

"I thought they were taking care of her," I whisper to Alak.

He winces. "According to everyone I spoke with, they tried. She's been refusing most of her meals, and I guess the rest is the effect of little light and restless nights."

I manage a nod, tearing my eyes away from the poor girl as she's helped up onto a horse, her hands bound together. Ega and Djimon mount their horses and flank her on either side. I make quick introductions between the humans and Fae and we're on our way, racing against time.

CHAPTER TWENTY

I'm a nervous wreck with Astra gone. It doesn't help that every corner of the fortress is crawling with soldiers, many of whom I don't know in the slightest. If Bram were still alive, he would be freaking out. Thankfully, my new Captain of the Guard—hopefully my soon-to-be general—is with me practically every moment of every day. When I'm not with Cal, I'm typically with Jess and her crew or Luc and his. Sometimes both. When I find moments to myself I dive into my spellbooks, looking for anything useful. I practice as many as I can and make sure my ingredients are fully stocked.

One afternoon I'm alone in my room, pages of spells spread out across my bed, when I feel darkness creeping across my thoughts. It's slinking around the corners of my brain whispering in my ear.

You're a failure.

You might as well stop looking for spells.

They'll never work.

You can't save your people.

They only die at your hand.

I don't even know why you try.

I squeeze my eyes shut and take a deep breath and release it slowly. I repeat the process a few more times, forcing the darkness from my mind. It works, but only barely. I need to move, to focus on something else. I shove papers off my lap and leap off the bed. I pace the room for a moment before the walls start to feel like they're closing in. My chest pinches and I fight to breathe.

"You're fine," I whisper to myself. "You can do this."

My words only halfway work to calm me, but they work well enough for me to realize I can't do this alone. I rush to the door and fling it open. Collin and Jameson are stationed outside my room and jump at the sudden movement. To be honest, I forgot they were there.

"Uh, at ease, gentlemen," I mumble as I slide past them out into the hall.

"Do you need us to take you somewhere, Your Majesty?" Collin asks, stepping forward. His eyes dart down to my feet which, I remember with a start, are bare. "Or are you not going far?"

I force a smile and wiggle my toes. "Not going far at all."

"We can still come," Jameson insists.

I wave them off. "Not necessary."

Jameson and Collin exchange a look, and I suspect they have strict orders to stick with me. Or maybe Bram's insistence and patrols stuck with them long after his death. Bram. I suddenly know where I need to go, and I need to be alone after all.

"I need to check something," I say, avoiding their assessing eyes. "I won't be long and I'm not going far."

Jameson clears his throat. "If you need us . . ."

"I'll yell for you."

I offer them a quick grin before I race off down the hall and around the corner to Bram's abandoned quarters. Of course he made sure he was nearby, even though he knew Cal would be with me. My heart feels tight, and I'm not sure if it's even beating as I place my hand on the door handle and push it open. It's startlingly quiet. I ease into the room and shut the door behind me with a click.

I take a deep breath and look around. Dust dances in a shaft of light that's snuck in through a sliver of space between the curtains covering a large window. I stride over and throw them all the way open, light flooding the small space. There's really not much to see. The bed is neatly made and the desk in the corner has neat stacks of unused paper and a bottle of ink. There's nothing but a half-melted candle on the bedside table. The only thing personal that remains is a trunk at the foot of the bed.

I swallow hard and make my way over, kneeling in front of it and lifting the latch. I'm a little surprised it's not locked, but Bram really didn't have much to protect or hide. Inside I find some clothes, a spare dagger in a sheath, a bottle of salve marked for sore muscles, a small book, a bundle of letters, something wrapped in a piece of cloth, and a leather pouch.

I pull out the letters first. There aren't many. A few are from his political contacts and soldiers under his care, but most are from his mother and sister. They feel very personal and I find myself setting them aside. The book proves to be a journal and I set it aside even quicker. Next, I reach for the cloth and slowly peel back the wrapping. I start when two amulets gleam up at me. A smile plays at the corner of my lips as I lift them.

"I forgot about these," I mumble to myself.

I raise them in the air, allowing them to catch the light. I recall the first time Winnie discovered these amulets and how excited she was that we found a solution to help the mysterious twins. I laugh softly. They're not so mysterious now. Astra became one of my closest and dearest friends. I barely knew her when I presented her with this amulet. She's grown into her magic so much since then.

So has Kato. My joy fades as quickly as it arrived.

I wrap the amulets and place them back in the trunk and reach for the pouch. I'm surprised to hear a soft clinking inside. I tip it and dump the contents into my hand. It's the ring Bram gave Astra when they were engaged and two stones. No, not just stones. I can feel the hum of magic. It's the Luvgim, I realize, my breath catching. I carefully slip the ring back into the pouch and set it aside.

I shift my hand so the Luvgim rolls across my palm. The magic calls to me like a song. I'd wondered what had happened to the Luvgim after Astra's rescue, but I never had time to ask. I clench my hand into a fist, squeezing the gems as hard as I can. They cut into my palm, but I embrace the pain and don't fight the tears that burn my eyes.

After a few moments I collect myself. Still clutching the gems, I close the trunk and push up onto my feet. I start to close the curtains but stop myself. This room needs a little brightness. A painful smile twists on my lips as I take one more look before heading back to my room. Collin and Jameson look relieved when I turn the corner. I slip past them back inside without a word—words honestly feel a bit too much right now.

I dump out one of my bags, adding to the chaotic mess already on my bed, and dig through until I find a long, thin strip of leather. It takes several attempts, but in the end I manage to tie the two pieces of Luvgim together and knot the ends together to make a type of necklace. I'm tempted to slip it over my own neck, but something tells me it would be a mistake. Instead, I place it into one of my travel bags.

I'm not sure why, but I feel better. I settle back on the bed and dive back into my spells. Cal comes in a few moments later and I offer him a weak smile. He scoots on the bed next to me, and I greet him with a kiss.

"Studying spells?" he asks, nodding to the book in my lap.

"Yep," I say, turning a page. "I want to be as prepared as possible."

Cal hums agreeably and takes my hand in his. I flinch and Cal scowls, turning my hand over in his. When he sees the marks left by the Luvgim he frowns.

"Ehren, what's this?"

I swallow and glance away. "It's nothing."

"Ehren."

I force myself to meet his eyes and give him what I hope is a reassuring smile. "I was looking through some of Bram's things"—his eyes soften—"and I grabbed something a little too hard."

Cal nods knowingly and slides off the bed. He walks over to his things and rifles through them a moment before resuming his seat on the bed, a bandage and jar of salve in his hand.

"Let me see," he says, holding his hand out for mine.

I take a shaky breath and comply. Cal cradles my hand tenderly as he carefully brushes salve on the wound. He's gentle as he wraps the bandage around my hand, securing it firmly. When he's done, he lifts my palm to his lips and presses a kiss to the wounds. My breath catches in my throat at his open affection.

"Cal," I say, my voice breaking.

He looks over at me, his caring eyes meeting mine. "I love

you so much, Ehren. I hate seeing you hurt, even if it's you doing the hurting."

I swallow, but I can't manage any words. I can only nod. Cal settles closer, his shoulder pressing against mine as he slides his hand into mine. He brushes a kiss across my cheek and my eyes flutter closed for a moment.

"You know if you ever need me, I'm here."

"I know," I whisper.

"I mean it, Ehren."

I lean over and kiss him. It's brief but firm, and I hope it properly portrays exactly how much I love him. Judging by the soft smile on his lips when I pull away, I succeeded. He holds my gaze for a moment before turning his attention to the forgotten book in my lap.

"Tell me what spells you think you'll use."

I smile and rest my head on his shoulder. "All right."

For the next hour, we spend time together flipping through the book. Everything feels calm and at peace, and it's exactly what I need.

THE NEXT COUPLE days pass without event, but I get more stressed hour by hour. In an attempt to do something productive, I convince Winnie to head back to the Summer Palace with Nyco, Sama, and few other soldiers. I'm not entirely sure what news Astra might bring back with her, but I feel better knowing Cadewynn is safe.

I'm pacing the edges of the training field when Cal spots me. He dismisses the troops he's working with and approaches me like one would a timid animal.

"If their travel went smoothly, they should back tomorrow," I say as soon as he's within earshot.

He tilts his head, doing the calculations himself, and nods. "That seems about right."

"But what if—"

"Nope," Cal says, cutting me off. "I'm not going to let you spiral."

I cock my head. "Do you have a plan to keep me from spiraling?"

Cal's eyes darken beautifully and he takes a step closer. "Of course I do." He leans in and his lips brush my ear as he whispers, "We're going to spar."

He takes a wide step back, watching his words register. I burst out laughing and he grins, his eyes shining. I step forward and loop an arm around his waist, pulling him flush against me. He starts to glance around to see if anyone is watching but stops himself, pushing aside the habit.

"What if I had other ideas?" I ask, my voice low.

Cal wraps his arms around me, linking his hands behind my back as he leans in and touches the tip of his nose to mine. "Oh, and what ideas are in your head, my prince?"

I inhale sharply and he grins, pressing his lips to mine. I kiss him hungrily for a moment before he pulls back. This time he does glance around. There are a few people lingering nearby but they quickly shuffle off, pretending like they don't notice us. Cal dips his head as crimson creeps up his neck.

"How about we make a deal?"

Cal raises his eyes to mine. "Go on."

I grin. "We spar for a bit to warm up, and then we continue with a different physical activity in a more private area."

Cal's eyes light up and he nods, pressing a quick kiss to my lips in reply. He steps to the center of the training area and unsheathes his sword. I take a deep breath and do the same.

He's quick and sure-footed and incredibly attractive to the point of distraction, so it doesn't take him long to best me. I roll my shoulders and we start again. This time, I focus better and am on the verge of winning when a large bird swoops onto the training field, shifting into a lean woman with dark skin.

My eyes widen as I stumble backward and Cal spins, assessing the possible threat. The woman, however, doesn't seem put off by Cal's raised sword as she approaches. She looks vaguely familiar but I can't quite place her. Judging by Cal's tense jaw and the fact that he's not lowering his sword, he can't either.

"Prince Ehren, I have a message," she says, her accent thick.

"Oh," I say, everything clicking into place. "You're one of the shifters that went to Athiedor with Kai."

The woman gives me a curt nod. Cal lowers his sword but doesn't put it away. Not yet.

"Is Astra . . . ? Is anyone hurt?"

The woman shakes her head. "No. Everyone, including the prisoner, is fine. I am merely to let you know they will be arriving soon." She glances up at the sky where the sun is already beginning to set. "Likely after dark. In addition to the prisoner, you will have four other guests."

"Who?" Cal asks, stepping to my side as he sheathes his sword.

The woman looks at him, her eyes trailing up and down his body, assessing him.

"Who?" I ask, bringing her eyes back to me.

"Four Fae. Do you need their names?"

Fae. Gods, she did it. Astra found the Fae and is bringing them here. Does this mean we have a chance?

"Breathe, Ehren," Cal whispers, placing his hand on the small of my back. When did I stop breathing?

I take a deep breath that borders on a gasp. "Thank you. I don't need their names."

The woman nods and glances between me and Cal. "If I'm no longer needed, I would like to refresh after my journey. Is there a place I can do so?"

I manage a nod but Cal is the one to step forward. He escorts the woman to the edge of the training field and calls for a servant. They chat for a moment before he returns to my side.

"I'm having them prepare rooms," Cal says. "I hope that's okay."

A small laugh escapes. "Cal," I mumble, slipping an arm around his waist. "You're welcome to do whatever you want."

I kiss him and he grins against my lips before pulling back. "Whatever I want, huh?"

"Please," I whisper, my voice shamelessly breathless at the thought of all the things I want him to do. I pull him into another kiss. "You promised me distractions."

Cal laughs and draws back, taking my hand in his and weaving his fingers with mine. "Well then, we should probably get to it or we won't have to time to finish everything I have planned before our guests arrive."

My eyebrows shoot up to my hairline. "They won't be here for a couple hours."

A seductive grin curls on Cal's lips and he tilts his head. "I know."

I swallow and stumble forward. "Yes, then, we should . . . we should go."

When Cal drags me into our room he sends my normal guards away, assuring them I'm in good hands. As soon as the door closes behind us, his lips are on mine and I don't have a care in the world.

CHAPTER TWENTY-ONE

"Holy fuck," Brock shouts in wide-awed awe as we enter the dining hall. "Are those Fae?"

The rest of the dining hall falls into muffled chatter as we approach the head table, everyone twisting in their seats to get a better look.

"Don't get too excited," I offer as we get within hearing distance. "This one"—I thrust my thumb at Ievis—"is an arsehole and the human realm is better off not being bothered by his existence."

"If all humans are as idiotic and tiresome as you lot, I would rather be back in my realm anyway," Ievis snaps.

Jess grins and glances to Astra over my shoulder. Astra sighs.

"Ronan and Ievis don't quite get along," Astra says, her voice tired.

"Oh, this will be absolutely wonderful," Jess says, her eyes shining.

Ehren, who's seated a few places down from Jess and her crew, leaps to his feet and rushes around the table to our side,

Cal trailing behind him with a smile. While his eyes are wide with wonder, he doesn't seem surprised that his sorceress is escorting Fae.

"I am Prince Ehren of Callenia," Ehren's saying by the time he reaches us. He glances over his shoulder at Jess and adds, "And this is my sister, Jessalynn." Jess offers the Fae a curt nod. "Welcome to our kingdom of Callenia."

Hycis is practically vibrating with excitement beside me.

"So, this is what a human prince looks like," she murmurs with unmasked delight as her eyes trail over Ehren. When she flicks her gaze to Jess, I notice Jess's hand shift to where she keeps a dagger on her thigh. The Fae's eyes track the motion and she chuckles. "Perhaps there is not much difference between your royalty and mine."

"Now, Hycis," Rynia says, stepping forward and placing a hand on her bondmate's arm. "Let's not stir up trouble quite yet."

Hycis grins wickedly. "Fine, I can wait a bit."

I don't bother hiding my grin. While I often fantasized about the best way to kill and be rid of Ievis on our journey here, Hycis and Rynia more than made up for the terrible Fae male. Their banter and relationship made me equal parts jealous and happy.

Astra rolls her eyes with a heavy sigh, but Alak is the one to speak.

"This is Hycis and Rynia," he says, nodding to each in turn. "They've been our main contacts for the berries."

Jess's eyes widen. "So we have more?"

Astra nods. "The servants are unloading the packages to be taken to the weapons room."

"We'll start turning them into poison as soon as possible, then," Jess says, glancing past me at the exit. She turns to

Kaeya and gives her a sharp nod. Kaeya rises, slinking out of the dining hall, and Brock shifts to take her seat directly next to Jess, glaring at the Fae in a protective manner.

"And what of the prisoner you went to fetch?" Jess asks, fiddling lazily with her goblet.

Astra's face falls. "We retrieved her."

"She's been taken to a secure room for now with Ega and Djimon standing guard," Alak adds, slipping an arm around Astra's waist and pulling her closer.

Jess opens her mouth to ask more questions but Ehren jumps in first.

"I'll send a few of my own guard in their place. I'm sure they're tired from traveling."

This time it's Cal that slinks off with a nod, pressing a quick kiss to Ehren's cheek before he disappears.

Ievis loudly clears his throat, drawing all the attention to him. "Is all important human business conducted in the middle of dining halls, or is it possible your kind does possess some level of decorum?"

"Oh, for fecks sake, Ievis!" I hiss, shaking my head.

He snarls and levels me with a glare. "That does not answer my question."

My eyes flash and I open my mouth to retort, but Astra steps between us, giving me an exasperated look.

"I do apologize for our lack of decorum," Ehren says with a winning smile. "I'll arrange for dinner to be brought to us in the briefing room while we go over whatever news you've brought." He turns to Jess. "I assume you can show our guests the way?"

She sighs but pushes up from the table. "Of course, dearest brother. I would love nothing more. Follow me."

Everyone falls into place behind Jess as she marches from

the dining room. My stomach twists with nerves, though I'm not sure why. We've all known that this moment was coming, but something about this meeting feels very . . . final, as if we're turning a corner. After this there will be no going back, and going forward means a path paved in blood and bones.

The briefing room isn't very large. It's meant for maybe half a dozen people, so when Ehren joins us with Luc at his side, it feels more than crowded. Brock volunteers to take guard outside the room, and Kai offers to stand with him. There seems to be some dissent among the Fae, but in the end, after a sharp look from Rynia, Hycis makes an exaggerated yawn and asks to be shown to her room.

"I suppose I could leave as well," Iefyr says, making to follow the other Fae, but Hycis places her palm to their chest and pushes them back into the room.

"You're important to this discussion, Iefyr," she insists.

"Am I?" they ask, arching an eyebrow. "I doubt it's time for me to play my part."

Astra offers them a soft smile. "You're still welcome to stay."

They shake their head. "I'm rather tired, to be honest. Ievis, I'm sure, will fill me in if needed."

Ievis offers them a sharp nod while I roll my eyes.

"Yes, Ievis will be the perfect person to explain how stupid our little human plans are."

"Ronan," Astra snaps.

I sigh through my nose and shake my head. "I'm heading to bed as well." I shoot Ievis a harsh glare. "This trip has been extremely taxing."

Without another word I shuffle out of the room, making sure to slam the door behind me, right in Ievis's face. I stomp past the guards in the hall, not even sparing them a glance as

Ievis tears the door open behind me, storming after me. I try to out-stride him, but I'm tired and my leg is aching after a day of riding in the cold. He cuts me off as we round a corner, his golden eyes boring into mine.

"I do not want to be here any more than you want me here," he snaps.

"Don't worry. You've made that quite clear," I reply. "We're worthless, pathetic humans who undid the perfect magic created by the amazing and flawless Fae when they saved us from the Dragkonians the first time. I've heard your laments over my race's stupidity the last few days, and I don't need to hear it any more. If you really don't want to be here, go home."

Ievis scoffs, crossing his muscled arms across his broad chest. Honestly, if he wasn't so damn infuriating I might consider him handsome, pretty even.

"You humans cannot solve this problem without my help."

"Why do you even care?"

He snaps his gaze to mine. "What?"

"Why do you care?" I repeat, emphasizing each word. "If we're so pathetic, why help us? Why not just let us die out due to our supposed stupidity?"

Ievis blinks, his forehead scrunched in a scowl.

"Ah, good, you didn't get far," Iefyr cuts in, marching up to us with a small smile.

Ievis turns to his sibling. "Do they need me?"

Iefyr places a gentle hand on their brother's arm and he relaxes slightly under their touch.

"I think they might. Either way, it would be good for you to be present, learn a bit about what's going to happen."

Ievis sighs but nods. "Fine."

Iefyr drops their hand. "Good." They turn to me. "Do you mind if I walk with you, Ronan? I've been given an idea of where my room should be, but Astra said you might be able to show me the way."

"Of course. Come with me."

We walk in silence for a while as we twist through corridors. We're both tired from our journey, and I know that while Ievis seems to exist solely to irritate me, even Iefyr has been negatively affected by their brother's attitude. We're rounding the corner to our hall when Iefyr finally speaks.

"He's not so bad, my brother."

A small huff of a laugh escapes my lips before I can stop it.

Iefyr smiles. "I know he can be a bit of trial, but he has his reasons. He has had high expectations stacked on him ever since we were very small. Once the other Fae discovered that we had unique magic, they sought to use us."

I come to halt, blinking at Iefyr in disbelief. "They took advantage of your magic when you were mere children?"

Iefyr nods, sadness shining in their eyes. "That they did. Thankfully we had each other, but life was not easy. Ievis is made of tougher skin than I am, and he became very protective of me very early on."

We resume our walk down the hall, but at a much slower pace as Iefyr continues.

"Ievis had a lot of pressure put on him to study and learn so he could create new spells, but I did not have so much luck."

"What do you mean?"

"Well," Iefyr says, drawing the word out. "My magic didn't take as much study since it was an inherent skill. It required practice, and practice could often be very draining."

We come to a stop in front of my door, but I don't bother going inside. Not yet.

"When you say draining . . ."

"I mean that I was forced to create portals that extended

far beyond even my capabilities." They meet my eyes and I can feel the heaviness in their gaze. "Portals that were supposed to stretch between realms."

I suck in a breath as understanding dawns. "The other Fae wanted to use you to get back to the human world."

Iefyr nods. "Indeed. Or, at the very least, they wanted to see if it was possible to bridge the worlds again, though I'm not sure why. From what I know of our history, the Fae never had much use for humans as a whole. From the stories they had Ievis studying, the Fae saw humans as more of a hinderance than anything."

"So, if they were using you when you were young to open a portal to my world, the realms had already closed themselves off. You weren't alive when magic was rampant in the human world."

Iefyr laughs softly, shaking their head. "No, it faded off long before I was born. Not all Fae are centuries old, you know."

Their eyes shine and embarrassment colors my cheeks.

"Of course I know that, I only—"

"It's fine," they say waving their hand. "My kind do tend to live longer than humans, and it is very hard to judge how old we may be since our aging slows as we reach maturity. Hycis and Rynia are far older, though I'm not sure by how much, and fit your human concept of long-lived Fae."

I swallow and look down at my cane, fiddling with it to avoid Iefyr's eyes as I ask, "So, if I may be so bold as to ask, how old are you?"

I slowly raise my gaze to Iefyr's and they smile at me.

"If you were to ask Ievis, I'm sure he would reply with a snide remark about it being none of your business."

My cheeks grow even warmer as I attempt to stammer an

apology. Iefyr throws back their head and laughs, the pleasant sound echoing down the hall.

"I, however, am not easily offended and have no reason to hide my age. Among the Fae one as young as I am is often considered inexperienced and practically a child, though I haven't considered myself a child in decades. My brother and I are nearing our fiftieth year. Since our aging and maturing process is slower, our age would be similar to a human in their mid-twenties. Our aging will slow even more in years to come and our appearances are likely not to show much more aging until we reach our two hundredth birthday, and even that change will be slight."

I nod, absorbing the information in silence. I had just assumed Iefyr and Ievis were much older, but it seems they're not that far from my own age.

"Either way, I hope you can understand bit better why Ievis is the way he is. He was crammed full of hateful information about humans at a very young age to the point where his mind may have been a bit poisoned against you. It did not help that I nearly died on multiple occasions trying to contact the humans via portal. It's a miracle Ievis has become level-headed enough to help you now."

A door opens and closes down the hall, drawing our attention to a servant who heads our way.

"Your room is ready," the servant whispers, looking at Iefyr with wide, terrified eyes.

Iefyr offers the servant a gentle smile. "Would you be so kind as to lead the way?"

The servant bobs their head in agreement and turns to lead Iefyr down the hall.

"Just be patient with my brother," Iefyr calls to me as

they're led away. "He's already coming around. I think it helps that he is quite taken with you."

I stand in the hall blinking after Iefyr, processing their words long after they've entered their room. When I finally enter my own room, my head is still spinning and I don't quite understand the warmth gathering in my chest. Gods, I need a good night's sleep.

CHAPTER TWENTY-TWO

"Okay," I say, breaking the awkward silence left by Ronan and Ievis storming out as well as Iefyr's quiet departure. I step up the table in the center of the room, all eyes shifting to me. "We have a lot to do. First, we need to get rid of the shadows."

It's an odd statement to make, but one we all understand. Astra nods and raises her hands, starlight flowing up and covering the entirety of the ceiling. I don't think I'll ever get used to the beauty of her magic. I force my eyes away and allow them a moment to adjust to the sudden brightness in the room.

"Thank you," I say, offering Astra a weak smile. "Let's start with explaining about the berries you brought and what plans you have with the Fae."

Astra nods and steps forward. She starts to explain the powers Ievis and Iefyr have and how they can help, Ievis returning a couple minutes into her explanation to lean against the back wall and glare at everyone. As she finishes up, trays of dinner arrive, making the space feel even more cramped.

"Hycis and Rynia know a good bit about the berries and have ideas on how to implement them to their fullest," Astra explains, eyeing a tray of food but not stopping to eat yet. "Since the berries are deadly to even the Fae, the actual creation and distribution of the poison will be up to us."

I nod, crossing my arms across my chest. "Not a problem. We already have a system in place. We'll just add in their input. Right, Jess?"

"Yep." She pops the "p" with a grin. "We'll happily make up the poison and take care of all that deadly stuff."

"Good," I say. "So I suppose that's covered for now. We can discuss more details once we're ready to move into battle and the spell is ready."

Ievis gives me a sharp nod. "Indeed. So is my part in this discussion done?"

"Unless you have additional input, yes," I say, holding my head high and staring the Fae down.

Ievis grunts and shakes his head. "Then I am done. So glad I could stand here and do absolutely nothing while you all jabbered away."

He moves toward the door and I call after him. "You're welcome to take any food with you."

Ievis turns his nose up as his eyes trail over the trays. "I think I may wait until morning to see if my options improve. Goodnight."

Once the door slams behind him, I turn to Astra. "Well, he's a delight."

She sighs and shakes her head. "You have no idea." She pauses to take a bite of food. "For the next part we'll need Kayleigh and a map of the palace."

I step to the table and unroll a scroll of a roughly drawn blueprint of the castle in Embervein before unrolling a second map of the palace and surrounding city and grounds, arranging both side-by-side on the table. While I work, Alak skirts off to retrieve his cousin.

Jess clears her throat and steps up to the table. "So, what are our plans?"

"I will move the small group of soldiers I have with me here to this location," Luc says, pointing to an access point on the edge of the city nearest the palace. He lifts his eyes to Jess. "And you will add some of your own soldiers?"

She nods. "We'll pair up my soldiers with yours evenly so they can be wisped away."

"And Alak'll fill in all the gaps with an illusion," Astra says. She looks over at Luc. "He can stay by your side and wisp you out."

Luc blinks, looking mildly surprised, as if he'd forgotten he also needed an escape plan. His expression softens and he offers Astra a small smile. "Thank you. That is much appreciated."

"Where do you need me?" Jess asks, her eyes darting over the map.

"I need you here, at the fortress," I say. My eyes meet hers across the table as I add, "If that's all right?"

She frowns and looks back at the map. My gut twists with nerves, afraid she'll call me out, prove I'm not fit for this job. She'll point out all the errors in my plan and show me to be the fraud of a prince I am.

"Or," she counters slowly, looking back to me, "why don't I take the rest of my army back to the Summer Palace? This fortress is getting rather cramped. I can free up some space by moving out any soldiers that won't be heading in to rescue the boy. Then they can also be ready to move out into battle as needed."

I consider her words and nod, a bit of relief surging through me at her suggestion. "Yes, that would work well. You'd be a little closer to us should something go wrong."

"Nothing will go wrong," Astra says, placing a reassuring hand on my arm.

I lift my eyes to meet hers and hold her gaze for a moment that stretches out. If only I could have half the confidence in myself that Astra and Cal have in me. Alak's return breaks the moment. The girl he brings in looks like a walking corpse.

"Was everything in Athiedor as expected?" I ask carefully, swallowing hard. This girl was supposed to be cared for, and if I find out Lord Dughlas broke his word, there will be hell to pay.

Astra offers me a tight smile. "Supposedly."

Kayleigh keeps her head down, refusing to meet anybody's eyes.

"Kayleigh," I say, my voice soft and gentle, "can you tell us where they're keeping your brother?"

Kayleigh's head jerks up, her eyes wide and wild. "Why?"

"We need to get him out of Kato's clutches." I work to keep my voice level and calm, but the girl still inhales sharply, shaking her head fiercely.

"No, no, no," she mumbles. "You can't"—she swallows— "use him."

"Kayleigh," I start, but Kayleigh cuts me off, yelling, "He's only eight! Eight!"

"Kayleigh," I try again, my voice quiet but firm. Her eyes meet mine and I can feel her terror. "We aren't going to hurt him. We're rescuing him. We want him safe." Her eyes dart to

Astra and then back to me. "Do you really think we'd hurt a child?"

She considers my words for a moment before slowly shaking her head.

"Saran is my cousin," Alak says. "I don't want him hurt any more than you do."

"You let Niall be killed."

Her voice is so quiet I barely catch her words, but I can see as they register with the others in the room. Bile rises in my throat and I look down, clenching my hands in fists at my side. Her brother died at my hand. He nearly killed me in the process, but it's still my fault he's dead.

My fault. My fault. My fault.

"Niall attacked us," Alak says, his voice just above a whisper, but it's enough to pull me from my thoughts. "He was actively trying to kill us. He was an active threat. Saran isn't."

"We really want to rescue him," Astra offers, her voice kind.

Kayleigh looks between them. "You promise?"

"I swear on my life I only want to get your brother from Kato's grasp," I say, my voice lined with determination. I will find a way to make this right. "He's a child and this war has already stolen too many. I won't let another suffer. I won't allow any harm to come to him, at my hand or the hand of anyone else."

Kayleigh meets my intense gaze and nods. "Fine." She shuffles to the table and squints down at the maps. She thrusts her finger at the map of the castle's interior. "There. Whenever we were in Embervein, he was being kept there."

I step forward and study the area. Jess follows suit, peering over my shoulder. The room she pointed out is only a couple turns away from the main throne room. I can't admit I remember it well, but I thought it was less of a room and more of an oversized storage closet.

"This isn't a bedroom," I mumble, shaking my head. "Or a cell. Why would Kato keep him here?"

Kayleigh shrugs. "He wanted him close but not always in the room with him. That room has no windows, so he was trapped. Of course, Kato claimed it was so they could have more shadows for Saran to converse with."

"Is anyone kept in there with him?" I ask.

"Caitlyn and I took turns staying in there with Saran. He didn't like to be alone. He—" Her voice breaks and it takes her a moment to steady herself. "He said the shadows were so loud sometimes and it scared him. He doesn't like to be alone." She clears her throat and glances away, avoiding all eye contact. "Now that I'm here, Caitlyn would likely be with him."

I nod. "Any guards we should know about?"

Kayleigh pauses, her forehead scrunched in thought. "Maybe? I know there was typically someone outside the door, but it was often Niall or one of his friends. He claimed it was for our protection, but now I'm sure it was to keep us in. I don't know if there are guards there now or who they would be."

"Let's assume there will be," I say with a nod. "Which means we need to be prepared for a fight inside the castle while Luc and Alak distract them from the outside."

"So who goes inside?" Astra asks. "We'll need to keep the group small or we'll be detected. And we'll probably want to wisp in directly and wisp out quickly."

"You, me, Cal, and"—I lift my gaze to the door—"Kai. Would Kai join us?"

Astra nods, already making her way to the door. "Kai already agreed to bring shifters with us, but they would be more help with wisping out soldiers if needed. I'm sure he'd be fine coming inside with us."

Astra sticks her head out into the hall and I hear the rumbles of their conversation but don't catch the words. When she pops back into the room, shutting the door, she nods. "He's on board."

"Good. Good," I mutter, looking back to the map. "Any chance we can wisp directly into the room with Saran?"

Astra steps forward and studies the map before shaking her head. "It would be risky. I don't know the area well enough." Her eyes scan the map. "The closest I could safely get us is here." She taps a nearby garden.

"Very well. Once Luc and Alak have drawn Kato's attention, we'll wisp into the garden and then sneak into the castle. As soon as we have Saran, we wisp out."

"Where will we wisp to?" Astra asks. "We can't go too far."

I turn and pull out a larger map of the area near Embervein. "We could camp here the night before"—I point to an area a few hours travel from the city—"and wisp back when we're done. It's close enough it shouldn't be too taxing on your magic, I hope, but far enough Kato won't follow and find us easily."

"We can even set up some illusion wards around the camp to further hide us, should any of Kato's Dragkonian scouts fly overhead," Alak suggests.

Astra nods. "I'll speak to Ronan and see if he'll let us borrow some magic for the wards. I can store it in my Syphon stone." She pauses before adding, "He may even want to come with us."

We all fall quiet, silence heavy in the room, our eyes on the map, as if we can suss out any dangers by simply looking.

"So that's it, then," Prince Luc whispers at last. "We have our plan."

I release a breath slowly and nod. "It would appear that way."

"When will you leave?" Jess asks, looking over at me.

"First thing in the morning," I reply without hesitation. I want this over and done. I can't stand sitting here doing nothing while my kingdom falls apart.

"Good. I'll gather my people and move to the Summer Palace tomorrow as well."

"I'll have Pax stay here and continue with the armies we leave behind," I say. Silence falls again and is only broken when Astra yawns. She dips her head sheepishly, a blush rising on her cheeks.

"Sorry," she mumbles. "It's been a long day."

I chuckle. "I suppose so." I lean forward and start rolling up the maps. "We should all get some sleep. We have even longer days ahead."

CHAPTER TWENTY-THREE

ASTRA

I've forgotten how slowly armies move, and the one we're taking isn't even all that large. We agree on sixty soldiers. Half belong to Luc and the remaining are a mix of shifters and Jess's army. Fifty will march alongside Alak and Luc to provide our decoy, while the remaining ten will stay back and guard the camp. We've also brought along a few Healers including a palace Healer, Healer Heora, Hanna, and, by extension, Pip, who never leaves Hanna's side.

A couple of the soldiers from Jess's army are skilled in camouflage magic, so we aren't entirely invisible, but we remain well hidden under a canopy of illusion. A few of the shifters stay in animal form, either watching from the skies or checking out our path ahead depending on their skills. At night, Ehren marks the borders of camp with warding spells, aided by someone from Jess's army. All the soldiers take guard shifts, and yet, despite our best efforts and precautions, nothing makes us feel at ease.

After a few days of travel, we slow on a hillside around

midday. Ehren pauses and pulls out his map, looking from the paper to our surroundings.

"Are we where we need to be?" I ask, stepping to his side.

Ehren takes a deep breath and nods. "I think so." He turns and looks at Luc over his shoulder. "We should start setting up the camp so the rest of us can move on."

Luc nods and makes his way over to the soldiers. The camp comes together quickly, tents going up in neat lines. It's almost too quick, and I can tell Ehren feels the same. He stands in the center, looking around, a lost expression on his face.

"This is going to work," I whisper, taking his hand.

Ehren looks down at me and offers a half smile. "I think so, too." He sighs and shakes his head. "I hate war."

I hum in agreement and rest my head on Ehren's arm and watch the camp settle. We're still standing there when Alak and Cal find us.

"You okay?" Cal asks Ehren, pressing a kiss to his temple.

Ehren pulls his hand from mine to take both of Cal's. "I am now." He brushes a quick kiss to Cal's lips before turning to me and Alak.

"Are we ready to go?"

Alak nods. "Yes. Luc has the army ready to move out."

Ehren forces a smile. "Let's get this done so we can be home by dinner."

WE KEEP ourselves hidden until we're right outside Embervein. There are plenty of soldiers patrolling the wall, so there's no doubt that once the army is spotted, Kato will send out his army. I give Alak's hand a squeeze before he turns and addresses our army.

"Remember, we're only the decoy," he says, his voice ringing over the distance. "If we can take out a few of Kato's soldiers, good, but that isn't our purpose today. Make sure our shields remain intact, especially above us. We have limited weapons that work well against the Dragkonians, so it's best not to engage them."

The soldiers' heads bob in agreement.

"Make sure you stay in your pairs of magic and non-magic. We may only have moments to wisp away and you must be close."

Alak turns to me, taking my hand. "Ready, love?"

I nod and let my magic flow to Alak. He takes a deep breath, closing his eyes, and more soldiers flicker into being around us. This close they're blurry and out of focus, but they'll work well enough to fool Kato. When the army is complete, Alak opens his eyes and offers me a sad smile.

"Excellent work," Ehren says, looking over the army.

"You'll let us know when you have the boy?" Luc asks, stepping to Alak's side.

I nod and lift my wrist to highlight my Syphon Stone. "I borrowed some Whisper magic from Pax. I'll let Alak know when Saran is safe."

Luc nods and offers me a wry smile. "And then we get the hell out of here."

I laugh. "Yes, exactly." I turn to Ehren. "Are you ready?"

He nods, taking Cal's hand. "Let's go."

We wait a moment while the masking wards are dropped, but once our presence has been noted, I reach my magic out and wisp us into the garden. We slink toward the palace entrance, but pause, ducking out of sight as Kato's soldiers rush past.

Ehren takes the lead, knowing the winding halls and corridors the best. More than once we're forced to hide as soldiers head to their stations, but that means our plan is working. We're nearly to the small room when a small group of men walk our direction. We duck around a corner and I cast a small illusion charm over us as we press against the wall.

I'm assuming you're here somewhere.

Kato's voice echoing in my head makes me jump. Ehren shoots me a concerned look, and I meet his eyes but don't speak. Not to him anyway.

I don't know what you mean.

Kato's chuckle echoes through my head. *I'm sure that isn't true. I see your bondmate, and I know you aren't far away. I can sense your magic. Why don't you come face me? I can show you my new throne.*

Do you really think I'm that stupid?

I know you're not, because I know you, Ash. You're power and brains, just like I am. You can still join me, if you'd like. Why don't we discuss it? Come to me.

What makes you think I'm in the castle?

I don't think you're at the castle. I know *you are. I'll meet you in the throne room.*

I swallow hard. I won't lie; it's tempting. Part of me wants to see my brother again, even though the brother I know and love isn't the person I'll be facing.

"Ash?" Ehren says, watching me with concern.

I shake my head and reply to Kato first.

I step through that door and I'm as good as dead.

I have a mere two dozen soldiers with me. Of course, they all have magic so they far outweigh your pathetic foot soldiers, but you could probably take them all. Come on, Ash. I know you'd enjoy the challenge.

Go to hell.

When he doesn't reply I turn to Ehren, my heart racing.

"What is it, Ash?" he presses, scanning my face.

I swallow and take a deep breath but it does little to calm me. "Kato knows we're here."

"Shit," Cal mutters while Ehren adds a few choice swears of his own.

"He's in the throne room. He wants me to come to him."

Ehren shakes his head and grabs my hand. "You can't go in there. Please, Ash, don't."

I squeeze his hand. "I won't. That's not why we're here."

"But if you don't go, Kato might come looking for you," Cal says, earning a sharp look from Ehren.

"We should split up," Kai jumps in. "Astra and I will go rescue the boy and you two go head Kato off and keep him distracted."

"No," I say quickly, shaking my head. "You have to stay with Ehren and Cal. They need you to wisp them out. I'll rescue Saran on my own."

Ehren opens his mouth to protest, but I smile and cut him off. "I'll be fine, but we don't have much time. We need to move."

"How will we know when you have the boy?" Ehren asks.

"I'll use the same Whisper magic I was planning on using with Alak. I should have enough to contact you all."

Ehren's shoulders sag with defeat. "Fine. Stay safe," Ehren whispers, pressing a quick kiss to my cheek before releasing my hand.

Ehren leads Kai and Cal toward the throne room and I split off, heading to the room where Saran should be. I get a little turned around without Ehren's guidance, but I manage to orient myself well enough. After a couple wrong turns I find the room. It's easy to spot since it's the only door I've stumbled across that has two guards. I pull back my illusion magic and reveal myself.

"Go alert Kato!" one of the guards shouts, drawing his sword.

"I'm afraid I can't let you do that," I say, pulling on my magic.

I send a hard blast forward into the chest of the second man. He slams against the wall and slumps to the ground. The first guard turns back to me, fear in his eyes, but that fear doesn't have him lowing his sword. In fact, it has him pulling on his own magic, red sparks trailing the fingers of his left hand.

"I didn't kill him," I say, praying to the gods my words are true and he's only unconscious. "And I don't want to kill you." A dagger of starlight appears in my hand and I raise it slowly. "But I will if I need to."

"Oh, I've heard how well you like to kill," he spits.

I jerk back. "That's not true. I never enjoy killing."

The man scoffs. "Tell that to my dead brother."

I don't get a chance to refute his claim before tendrils of red fire are snaking toward me. I dodge to the right and toss up a shield, the fire sizzling into it. I retaliate with a blast of light like I used previously, but he dodges. A second blast strikes his arm and he drops his sword. This only angers him and he lunges forward, hand extended. I duck under his grasp and stab my dagger into his side. He falters but doesn't fall. It wasn't a killing blow. I remove my dagger and step back. The guard spins to face me, holding a hand over the wound on his side, blood seeping over his fingers.

"Don't make me kill you," I plead, taking a step away.

"That's the only way you're getting through that door."

I take a deep breath and summon more magic. I won't kill

him. I won't. Instead, I squeeze my eyes shut and release a bright flash of blinding light. He screams and when I open my eyes, he's clawing at his eyes. My stomach twists with guilt as I stumble backward and open the door. I slip inside and close it behind me with a slight click, the man still screaming in the hall.

"Please, don't hurt us," a voice begs.

My eyes find a thin blond woman kneeling on the floor, a terrified boy clutched to her chest—Caitlyn and Saran.

"We don't want any trouble," Caitlyn says, her voice trembling.

I raise my hands, palms out. "I'm not here to hurt you." I meet Saran's tear-filled eyes. "I want to rescue you and take you away from here."

Saran sniffs and presses closer to Caitlyn, shaking his head.

"I swear on my life, Saran, I'm here to take you away from Kato to a place where he can't find you and force you to use your magic for him. Your sister said you don't like it."

"You know where Kayleigh is?" he asks, his voice sounding so small.

I nod. "I do. She's the one who told me where I could find you."

Saran exchanges a quick look with Caitlyn. She presses a kiss to his forehead and stands, placing herself between me and Saran.

"You're not going to take him and use him like Kato, are you?"

"No. We have no intentions of using him, only protecting him."

"And keeping him from helping Kato."

I pause, trying to find the right response. I don't really have time to negotiate.

"I understand," Caitlyn says, stepping closer. "As long as Kato has Saran he has an advantage over you. You take Saran away and it evens the playing field a bit, but what happens to him when you still lose?"

"We won't lose."

"I really want to believe that. I don't support Kato and I don't think I ever have. I'm here because I loved Niall very much." Her voice trembles but she doesn't stop. "He supported Kato and my choices were to abandon him or stay by his side and hope you still found a way to win. You know something of love, right?"

"I do," I whisper.

"Then you understand why I chose this side."

"Why remain on this side still?"

Caitlyn glances off, her expression heavy. "I've already lost so much. I don't want to lose any more." She meets my eyes. "I don't want to be on the losing side."

"You still think this side will win?"

Caitlyn sighs and shakes her head. "I've seen the Dragkonians. I can't imagine anything or anyone beating them, not even you. When you fall, Saran will be unprotected again. Kato may seek revenge."

"Kato won't hurt a child."

Caitlyn scoffs, her eyes hard. "He already has."

Boots echo through the hall, reminding me time is precious. I turn to Caitlyn. "What if I promised we have a way to end this war in our favor?"

Caitlyn meets my eyes as the soldiers come closer. "Do you?"

I nod. "We do."

Caitlyn inhales sharply and turns to Saran. "Go with her."

Saran's eyes widen and he shakes his head furiously. "Go. Find your sister. Stay with your cousin. Be safe."

I extend my hand and Saran cautiously places his in mine. I turn back to Caitlyn.

"I can take you, too. We can provide protection for you as well, and you can keep an eye on Saran."

She shakes her head. "Even if I don't agree with Kato, I think I still have good to do here."

"You're sure?"

"I'm sure."

The door flies open, slamming against the wall so hard Saran jumps, his eyes wide with terror. I turn and face the guards, tightening my grip on the boy's hand as I summon Pax's magic.

"Let the boy go," one of the newcomers demands, pointing a sword at me.

I smile and tilt my head. "You know, I don't think I will."

I pull the Whisper magic forward and send out my message in two directions, one to Ehren and one to Alak. No sooner are my words on the air than the soldiers charge forward. I look down at Saran and smile as I pull us both into a wisp.

CHAPTER TWENTY-FOUR

We navigate the castle quickly and quietly, making our way to Kato in the throne room. I hate splitting from Astra, but it was the best choice. We're almost to the throne room when we're met by Kato's soldiers. They're more surprised than we are and we're able to gain the upper hand quickly. More soldiers appear and we're backed into the throne room. Kato stands near the throne—*my* throne—a sneer on his lips.

"Really, Ehren? This attack seems weak and poorly thought out. Are you that desperate?"

I smile, cocking my head. "Well, you know"—I toss my sword in the air with a little flip, catching it again with ease—"I like making plans."

Kato laughs and holds out his hand, a sword of flame flaring to life in his palm.

"And you know how much I like to see your plans fall apart."

The next thing I know we're in a full-on battle. It's our small trio verses Kato and over a dozen magical soldiers. We are so severely outnumbered we don't even have a reasonable shot. If we were actually trying to take back the palace, our mission would be wasted. Luckily, that's not what we're here for.

I trade a grin with Cal as I spin into the fray, my sword clashing against a magical sword made of what appears to be glass. My opponent swipes wide and I duck, my footwork quick and efficient. He scowls and charges at me again, but I easily dodge his blow and land one of my own. He steps back with a hiss and adjusts his sword.

I have the boy.

Astra's voice startles me, but I recover quickly. Our mission was a success. We can get out of here. I make quick work of my opponent, knocking him off his feet and kicking his sword away, and catch Kai's eye. Kai gives me a sharp nod. I race toward him, ready to wisp and glance over my shoulder to make sure Cal also got the message. What I find paralyzes me. Cal's sword is on the ground far out of his reach and Kato is closing in.

I dash toward them but not before Kato jerks Cal to his chest, spinning him so he's facing me. Kato braces one arm around Cal, keeping him still, while he holds his fire sword to Cal's neck. Cal's eyes meet mine, his jaw set. Around us the battle stills, everyone's eyes trained on us.

"No!" I scream, charging forward.

"Stop," Kato demands, tightening his grip on Cal and pressing his sword closer.

Cal winces and I freeze, my heart pounding in my throat.

"What do you want?"

Kato laughs. "What do I want? You can't be serious."

I swallow and take a tentative step forward. "You already have my kingdom. What more could you want from me?"

Kato laughs again, shaking his head. "I never took you for a fool, Ehren."

Cal catches my eye again and shakes his head almost imperceptibly, flicking his eyes quickly to where Kai stands behind me. He wants me to leave him. I grit my teeth and tighten my grip on my sword. I look back at Kato. His eyes are dark—too dark to be considered natural in any way.

"Your sister. You—you want your sister."

A cruel grin crawls across Kato's lips. "Not such a fool after all."

"She's not here," I manage, gesturing wide.

"She's here somewhere, though, isn't she? I felt her magic."

"She's already gone," Kai says from behind me. I don't need to turn to know he's within arm's reach, ready to wisp me at will. "And she took your little shadow spy with you."

Anger radiates from Kato. "So your mission wasn't meant to take back the castle. You were after one of the keys to my success."

Kato pauses, tilting his head, and I barely dare to breathe as he weighs this new information. After a moment he hums and shrugs, adjusting the sword in his hand. "Well, if she's gone and your mission was otherwise a success, no point in keeping this one alive then."

"No!" I cry, lunging forward, my hand stretched out. I stop short when Kato pauses, his eyes meeting mine. I'm on dangerous, risky ground. One wrong word and Cal—*my* Cal— is dead.

"Please," I beg, my voice, my voice quavering. "I'll give you anything if you let him go."

Kato tilts his head. "Start by giving me a reason not to kill him."

My mind spins. Obviously, "I love him" isn't a viable answer. Kato doesn't care.

"I'm waiting, and I assure you, I'm not a patient man."

He adjusts his sword again and a small gasp escapes Cal as the fire brushes his skin.

"Take me!"

"Ehren, no!"

I ignore Cal's cry, not taking my eyes from Kato's. "If you let him go, you can have me."

Kato cocks his head in interest. "Why would I make such a trade?"

I take a bold step forward. "Astra cares more about me. If you take me and let Cal go, she'll return for me. I guarantee it."

"What would keep me from killing Cal and keeping you as well?"

I glance over my shoulder at Kai. He's still close enough to touch me. I look back to Kato.

"You kill Cal and I leave. You won't have me to trade, but you will make me a greater enemy." I set my jaw and meet Kato's eyes without fear. "You kill him, and I will make sure you suffer before I kill you."

I expect Kato to laugh at my threat, but instead he seems to consider my words. After a moment he nods.

"Very well."

I bury my shock and manage a nod. I take a step toward Kato and he snarls.

"Get rid of your sword."

I glance down at the sword in my hand. I'd almost forgotten I held it. I cheat toward Kai and pass it to him. Kai accepts it with a quick motion. My eyes fall to Cal's discarded sword. I sweep toward it and kick it to Kai as well. It only seems right to keep the duo together.

"If you're done collecting your armory," Kato says, his voice sharp, "shall we complete our exchange?"

I nod and step closer. I'm well out of reach of Kai now and mere steps from Kato. His jaw clenches as if he's reconsidering his decision. His soldiers close in, ready to meet any demand he might make. Without warning he thrusts Cal toward me. We make only the briefest contact before I shove Cal to Kai's waiting arms. Cal twists to look at me, his eyes wide and wild.

"Ehren!" he screams, reaching toward me.

"Bring my sister to me quickly," Kato says to Kai. "Every hour she lingers will mean consequences for your prince."

Kai acknowledges Kato's words with a sharp nod. Cal struggles against Kai's hold, screaming my name, but Kai's hold is firm. Cal keens my name again and I meet his eyes. Before I can consider even attempting to cross to him to wisp with him, one of Kato's men steps between us. I make eye contact with Kai and nod. In the blink of an eye, Kai and Cal disappear. It's just me now. Alone. I swallow hard and turn to Kato, straightening my shoulders.

Kato waves his hand and several of his minions march forward. None touch me, but the threat is heavy. Kato leers at me and steps closer, folding his hands behind his back.

"Now, what should I do with you, now that you're at my disposal?" he says, his voice low.

I tense, grinding my teeth together, but I refuse to show him any weakness.

"Hmm," he muses, slowly circling me, his men standing back to give him room. I keep my eyes straight ahead until he's back in front of me. He reaches out and places a finger under my chin, tipping my gaze up to meet his. "What shall I do with you? So many ideas."

I cock my head and offer him a cocky half-grin. "I suppose I really don't have a say in the matter, do I? I suggest you don't do anything too drastic, otherwise your sister may not see it as a fair trade."

Kato frowns and jerks his hand away. "That doesn't mean I can't have some fun. After all, I have some excellent Healers on hand."

Several of the others in the room snicker at his words. I wonder what horrors Kato has already inflicted for this audience. Kato steps back and assesses me.

"Why don't you start by kneeling before me?"

A growl escapes my lips before I can stop it. Kato grins, flames flickering in his eyes.

"Yes, I rather like that." He steps closer, his face a breath from mine. "Kneel before your king, Ehren."

Before I can protest, before I can even form a response of any kind, a sharp pain tumbles through me as Kato's fist buries itself in my stomach. I gasp and double over. Kato places a too-hot hand to my shoulder and shoves me down into a kneeling position, a crack sounding through the room as my knees hit the floor. As I struggle to breathe, he cards his hand into my hair and jerks my face upward.

"How does it feel to bow before a stronger ruler?"

I struggle to find my voice but I manage to put as much strength into my reply as possible. "Being forced to my knees surely cannot be considered true genuflection. Perhaps when you're used to taking things you haven't earned, forced submission is all you can achieve."

Kato snarls and hoists me up with such force I'm sure he's pulled several hairs loose. Once I'm on my feet he moves his hand from my hair to my neck, the heat of it far beyond what is natural. His touch burns but I refuse to struggle in his grasp and instead meet his eyes with defiance.

"I'm great and powerful. I've more than earned my place." He thrusts me back into the clutches of one of his men, who grabs my arms with more force than necessary, wrenching them behind my back at a painful angle. "You'll do well to remember your new place or even my Healers won't be able to mend your scars." He turns away abruptly with a wave. "Take him away."

The man holding me releases me, a sharp sword point pressing between my shoulder blades instead.

"Where should I take him, my king?" the wielder of the blade asks. "The dungeons?"

Kato glances briefly over his shoulder before lifting a shoulder in a slight shrug. "Perhaps." I'm shoved toward the door, but I'm stopped with a sharp jerk as Kato says, "No, put him in the room."

My stomach drops. I have no idea what he means, but I'm sure it can't be good. Kato cheats toward me and assesses me before nodding.

"Yes, the room. The dungeon is too predictable, and the room is more conveniently located. Besides, it seems we now have a vacancy." He turns away, acting with disinterest. "And send in a Healer. I'd like to start with a fresh canvas."

With another jerk I'm led from the throne room and down twisting corridors. It's my palace and not my palace all at the same time. Bile rises in my throat and I feel dizzy, but I refuse to show any weakness. We round a corner and I spot a couple sentries standing guard. I flick my eyes around to quickly take in my surroundings. At my best guess this is the room Astra was meant to check for the boy.

"Got a new prisoner for you," the man at my back says, prodding me forward with more force than necessary. "Kato wants him kept in here."

The guards grin, one of them stepping forward to unlock the door, pushing it open.

"Welcome home, Your Majesty," he mocks as I'm shoved inside.

The men all laugh as the door closes. There are no windows, but couple bright lanterns do their best to dimly light the area. My eyes adjust quickly and I take in the room. It's mostly empty—just a few pieces of furniture and a couple untidy, makeshift beds covered in tousled sheets. I hiss in pain when I turn my head to take in more of the room, my hand floating to slightly burnt skin at my throat from Kato's touch.

"I have a salve that might help that," a soft voice says.

I start and spin, ignoring the pain at the sudden movement. In the corner of the room stands a young woman. I narrow my eyes at her as she steps closer, light washing over her.

"Caitlyn?"

She offers me a sad smile and nods. "Yes."

She brushes past me to a small table and lifts a jar. She takes a tentative step toward me, stopping several feet away and extending the jar to me.

"A little will go a long way."

I reach out and accept the jar. A sweet, minty scent wafts up when I unscrew the lid. I sweep my fingers into the balm and gently rub it across my tender neck. The relief is almost instant. Once it's all covered, I replace the lid and pass it back. Caitlyn accepts the jar but doesn't put it back yet. Rather, she fiddles with it nervously, turning it over in her hands.

"Are you a prisoner as well?" I manage after a moment of awkward silence.

She raises her eyes to mine and shrugs. "I suppose." She sighs and turns away, walking to the table and finally setting the jar down. "Kato knows that I no longer support him, but I'm too important to let go." She looks up at me and offers a sad smile. "So, yes, I suppose I am a prisoner."

I nod and glance off, wanting to look anywhere else but at her. My gaze settles on the second unmade bed. "And you're trapped in here alone?"

"Saran was in here with me." She walks over to the bed and looks down at the blankets, something akin to affection on her face. "It was my job to care for him."

I smile softly. "So Astra succeeded in getting him out safely."

Caitlyn nods. "Yes."

I frown. "Why didn't you go with her? She could have taken you easily enough, and if you're truly a prison—"

Caitlyn cuts me off with a sharp shake of her head. "No. She offered but it was better I stay behind."

"Why?"

She offers me a smile sadder than any other. "Because it is my penance. I knew from the start that Kato's cause was wrong, but I said nothing. Even when I realized that Alak was a spy for your side, I did nothing to aid him." She sinks down onto the bed. "I chose, instead, to support my misguided fiancé against my better instincts. I allowed myself to be used and never said a word. It's better I stay here."

I'm tempted to argue with her, but something about the way she looks up at me stops my protests short. She's made her decision and has made peace with it. I nod and cross the room, sitting on the bed next to her, but leaving several inches between us. The minutes drag by as we sit in silence, but it doesn't feel awkward. We both jump when the door swings open and a young woman hurries into the room. Caitlyn leaps to her feet with a smile and I follow suit. The door slams shut and the woman shudders.

"Polly," Caitlyn says, stopping in front of the woman. "Have you come to check the prince?"

She nods, swallowing hard. "I have."

Caitlyn turns to me. "Polly is one of our Healers."

"Ah," I say with a nod, stepping forward. "So you've come to heal me so Kato can break me again later."

Polly flinches. "I wish I didn't have to, Your Majesty." Her face jerks up as panic washes over her. "Not that I don't want to heal you! That's not what I meant!"

I smile gently. "I understand your meaning." Her shoulders relax. "Now, where should we begin?"

Her eyes assess me carefully, lingering on my neck. "Let's start with the burns, since they're the most likely to scar if left unattended, and we'll go from there."

I nod and settle into a nearby chair to let her do her work. The warmth of her magic hums over me. In some ways it's comforting, easing my pain a touch more. But it's also terrifying. I have no idea what Kato has planned for me, but I am most positive it will be far from pleasant.

CHAPTER TWENTY-FIVE

ASTRA

There's an abrupt shift as we appear outside the Healing tent, leaving the chaos of the castle behind. I place a gentle hand on Saran's shoulder and usher him inside. Healer Heora rushes toward him, and he stumbles back a step, pressing against me.

"It's all right," I whisper, placing a reassuring hand on his shoulder. He glances up at me, eyes wide. "This is Healer Heora. She's a friend. You can trust her."

Saran looks back to Healer Heora, and she offers him a gentle smile.

"I only wish to check you over and ensure you're healthy. I won't do anything you don't like. I don't even need to touch you if you don't want me to."

Saran considers her for a moment and then nods slowly, stepping closer to her. He glances at me once more over his shoulder before turning back to the Healer.

"All right," he says, his voice quiet. "I feel okay. Master Kato made sure I was taken care of."

Healer Heora furrows her brow, still smiling. "I wouldn't

expect anything less of Master Kato, but one can never be too careful."

Saran nods and Healer Heora calls forward her magic. Saran eyes her cautiously but doesn't flinch away as her warm magic passes over him. The tent flap opens behind me, but I keep my eyes trained on Saran as he shifts his weight from foot to foot.

"Is he okay?" Alak asks, stepping to my side.

I offer him a sharp nod. "It appears that way. Healer Heora is assessing him now."

Alak nods, watching his cousin for a moment before turning his attention to me.

"How are you, love?"

I turn and meet his eyes, smiling. "I ran into little trouble I couldn't handle. You and the others provided a decent distraction."

Alak's shoulders sag with relief as he takes my hands into his. "Good. I was worried that—"

Alak is cut short by a scream outside the tent. My heart stills as fear floods through the bond. We rush outside to find Cal fighting off Kai.

"No!" Cal screams, jerking from Kai's grasp and spinning to face him. He raises his sword, pointing it in Kai's face. "You take me back right now!"

Kai doesn't even blink as he replies. "I can't do that."

"You have to!" Cal's voice breaks on the last word. He takes a shaky breath, lowering the sword and whispers, "You have to."

"Cal, what happened?" I ask, stepping forward, my eyes darting between Kai and Cal.

Cal spots me for the first time and straightens, rushing to me and grabbing my shoulders. His eyes are wide and wild.

"Astra, you have to make him take me back."

"Cal, calm down and tell me what happened." I look past Cal, searching for Ehren to ask for more details and my heart sinks. It's only then I notice Kai is holding Ehren's sword. I swallow and bring my gaze back to Cal. "Where's Ehren?"

Cal licks his lips, dropping his hands from my shoulders as he stumbles back. He rubs the back of his neck as he glances around.

"That's why I need to go back. I need to get him." He looks back at me, his breathing erratic. "I have to save him. He gave himself up for me and I can't . . . I need . . . He needs me to go back. He shouldn't have done it. Please, Astra." He falls forward onto his knees at my feet and grabs my hands. "I'm begging you. Let me go back."

I shake my head, trying to make sense of his words. I look to Kai who stands by quietly.

"Kai?"

"In the last moments before we were able to wisp away, Ehren was captured."

"No!" Cal yells, jumping to his feet and stomping up to Kai.

A few of the shifters who have been drawn by the yelling step forward protectively, but Kai holds up a hand, keeping them back.

"Ehren wasn't captured. *I* was captured, and Ehren, fool that he is, traded himself for me." Cal spins back to me, tears brimming in his eyes. "He traded himself for *me*."

"Kato has Ehren?" I ask, processing everything.

Kai nods. "Yes."

I pause, barely daring to breathe as I whisper, "Are we sure he's still alive?"

"He's holding him as a bargaining piece," Kai explains slowly.

"A bargaining piece for what?" I ask, though I already know the answer before Kai even says the words.

"For you. He'll trade Ehren for you."

I inhale sharply and stumble back. Alak catches me and loops his arm around my waist, keeping me upright.

"He said that every hour we delay to make an exchange Ehren will suffer," Cal whispers, his voice hoarse. He steps toward me as a tear slips down his cheek. "I would never ask you to exchange yourself for him. Never. But we cannot leave him there, Astra. You have to let me go back."

I meet Cal's eyes and I feel his desperation and sorrow. We both know what Kato is capable of, but we also both know it would be suicide to go back right now. As much as I want Ehren back, he'd kill me if anything happened to Cal.

"We'll get him back alive, Cal," I say as calmly as I can manage.

Cal shakes his head furiously, clenching his hands at his side. "That's not enough."

"Cal—"

"Kato's probably torturing him right now. Ehren could be suffering."

"Maybe I can—"

Before I can finish my response Alak speaks up. "We'll make a plan and get him back. No one needs to rush back at this moment."

I spin to face Alak. "Cal's right, though. Ehren may not have time."

Alak's face is full of emotion as he reaches out and brushes his hand down my cheek.

"I know, love, but if we rush in without a plan we could lose far more than Ehren," Alak whispers, his voice low enough no one else can hear. "And not just you, which would be unbearable enough, but the whole war. We have to be careful."

I swallow and nod, turning back to Cal slowly.

"Astra?" Cal asks, his voice barely above a whisper as his eyes flick over my face. I can't contain a wince as his eyes meet mine. He backs away shaking his head. "No. No. You can't— We can't wait."

I step toward him, extending my hand, but he jerks away.

"Cal, please."

He shakes his head, refusing to meet my eyes.

"We need a plan first, but I promise I'll do absolutely everything within my power to get him back."

Cal clenches his jaw and fixes his gaze on the ground.

"Look, mate," Alak says, stepping to my side, "I know how you feel." He slips his hand into mine. "When Kato took Astra, I feared for the worst, but Ehren made me wait and we came back successful."

Cal glances off.

"I love him, too," I say, my voice trembling slightly. "Not quite in the same way you do, I'm sure, but I love him very much. We'll come up with a plan to save him that won't cost us everything."

Cal finally meets my gaze, his eyes red-rimmed and leaking tears. "Then let me go back on my own. I'm not important. I'm expendable. Send me back"—he slams his hand on his chest for emphasis—"and let me get him out."

"I can't do that, Cal."

"Why not? If you truly cared about him, loved him like you claim, you wouldn't even hesitate."

His words feel like a slap sharper and more painful than any other injury I've endured. I waver on my feet, finding it suddenly difficult to breathe, to keep myself steady. Thankfully, Alak holds me firmly and Kai steps in.

"He gave himself up for you," Kai answers for me, moving closer to Cal. "He had me get you out. Do you really think he'd appreciate you undoing his actions when he made his choice so clear?"

Cal opens his mouth to speak but only clamps his jaw shut moments later, the fists at his sides tightening. He glances from me to Kai to Alak, shaking his head. With a loud huff of frustration he storms off. I watch him go, my heart sinking.

"He'll be fine," Alak whispers in my ear. I look up at him. "We'll get Ehren back and Cal will be okay."

I sigh and glance off in the direction that Cal disappeared and nod after a moment.

"I need to speak with Prince Luc," I say, pulling forward every ounce of authority I can.

"I'll find him," Kai offers

"Tell him to meet me in the main tent."

With a sharp nod Kai turns on his heel and marches off, his shifters not far behind.

"What do you need from me, love?" Alak asks, brushing his thumb across my knuckles.

I sigh and glance toward the tent behind us. "Go check on your cousin. Make sure he's fine and as comfortable as can be." I pause, glancing around the small battle camp. "We need to get him away from here as soon as possible, continue the original plan."

Alak nods. "Yes, but I'm assuming you won't be going back with him."

I shake my head, looking up into his emerald eyes. "Not until I have Ehren."

Alak exhales slowly before pressing a kiss to my forehead.

"I understand, love. I hope you also understand that I won't be leaving, either."

A small smile plays at the corner of my lips. "I wouldn't expect anything less."

"Good." He presses a quick kiss to my lips before releasing my hand and ducking inside the tent.

I waste no time making my way to the main tent. When I arrive, Prince Luc and a couple of his Guard are already inside with Kai, who is sharing details of what happened in the throne room. Luc eyes me, brow furrowed.

"I assume I am here to help you come up with a plan to get Ehren back?"

"If you can," I say. "But I also really need to get Saran out of here and safely out of Kato's clutches. If he gets Saran back—"

"—everything will be in vain," Luc finishes for me.

"Exactly."

Luc takes a deep breath. "Where do you need me most? Here, to take siege on the castle or back at the fortress or Summer Palace protecting the boy?"

I pause, considering my options. "Take Saran. I feel that the fewer people who go in to rescue Ehren, the better."

"Very well," Luc says with a nod. "We still have a few hours of daylight left. I will ready my men and we will leave within the hour."

I incline my head in gratitude and Luc returns the gesture before sweeping from the room.

"What do you need from me?" Kai asks calmly.

I sigh and gnaw on my lip. "I don't know." I raise my eyes to meet Kai's gaze across the tent. "I have no idea what to do."

In three smooth strides Kai crosses the distance between us and gathers me in his arms. I dissolve into his chest and tears break free. Kai holds me while I sob, tracing soothing circles on my back. When I finally manage to regain my composure, I pull back and look up at him.

"What do I do?" I whisper.

Kai forces a tight smile. "Rescue Ehren."

A small laugh escapes and I shake my head. "Because it's that simple."

Kai releases me and takes a step back. "Maybe it is."

I scowl. "What do you mean?"

"Your brother is most likely expecting a huge display. He's waiting for armies to charge in. He's expecting another battle."

"Is there another way?"

"You said it yourself just a few minutes ago—a small group is best. In fact, I think it's best if you don't go anywhere near the castle."

"Kai, I'm not staying behind."

"Your brother wants you. If you take a step into that palace, he'll know it, and this time you won't leave."

"Kai, I can't—"

I stop short as someone enters the tent behind me. I spin around to find Alak.

"What's wrong?" he asks, marching to my side. "I can feel something down the bond, but I can't place it."

"Kai doesn't think I should be one of the people to go in after Ehren."

"I agree," Alak replies without hesitation.

I blink and step back. "What? You know I can't leave him there."

"Do you trust me, love?"

"Of course I do."

"Good, because while I was sitting with Saran we chatted a bit and I think I have a plan."

I frown. "A plan that doesn't involve me?"

Alak's mouth quirks up into a small half grin. "It involves you being well outside the palace, in a safe place, where only our bond can reach."

I knit my eyebrows together as I struggle to process his words. When I finally unravel his meaning, a small gasp escapes.

"You mean for you and Cal to go in alone and rescue Ehren, and you'll use the bond to wisp all three of you away."

Alak nods. "That's the plan, yes. You should be somewhere a little farther north but maybe a little closer than the rest of our army. It also might help if we can find some sort of magic or spell for Cal in case the two of us have to split up."

I glance away. "We need to look through Ehren's things. He may have a spell prepared or bookmarked."

Alak takes a step closer, his eyes trailing over me. "Yes."

I manage a small nod and force myself to meet his eyes. "How soon will you leave?"

"I'll need a bit to restore my magic or I'll be useless. Creating an entire army and wisping Luc took a good bit of energy," Alak admits. "I also need some time to figure out the specifics of a distraction that will be fully effective and then time to find the spells we need."

"Can you be ready by morning?"

Alak nods and gathers me in his arms. "Dawn."

He presses a quick kiss to my lips. Kai makes a soft growling sound and Alak smiles and draws back, turning to him.

"While I'm in the palace rescuing the prince, I suppose you'll stay with Astra?"

Kai nods once, his gaze fixed on me. "Of course."

"Wait," I mumble, half to myself. "How will we meet back

up with the others? Ehren may need more help and healing than I can give him."

"If my shifters are with Luc and the others, I can guide the wisp to them."

Alak shoots Kai a curious look. Kai shifts uncomfortably under his attention and glances away.

"You don't need to know the details," Kai explains slowly, carefully. "Suffice it to say that blood magic and blood oaths are involved."

My eyes widen, but I hurry to bury my shock. I can feel Alak's own curiosity down the bond, but he doesn't press for details either.

"Then we'll make sure Luc knows to make camp somewhere tomorrow, and we can use that magic to get us farther away to safety," I say. "Kai and I will travel with Luc for a while to put plenty of distance between us and Embervein, but we can pause partway so you don't have to carry Cal and Ehren quite as far."

"We should find Cal and let him know the plan," Alak suggests, glancing toward the tent door. "I hope he didn't go far."

"I think I know where he is." I stand on my tiptoes and brush a quick kiss on Alak's cheek. "I'll catch up with you in a bit."

Alak gives me a parting nod as I leave the tent. Everyone is bustling about, prepping most of the camp to leave. I weave between the soldiers, heading to the edge of the camp. There I find Cal, sword in hand, running through some sort of one-person drill. He's drenched in sweat, face red from exertion.

At first I don't interrupt him, standing off to the side watching. I can tell by the shift in the way he's holding himself that he's registered my presence, but he doesn't pause. I'm not sure how much time passes before he finally stops, breathing hard, his clothes soaked through with sweat. He sheathes his sword before wiping his brow with a trembling arm and lifting his eyes to mine. Even from several yards away I can see the clear pain on his every feature. With slow, deliberate movements he crosses the distance between us, stopping a couple feet away. For several moments we stand there, just watching each other.

"I'm sorry," Cal says, breaking the heavy silence. "I shouldn't have spoken to you like that."

"It was nothing," I say, waving him off. "You were desperate and hurting, and had I been in your shoes, I might have reacted much the same."

Cal shakes his head firmly. "That's no excuse. You were hurting as well, and I lashed out. I know Ehren trusts you with his life, so there's no reason I shouldn't as well."

"Well, we have a plan," I offer with a small, forced smile.

He nods for me to go on and I quickly fill him in. When I finish he doesn't say anything, the silence dragging between us. When he speaks, his voice is quiet.

"So, first thing in the morning Alak and I leave?"

I nod quickly. "Alak is searching Ehren's things for any sort of spell that might help us locate him faster and for some magic for you as well." I reach out and grab Cal's hand, giving it a reassuring squeeze. "We will get him back."

Cal's chin quivers as he fights back the tears brimming his eyes. He opens his mouth to speak, but only shuts it a moment later, shaking his head. He takes a shuddering breath that's half a sob.

"It's not your fault, you know," I offer. Cal's eyes snap to mine. "Kai told me everything, and it's not your fault."

Cal shakes his head. "I was the one who got captured. I left

Ehren's side and Kato grabbed me. If I hadn't . . ." He trails off, his voice trembling. "I messed up and Ehren saved me. It's not supposed to work that way. I'm his Guard. I'm supposed to save him."

"Cal—"

"No, I messed up, Astra, and I take full responsibility." He pauses and glances off into the distance in the direction of the castle, almost as if he can sense Ehren. "If he dies because I failed to protect him, because I failed to protect myself, I will never forgive myself. I've lost so much already in this war, but I don't think I can survive losing him. Not when I've only just gotten him, not when I can finally call him mine."

I squeeze his hand again. "You will get him back."

Cal meets my eyes and manages a small smile. It doesn't go to his eyes, but it's a relief all the same.

"Now since there's not much more to be done tonight, why don't we go find some food?"

Cal's smile falters. "I'm not sure how much I can get down, but I'll try."

He doesn't try to pull his hand from my grasp, so I don't draw away. Hand-in-hand we cross the camp and only let go when we settle on the ground by a campsite. Alak brings us both dinner. We attempt for light chatter but the air is still tense. As promised, Cal manages a few bites, and in all honestly, I don't eat much more. Before we head to our respective tents for sleep, Cal catches my eye and I offer him a weak smile.

"We'll all be together again soon."

I pray to the gods my promise holds true.

CHAPTER TWENTY-SIX

RONAN

While Astra and Ehren go off to complete their plan to rescue Saran, I accompany Jess and her army back to the Summer Palace. Unfortunately the Fae also go with us. As soon as we arrive, a breathless Cadewynn races out to greet us, her eyes wide with delight as she takes in the Fae as well as their Unicorn. A guard whose name I don't remember accompanies her.

"Princess Cadewynn, meet Hycis, Rynia, Ievis, and Iefyr of the Fae," Jess says with a grin, motioning to each of them in turn.

The princess dips into a low curtesy. "The pleasure is all very much mine."

Hycis grins wickedly, stepping forward. "First a human prince and now a proper human princess."

Cadewynn's smile falters slightly as Hycis circles her. The guard stiffens, his hand on his sword as he takes a step closer. Hycis notices his movements and focuses her sharp glare on the young man.

"Do you assume I'm going to hurt your precious little princess?"

The guard straightens, meeting Hycis's eyes without fear. "I assume everyone is a threat until proven otherwise, and even then trust must be earned."

"Nyco," Cadewynn whispers. "I'm sure she's no threat or she wouldn't be here."

The guard—Nyco, I suppose—steps closer to her, slipping his hand into hers.

"I'm not going to let my guard down, Winnie, just because they're invited guests. Protecting you is my priority."

Cadewynn smiles softly and leans into him. Ah, so he's more than just her guard.

"Now that is adorable," Hycis says with a laugh. She takes a step closer so she's inches away from Nyco, her eyes boring into his. "Do you really think if it came down to it you could actually win in a fight against me?"

A smile curls on Nyco's lips. "I think I might surprise you, but even if I lost, it would be worth it if I could keep her safe for even one moment."

A hearty laugh breaks free from Hycis and she steps back to Rynia's side. "Oh, I do love you humans! Don't worry, little soldier, your princess is safe."

"Perhaps we should all head inside out of the courtyard?" Cadewynn suggests tentatively, her eyes flitting over our traveling party. They settle on Jess. "Are Kaeya and Brock back, as well?"

Jess nods. "They've taken the army around to the barracks but Kaeya, at least, will join me soon with the weapons and berries."

"We have the berries?" Cadewynn asks, her eyes going wide.

Ievis scoffs. "Why else did you think we were here?"

Cadewynn blinks and I step forward, pushing in front of Ievis. "Ignore him. He gets grumpy when he hasn't had a chance to get in a nap. He's old and frail, you see."

Ievis growls and mutters something under his breath that I'm positive is swearing in his Fae tongue, but Iefyr lets out a small laugh. The tension is broken, however, and Cadewynn's gentle smile returns.

"All right then. Follow me inside and we'll get everyone settled. Then we can go over our plans with the weapons and how to take down Kato and his Dragkonians."

Each day Jess and Kaeya take up residence in a corner of the dining hall, weapons spread out across several tables. Cadewynn, along with her partners Nyco and Sama, often flits into the room with scrolls bearing research on poisons and how to adapt them to various weapons. I switch between studying in the library and sitting with my books in the dining hall, observing the process. Occasionally they ask for my input.

The Fae tend to keep a healthy distance from the weapons and poison, but are too invested to leave the room entirely. Hycis and Rynia sit at the same table as the weapons but on the opposite end, playing a game of dice, while Iefyr sits next to them reading a book of human faerie stories for nothing more than amusement. Ievis paces the room, huffing in disgust on occasion just to let us know he thinks we're all wasting our time. I do my best to ignore him, focusing on my own research about the barrier and magic that was used against the Dragkonians before. Thankfully some of the older books stored in the libraries of other

Athiedor Lords have preserved stories from the time of magic.

"Oh, that's interesting," I mumble, my eyes scanning the page of text in front of me.

"What?" Iefyr asks, lifting their eyes from their book.

"I think I found another account that describes the original barrier in greater detail than the previous accounts," I reply, turning the page.

"Oh! Let me see!" Iefyr says, bouncing up from their seat and reaching eagerly for the text as they slide into the spot next to me.

"Yes," Ievis growls under his breath. "I am sure the human text has new information that has never—"

"Please be silent, Ievis," Iefyr chides, already scanning the text. "This is why we came."

"Well, is there anything new?" Ievis asks, coming to a halt behind his sibling, which is far too close to me.

Iefyr shrugs, not bothering to look up. "It's a different perspective, and a new perspective always helps."

Ievis rolls his eyes, clearly not convinced. I shake my head and push up from my seat, eager to escape the squabbling siblings. I leave my book with Iefyr as I head down to where Kaeya and Jess are working with the weapons. Jess is carefully coating weapons in poison, treating the sticky substance with care even though it poses no real risk to her. Kaeya sits next to Jess, filling darts with the same focus.

"Will that be enough to take down the Dragkonians?" I ask, nodding to their work.

"Do you mean the poison itself, the amount we're putting on each weapon, or the actual weapons?" Jess asks, not bothering to look up.

"Yes," I say with a grin.

Jess groans and rolls her eyes but Kaeya smiles.

"The poison, even diluted as it is, will most assuredly bring down a Dragkonian," Hycis says, stepping to my side but maintaining a safe distance. "These berries are very deadly to us and thereby the Dragkonians. Even in such a small amount it is incredibly lethal."

"Your soldiers will have to possess the necessary skill to actually hit the Dragkonians for it to work," Ievis cuts in, pushing between Hycis and me to glare down at the weapons with clear distaste.

"What makes you think our soldiers are lacking?" I challenge.

"Well, not *your* soldiers," Ievis drawls, meeting my eyes with heat. "You do not even have an army here. Actually, what is your role again? Reading insignificant prophecies and histories that help no one?"

"I'm the Athiedor Ambassador," I grit out.

"Is it typical for ambassadors to spend their days lounging in libraries?"

"Out!" Jess snaps, cutting me off before I can reply.

"Pardon?" Ievis says, glaring at Jess.

She points at the door. "Out. Both of you."

"I—" I start but Jess silences me with a wave.

"No. I'm done listening to you two bicker. Go to separate rooms of this gods' forsaken castle. Maybe even the same room and fuck it out."

My eyes widen in horror and Ievis curls his lip in disgust.

"How dare you suggest I debase myself with—"

Jess raises a dagger coated in poison and points it Ievis's way and he falls silent. "All I'm suggesting is that you remove yourself from the room where I am working with something that could very much kill you. It would be horrible if my hand were to slip."

Iefyr tenses, their eyes darting between me and their brother and the dagger. Hycis's eyes shine with glee as she drops a hand onto Ievis's shoulder.

"I think she wants to be taken seriously, don't you, Ievis?" she whispers in his ear.

Ievis snarls, shoving her hand away as he leans in toward Jess. "Are you threatening me?"

She twirls the dagger in her hand. "Do I need to?"

Ievis growls. "So be it." He turns to me. "Show me to your library."

I blink at him. "Come again?"

"Your library," Ievis repeats, emphasizing each syllable.

I tilt my head, meeting Ievis's eyes. "My little human library?"

Ievis clenches his jaw, his eyes flashing like molten gold. "Yes."

I hold his gaze for a moment before I burst out laughing. "It would be my pleasure."

I stride from the room, humming as Ievis stomps behind. He keeps a decent distance from me as we weave the familiar corridors. When we enter the library, he pauses in the doorway, his eyes trailing over the shelves.

"I did not realize humans put this much stock in knowledge," he admits.

I study him for a moment, trying to decipher the meaning behind his words. His tone is flat, but I'm sure there's an insult buried beneath them. He shifts his gaze to me.

"Well, do we just stand here and absorb the knowledge by being in proximity to the books? Because if that is the case, humans use libraries very differently than the Fae."

A grin twitches at the corner of my lips but I refuse to give in and smile at the bastard.

"Of course not." I make my way to the nearest table where I already have a pile started from earlier and sink down into a chair. "Grab a book and read."

Ievis moves across the room so quietly I don't even realize he's left the doorway until he takes a seat across from me. He reaches and pulls a book from the pile, opening it to a random page. I do my best to focus on my own text, but when I glance up at Ievis I'm surprised to see his brow scrunched in frustration, his jaw clenched. After a moment he slams the book shut and glances away.

"You can't read the language," I mumble, drawing the full ire of his gaze.

"It is not as if I had much use for human drivel growing up," he snaps, crossing his arms. "And even if I did, it likely would not have been this particular language or dialect."

"But you speak our language."

Ievis rolls his eyes. "Not exactly. Our tongues are typically able to translate the spoken word so you understand us, and our brains process most audible language in a way that we can understand it. Call it magical Fae charm, whatever you want. It's an inherent part of my people. The written word, however, is different."

"Iefyr seems to have some understanding of our written languages."

Ievis bristles. "We had different instruction."

I lean back in my chair. "Well, I can teach you, if you'd like."

Ievis scoffs, shaking his head. I roll my eyes.

"Wait. I forgot. I'm much more inferior than you, so what could I possibly have to offer?"

"There is no point for me to learn to read your language. I

will not be here long enough for it to be of any use. I am only here to help create a spell to contain your Dragkonian problem before it spreads to my realm. Once I am done, I will leave your human world forever and all knowledge of your language will be no more than wasted time. It is not as if your books contain any knowledge about my people that would be helpful."

"You don't know that."

"What do I not know?" he challenges, his voice edged and dangerous. "That I will be rid of this realm forever shortly, or that your books contain some sort of special knowledge?"

I shrug, a taunting grin playing on my lips. "Both, I suppose."

He opens his mouth to argue, but I cut him off. "Look, I know you think very little of humans, but we do have accounts and histories of magic when it was alive. We have records of the original defeat of the Dragkonians. It took some searching of ancient magical libraries, but we have them."

"The Fae also have accounts, and I can assure you our records are much more accurate."

"You're so sure of that?"

"Of course."

"So you don't think there's even a possibility for the smallest margin of error?" I lean forward onto my elbows, meeting Ievis's intense gaze. "You don't think there might be even the tiniest detail that could be wrong?"

Ievis pauses, working his jaw. "I suppose there could be small errors, but I have no doubt your human texts contain more error than fact."

I laugh, the sound echoing off the library walls. Ievis shifts uncomfortably in his seat.

"Okay, fine," I say, eyes shining. "Let's assume that your texts are infallible and contain no errors and that the human versions of the same stories got a few things wrong. It's still possible that the human records could contain details the Fae didn't see fit to include. Would you concede that *this* is at least a possibility?"

Ievis draws a long breath through his nose before nodding sharply.

"Therefore, it follows that maybe you haven't found the answers you need for your spell because you don't have access to all the information?"

Once again Ievis nods, but it looks as if the motion pains him. I grin.

"It does not mean that your books have the answers, only that they might," he says through clenched teeth.

"True," I concede. "At least it gives you another place to look. Besides, the places where the stories overlap are likely to show us what parts are the most factual."

Ievis sits up straighter, his eyebrows arching up. "Repeat that."

Now it's my turn to look confused. "Repeat what?"

"The last thing you said, about the stories overlapping."

I scowl, playing over my words in my mind. "You mean that the overlapping parts show us the factual parts of the story?"

"Yes. That."

"Okay, what about it?"

"The Fae records and the human records would both show their own form of bias," he says slowly, as if the words are being pulled from him against his will. "The humans would want to make themselves out to be the heroes and would gloss over the part the Fae played."

"And likewise with the Fae. They would want their histories to show their power instead of showing how they had to rely on humans."

Ievis nods. "Exactly."

My eyes widen as I catch where Ievis is going. "So, the places where the records agree show us a better picture of what actually happened. We can fill in the gaps with the parts from each side of the story that complete it the best."

A smile crawls across Ievis's lips. At first I'm startled by the beauty of it. Even though I've seen little more than snarls and scowls on his features up until this point, the smile fits him. It makes him truly beautiful, showing another side of him. A side I find myself longing to see more of. The realization sends reality slamming back, and I shake my head, clearing the thought. I quickly turn to my text, flipping through aimlessly to give my hands something to do.

"We need to place the stories side-by-side and then we may be able to find our answers." I raise my eyes to his. "You brought Fae texts with you?"

"I did," Ievis says slowly, something new and intense in his gaze. "They are in my room."

I swallow, suddenly needing to take a moment to breathe as I lose myself momentarily in the molten gold of his eyes.

"Should we—"

Footsteps racing down the hall and echoing yells cut me short. I fumble for my cane, pushing away from the table, but Ievis is already moving toward the door before I'm even out of my seat. He throws the door open to the chaos of servants rushing by.

"What's happened?" I call out to a servant boy as I step to Ievis's side.

The boys pauses, looking up at me with wide, horrified eyes. "There's been an attack."

"An attack here?" Ievis demands, making the boy shrink back.

"Not the castle," the boy says, shaking his head. "In the village. Oxwatch. I-I don't know the details." He glances off down the hall toward where the others disappeared. "I need to go. They said they need us all."

"Go on," I say, motioning the boy away. Once he's gone, I turn to Ievis. "I think we may need to rejoin the others."

Ievis nods. "For once, human, we are in agreement."

Well, there it is. Ievis agreed with me. The world is surely coming to an end.

CHAPTER TWENTY-SEVEN

RONAN

The previously quiet dining hall is currently full of chaos. The tables have been smashed against the edges of the room to make room for the wounded villagers being dragged in by soldiers.

"Bring more blankets," Jess yells above the cacophony. "Set those with worse injuries on the left side and those with light injuries along the right wall."

People scurry around, trying to follow Jess's demands. Someone shoves past me, and I fall against Ievis. He stiffens but doesn't push me away. I straighten so I'm not pressed right up against him, but I'm close enough I can feel his warmth.

"What of those who have escaped with little to no wounds?" one of the soldiers asks.

Jess blinks and I step forward. "We can get them set up in the library for now."

Jess shoots me a grateful look and nods. "Yes, the library. Send the refugees who don't require Healers to the library."

The soldier nods and dissolves back into the crowd. Jess leans over and whispers something to Kaeya who nods and calls to some of the soldiers. She leads them over to the table covered in poisonous weapons, and they each take an armload before rushing from the room. Jess looks back to me, approaching slowly.

"Can you oversee setting up the refugees in the library?"

"Of course," I say with a nod.

"Thank you." She pauses, glancing around and taking a shuddering breath. "I don't know what I'm doing here."

"It looks like you're doing well and have a handle on things."

A small laugh escapes as she shakes her head. "Well, at least I'm keeping up appearances."

"What's the plan? Anything else I can help with beyond getting the refugees situated?"

Jess shrugs, glancing off. "I have Kaeya taking a group of soldiers to clear out the attacking soldiers and Dragkonians in Oxwatch, but I fear the village may already be lost." She takes a deep, fortifying breath. "I'm trying to figure out what to do with all these people in the meantime since they don't have homes to return to."

"I'll go talk to Cook and make sure we have food ready for everyone and then I'll head back to the library and make sure everyone is as comfortable as can be."

Jess nods absentmindedly. "Good. That gives us a place to start, at least."

"Where is Iefyr?" Ievis says, stepping forward and making me jump. I had forgotten he was here.

"They said something about getting people out, but I don't know—"

"You let them leave and run directly into danger?" Ievis snarls, stepping into Jess's face, teeth bared.

"Look," Jess says, shoving the Fae out of her face without

fear. "They're quite capable of making their own decisions. If they want to run into the fray, it's not my job to stop them."

Ievis growls and storms away. I glance after him as Jess mutters, "Gods, I hate that Fae." Before I even realize I've made a conscious decision, I'm stumbling after Ievis. I'm moving against the flow and Ievis is much faster than me, so I lose him quickly.

"Ievis!" I yell, praying he can hear above the chaos. "Ievis!"

I push through the crowd and open my mouth to yell again but crash into a hard body. I look up into Ievis's scowl.

"What?"

I grab his forearm and pull him to the side, out of the rush of the crowd. "Where are you going?"

He clenches his jaw, jerking from my grasp. "I am going after Iefyr."

"Where exactly do you think they are?"

Ievis levels me with a glare and the pieces click into place.

"You think they went into the village to create a portal back to the palace."

"They're stupid enough to try. They forget that they're not invincible." He turns and starts to march away. "I have to stop them."

"Let me come with you."

Ievis laughs bitterly. "You are too weak and will only hold me back."

His words sting and I stumble, as if my body is eager to prove his words.

"Just because I have to use a cane—"

He spins back around, cutting me short. "Is that really what you think I meant?"

I frown. "I . . . Isn't it?"

Ievis shakes his head, something I can't quite place on his face. "I would never— No. That is not what I meant."

"Oh, so this is because I'm human."

"That is part of it," Ievis admits. "Besides, are you not needed in the library?"

He's walking away before I can say anything, quickly lost again to the crowd. I sigh, conceding his point. I make a detour through the kitchen and check in with Cook. As expected, it's equally chaotic as the dining hall, but Cook doesn't seem to mind my presence. She already has all hands on deck to provide tea and food for our onslaught of guests.

When I make it to the library I'm met with wide eyes and scared faces. Many of the refugees filling the walls are mere children. I force a smile and make my way through the crowd. Once I've assessed the situation, I help everyone get settled. Eventually people stop coming through the door and our number settles. The library is crowded but there's still some space to spread out. Servants sent by Cook appear and help pass out blankets and, later, tea and biscuits from the kitchens.

I feel helpless and useless. I'm standing in the center of the room, my eyes trailing over the crowd when Ievis and Iefyr return. They're a little dirty and appear to have some minor injuries, but they're both alive. Iefyr looks tired, leaning heavily on Ievis, with a decent scratch on their left cheek, but they're smiling softly. Ievis's sleeves are rolled up to his elbows, revealing strong forearms covered in black swirling ink. Iefyr stops to chat with a little girl near the entrance of the library, but Ievis's eyes search until they find me. He says something to Iefyr who gives him a nod before he heads my way.

"I see you found Iefyr okay," I say, nodding to where they now sit among the refugees.

Ievis nods, glancing off. "I did."

"Good." I swallow, my throat suddenly thick. "I'm glad you're both all right."

Ievis looks back at me, tilting his head. "Are you?"

"Of course. Why wouldn't I be?"

Ievis hums, crossing his arms, his expression blank. "I was under the impression you did not care for me much."

His response takes me off guard for a moment, but I recover quickly. "From what I understand, you still have quite the part to play. It would be a pity if I've had to suffer with your presence all this time only for you to die tragically before you can even fulfill your duty."

A smile twitches on the corner of his mouth. "Yes, that would be quite the tragedy indeed." He holds my gaze for a moment before pulling his eyes away. "So what exactly is the plan?"

I sigh, shaking my head. "I don't know. I'm trying to get them as comfortable as possible, but after that, I'll be as useless as you typically assume me to be."

"What about your stories?"

"My stories?"

Ievis glances at me out of the corner of his eye. "Stories make for good distractions, don't you agree?" I nod and he continues. "So tell them a story. Distract them."

I lick my lips, my mind already sorting through the stories I know by heart. "All right, I can do that."

I walk over to one of the easy chairs nearest the fire where several children are huddled. I ease into the seat. Ievis follows me and stands behind the chair, leaning forward to rest his arms on the back directly behind my head.

"Would you like to hear a story about how a little Athiedor peasant girl saved the Prince of the Fae when he was turned into a snake?"

The children's heads bob up and down eagerly as they shuffle and shift so they're all facing me. I grin and lean forward, leaping into the story. Behind me Ievis mumbles things under his breath, quietly correctly parts of the story as I go. The crowd grows and soon my voice is echoing off the library walls so everyone can hear me. When I finish, Ievis shakes his head.

"That is not even remotely what really happened."

I twist in my chair and grin up at him. "No?"

"No."

"Then why don't you tell us the correct version?"

Several of the children pipe up, begging for Ievis to tell his version, not put off in the slightest by his scowl.

"Go on, Ievis," Iefyr encourages, settling on the floor and leaning against a nearby chair. "You always were my favorite storyteller."

Ievis mumbles a curse under his breath, but concedes without argument, diving into his own version of the tale. At first he's as stiff as ever, his voice flat and dull, but as the story advances, it takes on a life of its own. I've heard a good many storytellers in my lifetime, but Ievis is by far one of the best. I'm quickly lost in the cadence of his voice, reliving a story I thought I knew well, experiencing it in a different way from a fresh perspective. When he finishes, I'm almost disappointed he's done. Clearly I'm not the only one either, because the children immediately beg him to tell another. He scoffs, shaking his head, but there's no hiding his smile or the shine in his eyes.

When he caves to their pleas, he moves around the chair and perches on the armrest. I shift a bit to give him more room, but I don't shy away from his proximity. He finishes his second story just as dinner arrives from the kitchen.

"You're quite good at telling stories," I say quietly as our previously captive audience scampers away to get in line to receive their food, Iefyr going along with them after shooting their brother a gentle smile.

Ievis shrugs but doesn't bother trying to deny it. "Iefyr always liked stories but wasn't allowed to read them because they would 'interfere with their studies.' I had access to them, so I did what I could to share what I could."

"You're a good brother."

He turns abruptly to face me, twisting around so sharply he nearly falls off the armrest. "No, I was not."

I frown.

"I could have done so much more for them, but I failed them over and over and over again."

"What happened to them wasn't your fault."

"What do you know of it?" he scoffs. "You have no idea what our childhood was like."

"I admit I don't know the details, but from what Iefyr said —"

His eyes flash and I stop short.

"What did Iefyr tell you?"

I swallow. "Not much." Ievis holds his glare and I continue. "They mentioned that you two didn't have a normal childhood. That you were used for your magic from an early age."

"Did they mention that I failed to stop the other Fae from experimenting on them? That they nearly died because I was too weak, too cowardly to fight for them?"

My stomach twists with unease. "No, they didn't mention that."

"Then you have a very incomplete tale."

"Iefyr only spoke good things about you, Ievis," I say softly, placing my hand on his arm. He tenses but doesn't move away. "Clearly they don't hold anything against you."

Ievis looks down at me, and my breath catches in my throat. Emotion flickers through his eyes for a moment before he schools his features, jerking away from my touch and standing in one sharp movement.

"As if I need the platitudes of a human," he snaps.

A few curious eyes turn our way. He grits his teeth, purposely looking anywhere but at me. Frustration bubbles up in my chest mingled with anger. I push up with my cane and grab his shoulder with my free hand, twisting him to face me.

"Fine. If you want to believe you're a fuck-up, far be it from me to convince you otherwise, but you realize you just called your sibling a liar."

His eyes darken and he opens his mouth to speak but I don't let him.

"Hate me and my realm all you want, but you're stuck here for the foreseeable future, so get over yourself."

I pull my hand away and push past him before he can respond. I'm halfway across the room, weaving between the clusters of people scattered around eating their meager dinner when Jess enters the library. Everything about her from her expression to her stiff stance tells me something is wrong. I quickly cross to her, and she pulls me out into the hall. She glances both ways, making sure there's no one close enough to overhear.

"What is it, Jess?" I press. "What's happened?"

The library door opens behind me and Ievis slips out. His mouth is set in a tight line as he steps to my side, keeping a good couple feet between us.

"There have been more attacks."

"Attacks? Plural?" I ask, my heart dropping into my stomach as she nods. "How many? And where?"

"The reports are still coming in, but several villages to the south were attacked. We had soldiers near one so the damage was minimal, but another was almost completely lost. A handful of people escaped." She pauses, swallowing hard. "But the refugee camp was hit as well."

"What refugee camp?" Ievis cuts in. "Isn't the entire kingdom a refugee camp at this point?"

Jess shoots him a sharp glare and straightens her shoulders. "There was a main refugee camp located in the west that was recruiting soldiers for our army."

"Pax was there," I mutter. "That was his camp."

Jess looks to me and nods. "Yes."

"Were there any survivors?"

Jess's eyes darken. "We don't know. Somehow someone in the camp got a message out to Pax, but after that they lost contact. According to what Pax heard, it doesn't seem likely."

"This was a personal attack. Between the attack on Oxwatch and the attack on the refugees, it appears Kato is making this personal."

"That's what it looks like. I also wouldn't be surprised if the attacks to the south have a personal connection of some sort that I don't know about. There didn't seem to be anything particularly strategic about it."

Ievis looks between us. "Why would this be a personal attack? The nearby village I understand, but what is the connection to the refugee camp?"

I sigh and turn to face Ievis. "The leaders of the camp are close personal friends of Kato and Astra. Or they were. There's no way that Kato didn't know, so if he attacked them, it was personal."

Ievis arches his eyebrows but doesn't say anything more. I turn back to Jess.

"What's our next move?"

"I'm sending out all the soldiers I can spare. Basically my whole army is heading out in the morning with some leaving tonight to go aid the villages in the south. Pax is preparing all the soldiers in case Ehren wants him to go search for survivors from the refugee camp."

I frown. "Do we have contact with Ehren?"

Jess nods. "We have a few shifters to take messages back and forth. I've already sent a message, so hopefully we'll hear back soon."

"And you have enough protection here should all those soldiers leave?" Ievis asks, inching closer in what could almost be confused as a protective motion.

She sighs and looks down the hall, her eyes unfocused. "Thankfully, Luc left enough of his army here along with several more of Kai's shifters, so we'll have some protection, but I don't want to rely entirely on a foreign army, so I'm keeping back a handful of soldiers. I sent Kaeya among their armies to ask for volunteers to go out to the areas where our armies are already spread thin, but I don't know the numbers yet."

"What do you need from me?" I ask.

"I need to go back to the fortress and organize things a bit. Things are in flux, and if Pax leaves, we need someone in charge over whoever is left behind. Can you hold the fort down here until either I or Ehren return?"

I nod. "Of course."

Her shoulders relax. "Thank you."

A wide-eyed servant rushes around the corner and stumbles up to Jess, handing her a paper. Jess scans it quickly and turns back to the servant.

"Tell him I'll be there soon."

The servant nods and scampers off. Jess turns back to me with a sigh.

"I thought the Valley was boring and that war might be a welcome reprieve," she says with a forced smile. "It's a lot bloodier, messier, and exhausting than I anticipated."

"Hopefully Ehren and Astra will be back soon to help with the burden," I offer.

Jess shrugs. "I suppose. Anyway, I need to get back to organizing armies." Her eyes dart to Ievis. "If you discover anything that can help, let me know immediately."

Ievis offers her a sharp nod. "Of course."

With a parting nod, she disappears down the hall. Once she's gone I turn to Ievis.

"Look, I know you hate me but we need to find a way for you to complete your spell. We can't sustain losses like this much longer."

Ievis hesitates but eventually nods. "Fine. Shall we go back into the library?"

I glance toward the door. "I need to grab some texts, but I doubt I'll be to concentrate in there with all these people. I might need to go to my room and be alone for a bit."

"Entirely alone? Or should I join you?"

My eyes snap to his. "You would want to be in close proximity with me in my own personal space?"

He shrugs. "I have been in worse situations before. And, as you pointed out earlier, our answer may be found by looking at our texts side-by-side. I cannot read your human language, and I highly doubt you know the language of the Fae. If there is truth in this idea, we need to work together."

"I agree. So . . . truce?"

Ievis nods once. "Truce."

"Very well. Let's gather our things, maybe grab a bite of food, and then we'll reconvene in my room."

Something close to a smile twitches on Ievis's lips as he agrees. Fifteen minutes later we've left Iefyr in charge of the library and we're sitting cross-legged on the floor of my room, texts spread between us, ready for a long night.

CHAPTER TWENTY-EIGHT

EHREN

Kato keeps his promise to make me suffer for every hour Astra doesn't show, or at least it appears that way. I don't have a reliable way to track the time, but guards burst into the room frequently enough to make me believe Kato is keeping track. The first couple of times I'm dragged into the throne room for a bout of torture, sunlight still shines through the windows. My third march down the hallways reveals the sun sinking down into the horizon. My last several visits have been during the night. I haven't managed to get more than a few brief moments of sleep, and I'm exhausted.

Another promise Kato keeps is the Healers. So far I've met four. Polly has visited me several times, and she's by far my favorite. She at least seems to be on my side and has a lot of power in her Healing. Even when she can't rid me of scars, she eases my pain.

Tabitha is another confident Healer. She's middle-aged and stoic. She glares at me as she Heals, clearly put out by having to assist me. I don't know if she supports Kato fully or if

285

she's here by force. I can't get a read on her. She's thorough, though, so I don't hold her attitude against me.

Dax is clearly on Kato's side. He watches every torture session with glee and barely Heals anything when he's called forward. He stops any bleeding and helps to mend a broken wrist, but he does nothing for the pain. He presses far too firmly on each wound, grinning when I flinch. I have no doubt the burns he "Healed" on my back are still mostly there and will leave behind nasty scars seeing as how they still hurt when I move.

Jack is young. He can't be more than fourteen. He's terrified and shaking every time he kneels before me, whispering apologies under his breath the entire time. His magic is weak and his basic knowledge of healing in general is lacking. He's only Healed me twice, but both times he barely stopped the bleeding. The gash on my right side still aches, and I'm pretty sure it might split open at any moment.

I don't find it comforting in the slightest that all four Healers are present when my guard shoves me into the throne room this time. At least that damn Dragkonian isn't present. I barely retain the shudder at the memory of his black fire and darkest magic from my last session. He twisted magic into its darkest element and created wounds that went beyond anything that could be Healed. Poor Polly wept the entire time, whispering apologies that she couldn't do more.

"I wonder how much my sister cares for you," Kato drawls as my guard shoves me down onto my knees before Kato's throne—*my* throne. "After all, you think she would've at least *tried* to get you back."

I clench my jaw and lift my chin defiantly. "She's not a fool."

Kato chuckles. "I suppose not. I will give that to my sister

—she's never been a fool—but I did expect a bit more bravery on her part."

Anger roils through me at his words. "She's far more courageous than you'll ever be," I snap.

Kato straightens in his seat and snarls, "Excuse me?"

"You are a coward."

This time Kato leaps from the throne and lunges toward me. He grabs my shirt and yanks me to my feet.

"I am no coward!"

"Then prove it," I say, my exhausted mind pulling together a plan. "Only a coward would be content to keep torturing me like you've been doing."

Kato releases me with a jerk. I barely contain my wince as pain laces through me.

"And how would you do it differently?"

"I wouldn't do it at all."

Kato huffs and shakes his head. "Of course not." He takes a step back and spreads his arms wide. "All hail the high and mighty Prince Ehren."

Several of the onlookers chuckle to themselves as Kato grins.

"If I were to ever do anything remotely close to this, I'd give my captive a weapon."

Kato scoffs and arches an eyebrow. "A weapon? You really expect me to arm you? Now who's a fool?"

Another round of laughter echoes through the room. Kato crosses his arms and eyes me as if he's trying to figure out my plan.

"You have men stationed every few feet. Even if I managed to best you after hours of torture and no sleep, how far could I get?" I shrug, my shoulders aching with the motion. "Of course, if you're afraid—"

"I am *not* afraid," Kato roars. His gaze snaps from me to those standing around. "Get him a sword."

The silence in the room is thick as most of the occupants blink at Kato, trying to process his demand. Kato's nostrils flare at the lack of response.

"Get him a sword!"

The trance breaks as everyone scrambles about. A soldier stumbles forward and offers his sword. I accept it, weighing it in my hand. It's heavier than mine and is a bit awkward, but I've worked with worse. Of course in those previous circumstances I hadn't been undergoing hours of torture and wasn't fighting with no sleep. I'm determined to make it work. I have to.

"Are you satisfied with your weapon?" Kato asks.

I turn the sword over in my hand and grin at Kato. "Satisfied enough."

"Good."

Kato holds his hands out to the sides and a flame sword appears in each. We take our positions and Kato launches forward first. I dodge his first blow and block the second that follows immediately after. I duck under two back-to-back swipes and make a strike of my own.

He's fast and has two swords, so I have to stay focused, which is easier said than done seeing as how I'm exhausted and every movement has my body screaming in protest. I'm doing more dodging than striking, but that works in my favor because it allows me freedom to move as needed without arousing suspicion. After only a few steps, I've manipulated my position so there's fewer people between me and the door. If I can keep Kato distracted enough, I might be able to get even closer and make a run for it. I don't need to go far. Down the hall to the right behind a tapestry hides one of the many secret pathways the servants use to navigate the palace unseen. Since I was a bit mischievous as a child, I know the pathways well enough that if I can get to the door, I can hopefully escape the palace. I can save myself so no one has to risk their life to rescue me.

I'm nearly into the position I need when Kato wisps behind me. I stumble back and only barely manage to block his strike before the sword in his other hand heads my way. I pivot, ducking to avoid the blow, but lose my footing. My ankle twists under my weight and a sharp pain shoots up my leg. I topple to the ground face first, my sword skirting across the floor. Several of the spectators cheer. Kato hovers over me as I flip over and reach my right hand out to grab my sword. My fingers stretch, brushing the hilt, when Kato's fire sword crashes down.

The next few moments slow as my brain struggles to process what happens. Kato's fire is between me and the sword, the fire blade passing through my wrist. I jerk my arm back, but my hand stays behind, entirely severed. I can only blink in shock as I lift my eyes to Kato. His gaze is locked on the damage he's done, eyes wide in what looks like shock. His attention darts to me and I'm startled by what I see. The inky blackness that was prevalent in his eyes before is gone, replaced by the same bright amethyst I've seen in Astra's eyes. His expression is panicked as he stumbles back a step, clearly horrified by what's happened.

I'm still processing what his reaction could mean when reality seeps back in and time catches up. Pain radiates from my wrist and a scream escapes my throat. I clutch my wrist to my chest, curling into a fetal position on the floor. My ears ring and the world around me feels fuzzy and out of focus, but I still catch the panic in the room.

"Healer! Get over here now!" Kato yells.

Hurried footsteps rush my way and someone takes my wounded arm in their hand. I force my eyes open and look up into the terrified eyes of Tabitha. She licks her lips and glances from my wound to my hand. My hand, that is no longer attached. When she picks up the discarded appendage, bile rises in my throat and I can't keep it down. What little I had in my stomach comes up covering Tabitha and I both.

Tabitha isn't put off by my sick, however, and whispers something, her warm magic caressing my wrist. Whatever she does doesn't reattach my hand, but it does something to the wound that makes the pain a little less overwhelming. I can still feel darkness edging in. I close my eyes, fighting to hold onto consciousness. Gods know what Kato might do if I pass out.

"Heal him!" Kato roars.

"This magic is beyond me," Tabitha says, her voice trembling. "I can—"

She doesn't even get a change to finish before Kato sweeps forward. I hear a sizzling sound followed by a wet thud as gasps mingled with screams echo around the room. I crack my eyes open again to find Tabitha's decapitated body inches from my own. A mangled cry escapes my lips as I struggle to scoot away, eager to put distance between her body and mine.

"You!" Kato yells, pointing to someone else along the edges of the room. "Heal him."

The world jerks out of focus lend I struggle to breathe. I squeeze my eyes shut, my head pounding. Someone else takes my wrist and more magic washes over me. This time the pain lessens significantly. I open my eyes and look up at a terrified Dax. His magic is strong, much stronger than he'd been letting on. He holds up my hand and presses it against my wrist, muttering under his breath. His magic is warm, almost refreshing, but when the glowing stops, my hand still isn't attached.

Dax swallows hard and looks up at Kato, shaking his head. "Magic cannot heal this. It's too severe." His voice is steady but thick with fear.

Kato snarls and swings his sword. Dax doesn't even have time to react before his body joins Tabitha's. I'm still staring in horror at their bodies, blood pooling around them, when Kato motions to the next person along the wall, ushering them forward. I glance over and see Jack walking toward me, his eyes wide and filled with tears, his entire body shaking.

"Stop!" I croak, my voice hoarse. It takes every bit of energy I have to push up into a semblance of a sitting poison. "Stop."

Kato turns his sharp gaze to me, flames flickering in his eyes.

"You don't want to be healed?"

I shake my head. "If they couldn't heal me"—I nod toward the bodies but don't look directly at them—"I doubt there's anything that can be done."

Poor Jack glances desperately between me and Kato, his hands clutched in front of him as tears spill down his cheeks. Kato growls and shifts his swords into a huge ball of fire and throws it at the far wall. People scream and dive out of its path, barely avoiding decimation before it disappears into the stone, leaving behind curling black scorch marks.

"Fine. You don't want to be healed? Then fine. So be it." Kato turns and storms back up to his throne. "Get him out of my sight."

No one moves. I doubt anyone is even breathing. Kato's head snaps up.

"GET HIM OUT OF MY SIGHT!"

Suddenly everyone is moving at once. I'm yanked up from

the ground, someone on either side pulling me from the room. I'm dizzy and unable to stand on my own so they drag me through the halls. When the door to my prison room opens, I'm thrown in mercilessly into a heap on the floor, the door slamming behind me a second later.

"What happened?" Caitlyn asks, rushing to my side.

I wince and raise my head, lifting my hand, or the lack thereof. Caitlyn gasps, her hand flying to her mouth.

"Oh, sweet gods! Ehren, what did he do to you?"

"It was my fault." In the quiet of the room I notice my voice is hoarse, probably from screaming.

She shakes her head. "No, he's an evil bastard. Here, let's get you into the bed."

Caitlyn loops her arms around my waist and helps me to my feet. I collapse against her and she stumbles, forced to bear the brunt of my weight. I'm afraid she might drop me, but while she's slight, she's determined. We make it to the bed and I fall back against the wall, my legs stretched out in front of me.

"What happened?" she asks, pouring water from a pitcher and handing it to me.

I gulp down the water and try my best to describe my plan and how it went terribly wrong. I'm getting to the part where he killed Dax when we're interrupted by voices outside. The door opens slowly and Polly steps inside as the door slams shut.

I shake my head violently. "No, please tell me Kato didn't send you."

Polly smiles softly and shakes her head. "No, he doesn't know I'm here."

I sigh and relax against the wall as she makes her way across the room.

"I thought maybe I could help a bit, even if I couldn't heal you completely." She holds up a small jar of some sort. "May I put some of this on your . . ." She pauses, struggling to find the word.

I save her the trouble. "Yes, that's fine."

She nods in reply and removes the lid, a harsh aroma filling the air. Caitlyn gags and moves away.

"I know it doesn't smell the best," Polly says as she lifts my wrist, covering the wounded area in a thick, yellow salve. "But it will work to heal the flesh to reduce scarring as much as possible while helping to keep the pain manageable."

Even as she speaks I can already feel the positive effects. The pain that was once there is becoming a numb reminder. She seals the salve on my skin with a bit of magic and steps back, placing the lid back on the jar and handing it to Caitlyn.

"Have him put more on when that wears off in a couple hours," she says and Caitlyn nods. Polly turns back to me, pulling a small vial from her pocket and removing a cork. "This is a bit of medicine to be taken orally." She offers it to me and I accept it, eyeing it carefully. "It's bitter and will make you sleepy, but it will help heal you all the faster."

I look up from the vial and meet Polly's eyes. "What happens if I'm asleep when Kato sends for me again?"

Polly shakes her head. "He won't. After they removed you, Kato declared he was done and sent everyone to their rooms."

"You're sure?"

Polly nods. "Very sure."

I take a deep breath and down the medicine. It's extremely bitter and makes me gag.

"I'll come back in the morning and check on you," Polly says, already making her way toward the door. "Until then, just rest."

She offers me a weak smile before the door opens and she's ushered away. Once she's gone I have Caitlyn help me into a supine position, the medicine already tugging on my consciousness.

"Rest," Caitlyn whispers, tucking a blanket around me.

I nod, my head heavy as I close my eyes. For the first time I think of what might have happened if Cal were here instead of me. I shudder at the thought. I can't stand the idea of Kato hurting Cal in any way. Though, it's more likely that Cal would've been in far more danger than me. In Kato's eyes he's expendable. To me he's so much more; Cal is my world. I'm happy to sacrifice everything for him, risk everything for him.

I want to get back to him. No, I *need* to get back to him. Though, I was already broken before. What will Cal think of me now? I'm no longer whole. I was barely together before and now . . .

"What if he can't love me anymore?"

I don't realize I've voiced my fears aloud until Caitlyn replies.

"Who?"

I blink my eyes open and stare up at Caitlyn as she hovers over me.

"Cal." My tongue feels thick and heavy.

"Oh now, love," Caitlyn whispers, brushing hair out of my eyes. "If he loved you before, I can't imagine this would change anything."

"But I'm nothing," I mutter, my words slurring under the influence of the medication. I squeeze my eyes shut. "He deserves so much better than me."

Caitlyn sighs. "When you really, truly love someone you stay, no matter what. It's why I'm here." She goes quiet for a moment and I think maybe she's done. When she speaks again, it's barely a whisper. "Perhaps I made a mistake sticking by Niall for so long." She clears her throat. "But no matter. Cal will still love you, the circumstances be damned, if he's a decent person."

"He's more than decent," I murmur, burying my face in my pillow. "Which is why he deserves so much better than me."

I want to tell her more about Cal, how he's the best human to ever exist. I want to let her know everything he means to me. But I can't quite get the words out, the medicine finally pulling me under. So I give in to its caress, falling into its pleasing warmth as visions of Cal dance in my head.

CHAPTER TWENTY-NINE

ALAK

I doubt Astra got a wink of sleep last night. I know I hardly got any. I spent hours combing through Ehren's books, jotting down spells. Cal joined me for a while. He's the one who discovered Ehren's Syphon Stone ring and the Luvgim stones at the bottom of Ehren's bag. Astra helped me fill them with spells and magic before handing them off to Cal along with a quick tutorial on how to use magic with the Luvgim.

We're all up and dressed before dawn is even a whisper on the horizon, the camp packed and gone in what feels like mere moments. Most of the soldiers moved out yesterday under Luc's guidance, but a few shifters stayed back so they could take our supplies. By the time soft colors of early morning paint the sky, we're ready to be on the road. Cal and I are taking nothing but our swords, Cal bearing Ehren's as well. The rest of our belongings, horses included, are heading north with the shifters.

"This will work," I whisper, pressing a reassuring kiss to Astra's cheek.

She sighs and looks past me to Cal. When she looks back to me she nods and forces a tight smile. "Yes, it will."

With one last parting kiss she turns and joins the caravan. They need to put as much distance between them and the palace as possible before they'll need to make camp and wait for us to join them. I turn and offer Cal a smile.

"Ready?"

He doesn't even attempt a smile as he nods, his hand absentmindedly reaching for the Luvgim looped around his neck on a thin leather strap. For the first couple hours we walk in silence, the sun rising higher and higher in the sky, but doing little to warm our way. I can tell Cal is frustrated with our slower pace, but without our horses we're limited. A little before midday, we break for lunch. When I offer Cal his portion of the food, he looks away.

"If Astra were here she'd make you eat something."

Cal stares off. "I can't eat. Not while Ehren is a prisoner."

"You have to eat something. You need your strength so you can fight." I hold out a piece of dried meat. "For Ehren."

Cal stares down at it. I think he's going to turn it away again, but he accepts it after a moment. He only eats about half of his portion, but it's better than nothing. It's not long before we're back on the road. Cal keeps his gaze fixed on the horizon, eager to get to Embervein. When the city finally appears in the distance, his shoulders visibly relax. We stop on a hill outside of the city.

"Are you ready?"

Cal nods. "Yes."

"And you remember the plan?"

"You'll create a distraction and draw Kato's attention while I find Ehren." His hand drifts to the Luvgim at his neck. "I'll do whatever I need to free him and, once I have him, we meet in the hedge maze in the eastern garden."

"Yes, but be careful. I don't think Astra or Ehren would ever forgive me if something happens to you. If things start to go wrong, head to the maze even if you don't have Ehren yet. We can regroup and come back with another plan."

Cal meets my eyes with a steely gaze. "If I don't get Ehren out, I'm not coming out either."

I swallow hard and nod. If it were Astra trapped in the castle, I'd feel the same. I turn my focus toward the castle and stretch out my magic. I'm not surprised to find it heavily warded. I release a bit of my Syphon magic and let it play along the edges of the ward, absorbing the tiniest bit of the magic. It stings as the magic transfers to me, but I don't pull back or slow down. After a moment the magic starts to settle alongside my own, and I realize it's not simply one ward or one spell but rather many woven together by several people. I can taste all their different magic. But the magic I'm absorbing isn't raw, usable magic. It's old and stale, so while I can draw it away and break down the ward, it's not magic I can use.

Once I've weakened a portion of the warding into a thin enough veil we can pass through, I extend my hand to Cal. He accepts without a word. I pull us into a wisp and we push through the weakened warding. The magic that remains crackles against our skin, but it doesn't burn or resist us so I consider it a win. We land in a familiar corridor outside the library. I know that breaking through the wards alerted someone to our presence even before I hear the guards.

"They know we're here," I whisper. "We need to be quick."

Cal nods and glances off down the path he's meant to take. He draws a deep breath and closes his eyes. The Luvgim glows and blue light sparks at his fingertips. After a moment, he vanishes thanks to a simple camouflage spell. I know it won't last long, but it will allow me to pull the attention away from the throne room and the area of the castle where Ehren is likely to be stashed so Cal can sneak in and find and rescue him.

It doesn't take long for our plan to work. Soldiers are already filling the area where I stand, drawn by the warning sent out by the wards. I pull on my own magic and create a shield, blocking their magical blows. Every so often I send out attack magic of my own, though it's never been my strong suit.

I'm soon well outnumbered by more than a dozen magic wielders, but they're not trying to take me down. They're attacking me, no doubt about that, but they seem to be holding back. It's only when I feel the tug of my magic draining I realize what they're doing. They want my magic weakened before they make a firm attack. This knowledge gnaws a pit in my stomach as I block a water-based attack.

"Where's your coward of a king?" I demand. "I have a message for him."

A few of the magic wielders exchange a look, one of them stepping forward.

"What's the message?" he asks.

I cross my arms. "I'm to deliver it to him and him alone."

One of the others steps forward and whispers something in the first man's ear. He nods and turns back to me.

"Who's the message from?"

I scoff. "Who else would the message be from? His sister. Of course it's a message from his sister."

The man nods and turns to someone else in the crowd and motions with his hand. The girl closes her eyes and takes a deep breath. I'm not sure what she's doing, but I can feel the crackle of her magic on the air. A moment later she opens her eyes and stares at me.

"He's coming."

The words are barely out of her mouth before the air nearby bursts into flames. I stumble back, the heat licking at my skin despite my shield. Kato appears, a snarl on his face as he takes me in.

"Well, well, well. The little traitor returns."

"I was never the traitor."

Kato laughs bitterly. "You only lied and pretended to be on my side for weeks before turning around and betraying me. If that's not a traitor, what is?"

"I never betrayed you because I was never on your side. Not after you turned your back on Astra."

"She turned her back on *me*," he snaps, taking a wide step forward so he's less than a foot away, his magic vibrating against my shield. "When she chose everyone else instead of staying by my side, she betrayed *me*. We could be on the same side, and we could both be building this kingdom together. You could be there with us. I would have let her keep you."

"But you would have made her turn her back on everyone else."

Kato waves his hand dismissively. "They don't matter."

"Your sister disagrees."

"Is that your message? Were you supposed to risk your life to let me know that nothing has changed?"

I laugh and shake my head. "My message is that you've underestimated your sister for the last time."

A blast of magic shakes the castle and Kato's eyes darken like thick smoke.

"How many people did you bring with you?"

I cock my head. "What makes you think you think I didn't come alone? Maybe you have a whole slew of traitors in this castle."

Kato snarls and lunges forward. He breaks through my shield with little effort, his fingers curling around my neck. His grip is heated and tight against my throat, but he's not actively burning my flesh or cutting off my air supply. Not yet.

"Is my sister here? Answer me honestly."

More magic shakes the castle and I wonder exactly what type of spells Astra taught Cal to use with the Luvgim.

"Wouldn't you like to know."

His grip tightens, his touch searing into my skin. I hiss in pain but manage not to struggle in his grip.

"I could kill you right here, right now," Kato says, his voice low. "I wouldn't even think twice about it. I already meant to kill you when I took out Bram. I have no qualms about finishing the job today."

Mentioning Bram was probably one of the worst things Kato could have done in the moment. Anger roils through me and I set my jaw, my eyes flashing.

"You can't kill me," I gasp.

Kato's grin is cruel as he says, "Oh, and why not?"

An even crueler grin curls on my lips as I allow my Syphon powers to reach out. My magic hisses as it wraps around his magic. It's dark—much darker than I remember—and rancid on my tongue. I latch on, twisting my magic with his and then I pull. His eyes go wide and he jerks back, but it's too late. I already have a hold. I pull more of his magic and he stumbles back, wincing.

"You forgot, didn't you?" I say, taking a step forward. "You forgot exactly what I can do."

He reaches for his magic but I cut him off, drawing a heavy dose of his fire magic. He gasps and drops to his knees. His magic is intense and I can't take much more without overwhelming myself. As a Syphon it's possible to absorb too much magic, having the same effect as using too much. I hold out my hand and release some of Kato's, a flame coming to life in my palm as easy as breathing. The others around us gasp and their eyes dart around nervously. I hold out my other hand and a twin flame appears.

"You really shouldn't mess with a Syphon."

I clap my hands together and unleash the full brunt of Kato's power, a flash of fire blasting out and crashing into the floor near Kato. The flames don't disappear however, and I take hold of them, twirling my fingers. The flames twist and spiral, surrounding Kato and locking him in a cage of his own fire. He stands and his lethal gaze meets mine. He reaches out and touches the flames around him, and they curl into his palm until they're all dissolved.

"You can't defeat me with my own power."

"No?"

Kato snarls. "No."

I barely manage to dodge the fireball he throws my way, but thankfully I'm quick on my feet. I reach out with more Syphon magic but this time I don't go after him. Instead I taste the magic of those watching. *Telepathy. Smoke. Telekineses. Shielding. Metal Manipulation. Water. Attack. Speed. Air. Attack. Fire. Glass Creation and Manipulation. Poison Creation. Shadows. Plague.* Normally Syphons can only feel out the magic and need to physically touch their victims to draw away their power, but my bond and connection with Astra has strengthened my power immensely. Even though she's not here, the bond is enough to affect my magic.

I draw a little from each bystander and twist their magic together with mine, crafting a new magic. It rises before me as a beast, an illusion that has footing in the real world. The elements flicker together as the creature fills the space. It towers above us, its head scraping the ceiling. Swirling shadows, air, water, and other magics compose the body, but it has eyes made of fire and claws made of glass.

I raise my hand in a silent command and the beast attacks, magic spilling forward, twisting around my attackers. They scream as their flesh burns, as boils scatter across their skin, as magic scrapes against their cores leaving them raw. Kato seems less affected, a shield of smoke protecting his body from the worst of it, but even he stumbles back before vanishing.

Once he blinks away, I know my time is limited. He's going to check on Ehren, to see who else came with me. It's time to go. I call back my beast and wisp away, appearing in the center of the maze. I collapse, leaning against the hedges, feeling drained. My own magic is fine at its core, but the sudden absence of all the borrowed magic leaves me shaking like I'm going through withdrawals. A soft whisper down the bond tells me Astra can feel the change. I send back what I hope is a reassuring rush of magic letting her know I'm okay for now.

Loud sounds echo from inside the castle and I press my shaking hands against my thighs. I wonder if I should head inside and try to find Ehren and Cal, but, no, that's not the plan. I push up from the ground, my heart racing. I reach out my magic and try to gauge my surroundings, the threats. Someone is in the maze. No, two people are in the maze. I ready my magic just in case they aren't the two people I'm waiting for. I hope they are, because I don't know how much longer I can wait.

CHAPTER THIRTY

EHREN

I wake groggy, my mind clouded and fuzzy to the point I have no sense of the time. Caitlyn tells me it's mid-morning and offers me some dry toast and tea. I manage a few bites before my stomach starts turning. It's all I can do not to look at my missing hand, but once I do, my appetite vanishes entirely.

Polly returns shortly after to check on my healing. There's nothing more she can do, but she offers me a little more of the medicine to help with the pain and covers my wound in fresh bandages. I take a smaller dose so I only pass out for about an hour, waking early enough to eat some lunch.

The room feels increasingly smaller and I pace back and forth across the small expanse of the room like a caged animal. Caitlyn watches me with concern, though she never says anything. I have to get out of here. I need a distraction. I'm trying to figure out how I can escape when the sound of running pounds down the hallway.

"Something's happening," I whisper, marching to the door and pressing my ear against it.

I can make out muffled commands but nothing distinct. I growl in frustration and spin around to face Caitlyn.

"I have to get out there." She starts to shake her head but I cut her off. "No, I *need* to get out there. If someone came back for me, I have to find them before anyone else gets hurt. I won't allow any lives to be lost in exchange for mine."

Caitlyn considers me for a moment before her shoulders drop in resignation. "All right. I have an idea, but you'll have to be ready to run."

I lick my lips and nod. "I can do that."

She takes a deep breath and screams. The sound is shrill and I wince as the sound fills the tiny room.

"Shut up in there!" a voice calls through the door.

"There are people in here! They're trying to take the prince!"

I shoot her an impressed look and she shrugs, a small smile playing on her lips. Keys jingle, unlocking the door with a click, and I prepare to run. As soon as the door cracks open, I slam my fist into the face of the guard. He stumbles back but he's not alone. Another guard races forward, sword drawn, but I'm ready for him. I kick hard and fast between his legs. When he gasps and bends over, I snatch the sword from his hand. The first guard recovers and comes at me but I fight him off with the stolen sword.

Thank the gods my dominant hand is fine and my injuries have healed enough that that I can fight without being in too much pain. After a few well-placed blows, I manage to strike his leg. He screams as the blood gushes out. I quickly spring past him into the open hall. Without hesitation, I race away, my injuries singing, but I force myself to focus on my escape rather than my pain, saying a quick prayer that they don't punish Caitlyn too harshly for the part she played.

I stagger down the hall, my head swimming as I struggle to gather my bearings. A blast of magic rattles the walls, making me feel a bit disoriented. This is my castle and I know it well. I can do this. I pause and take a deep breath, looking around again. It slowly registers where I am and I take off again. Another blast of magic echoes around me, closer this time, and I stumble forward, my right shoulder slamming into the wall with a hiss as pain lances up my side. I push away with a grimace and plow onward. As I round the corner, my heart leaps into my throat.

Cal at stands at the far end, spotting me at the same time I do him. Without hesitation, we both race toward one another, our bodies slamming together in an embrace when we meet. His fists clutch the folds of my shirt, holding me tightly against his chest.

"Gods," he breathes in my ear, "I thought . . . I thought . . ."

"I know," I whisper, brushing my lips across his cheek. "I'm alive."

Cal swallows and steps back a half step as he releases me. My eyes fill with tears as they meet his. I brush away one of his tears as it breaks free.

"Hey, I'm okay." I hear shouting nearby and quickly add, "We should probably get moving, though. What's the plan? We do have a plan, right?"

Cal nods, licking his lips. "We're supposed to meet Alak in the hedge garden. He—"

Cal breaks off suddenly and I realize a moment too late why. He's reaching to grab my hand, but not my left. The hand he means to grab is gone. He inhales sharply and staggers back a step, his eyes widening in horror, his breathing erratic.

"Ehren," he whispers, his voice barely audible. He shakes his head as pain tumbles across his features. "What did he do?"

I force a smile and raise my right arm, fighting every instinct I have to keep from cringing. "Oh, this? It's nothing."

Cal lets out a small sob as he closes the distance between us to pull me against him.

"It's okay. It doesn't really hurt much anymore," I mumble, though I know Cal can hear my own self-torment in my words. "I guess it's a good thing I'm left handed."

When Cal draws away, murderous fury replaces his previous sorrow. "I'll kill him for hurting you."

"One day. Soon, I'm sure, but right now, we really need to get out of here before you're caught."

Cal still seethes but he nods, glancing around. He reaches toward his throat and I notice the glowing Luvgim for the first time. He whispers something before looking back to me.

"We should be invisible, or at least camouflaged for about ten minutes, but we need to move quickly."

Cal grabs my remaining hand and pulls me through the corridors. Each twist and turn drives a new dagger of fear into my gut. Now that the rush from my initial escape is waning, I'm acutely aware of all my injuries, my body weak from the trauma I've endured over the past day. I have no idea how well I can hold up in another fight. I barely survived the last one. When we finally dash into the garden and enter the hedge maze, I nearly sigh with relief.

Alak stands in the center, his sword raised and magic twirling at his fingertips. When he registers that it's only us, his shoulders loosen as he lowers his sword.

"We need to go," he says, extending his hand, but he stills when he notices my injury. His eyes flick up to meet mine, and I shake my head, begging him not to call attention to it as I drop Cal's hand and place my good hand in his. Alak swallows, his jaw tense as he extends his other hand to Cal.

No sooner has Cal gripped Alak's hand than we're jerked away from the garden, spinning into the in-between. When we land, a forest folds around us, Astra and Kai appearing in front of us. I purposely shift so my missing hand is less obvious and half-hidden behind my back.

"Thank the gods," Astra whispers, rushing forward to pull me into her arms. A small sob escapes as she buries her face in my chest. "I thought you might be dead."

I rest my chin on her head. "I'm harder to kill than that."

"We shouldn't stay here long," Kai cuts in, glancing around as Astra pulls back.

"Kai's right," Astra says. "We need to meet up with the rest of the camp. If everything went as planned they should have everything set up for our arrival."

"Are you wisping us there?" I ask.

Astra nods. "Kai sent his shifters along with Luc's army and he has a bit of a unique link to them that we can follow."

I throw Kai a curious glance but decide now is not the time to ask.

"Ready?" Astra asks.

We all nod and Cal grips my hand tightly as Astra's magic wraps around us. The forest fades and a bustling camp appears in its stead. A nearby solider blinks at us but recovers quickly, her shoulders straightening.

"Can you take us to Prince Luc?" Kai asks.

"Of course. This way," she says, directing us through the tents.

Cal tightens his grip on my hand. I squeeze his in return and he glances over his shoulder, a small smile on his lips. When we halt in front of a tall tent, Luc steps out.

"You made it back." He smiles, but it's tired. He glances to me and I'm grateful he doesn't look down and notice my hand.

I can't take any more pity right now. "Your tent is set up for you in the eastern corner of the camp so you can rest. A Healer will be there shortly if you need her."

"I—"

"Yes," Cal cuts me off sharply, his hand gripping mine so tightly it's almost painful. "Send a Healer."

Luc nods and forces a smile. "Right away." He turns to Astra. "Perhaps we could talk a moment while the prince is with his Healer?"

Astra nods before looking up at me. "I'll check on you in a bit."

I barely manage an agreeing nod before Cal tuns on his heel, pulling me between tents and campfires until we reach the tent marked with my crest. Once the tent flap closes behind us, he releases me before collapsing to his knees, hands covering his face as his body shakes with sobs.

"I failed you. Gods, I failed you."

My heart shatters as I kneel down in front of Cal, grabbing one of his hands.

"Hey," I whisper as I pull the hand away from his face. "You didn't fail me."

"But I did," he chokes, refusing to meet my eyes. "I allowed you to be taken and now—" A sob cuts him short as he glances down to where my hand should be. "It should have been me."

"I'm glad it wasn't you. I happily took your place."

Cal's eyes jerk to mine. "No. You're the prince—*my* prince —and I swore I'd always stay by your side, that I'd protect you, but I fucking failed and now you're suffering."

My chest is tight as I wrap my arm around Cal to draw him close, but he resists, pulling away. I scowl in confusion, dark thoughts fluttering through my brain.

"Can you not . . . accept me like this?"

Cal's eyes meet mine, wide and full of far too many emotions to sort. "Ehren . . ."

I stumble to my feet, taking a step back. Cal gapes at me, not speaking. My heart pounds against my ribcage, my chest constricting, making it a struggle to breathe. Cal's lips part like he wants to speak but no words come out. He almost looks relieved when the tent flap sweeps back and a Healer steps inside.

"Your Majesty," the Healer says inclining her head. "Prince Luc sent me. What injuries have you sustained?"

"His hand," Cal rushes, stepping forward with urgency. "Heal his hand."

"Cal," I say, my voice cracking as something akin to grief surges through me.

The Healer knits her eyebrows in confusion before glancing down to my hands. Her eyes fall first on my left, clenched at my side, and then widen as she takes in the missing appendage on my right. Her face holds a fresh brand of confusion and terror when she looks back up at me.

"I-I don't think . . . ," she stammers, wringing her hands.

"You *have* to," Cal demands, stepping forward, his voice laced with venom. "You must. It's your duty."

She glances back at me, everything about her apologetic. "I can try but . . ."

"It's okay," I whisper, not able to raise my voice any louder as I place my good hand on her shoulder. "I don't expect you to heal it."

She swallows and bows her head. "I'm sorry, Your Majesty." She lifts her eyes to me, keeping her head inclined, but I still see her pity. "Is there anything else I can assist with?"

I shake my head, forcing a weak smile. She nods and excuses herself, backing out of the tent.

"What did you do?" Cal yells, his hands in fists by his side. "Bring her back. Make her heal you."

"Cal."

"No. No, I won't accept this. I'll go get her. Or I'll find another Healer. A better one."

Cal tries to brush past me but I block his way.

"Move," he orders, refusing to meet my eyes.

"No."

"Ehren—"

"Cal," I start, but my voice cracks, lost to a sob. I can't do this anymore. I drop to my knees as tears break free. I expect Cal to leave, but instead he stands frozen to his spot. Then he eases to the ground slowly. He reaches toward me but pauses, his hand hanging in the air between us as if he can't decide what to do with it, as if he can't bring himself to touch me. I look at him through my tears and nothing but pain is on his face.

"I won't break if you touch me," I manage.

The words are barely out of my mouth before Cal's arms engulf me, pulling me into his lap. He buries his face in the crook of my neck, and I feel his own hot tears against my skin. Time stills as we clutch each other and weep.

After several minutes, I finally draw back enough to look into Cal's swollen eyes. "Can you still love me, even if I'm broken inside and out?"

Cal makes a sound somewhere between a laugh and sob, making a smile twitch at the corners of my own lips.

"Of course. I'll always love you, Ehren. This changes nothing. I only hate to see you suffer. I don't understand why you sent the Healer away."

I sigh, shifting so I'm more beside him than on him, and

rest my head on his shoulder. He moves with me, placing his arm behind me for support.

"Trained Healers already tried."

"What Healers? How?"

"Kato had Healers on standby, but the damage was permanent. Kato tried two Healers, actually, and a third came on her own. None could heal me. Two of them actually paid for their failure with their lives." I pause, looking up at Cal. "I saw fear in his eyes, Cal. True regret and horror at what he had done. I think—"

"No," Cal says firmly, shaking his head. "I see where you're going with this and no. I will not feel sympathy for the man who did this to you, the man who killed Bram and Makin."

My stomach twists and I fight the urge to vomit.

"I know. I didn't think I could either. Maybe I still can't. I don't know. I'm conflicted. But the old Kato is still in there, fighting." Cal grits his teeth and looks away as I continue. "We rescued Saran because he was trapped and being used. It may be a similar situation with Kato."

Cal jerks away, standing with his back to me.

"It's not the same. Kato chose to surrender to the dark."

"It may not be that simple," I insist, my voice soft as I look up at him.

Cal shakes his head and when he turns to look down at me, tears of fury fill his eyes. "No, I won't, Ehren. You *cannot* ask me to forgive him, to save him. He took—" Cal's voice breaks and it takes a moment for him to compose himself enough to continue. "He took Makin." Cal drops back down, reaching a hand out to caress my cheek. "He hurt you." I turn my head to kiss the palm of his hand. "I can't forgive him."

"Come here," I mutter, reaching out my good arm. Cal practically crashes into my embrace.

"I'll never ask you to forgive him," I whisper before pressing a kiss to Cal's cheek. "Never. I do ask that you consider helping save him if we can find a way." Cal tries to pull away again, but I manage to hold him firm. "He'll suffer consequences for his actions; I swear it. But he's Astra's brother, and he was once our friend."

When Cal tries to pull from my grasp again, he succeeds.

"So, you choose Astra over me?"

My eyes widen as I shake my head. "No. Cal, no. That's not —I didn't mean . . ."

Cal swallows and stands, striding toward the exit. I try to push up and follow him, but I momentarily forget about my missing hand and I fall forward instead, crashing to the ground. I hiss in pain as my other injuries hit the ground. I struggle to find my balance, but Cal is helping me up before I have a chance to work out how to right myself. Once I'm standing, Cal meets my eyes, his gaze hard. I manage a smile and reach my hand to touch his face but he steps back, away from my reach, shaking his head.

"I—I think I need a moment."

He's gone before I can protest. I blink at the space where he stood moments before, my heart aching with fresh pain. I struggle to breathe. I clench my eyes shut and place my fist over my heart. This pain is far worse than any I experienced under torture. I can't take it.

I don't know how long I stand there, shattered and hurting before Astra finds me. She rushes into the tent and freezes. I open my eyes and meet hers.

"What's wrong?" she asks, her voice soft.

Unable to say the words, I simply lift my wrist. Her eyes move slowly to my missing hand before going right back to my eyes. The horror on her face breaks me even more.

"Ash," I whisper, my voice hoarse and trembling.

"Ehren," she sobs, rushing to throw her arms around me. "I'm so sorry."

I lean my head down and press a kiss to the crown of her head before resting my chin there.

"It's not your fault."

She doesn't argue, but she doesn't concede either. She only pushes closer, her hands gripping my shirt as tightly as possible. After a moment, she pulls back and glances around, frowning.

"Wait. Where's Cal?" She looks up at me and what little resolve I had gained at seeing her falls away. She takes note and asks again with more force, "Ehren, where is Cal?"

"He left."

She shakes her head stepping back. "No, that's not . . . no."

"He's gone, Ash," I say, my voice cracking as fresh tears break free. "He can't handle everything."

"No, you didn't see him when you were taken. He was nearly rabid with fear and fury. There's no way he would just leave you. Not now. Not like this."

I look away.

"What aren't you telling me?"

"Kato's still in there." I look at Astra as her mouth drops open. "*Your* Kato. The Kato I met in Timberborn. The one who joined my Guard."

Astra takes a shaky breath, lifting a trembling hand to her mouth. "What?"

I nod and finally manage a tight smile. "He's still in there. He doesn't have much control, but I could see him fighting to get out."

"What does that mean?" Her voice is barely a whisper. "Can I—can we save him?"

My smile grows and it's almost sincere, almost believable. "I think maybe we can."

A sob escapes her lips as she blinks away tears, happy tears for a change. She meets my gaze, her eyes shining with hope.

"You really think we can save him?"

I reach out and gently wipe a tear from her cheek. "Yes."

She shakes her head in disbelief, a laugh bubbling out. I try to smile. I try to be happy for her, but Cal's face flashes in my head. Astra watches me a moment before her eyes widen with realization.

"You told Cal."

I nod and look away.

"And he didn't take it well."

"No, he didn't take it well at all." Astra places a hand on my arm and I look back into her eyes. "But it's not going to stop me from trying to save Kato if we can."

Astra studies me for a moment. I can see the thoughts spinning in her head as her eyes go out of focus, staring off at nothing. Her lips move as if she's speaking, but no words come out. Clarity dawns as she drags her eyes back to mine.

"Ash, what is it?"

"You shouldn't have to suffer because of me. Kato has done enough. I've done enough."

I frown, trying to make sense of her words. She takes a step back.

"I'm sorry, Ehren." She forces a smile that doesn't go to her eyes. "Don't worry. I'll fix this." She glances off, her gaze unfocused. "I think I need to go to the source."

I realize a moment too late what's happening. I reach out to grab her, but my hand finds nothing but air.

"No. No. No."

I plunge from the tent, screaming Alak's name. Several

others turn wary eyes my direction as I race through the camp, eyes darting around wildly in search of Alak. When Alak finally rounds a tent, he looks dazed and confused.

"Where did she go?" he asks, stumbling toward me.

"I think she went to confront Kato."

"No. No, she wouldn't do that without me." Alak shakes his head vehemently, but his voice is weak and unsure. "She wouldn't leave me behind. We're stronger together."

"Are you sure?"

When Alak lifts his eyes to mine, I can tell he's not sure in the slightest.

"What happened? Why did she leave? Is it because of your hand?"

I absentmindedly grab my right wrist, and Alak winces, glancing away a little guiltily.

"I spoke with the Healer," he mutters. "She mentioned she wasn't able to heal it."

I manage a nod. "That's fine. It's not like I can keep it a secret. But yes. It was linked to her disappearance at least a little. I might have mentioned that the way Kato reacted when I lost my hand makes me think he isn't completely gone and might be able to be saved."

"What?"

"And when she found out Cal left me beca—"

"Cal left you?"

I bite my lip and nod as fresh pain washes over me. "He and I had a disagreement and he stormed away."

"Because of Kato? Because you want to save him?"

I nod.

"Shite."

"I know."

Alak rakes his hand through his hair as he turns, looking

around the camp. "What do we do? Do I go after her? Do I wait here for her?"

My shoulders sag. "I have no idea."

Alak sighs and turns his head toward me. "She gave no indication of her plan?"

"She said something about going back to the source, but that's it."

Alak sighs again, closing his eyes for a moment.

"I have a bad feeling about this, but Astra wouldn't confront Kato on her own. Not after we just got back from rescuing you. Not after everything we've risked to get to this point."

Alak turns away, his hands on his hips as he surveys the camp. "I'll pass word on to Luc and the others to be on alert. There have been more attacks, so we can't stay here. We're needed back at the Summer Palace."

All the blood rushes from my face. "More attacks?"

Alak nods grimly. "Luc received word while we were rescuing you. He spoke to Astra, and I heard the details second-hand. Oxwatch and several other villages were attacked at the same time, the refugee camp as well. It's likely gone with no survivors. I'm sure Luc can give you more details once you've had a chance to rest and recover a bit."

I nod numbly, my mind already swirling with my failure, with all the ways my kingdom is falling apart.

"If Astra knew the plan, stick to it," I say. "I'm sure if she needs it changed, she'll let us know."

Alak turns to me and offers me a sloppy half smile. "Maybe you're right. You should really go back to your tent and rest."

"No," I object, scowling. "I'm the prince. Technically, I'm the king. I'm not going to sit on the sidelines and wait while more people die in attacks. I need to meet with Luc and—"

"Ehren," Alak says, his voice quiet but firm. "You were literally rescued less than an hour ago from what I assume was hours of torture. You're missing a hand for gods' sake." I flinch and he sighs. "Please, rest a little. I'll send food your way. As soon as we have a solid plan or an answer, I'll come get you. I swear it."

I open my mouth to argue, but exhaustion is already taking over. I drop my shoulders and nod.

"Fine. I'll be in my tent."

Before I can talk myself out of it, I turn and stride back to my tent. It feels so empty. I settle onto the makeshift bed and let my tears break free. I grasp the blankets in my fist as I bury my face in the pillow and sob so hard my muscles ache. At some point I fall asleep, but my dreams offer no comfort, only more pain.

CHAPTER THIRTY-ONE

ASTRA

Leaving Ehren may have been a decision made in the heat of the moment, but part of me knows I would always end up back home. Timberborn is a ghost of itself, a mere shadow of the town I grew up in. It's not abandoned—I can see evidence of life scattered around—but it might as well be. My feet are heavy as I walk the familiar path through the village square, taking in the broken and crumbling buildings. I wonder how much of the damage is from the earthquake the night of my birthday and how much is from the disasters brought on by Kato and Ehren's father.

I pause momentarily outside Mara's house. I have so many good memories from inside those walls. I walk up to the door and consider knocking. I want to know if Mara's parents are okay, if they know how amazing their daughter is. I wonder if they know the difference she's made in the lives of many. In the end, I walk away. They're not why I'm here. Perhaps I can visit them another day when I have more good news than bad to share.

My footsteps slow as I approach my destination. The curtain of my childhood home is drawn across the doorway with all the windows closed off as well, but I can hear movement inside. I take a rallying breath and knock on the doorframe before pushing the curtain aside. It takes my eyes a moment to adjust to the dimness inside, but when they do I find three pairs of eyes blinking back at me in disbelief.

"Astra?" my mother whispers, clutching a hand to heart.

I manage a small smile as I turn my attention to Rick and Tabitha who sit by the flickering fire, eyes wide.

"Where's Beka?"

My mother's jaw tightens. "She isn't here."

"She left to join the resistance," Tabitha pipes up, earning a glare from my mother.

"The resistance?"

Tabitha nods. "She has earth magic, and after Kato sent people to attack us and steal all the magic away—"

"We don't know that Kato sent anybody," my mother cuts her short.

"Yes, we do," Rick says. "He came to destroy us." He eyes me, his expression cold. "Is that why you're here? To take us away? To force us to join *your* army?"

I offer my siblings a weak smile. "No."

Tabitha's eyes brighten. "Are you back to stay?"

My smile fades as I shake my head. "I only came back to get something I need."

Tabitha's face falls. "Oh. It's lonely with everyone disappearing."

My mother clears her throat. "Are you at least staying for dinner?"

"I suppose, if it's allowed."

My mother's hesitation combined with the warring emotions crossing her face answer all my unasked questions.

"I won't be long, and then I'll be out of your way."

"Stay," my mother says quickly. She straightens, holding her chin up. "Stay for dinner."

It's a small moment, but it's enough for me. At least, it's enough for now. "Thank you."

I turn and look at the ladder leading up to the loft. I promise Tabitha and Rick I'll be back in a moment to catch up with them, and I head up into the loft. I freeze at the top of the ladder as my eyes adjust to the heavy shadows. It hasn't changed at all in the months I've been gone. My cot still sits against the far wall with Kato's in the corner.

For a moment I allow myself to pretend that the world isn't falling apart. I pretend that I'm just getting home from a day in the library archives. Kato will be home any minute from a day of training smelling like sweat and dirt. There's a good chance Pax will come with him and they'll be laughing and joking around. They'll pull me into their jokes, and we'll sneak off after dinner to meet up with Mara. Who knows what mischief we'll get up to?

I sigh and blink away the memories and longing, climbing the rest of the way into the loft. I cross the distance to Kato's cot and kneel next to it. I take a deep breath, holding it while I say a quick prayer to the gods. I slip my hand under the cot and slide it around until my fingers make contact with something soft and firm. I let out the breath and close my eyes in relief as I grasp the item and pull it out.

For our eleventh birthday Mara gave us each a journal. Kato's was black leather and he used a small dagger to carve his name on the cover. I allow my fingers to trace over his childish script, the memory as fresh today as it was seven years ago. I shake my head and shove the journal in my dress pocket and head back down the ladder. Now is not the time for reminiscing.

I spend the time until dinner with Rick and Tabitha by the fire. They fill me in on everything that has happened, my mother huffing in frustration from the kitchen in regular intervals. Once we've eaten, my mother convinces them to head to the loft, though, judging by the quiet whispers and muffled giggles, they don't go to sleep for a while. I smile softly to myself, remembering nights like this well, only the whispers and giggles were between me and Kato. My mother busies herself cleaning the kitchen, and when she finally takes a seat next to me, she won't make eye contact.

"Why are you here, Astra?"

"Surprised to see the daughter you rejected and disowned?"

She sighs and stares into the fire. "I never wanted to disown you. That was all your father."

"And where is he now?"

My mother finally looks at me, her face expressionless. "He's dead."

I start and blink at her. "Dead? How? When?"

She shifts her gaze back to the fireplace. "He was killed while traveling a couple months ago when his inn mysteriously caught fire in the middle of the night."

"Fire?"

"Yes. It was quite strange. I can't imagine why a random fire would consume an inn. The strangest part seems to be that it was mostly contained to his room."

She gives me a pointed look that says she clearly thinks Kato was involved. Honestly, I'm inclined to agree. For several minutes, only the crackling of the fire fills the silence that falls between us.

"You came for Kato's journal, didn't you?"

I turn toward my mother. "You know about his journal?"

She laughs humorlessly. "Very little about you children escaped my notice. I know you and Kato snuck out onto the roof on a regular basis. I know about the times you snuck off to Pax or Mara's houses, sneaking back into your rooms before the sun rose. I know that you taught Kato to read and write more than was needed for a soldier and, in exchange, he taught you how to use weapons. So, yes, I also know about the journal."

I pull it from my pocket and let it sit in my lap. "Have you read it?"

She shrugs. "I glanced through it. I hoped to maybe find where I went wrong, though I suppose things were never right."

"What do you mean?"

She sighs, finally meeting my eyes. "I never wanted to have children, let alone twins." Her words sting for multiple reasons, but I force myself not to react as she continues. "When I was forced to marry your father I did everything I could to keep myself from getting pregnant. For a couple years I was successful. Maybe it was Fate working her cruel magic and I couldn't have avoided it, but whatever the reason, you and your brother came along.

"I thought maybe I would adjust, but honestly raising twins took its toll. As much as I wished otherwise, I resented you. Of course there were moments along the way where it wasn't so bad, and by the time Beka came along I had accepted my lot. But those early years were hard for me. Thankfully you and Kato had each other, so I didn't feel like you missed out on much by having me as a mother."

The kind part of my mind wants to comfort my mother, tell her it was all okay, but another part of my mind wants to tell her she was all the failure she thinks she was. Before I can decide which path I wish to take, the curtain in the doorway is thrown aside and a rush of winter air sweeps inside, causing the flames in the fireplace to flicker. I call forth my magic as I stand and face the door where a cloaked figure looms.

"Who are you and what are you doing here?" I demand, lethal magic dancing at my fingertips.

The figure raises their head and lowers their hood as they step further into the room, the curtain falling closed behind him. It's an older man with already graying hair and a face lined with wrinkles. A pair of twinkling gray eyes meet my own as the stranger smiles.

"Astra Downs, I have been searching for you. I should have known you would return to your roots. After all, it's at the roots we often begin our strongest growth," the man says gently with a thick Athiedor accent.

"Who are you?" I demand again, not lowering my magic.

"Ah, yes. How rude of me. My name is Gavin Thornburrow, and I simply wish to speak with you. I believe you can help me find my grandson."

I shake my head, pulling in my magic so it's no longer visible but still readily accessible.

"Your grandson?"

The man nods. "Indeed."

"How did you know I was even here?"

He motions toward the fire. "Perhaps I could come in? Tell my tale? I swear to the gods I mean no harm. If you don't like my explanation, feel free to toss me back into the night, but my extremities are quite cold."

I glance to my mother who stands tense beside me. She looks to me and shrugs.

"This seems like your problem, not mine."

I sigh and nod. "Come on in. You can tell your story while you warm up. Do you need any food?"

My mother glares at me as the man nods.

"If you have any to spare."

Without a word my mother stomps away to gather up some of what remains from our dinner as the man eases to the ground with a groan. I take a seat next to him, putting enough distance between us that he can't easily reach out and touch me. I scoop up the journal from where it had fallen on the floor and tuck it back into my pocket as my mother passes the man the food.

"Thank you for your kindness, ma'am," he says softly, looking up at her. My mother nods curtly before the man continues. "Any chance that Mistress Astra and I could chat in private?"

She glances briefly to me, as if my opinion has ever mattered, before she heads into her room. Once she's gone the man turns to me.

"I suppose I should start at the beginning?"

"I honestly don't care where you start as long as it ends with you telling me why you're here and how you knew to come here."

The man chuckles. "Quite right. Well, to start with I'm a Seer."

My eyes widen and I relax a little. It would make sense for a Seer to know my location even though it's a little off-putting given I didn't know myself I would be here until I arrived. The man takes a bite of food before continuing.

"I always had the gift, even as a child."

"You had visions before magic returned?"

"Well," he says, pausing to take another bite. "I've never really had clear-cut visions. They're more inclinations and feelings, some clearer than others. Sometimes I know when I should arrive at a place with an exact purpose and other times it's more of a general feeling that something very good or very bad is about to happen. Sometimes the details are all in place and other times I only have a vague awareness that something is about to happen. Often times the visions, if that's what you want to call them, don't even make sense until the event is upon me or after it has passed."

"So that's how you knew I would be here? You had a feeling?"

"Aye. I had a feeling that if I were here tonight at the correct time that I'd be able to reach you."

"You've had this feeling before?"

He nods. "And yet my timing was off. One thing I know without doubt, that I've known for some time, is that you can reunite me with my grandson."

"Does your grandson want to be reunited with you?"

The man sighs and, for the first time since he walked through the door, he looks unsure of himself.

"I do not know," he confesses slowly. "The last time I saw my grandson he was a toddler."

"How old is he now?"

"Twelve."

"Why are you looking for a grandson you haven't seen in a decade?"

The man hesitates, searching for an explanation. He finally

settles on "Perhaps I should tell a bit more of my story and fill in the blanks."

"If you think it'll help."

"I think it might. As you can imagine, growing up a Seer in a time without magic was quite the experience. Most people I met either believed I was making everything up, that I was insane, or that I was simply lucky and good at guessing. Occasionally I would stumble across someone who saw my power for what it was—true and rare magic. My wife was one such person and I loved her dearly. She struggled to conceive but she finally gave birth to a daughter, and she was our world. Of course, growing up in my home, my daughter also knew that my magic was very real. Which is why she blamed me when her mother died."

A small gasp escapes my lips. "Surely you had nothing to do with it?"

He shakes his head, his eyes heavy with sadness. "I did not. It was an accident with a horse and cart that took her life, but my daughter, who was fourteen at the time, thought I should have been able to See and prevent it. She never truly forgave me and ran away a couple years later with a group of traveling merchants.

"As you can imagine, I began searching for my daughter. Thanks to my powers I came close to finding her many times, but she was always gone when I arrived." He chuckles. "Sometimes I think she had a little power of her own to avoid me so well. By the time I found her, many years had passed. She was married to a farmer in a small village in Southern Callenia and already had a young son. We managed to reconcile enough that she allowed me to stay. I saw that her husband was a good man and I enjoyed spending time with my grandson."

The man pauses, staring into the fire with a glazed expression, a smile playing on his lips.

"He was such a bright boy, even then. He laughed and played and had such an adventurous streak." He laughs. "He certainly knew how to keep us on our toes."

"What happened to him?" I ask, dread pooling in my stomach.

"Nothing. Well, not then. One thing led to another and I noticed that the boy seemed to be able to predict certain things. He picked up on patterns far faster than other children his age. One day he even caught a cup falling from a table, which wasn't a grand feat except that he started to reach for it before the cup had been knocked over."

My eyes widen. "He was a Seer."

"Aye, that he was. He shouldn't have had access to his magic so far from Athiedor soil, but for whatever reason he did. When I pointed it out to my daughter, she became furious. Told me I was mad and forbid me to fill her son's head with such nonsense. She forced me from her home and made me promise never to return."

He sighs, shaking his head. "My intent was to respect her wishes, and I left, never expecting to see my grandson again. I wandered around Callenia and Athiedor, doing what good I could with what little Seeing power I possessed. I like to think I saved a few lives and changed a good many more. When magic returned, my own power grew and was almost overwhelming. I was plagued with headaches as incomplete visions flashed through my head. Out of concern for my grandson, I returned to the village and found my daughter inconsolable."

He meets my eyes and I notice the tears glistening there. Sympathy surges through me.

"Was he . . . okay?"

"He was gone. My daughter told me that when magic returned, the boy went nearly mad. Her once lively and happy child could only weep and scream. Visions plagued his dreams to the point he couldn't sleep. He would claw at his head, crying out. At first, she said he rambled endlessly, shouting random things that didn't make sense until after they had happened. He couldn't control the visions. She said . . ."

His voice breaks and he takes a moment to compose himself before he continues.

"She said he tried to end his life a couple times and she only managed to stop him because of a sense that something bad was about to happen. Then one day, she noticed he was a little calmer. He stopped speaking altogether, though. He wouldn't say a word. He would disappear during the day and return home in the evenings. One day she followed him and discovered that he'd found a friend. When he was with her, he was calm, albeit stoic and reserved.

"A few days before I arrived, she woke up and found him missing. She searched frantically through the village and went to the home of the little girl. She discovered a note from her son tacked to the door, telling her that he had Seen the future. He, his friend, and her Healer grandmother needed to leave for their safety. He said that soldiers were coming and he had somewhere very important he needed to be. That he needed to help save one of the twins."

I still as the man looks over at me. Chills skirt over my skin and my breath catches in my chest, kept there by my rapidly beating heart.

"What is your grandson's name?"

The man offers me a sad smile. "He was named Philip after his father, but most people call him Pip."

For a moment it feels as if the world is tilting as everything tumbles into place. I shake my head in disbelief, staring at the man, my mouth gaping.

"Pip is your grandson?"

"Aye, he is. And he's a good boy. I take it you do know him after all?"

"I know him well. Him and Hanna, the little Healer girl. He helped save my life and the life of my friends. I— He—"

All words fail me as the man smiles.

"You know where he is now?"

"I do."

"Would you be willing to take me to him? I swear to you I only wish to help him."

I slowly manage a nod. "I can. I was planning on going back in the morning. If you like, you can wisp along with me."

The man's smile widens. "Thank you, Astra. You have no idea what this means to me." He stands, stretching. "I don't suppose you would mind if I borrowed some blankets to make a bed by the fire?"

I stand as well. "Of course not. Let me get you situated."

A few minutes later, the man has a makeshift bed made by the fire. I start to head upstairs to sleep on my cot one last time when I pause, a thought occurring to me. I turn back to the man, who's watching me, waiting for my question.

"Why is it Hanna is able to calm him when no one else could?"

The man's smile lights up his eyes. "You should understand better than most, I would think, why she can calm him. After all, you too have a bondmate."

I gasp. "They're bondmates?"

"Indeed. Though I suspect they have not completed the soul bond as you have, given they've been on the run, but I suspect their bond works well all the same."

I feel numb as I nod, words failing me for the second time tonight. I manage to mumble a quick goodnight before heading up into the loft. When I reach my cot I'm surprised to find Felixe curled up fast asleep, his head resting on a letter. I smile and slip the paper from under him, careful not to wake him. I glance over Alak's worried words. I carefully fold the letter and slip it in my pocket with the journal. Tomorrow is going to be an interesting day.

CHAPTER THIRTY-TWO

EHREN

I reach a hand that doesn't exist toward a body that isn't there. It takes a moment for the grogginess of sleep to clear from my mind enough for me to register that I didn't dream my rescue. I'm free from my prison, but I'm not home. Home is with Cal and he's not here.

I sit up with a groan, my muscles and wounds screaming at me in protest. A quick glance to the cool cot beside me indicates Cal never joined me at all. I shutter my eyes as fresh guilt and pain swarm me. My eyes snap open at the sounds of footsteps approaching the tent.

Cal ducks inside and I leap from the bed, stumbling into him and bringing us both tumbling to the ground. Cal chuckles and untangles himself from my wayward limbs so we can kneel on the ground, our knees touching as we face each other.

"I guess you've forgiven me?" he asks, fighting to keep eye contact.

"Forgive you? What is there to forgive?"

"I abandoned you," he whispers, looking down at the hands folded in his lap. "I couldn't stand it when you were gone, and I finally got you back only to storm out and leave you." His eyes flick to my wounded wrist, and he reaches tentative fingers to trace along the bandage. "You needed me and I wasn't here."

Cal finally meets my eyes and I lean in and kiss him gently. "You're here now, right?"

Cal swallows, nodding as he forces a smile. "I'm not going anywhere." His whole body tenses as he adds, "If you think Kato is worth saving, then I have to believe it too, but I'm not sure if I can actively participate in his redemption."

"I would never expect you to, Cal. I would never ask that. *Never.*"

Cal nods as his smile turns more genuine. "I love you, Ehren."

I lean forward and press a kiss to Cal's lips. "I love you, too. More than anything. It was the thought of you that kept me going when I was locked away."

Cal grabs my hand, intertwining our fingers.

"I nearly went mad with worry," he confesses. "I thought I might never see you alive again, and I couldn't handle it." His grip tightens. "I need you like I need air to breathe."

Tears fight to break free as I draw Cal into another kiss, this one soft and slow, but filled with a sweet urgency. He leans into the kiss, shifting so he's more beside me than in front of me. After a moment, I pull back, my eyes shining.

"I can't live without you either," I whisper, pressing my forehead against his. "That's why I couldn't let Kato take you."

"You traded yourself for me." His voice is so quiet I wouldn't have heard him if I wasn't so close.

I pull my hand from his to trace my fingers along his cheek. "Yes, and I'd do it again in a heartbeat."

Cal's lips crash against mine and I surrender to him, wrapping my arms around him, my hand on his neck, holding him close. When Cal shifts again and pulls me tighter against his chest, I wince. Cal jerks back, his eyes searching me.

"What's wrong?"

I force a smile. "Nothing."

"Ehren."

I sigh and stand, turning my back to him.

"My hand isn't my only injury."

"What?"

I glance at Cal over my shoulder as he blinks up at me.

"I—Kato had his fun."

Cal stands in one smooth motion, his eyes hard. "What did he do? Show me."

I swallow and consider Cal for a moment before I nod. "I may need your help. I need to take off my shirt and I haven't exactly had time to practice with one hand."

Pain flickers across Cal's face as he nods and closes the distance between us. I can't meet his eyes as he lifts my shirt over my head, a sharp gasp signaling the moment he sees the remnants of the gashes, burns, and bruises across my chest.

"Ehren, what did he do?"

His voice is filled with fresh agony. When I meet his tear-filled eyes, I immediately glance away. I can't handle the emotion there; I'll drown in it.

"I don't really want to talk about it."

"The Healer—"

"No, Cal."

"But, Ehren . . ."

His voice is pleading, begging, desperate. I force my eyes back to his as a tear slides down my cheek.

"These wounds are meant to last. Akaash helped to inflict

them and sealed them in a way that magic cannot heal. Trust me, a skilled Healer already did what she could."

Cal shakes his head, his jaw clenched. "How can you forgive Kato for this? How can you think he has something redeemable about him?"

A weak smile twitches on my lips. "Because, for a brief moment, I saw the regret and panic in his eyes." I trace my fingers down Cal's face and his eyes shutter closed as he leans into my touch. "He could have kept me from escaping, but, in the end, he left me with only two guards and someone he knew might help me escape. He could have left me to suffer more than he did, but he made sure I had Healers."

"Still . . ."

"I know. I know. If it comes down to it, and we have to kill him, I won't stop it."

Cal nods, staring deep into my eyes. "If he even attempts to harm you again, I'll kill him without hesitation." Cal glances away and takes a deep breath. "I'm sorry for what I said last night."

A smile twitches on my lips. "Which bit?"

Cal glances back to me, the corner of his mouth turning up slightly. "I said a few foolish things didn't I?"

"Nothing I can't forgive," I murmur, pressing a quick kiss to his lips. "Nothing you can't make up to me." I waggle my eyebrows and Cal laughs, kissing me in turn.

"I *will* make it up to you." He sighs as he draws away, rubbing the back of his neck. "I was referring to the part where I accused you of choosing Astra over me. I didn't mean it."

A shadow crosses my face as my heart aches at the memory. "Oh. That."

Concern shines in Cal's eyes. "I know you love her as much as you love me, though not in quite the same way. I would never ask you to choose between us, and I never expect you to." I manage a nod. "Maybe we should forget all this and go find some food?"

I press my hand to stomach as I grin, and my smile is nearly sincere. "Now that's an idea I support completely."

Cal breathes a sigh of relief. He helps me change into a new set of clothes before changing himself. He offers me my sword and assists me in attaching my sheath. I'm glad I have him because I can't imagine trying all of this with one hand, though I suppose I'll have to learn soon. Once we're ready to go, we head outside, Cal pulling back the flap as we step into the sunlight. I take Cal's hand and weave my fingers into his.

"You know," I say after a few moments of silence, "you never have to ask."

Cal frowns at me. "Ask what?"

"Ask me to choose between you and anyone else." I meet his eyes. "I will always choose you. Always."

Cal's lips part as he comes to a halt. His eyes scan my face with a sense of desperation. Then his lips find mine. The rest of the camp melts away. I don't care about my wounds. I don't even notice my missing hand. It's just me and Cal. When he pulls back, tears shine in his eyes as he smiles.

"I will always choose you, too. I always have and I don't imagine I could stop now."

I smile and bump my shoulder against his. "I expected as much."

Cal's rich laughter floods over me as he takes my hand again. We resume our journey to find food, both of us smiling like fools. Those smiles fade when we see the look of concern on Alak's face.

"She's still not back?" I ask.

Alak shakes his head as Cal looks between us.

"Astra's missing?" Cal asks and I nod as Cal frowns. "Where did she go?"

"I don't know," Alak replies with a heavy sigh. "Felixe took a letter to her last night but he hasn't returned. Bloody fox likes her better half the time."

"Have you tried following the bond?" I ask, guilt swirling in my stomach. It's my fault she's gone. It's my fault Alak is concerned.

"Not exactly, but there's this sort of block on it. I could push through it and go to her, but I get the very distinct feeling she doesn't want me there—wherever 'there' is."

My heart races as my thoughts spin, growing darker and darker by the second. "She could be in danger."

Alak nods grimly. "It's possible given the current state of things, but I think I'd sense it. I have before, and that was prior to our bond being completed. Kai's about two seconds away from sending out every shifter in his command to search the whole of the continent for her, though."

Cal angles his body toward me to study my face. "Why did she leave?"

I force myself to meet his eyes. "I don't know for sure. She said she wanted to fix everything."

"Fix everything—you mean me? Us?"

Panic swims in his eyes as he tightens his grip on my hand.

"That was part of it, but, Cal—"

He starts to jerk away, but I refuse to let his hand go.

"Cal, it was more than that." He keeps his gaze fixed away. "I told her I thought Kato could be saved and she left. I think she's trying to find a solution."

"How sure are you he can be saved?" Alak asks.

"I don't know, but I caught glimpses of the old Kato when he . . ."

I let my voice trail off, and Alak glances down to my hand. Even Cal's eyes drift down, his jaw clenching.

"Ah, I see." Alak clears his throat and straightens.

"I know what I saw. I don't know how to reach that part of Kato without one of us going through more life-altering trauma, but my guess is that's why Astra left. She's trying to find an answer, a way to stop all this with less bloodshed."

"I guess all we can do is continue with the plan and hope she shows up," Alak says with a sigh.

"What is the plan?"

"We go back to the Summer Palace," Cal replies. He traces his thumb over my knuckles as he finally looks directly at me, his expression softening as his eyes meet mine. "We get you back to safety within the wards and then we regroup and figure out our next move."

I smile softly and a mirroring smile plays on Cal's lips.

"First, I believe I was promised breakfast."

"That I can help you with." Alak grins, motioning for us to follow him. "Though," he adds as we walk, "things back at the Summer Palace aren't quite as we left them."

"That's right. Last night you said something about attacks?"

Alak nods. "It seems Kato decided to attack multiple places at once, likely to spread out our resources and armies."

We stop at a smoldering campfire with a few people still lingering around, but they meander off as we approach. Our conversation pauses as we take our seats and scoop out portions of porridge from a bowl being kept warm over the fire. Once we're settled, I look back to Alak.

"How did you receive the message about the attacks?"

"Jess sent it with one of Kai's bird shifters. It seems she's handling everything well, but she's eager for our return."

I nod, suddenly finding my porridge very hard to swallow. I had hoped everything would remain relatively quiet while we were rescuing the boy. The boy. My eyes dart around the camp.

"What is it?" Cal asks, tensing up, his hand going to the hilt of his sword.

"Saran. Where's Saran?"

"He's in the Healers' tent," Alak answers. "It seems he's quite taken with Hanna and Pip." He pauses, smiling. "Well, more one than the other, but he's with them all the same."

"But he's okay? He made it out all right?"

"He's fine," Alak assures me. "He didn't have any injuries. Well, nothing physical, anyways—you can't really be a prisoner forced to use magic against your will and be entirely okay —but he's getting there. I think he'll be even better once we get him farther from Kato and to a place where he feels safe and secure."

"Hopefully the Summer Palace can be that place."

Alak hums, nodding as he stares down into his bowl. I cock my head.

"There's something you're not saying."

Alak sighs and raises his eyes to mine. "I was wondering if it might be possible to send Saran further away than the Summer Palace if he wants. Maybe even to Gleador."

I only hesitate a moment before I'm agreeing. "Of course. As soon as we get back we'll arrange for him to be sent away. Maybe we can send Kayleigh with him."

"Can she be trusted?" Cal cuts in.

I shrug. "I doubt she'll go back to Kato."

"She won't," Alak insists, his voice firm. "I know she won't. If you give her the chance to leave and get Saran to safety, she'll take it. I'm pretty sure Kato wants her dead, anyway. You can even look at it as a banishment for her crimes if it makes you feel better about it. She has to leave Callenia but can still seek refuge in your name since she helped rescue Saran."

I mull his words over, nodding slowly. "Yes, I think that would work, assuming King Naimon is amiable." I turn to Cal. "What do you think?"

He smiles softly. "I think you are making an excellent king." He leans in and brushes a quick kiss to my cheek.

"Well, then," I say as Cal draws back, not even bothering to hide my grin. "I say we have a plan. We'll get back to the Summer Palace and get it all sorted. It shouldn't—"

I'm cut short by a gentle burst of magic not far away. I smile as Astra comes into view, though my expression fades into confusion when I notice she has someone else with her.

"Shite."

I turn and look at Alak who has gone entirely pale, his eyes wide. I look at Astra and notice she's looking at Alak with equal confusion, whereas the man next to her now wears a knowing smile. A quick glance at Cal tells me he's also lost. When I look back at Alak he's literally shaking.

"Who is that?" I ask, my hand immediately going to my sword.

Alak swallows hard and the look in his eyes when he turns my way chills me to my bones.

"That," he says, slowly, "is the man who saved my life."

CHAPTER THIRTY-THREE

ALAK

The world grows fuzzy and out of sync. Everything is too bright and my ears are ringing, the sound only drowned out by the pounding of my heart. It doesn't make sense. There's no way that the man standing in front of me right now is the same one I met that fateful night six years ago. Over the years, I've almost managed to convince myself that I dreamt the whole thing, the scars on my wrists the only evidence remaining. But that man, dream or no, was never meant to cross my path again. It's not possible. And yet . . .

He has a few more lines on his worn face and a bit more gray speckled through his hair, but the kind eyes are the same. It's him. I have no idea how or where Astra found him, but it's the same man. I swallow hard, trying to keep a hold on reality, shifting my gaze to the man's right to Astra's wide eyes and parted lips. For the first time since their arrival I focus on the bond, letting her surprise and bafflement wash over me. She didn't know who he was to me. So why is he here?

"How did he save your life?"

Ehren's voice draws me from my daze, but my tongue is too

thick to answer. I shake my head, trying to clear my racing thoughts and bring forward something coherent. But I don't need to speak; the man speaks for me.

"It's good to see you again, young man," he says, his voice soft and kind as he takes a step closer. "I take it you found life worth living after all?"

I manage a nod, a hoarse "yes" slipping from my lips. Ehren glances quickly between me and the man, his brow furrowed as if he's trying to decipher some complicated puzzle. Astra is barely daring to breathe.

"Astra?" Ehren says, finally looking to her for answers I know she can't provide.

She tries anyway.

"I went home to get this." She pulls a worn black book from her pocket. "While I was there, Gavin found me and asked me to bring him with me."

"He found you?" I say, my voice rough.

Astra's head bobs in affirmation. "He did." She takes a step closer to me, her eyes never leaving mine. "I had no idea who he was to you."

I swallow and nod.

"But he's safe?" Ehren cuts in. For the first time I realize he has a hand on the sword strapped to his side, ready to defend and protect if needed, despite having been rescued himself less than a day ago.

"I mean you no harm at all," Gavin replies calmly. "I merely wish to be reunited with my grandson." He turns to me with a small smile. "To reunite with Alak is only an extra blessing."

Ehren scowls. He opens his mouth to speak but is cut short by another voice behind me.

"Is that him, Pip? Is that your grandfather?"

I turn to discover Hanna and Pip standing a few feet behind

me. Hanna's eyes shine bright and she's grinning. Pip, on the other hand, looks even paler than usual, his dark eyes wide and unblinking. Hanna reaches over and takes his hand, and he grips hers tightly.

"Hello, Pip," Gavin says, taking a tentative step toward him. "Do you know who I am?"

Pip swallows hard and nods.

"Did you know I was coming?"

Pip only stares at the man and I can practically hear his racing heart from here. Hanna rests her head on his shoulder and he relaxes slightly before managing another sharp nod. Gavin gives his grandson a smile and takes a tentative step closer.

"That's good. I heard you had the strong gift of Sight. I was hoping we could chat?"

Pip inhales sharply, looking like he could run at any moment. He swallows hard before nodding.

"We have a tent," Hanna offers, pulling her head from Pip's shoulder. "We share it with my grandmother. Perhaps we could go there?"

Gavin gives Hanna a grateful nod. "That sounds lovely. Thank you, my dear."

Hanna grins at the man as he joins her. As they walk away, Pip stays so close to Hanna their shoulders touch. Once they disappear around the corner, I turn my attention back to the group to find all their eyes on me. I clear my throat and fiddle with the ends of my sleeves, suddenly very aware of the scars hidden on my wrists.

"Are you okay?" Astra asks, approaching me carefully like I'm a wounded animal.

I attempt a smile but fail. "I'll be fine."

She reaches for my hand, forcing me to release my grip on

my sleeves as she weaves her fingers with mine. "If I'd have known, I would've given you a warning."

I sigh through my nose and press my forehead to hers, closing my eyes. "I know, love. I know."

We stay like that for a moment until Luc's voice breaks through.

"Is everything all right?"

I press a quick kiss on Astra's nose before I pull back and turn to face Luc, managing a weak smile. "All good."

Luc's worried eyes fall on Astra. "You're back with good news, then?"

Astra lifts her shoulders in defeated shrug. "Not good news but nothing bad either. I hope that maybe I found something that can give us answers."

Luc nods as if this answer is acceptable enough to him before he turns his attention to Ehren. "How are you this morning?"

Ehren offers Luc a weak smile. "Healing."

Luc takes a step closer. "I was thinking about the message I received from your sister. I assume you heard about the attacks?"

Ehren nods. "Yes, Alak told me."

"Good." Luc shoots me quick smile of thanks before focusing on Ehren again. "Her message mentioned sending her own army to assist, but I was thinking how I have armies stationed not far from the area where the refugee camp was located. I believe it might make more sense for me to take the soldiers I have with me here and join with one of my larger armies now instead of going all the way back for reinforcements, yes?"

"That might work, if you feel safe doing so," Ehren replies slowly. "Do you have maps of the area?"

Luc nods. "I do, however, I was hoping to take someone with me that has already been there." He turns to me, inclining his head. "If you would be willing."

I exchange a quick look with Astra. I don't want to be parted from her again so soon, especially right now when I'm feeling particularly vulnerable. But war means making sacrifices, and I know I can be back by her side in a moment's notice if needed. I force a smile that I can only hope comes across as convincing.

"Of course. I'd be happy to accompany you."

Luc smiles. "Thank you." He allows his gaze to travel over the others before taking a step back and inclining his head. "If you will excuse me, I will notify my soldiers of the change. I assume we will be on our way soon?"

Ehren clears his throat, glancing at Astra who gives him a quick nod, before he replies. "Yes. We're mostly done here. Give us another moment or two and we'll help pack up so we can all be one our way."

"Excellent," Luc says. "I will pass that on to Kai. I believe he was wondering as well."

"Kai!" Astra says, her eyes widening. "Perhaps I'll come with you and talk to him myself."

Luc offers her a polite smile. "I would enjoy your company."

Astra grins and steps to his side, accepting his offered arm. "Thank you." She looks back at me as they start to walk away. "I'll catch you again before you leave."

I smile in response and she turns her attention back to the prince on her arm. I take a deep breath and face Ehren, who's still studying me closely.

"If you need anything, you'd say something, wouldn't you?" he asks.

I swallow. "I would. I assure you, I'm fine, or at least I will be soon. I just . . . I wasn't expecting to see someone from my past, from one of the darkest moments of my life at that."

Ehren's eyes widen with recognition as the pieces click into place. "You said a Seer saved you."

Judging by the curious look Cal gives Ehren, he doesn't know my secret. Ehren never told him about my past. I step closer to the two and extend my arm, wrist up, and allow the illusion I usually keep in place to fall away. Cal stares down at my wrists, his eyes widening when he realizes what it is he's seeing. He slowly raises his gaze to me, and I hurriedly shove my sleeves back over my hands as the illusion snaps back into place.

"I'm glad he saved you," Cal says, his voice earnest.

I manage a somewhat sincere smile. "Thank you. I am, too, though at the time I didn't understand why anyone would bother saving me." I glance off at a group of soldiers who are starting to disassemble the camp. I gesture toward them, "We should go get ready to leave."

"Yes," Ehren says quickly, sliding his hand into Cal's. "Yes, we should."

We split up and head off to pack up our things. I'm nearly done when Astra joins me. She helps me finish up and we head to our horses.

"Are you all right with me going with Luc? I can ask him if it's okay for you to come along as well," I ask as we attach our bags.

She sighs, focusing on her bag for a moment before raising her eyes to mine. "It's fine. I only wish I hadn't run off last night. I missed you."

The corner of my mouth tips up into a smile. "I missed you, too, love." My smile falters. "I was worried."

"I'm sorry," she says, avoiding my eyes. "I know I should have let you know I was leaving, but I wanted to go before I managed to talk myself out of it."

"I get that."

"And to answer your question," she continues, lifting her gaze to mine, "I wish I could go with you and Luc, but I feel like I'm needed by Ehren's side."

I nod. "I understand."

She moves closer and takes my hands in hers, gazing up at me. "Promise me you'll stay safe. Don't take any unnecessary risks."

I lean down and brush a kiss across her lips. "I promise."

"Ready to go?" Luc says from behind us.

I turn and offer him a weak smile. "As ready as I'll ever be."

Luc glances at Astra before looking back to me. "I'll be with my army ready to head south. Please, take as long as you need to say your goodbyes and meet me there," he says with a gentle smile before turning and walking away.

I give Astra one more goodbye kiss and mount Fawn before riding to meet Luc and his army. Luc greets me with a smile. Since our group is a bit smaller, we move out before the rest of the camp, traveling mostly in silence. Well, Luc and I ride in silence; the others may start off quiet but quickly dive into conversations in Ascarian. I expect Luc to join in, but he only watches the chatting soldiers with something close to envy.

"Are you and your sister close?" I ask, suddenly eager to chase the shadows from his face.

Luc blinks over at me, seemingly surprised by my question, but that surprise quickly fades into a gentle smile.

"Quite close."

"I suppose you miss her?"

Luc nods with a sigh, fixing his gaze ahead of us. "I do, yes.

Very much. Nicolette is very strong. There are many times I have leaned on her, though she is the younger sibling. While I appreciate the strength I am finding on my own, I do often wish she could be here." He glances over at me. "Do you have any siblings?"

I chuckle and shake my head. "My parents didn't even want me, let alone more children. Well," I amend, tilting my head, "my mother made me feel loved and wanted enough. If she hadn't been tied to my father she may have wanted more children, but I'll never know."

"Your parents, they are dead?"

I study Luc for a moment, debating how much to tell him. I settle on, "They died when I was a child."

"I am sorry for your loss," Luc says, inclining his head. "I can tell from the way you speak of your father that he was likely not a good man, but I am sorry all the same. Facing death as a child is never easy."

"Thank you."

We fall silent again for several minutes before Luc asks where I got Fawn. I grin, telling him the story, and we fall into easy conversation. Neither of us had perfect childhoods, but we both manage to share plenty of happy memories. We even chat through a shared lunch. By the time we stop to make camp for the night, I feel like I have another good friend.

CHAPTER THIRTY-FOUR

RONAN

Although most of the refugees have vacated the palace seeking refuge elsewhere or have been assigned one of the spare rooms to share, many of them seem to find comfort in the library. I can't blame them. I also find comfort in the pages of a book. However, their constant presence makes it difficult to continue my research. This is why I've found myself in Ievis's room again.

"Are you napping?" I ask sharply when I look up from my book to find Ievis stretched across his bed, eyes closed as a book rests propped up against his knees.

"Shh," he replies, swishing a hand through the air without bothering to open his eyes.

I slam the book I'm reading shut with a snap. "I'm not going to do all the work while you sleep."

Ievis growls and opens his eyes, pushing up into a sitting position and tossing his book to the side. "I was not sleeping. I was *thinking*. Your incessant jabbering is interrupting my process."

I huff in aggravation and reopen my book, flipping to find

the page I was previously reading. Normally I'm a calm and collected person, but something about Ievis sets me on edge, making me act rashly and do things I wouldn't normally do, like closing a book without a bookmark.

"For what it is worth," Ievis says, lying back down, "I think I may be close to a solution."

I jerk around in my seat to look at Ievis. "You are?"

Ievis nods, his eyes fixed on the canopy above his bed. "There is something in this text I was reading that triggered a memory of some sort. I know I learned about this account, and there's something important there. I just have to remember what."

His voice is edged with frustration. I hesitate a moment before pushing up from the desk and making my way over to him, leaving my cane resting against the desk.

"What are you doing?" he asks, eyeing me curiously, brow furrowed as I sit on the edge of his bed.

"I thought maybe I could help you sort it," I reply, motioning to the abandoned book laying page down between us.

Ievis scoffs. "How could you help me? You cannot read the language." He nods to my stack of books. "And I am quite positive we had very different educations."

I sigh, pinching the bridge of my nose. "Yes, you've made it quite clear that your education was massively superior, but we also agreed that our solution may lie in the common features of your texts and mine."

Ievis blinks up at me, looking almost bored. It takes every ounce of self-control I have to maintain my temper.

"So maybe you could tell me what sparked this memory, and I can see if there's any connection in what I have available?" I say through gritted teeth.

Ievis studies me for a moment longer before he sighs, rolling his eyes.

"Fine," he mumbles, shuffling into a sitting position and grabbing up the book. "This is an account of Fae creating a locking spell."

He passes me the book, and I take it, looking down at the page. I can't even begin to understand the curling Fae script, but the account is accompanied by a sketch of three Fae standing side-by-side, glowing hands extended between them.

"It is not the exact spell that was crafted for the Dragkonians," Ievis continues, "but it's similar. It was created to trap a different brand of evil."

I nod, turning the page to find a sketch of a three-headed beast looking up at me. My breath catches as I stare down at the picture. I turn and face Ievis, holding up the book.

"Is this what they're trapping?"

Ievis nods. "Yes, why?" He sits up straighter, his eyes shining. "You recognize it?"

My heart flutters wildly in my chest as I scoot off the bed. "Maybe."

I kneel next to the desk and dig through the pile of books I brought with me. I find the one I need and pull it from the stack. I flip through the pages until I come to the entry I need, pausing to scan the page.

"You think that's the same beast?"

I jump, not expecting Ievis to be right behind me. I glare at him over my shoulder.

"How do you move so quietly?"

He shrugs like it doesn't matter, but there's pride gleaming in his eyes. "Most Fae can move with great stealth." He nods to the book. "So, the monster?"

I turn my attention to the text and try to ignore how closely the Fae man is sitting to me. His chin is practically resting on my shoulder as he peers down at the page.

"I don't know how many three-headed creatures there are, but this story is about a beast called the Grugog. According to legend, it terrorized parts of Athiedor, nearly destroying the entire kingdom. It could breathe hellfire and its bite contained venom Healers couldn't combat in the slightest."

"That sounds like the same creature. Though, we called it —"

The name doesn't quite translate into human language. I haven't heard many words in the Fae tongue and in this moment I'm glad. Even though I know the Grugog was a horrible creature, whatever the Fae call it sounds beautiful. I have the sudden desire to hear more phrases from Ievis's mouth and heat swirls in my belly at the thought.

"Are you all right?" Ievis asks, jerking me back to reality.

"I'm fine," I mumble, my cheeks heating.

"Are you sure?" Ievis asks, pressing the back of his hand to my flushed face and my heart stops. "You seem warm."

I swallow and work hard to keep my breathing steady. I force myself to pull away from Ievis and grab the corner of the desk to pull myself up. Ievis stands with me, eyeing me with something close to curiosity.

"I'm fine," I repeat. When it's clear Ievis doesn't believe me, I glance away, my face heating even more. "I was merely taken off guard by your Fae language. The Fae name for the Grugog didn't translate."

Ievis grins smugly, crossing his arms across his chest. "You enjoy my native tongue."

I'm not sure if my face can get any redder, but if it's possible, it does. I convince myself this time it's due to frustration and most definitely not attraction. Not to Ievis. I can't be attracted to him. I merely appreciate the language from a purely academic standpoint.

"It's different," I grumble. "I wasn't prepared."

Ievis's grin turns wicked and he says something else that doesn't translate. The Fae words pour from his mouth like sweet honey and wrap me a warmth that stirs far more than they should. I inhale sharply and swallow hard, my heart racing.

"What . . . ? How did . . . ?" I stammer.

Ievis laughs, and gods, it's a beautiful sound, even more enchanting than the language. I glare at him and his mouth falls into a smirk.

"My language translates naturally when there are words available, but I can choose to keep it from translating if I wish."

"That's . . . interesting," I manage.

Ievis steps closer, his golden eyes gleaming. "Do you want to know what I said?"

I take an unsteady breath and turn my attention to the book in my hand, setting it open on the desk. "I'm sure it was an insult of some sort." I swallow, willing my rapidly beating heart to slow. "Perhaps we should get back to the task at hand? We can discuss more about your language later if you feel the need."

Ievis's eyes spark with something I can't quite place, but whatever it was is gone the next second.

"Yes," he says looking down at the open page. "So assuming the creature is the same, how can that help us?"

"Well," I say, turning my back to the Fae and standing over the book, "our story tells of 'great warriors' locking the beast away in a cage made of gold from the gods."

Ievis scoffs and I glance at him over my shoulder. "What?"

He shakes his head. "There were no 'great warriors' or 'gold from gods.' They were normal Fae crafters using gold from our realm. Would you like to know what my stories say?"

I nod and Ievis heads back to the bed, sitting on the edge. I follow, taking my book with me, and settle next to him as he pulls his book off the bed behind him.

"The Fae crafters used gold found in the Great Mountains," Ievis explains, shifting the book so it's partly on his lap and partly hanging off. I scoot closer, my leg pressing against his so we can properly share his book while I set mine to the side. He hesitates a moment before continuing. "It was a complex spell that required them to work together, but it was not too taxing. They put the spell directly on the gold."

I frown down at the page, nodding. "That matches well enough with the story I heard, simply inserting the Fae and their gold." I look up at him. "What is it about this story you think might be useful?"

Ievis sighs. "That is the thing. I do not recall. Something about the spell was different. It was more than the spelled gold that contained the beast, but this particular account doesn't give any more details. I'm sure something is missing."

"Let's see if my story says anything that sparks your memory."

He nods, and we switch the books in our laps, placing mine where his was as he sets his book to the side. I scan over the story, mumbling as I read the introduction that matches more or less with what Ievis shared. When I get to the part of them enacting the spell, I sum up what I'm reading.

"They took the gold from the gods—"

"Fae Crafters."

"Right, Fae Crafters, and made a cage. They spoke the words of the gods—"

"Typical Fae spell."

I glare up at Ievis. "Can you let me finish?"

He huffs and rolls his eyes. "Fine. Continue reading your inaccurate tale."

I clear my throat and find were I left off. "Okay, they spoke the words of the—the spell, and forced the creature inside, tethering the Grugog with the spell."

Ievis sits up straighter, nearly kicking the book from our laps. "They what?" I look up at him but he's staring down at the book, lips parted. "What *exactly* does it say?"

I place my finger on the page and trace the words as I read. "'They spoke the words of the gods, tying the beast to the core of the cage. As long as the spell held, the beast would be contained, for it could not part from the leash of the spell. It and all its kind would remain linked by the words of the gods to the gold, trapped well within its walls, or dead if they were spread without.'" I look up at Ievis. "Does that mean something to you?"

I'm not even sure Ievis is breathing as he whispers, "Yes."

"What does it mean?"

Ievis slowly raises his eyes to mine. "It means that while I need to make a spell to close off the Isle, the key is not in the warding. It is the Isle itself."

I shake my head. "I'm afraid I don't understand."

"The spell that contained this beast was not in the gold. Not entirely. The spell worked because it locked the beast inside."

"Through the gold," I say, thoroughly confused.

Ievis growls and stands abruptly, the book crashing to the floor. I don't try to pick it up, lost in watching Ievis as he rakes his hands through his hair in frustration. He turns to me, his gaze fierce.

"The spell linked to the gold, yes, but what kept the beast

in the cage was not the gold itself. The spell tied the beast to the cage, so even if the door was left open, the beast couldn't leave. The magic worked as a leash."

His meaning clicks and I gasp, standing to my feet. "So the key to the spell to lock away the Dragkonians needs to be the same? We don't need a warding spell strong enough to keep them locked in. We need a spell that tethers them to the island."

"Yes," Ievis breathes, taking a step closer to me.

"The story says that all the beasts outside the cage died. Does that mean—"

The words catch in my throat as Ievis steps closer, stopping barely an inch away, looking down at me with a strange intensity in his golden eyes.

"Yes," he says, his voice lower and rougher than normal. "We can trap the Dragkonians on the Isle who are already there and kill any that are not."

"So, we did it. We found the clue we needed," I say, my words barely a whisper.

Ievis leans in, stopping just shy of touching me. "We did." He hesitates a moment, then, "Ronan—"

"Yes," I gasp.

His mouth crashes on mine. There's absolutely nothing gentle about the kiss. It's bruising and intense, and yet it's by far the best kiss I've ever experienced. Ievis shoves his hand into my hair, pulling me closer. A small moan escapes me as he angles my head up and nips my bottom lip. I reach an arm around him and clutch the fabric of his shirt in a double attempt to steady myself and keep him flush against me. He pushes forward and I stumble back, my legs hitting the side of the mattress. I fall back on the bed with a startled gasp, and he looks down at me through lidded eyes. He releases me with a jerk and staggers away, forcing himself from my grip.

"Ievis?" I ask, breathing hard.

He turns away and I stand, placing a hand on his shoulder. He jerks away with so much force it nearly tips me over.

"You should leave."

"What?" I ask, blinking as I try to clear my head and calm my thoughts.

Ievis spins to face me, fury on his face so fierce I flinch away. He's the perfect picture of an angry god.

"Get out!" he snarls. "Now!"

I start to reach for my cane but Ievis cuts me off with a growl. "Out!"

I swallow hard and stumble from the room, my head spinning. The door slams behind me, and I trip down the hall, using the wall as support. My hands tremble as I open my door. I quickly cross my room and collapse on the bed, my whole body shaking at this point. Tears burn my eyes and I'm furious at myself. I can't believe I let that happen. I can't believe I let my guard down.

Though, I remind myself, Ievis was the one who kissed me. I didn't initiate it. I didn't realize that I wanted it until the opportunity presented itself. So why did it hurt so much when Ievis changed his mind? Why is my heart beating so fast in my chest that I feel like it could break free? And why, more than anything, do I wish it would happen again?

CHAPTER THIRTY-FIVE

ALAK

When we get close to one of Luc's armies, Luc sends a messenger ahead. We arrive later that evening, the camp of soldiers ready to receive us. A man rushes forward falls to his knees before Luc as the prince dismounts. Luc says something in Ascarian and the man nods, standing. They exchange a few more words before the man leaves and Luc turns to me.

"The army can be ready to move out if we need it, but they are helping to keep some of Kato's soldiers from advancing on a town a little to the East."

I nod, considering his words. "Do you still want to move the army to search for the refugees?"

Luc glances away almost guiltily. "I do not." He looks back at me and quickly adds, "I do wish, however, to find the refugees. I simply do not think moving my entire army would be the best decision. It would not be—what is the word? Subtle? Yes, it would not be subtle."

I nod. "I trust your judgment."

Luc looks a bit surprised by answer. "You do?"

"Of course. These are your soldiers, your people. You've studied war and how armies move more than I have, and if you believe your army is in the best spot possible, then I have no reason to doubt you."

Luc inclines his head, a little color rising on his cheeks. "Thank you." He glances over his shoulder, his eyes trailing over the camp. "There should be a war planning tent in the center of camp. I believe we can craft a workable plan of what should be done next, if you would like to come along."

"Of course. I will help in any way I can."

I allow a soldier to take Fawn, and I follow Luc through the winding rows of tents. When we arrive at a larger tent, the guard outside gives me a wary glance, but with a word from Luc he allows me entry. Inside is a large table covered with maps. A large, broad-shouldered man in armor looms over one, while a couple other high-ranking soldiers standby.

"Prince Luc," the man says, bowing his head.

"Général Dubois," Luc replies with a nod. He gestures to me. "This is Captain Alak Dunne, magical instructor of Callenian troops under Prince Ehren."

Hearing the title of captain before my name is startling, but I manage not to react. The general eyes me with a certain amount of distaste before turning his attention back to his prince. He begins to say something in rapid Ascarian, but Luc stops him, raising his hand.

"Please, Général, if we could speak Callenian in the presence of our ally, I would greatly appreciate it. If it is difficult, I can translate?"

The general seems truly affronted but complies nonetheless.

"My apologies," he says in a heavy Ascarian accent, not sounding the tiniest bit apologetic. "As you can see, where our army is stationed is important. We are protecting these villages and protecting one of the main routes the Fire King would likely use to get to the mountains. If we give up our position, it could create easy access for the Fire King to not only take the village but also cross the mountains into Ascaria."

Luc nods, peering down at the map. "I feared as much." He looks up at the general. "I think it may be best for the main army to stay here, but I still wish to seek out the refugees."

"My prince?" Général Dubois says, raising a thick eyebrow. "You wish to go alone?"

Luc smiles, shaking his head. "No, I would take Alak"—he gestures to me—"along with some of your fastest messengers and maybe a handful of soldiers in case we run into trouble."

It's clear by the general's frown and furrowed brow that he doesn't agree with Luc, but in the end he concedes.

"Very well, Your Majesty. When do you plan to leave?"

"Morning," Luc says assertively. "We will rest here tonight and move out first thing."

"Is there anything else I can do for you in the meantime?"

Luc considers the general's question for a moment before nodding. "If you could allow Alak and I a moment to look over the maps in private, I would appreciate it."

The general starts at the strange request and even I can't quite hide my surprise. The general recovers quickly and leaves with a low bow, motioning for the other two men to follow him. Once we're alone, Luc turns to me.

"I thought it might be a good idea to confirm our path," he says, stepping closer to the map. "Can you show me again where the refugee camp was located?"

I step to Luc's side and scan the map. It's highly accurate and, like Ehren's, has various figures representing the different troops and battle areas. Even with all the additions to the map, it doesn't take me long to find the spot.

"There," I say, pointing to the area. "It was in this wooded area near the mountains."

Luc hums, nodding as he takes in the map. "It looks like we have a fairly clear path there. If the reports are correct and my men have kept the map accurate—I have no reason to doubt them—we should be able to get to the area in a day or so."

"What do you hope to find when we arrive?" I ask, almost afraid of his answer.

"Well," Luc replies slowly, reaching out to adjust one of the figures representing his army, "the initial message indicated the camp was lost." He pulls back his hand and turns his full attention to me. "I am hoping we will find evidence of survivors."

"Do you think there are survivors?"

Luc sighs. "I hope so, though I fully confess that the report I received was not exactly promising."

My stomach twists at the thought that no one survived. That camp wasn't soldiers. It was innocent people. Children. There was no need to destroy it.

"We should probably get some rest," Luc says, glancing toward the tent exit. "I'm sure my general is more than eager to stare down at his map some more and have me out of his way." He shifts his attention to me and offers an attempt at a smile. "There is a tent set up for us—well, for me—but if you'd like to join me, I could use the company."

"If I wouldn't be a bother."

Luc huffs a small laugh, shaking his head. "No bother at all."

We step outside and the general calls for a soldier to lead us to Luc's tent. When we arrive, we find our bags already inside. Luc steps over to a washbowl and rinses his face while I look around. It's a larger tent, much like the ones Ehren and Astra were using when I joined them after escaping Kato. There's only one bed, but it's more than large enough for both of us with plenty of space around it should I decide to sleep on my bedroll instead. When my gaze comes back around to Luc, I find him watching me with a furrowed brow.

"Are you sure you're okay with me sharing the tent?" I ask, trying to decipher the tense expression on his face.

"It is fine. I have not changed my mind, only . . ." he trails off, looking to the side, red rising on his cheeks.

"Luc, I can go. I have no problem sleeping among the soldiers."

"No, no," he says quickly, waving his hand. "You are fine in here, I only ask that I may have a moment alone to change out of my clothes?"

He raises his eyes to me, and I smile.

"Of course. I can go check on Fawn."

Luc visibly relaxes and offers me a sincere smile. "Thank you."

I give him a parting nod and leave the tent. It takes a bit of exploring to find the horses, but I swear Fawn is happy to see me. After I chat with her a bit, I wander the camp, partially because I'm lost and don't know a lick of Ascarian to ask how to get back to the tent, and partially because I want to observe the soldiers. They're really not all that different from Callenian soldiers. They laugh, play games, and share stories.

When I finally find my way back to Luc's tent, he's changed clothes and looks refreshed. Dinner is waiting, so we eat quickly and then settle in for the night. When I offer to use my bedroll, Luc waves me off and insists we share the bed. We both fall asleep quickly, and I'm happy to report the foreign prince doesn't snore.

WE'RE on the road again at dawn, accompanied by a couple of messengers and roughly a dozen soldiers. Luc leads the way with me riding at his side. The Ascarians behind us slowly devolve into chatter, but Luc remains mostly quiet, his focus on the trail ahead. When I speak to him, he always willingly replies, but he never really starts any conversations, not even when we stop to break for lunch or when we make camp for the night.

The second day is much the same. Luc is a bit withdrawn, and I begin to wonder if I've done something to offend him. When we stop for lunch, I decide to broach the subject.

"Luc, is everything okay?" I ask, not exactly sure where to start.

Luc blinks at me. "Pardon?"

"You seem quieter than normal," I try again. "Did I do something to offend you?"

Luc shakes his head. "Ah, no. When I get stressed or anxious, I sometimes shut down." He offers me an apologetic smile. "It has always been this way. My sister, Nicolette, is usually the one to draw me out of my head, but as she is not here, I am afraid I may be getting lost in my own mind. I apologize for my rudeness."

"I didn't find you rude at all," I assure him. "I only wanted to make sure I hadn't done anything. Is there something I can do to help?"

Luc hesitates for a moment, tilting his head in consideration. "Perhaps, just speak to me? Distract me from my thoughts."

I smile. "I can do that."

"*Merci beaucoup*," he replies, inclining his head. "You are a good friend, Alak."

The rest of the day passes a little faster. I do my best to engage Luc in conversation, and he makes an effort to stay in the moment. It's early evening when we reach the familiar woods where Bram and I discovered the refugee camp not all that long ago. We slow our horses and I dismount, searching for the magical trail I found before, but it's gone. We tramp through the trees, my heart sinking lower and lower the closer we get to the camp location, but nothing prepares me for what we find.

The campsite is nothing but embers. Even though the attack happened days ago, smoke still curls in the air. I stumble forward in a daze, ash crunching beneath my feet. I vaguely hear Luc talking to his soldiers in Ascarian behind me but can't focus on him right now. Bile stings my throat as I remember the families that had taken refuge here. How could Kato do this?

"Can you detect any magic?" Luc asks, stepping to my side.

I swallow hard and reach out with my magic, but there's nothing there to find. The magic is as dead as the rest of the camp. I can't bring myself to say the words, so I shake my head instead.

"Hm," Luc says, taking a few steps forward, his face scrunched with concentration. "I expected . . . more."

"More what?" I ask, snapping out of my daze.

"More . . ." He pauses, waving his hand as if searching for the word. "Destruction? No, no. More evidence, I suppose."

I frown. "I don't understand. This"—I motion to the ashes—"seems like some fairly devastating evidence."

Luc turns to me, waving his hands wildly. "No, no! You misunderstand me. This is devastation indeed. How can I explain?" He pauses, his brow scrunched in thought before trying again. "Tell me, Alak, what do you see that's been destroyed?"

I don't understand what Luc is getting at in the slightest, but I let my eyes trail over the camp.

"Broken and burnt tents, abandoned campfires, life lost."

"Look for the bones. How many bones do you see?"

My frown deepens, but then I realize what Luc is saying. My heart picks up speed and I stumble forward, frantically looking over the camp. Yes, there are skeletons mixed among the ashes, but not many. Not many at all when you consider how many people were here. I turn to Luc, my eyes wide.

"They got away. At least some of them did."

Luc nods. "Yes, I believe so. Do you have any idea where they might have gone to escape?"

I start to shake my head but stop. "The mountains. The path would have been traveled well enough by the soldiers that left for Pax's army."

"Can you lead the way?"

I lick my lips and nod. I've only made the trip once before but I'm sure I can do it again.

"Good," Luc says. "We still have daylight left. Let's make of it what we can. We will need to find the refugees soon, as I am sure their supplies are little, given the rush with which they would have had to leave."

Luc turns and says something in Ascarian to one of the messengers. The man nods and bows before mounting his horse and riding off.

"He will secure extra rations and support. Hopefully, we will arrive in time."

We quickly mount our horses and head off toward the mountain pass. As we ride I pray to the gods we find more than bodies on the road ahead.

CHAPTER THIRTY-SIX

RONAN

I sleep restlessly all night and wake with my body feeling exhausted but my mind rushing with thoughts. Several of my books are still in Ievis's room, but I have enough in mine to occupy me. I know I should probably head out into the castle and see if I'm needed, but I don't have the energy. I need to be alone right now.

Around noon, my hunger wins out. I could ring for a servant to bring me lunch, but I figure they have better things to be doing. I limp across my room and open the door, nearly tripping over my cane resting against the doorframe. I pick it up and hold in my palm for a minute. At least Ievis had the courtesy to return it. I glance toward his door further down the hall. Maybe . . .

I shake my head and resume my path to the kitchens. The main lunch appears to be over. My stomach grumbles, so I head to the Come and Go room instead, knowing that there should be a little something. A few soldiers linger about, munching on sandwiches. They greet me as I cross the room and take a sandwich of my own.

"What's it like working with the Fae?" one of the soldiers asks, catching me off guard.

I shrug, taking a bite of my sandwich so I have a moment to form an answer.

"The one seems nice," another soldier offers. "Iefyr, I think their name is?"

Another solider nods in agreement. "Yes, they seem nice. I heard they rushed into Oxwatch and helped transport people out."

"The others seem very unfriendly and dangerous," the first soldier says, turning his attention back to me. "Are they?"

"They're a bit different from what we're used to, but we're in no danger from them," I manage. The soldiers don't seem terribly enthused by my response, and I suppose I can't blame them. As one of the few who's had regular contact with them, they want actual insight.

I sigh and recall the frustration on Ievis's face when he was trying to remember the connection of the spell, the light in his eyes when things started clicking into place, the soft warmth of his lips on mine. My face heats, and I shake my head, pushing the thoughts away.

"The Fae can be a bit much at first, but once you get to know them, they're similar to us at their core." I look up into several pairs of curious eyes. "They may outlive us by centuries and have magical knowledge we could never dream of, but they feel and fight and, I suspect, bleed much like we do."

"But what are they *like*?" the man presses.

"I can't sum them all up at once. They're individuals, not one, solid heap of Fae," I snap, more bite to my words than I intend. They all blink at me, clearly surprised by my brashness. I sigh but don't bother to try again. There's no way to describe the Fae in a way that will satisfy them.

"If you'll excuse me," I say, grabbing a couple more sandwiches from the tray, "I have things I need to attend to."

I turn and leave without another word, feeling only slight guilt. I briefly consider finding Jessalynn and the other Fae to see if I can be useful, but honestly, being around people right now feels like it would be a little too much. I'm working on balancing my cane and the sandwiches so I can open my door when another door clicks open down the hall.

"Oh."

I look up to find Ievis frozen in the doorway of his room. His scowl drops to my hands.

"Do you need help?" he asks cautiously, stepping all the way out into the hall and shutting his door.

I stubbornly shake my head and try the door handle again, nearly dropping everything in the process.

"Ronan," Ievis says, walking my way.

"I don't need you," I mumble, trying again. This time, I do lose hold on the sandwiches. They go tumbling toward the ground, but a strong hand catches them before they hit the floor.

I straighten and lift my chin defiantly. "Thank you." I open my door and step inside, extending my hand. "My sandwiches?"

Ievis glances at the food in his hand before sighing in resignation and handing them over. I start to shut the door with my foot but Ievis presses his palm against the wood, stopping me.

"Can I come in?"

I swallow and every instinct tells me to turn the Fae man away. After all, there are stories that warn against exactly this sort of thing. We're taught not to invite the Fae in, because once they have access the can enter at any time against our will. Which makes me curious.

"Is it true then?"

Ievis frowns. "Is what true?"

"That a Fae has to have permission to enter someone's private area?"

Ievis studies me for a moment before he bursts out laughing. If he wasn't so aggravating, I would be very attracted to him right now.

"Good bye," I huff, trying to close the door again, but once again Ievis stops me.

"I am sorry," he says, delight still ringing in his voice. "I had forgotten that you humans believe that old story. I feel confident it was made up to make humans feel safe against Fae intrusion." He sobers, the grin falling from his face. "No, I only request access because I will not force my way into a place where I am not wanted, but I could use your help."

I blink at him. "My help?"

He purposefully glances away. "Yes. I have been working on creating the spell we need, and I have hit a bit of a block. I could use an outside perspective." He looks up and meets my eyes, my heart skipping a beat as he adds, "Your perspective."

"I don't know, Ievis. You've made it quite clear that I'm more a hinderance than anything."

Ievis takes a step closer, forcing my door open a bit more and pushing into my doorway. I stumble back a step.

"You are definitely many things," Ievis says, his voice steady and his expression betraying nothing. "You are a distraction. You are a scholar. You are a frustration. You are everything I was cautioned against. But of all the things you are, not one of them is a hinderance."

I forget how to breathe for a moment, my hold on the sandwiches tightening to the point I know I'm crushing them, but I don't care.

"I'm not?"

"No." Ievis steps into my room so he's less than a foot away. "You . . . inspire me. Without you I would still be pointlessly searching for answers. Because of you, I may actually be able to create the spell before the world burns."

I force myself to step back, though it's the last thing I want to do. "You would have figured it out." I force a tight smile. "Let's not forget your superior Fae education."

Ievis's jaw tightens. "Ronan—"

Before he can finish what he wants to say, footsteps pound our way. Ievis frowns, stepping back out into the hall. A breathless young servant boy comes to halt, staring up at Ievis with wide, terrified eyes.

"Can I help you?" Ievis says, his voice an irritated growl.

"I n-need Lord M-McDullun," the boy stammers.

Ievis rolls his eyes and motions to me as I step forward.

"I'm here. What is it? Is there more trouble?"

"I don't think so. Not directly," the boy says, glancing nervously at Ievis. "There's an issue in one of the gardens. An archway was glowing."

"An archway . . . The portal?"

The boy nods, finally putting his full focus on me. "Yessir. Mistress Jessalynn knew how to open it well enough, but the man that stepped through was asking after you."

"That must be Master Arcanis," I say as much to myself as the other two. I look up at Ievis. "I should go speak to him."

I start to take a step toward the door but pause, glancing down at the sandwiches in my hand. Ievis makes a sound somewhere between a growl and a sigh and snatches them from me, tossing them to scatter across my desk.

"That was my lunch!" I cry.

"I will get you something better than stale sandwiches," Ievis counters. "We should go see this Master Arcanis."

I cock an eyebrow. "We?"

Ievis stands straighter, meeting my gaze with a fierceness that dares me to defy him. I'm tempted to deny him on principle, but in the end I give in.

"Fine." I turn to the boy. "Lead the way."

The boy takes off down the hall, Ievis and I trailing behind. I do an excellent job ignoring him the whole way, despite the fact I can feel him staring at me the entire time. The boy stops outside the Meeting Room and I pause in the doorway, steeling myself in case Master Arcanis has bad news.

"It will be fine," Ievis whispers in my ear, his voice low and reassuring. "Even if what he bears is bad news, we are almost at a solution."

I manage a nod and step through the door. Jessalynn is at the far end, seated in one of the chairs usually occupied by Astra or Ehren. Master Arcanis sits in one of the seats to her right. They both stand when we enter.

"Lord McDullun," Master Arcanis says, inclining his head. He turns his attention to Ievis. "And a Fae?"

"This is Ievis," I say, gesturing vaguely toward the Fae male.

"A pleasure to meet you," Master Arcanis says.

Ievis grunts in reply, crossing his arms.

"Ignore him," I say, shaking my head. "Do you bring good news or . . ."

Master Arcanis smiles, and it settles some of my worry. "Good news." He places his hand on a box sitting on the table. "I have your portal stones. Would you like to see them and hear a bit about how they work?"

I nod numbly. Master Arcanis resumes his seat, and I take

the one next to him. Jess rolls her neck and glances between the two of us.

"Well, unless you need me, I'm going to go finish what I was doing before you sent the entire castle into a panic," she says, shooting Master Arcanis an annoyed look.

"I do apologize again," Master Arcanis says, giving Jess an apologetic smile.

Jess waves him off. "It's fine." She takes a few steps toward the door but pauses, looking up at Ievis. "Are you just going to hover over them?"

I tilt my head back and look up at the Fae. If looks could kill, Jess would be a pile of dust. Jess, however, doesn't look put off by him at all and stares him down. He lets out a huff and looks down at me.

"I will be in your room when you are done."

Before I can respond, Ievis turns on his heel and leaves. Jess waggles her eyebrows at me. I try to brush her off, but I can feel my face heating. Jess grins and leaves with a wink. I turn my full attention to Master Arcanis. He opens the box to reveal several small stones lined up on black velvet.

"These stones," he says, tapping a couple of clear stones in the top row, "link directly to the portal on the Isle of Naskein. These"—he points to a collection of light blue gems with symbols etched in the center—"will link any two portals. If you plant a stone here and then another on the edge of a battlefield, you will be able to evacuate easily. The stones with matching symbols link to each other."

I nod, barely breathing as I count the blue stones. Twelve stones, six pairs. That means we can create six portals. The lives we can save. I raise my eyes to Master Arcanis.

"Can more than one portal be in the same location? For example, could we have three portals set up on various points near a battlefield and have them all link back to the Summer Palace?"

"Yes, that is possible. Though, you would not want them to be too close, lest their magic interfere."

I nod. "How far apart would they need to be? Opposite sides of the castle?"

"No, not quite that far. They could be in the same courtyard. I would think a few yards between each would suffice."

My mind is already working out the possible locations for the portals. "So we could put them in the same garden as the portal that already exists? That way if people were portalled to the Summer Palace that needed to be moved to the Isle, we could do so here?"

"Yes, and furthermore," he says, pointing to the last four gems in the box, each a bright red, "these gems link to other portals I have already set up. They're specifically meant for longer distances that don't quite suit the other gems."

"Where do they link?"

"These two both link to Gleador, one in Koshima and one in the Valley." He points to each in turn before moving on to the next one. "This one links to a small town in Oyrain not far from the capital that has agreed to house anyone who needs refuge. And this"—he gestures to the last stone—"links to a portal in Clan Bashmore."

The name strikes me in a way I don't expect, and I work hard to school my features. "Bashmore?"

"Indeed," Lord Arcanis says with a nod. "Young Lord Bashmore was quite insistent that a portal be placed near the main fortress on his land. He said there were people on the frontlines he cared for, and he would do whatever it took to save them."

My heart flutters. Even though Cillian and I couldn't work things out, even though we aren't meant to be, he still cares. A smile plays on the corners of my lips. Even if we can't be lovers, our friendship will never fade, and honestly, I think that means more to me than anything.

"Thank you," I say to Master Arcanis. "I appreciate you arranging this for me."

"It is no problem at all," he insists, closing the box. "I am happy to aid the war effort in a way that promotes peace."

He pushes up from the table, and I rise with him.

"Would you like me to have a room prepared for you?" I ask somewhat awkwardly as Master Arcanis passes the box to me.

He shakes his head. "No, that will not be necessary. From what I understand, the palace is overcrowded as it is. No, I think I will take a moment to talk with Mistress Jessalynn, and then I will be on my way."

I walk him to the doorway and offer to help him find Jess, but he turns me down. Not having anything else to do, I head back to my room, the box of precious stones tucked under my arm. I'm stuck inside my thoughts so deeply that I startle when I enter my room and find Ievis in the middle of my floor sitting crosslegged on a blanket laden with food. If I didn't know any better, I would think Ievis managed to wrangle us up a picnic.

"I thought you might be hungry."

I huff and close the door, moving to set the box on my bed.

"Well, seeing as someone literally threw my lunch across the room earlier, yes, I'm hungry."

"I got you food."

I pinch the bridge of my nose. "I can see that. But the question is why? *Why* did you get me food?"

"As you said, I ruined your pathetic excuse for lunch so I—"

"No, Ievis," I cut him off, my anger rising. "Why are you bothering with any of this? What changed between yesterday and today? If you recall, you kicked me out of your room quite viciously. You didn't even—" I pause to swallow, nearly choking on my own emotion. "You didn't even let me get my cane."

Ievis bows his head, looking more nervous and unsure than I've ever seen him. "As soon as I calmed down, I brought your cane to you."

"No, you didn't bring me anything. You left it outside my door for me to find. You couldn't even be bothered to knock and hand it to me directly."

He slowly raises his eyes to mine and my breath catches at the raw sincerity shining there. "I am very sorry."

He stands and takes a tentative step my way. I'm tempted to move away, but I'm frozen to my spot.

"I was raised to hate humans. I was told about all the things that were wrong and unnatural about finding attraction in humans. Iefyr always found humans fascinating and tried to convince me otherwise, but it is not easy to undo decades of indoctrination. At first, when I realized I was drawn to you, I convinced myself it would be okay, as long as we didn't take it too far, as long as I buried those feelings and refused to give them air. I believed I could smother the part of me that found attraction in you, so I pushed you away the best I could. In the end, I gave into my baser instincts. I hated myself for being so weak."

He pauses and swallows, my eyes tracking the smooth movement of his throat. I'm inexplicably drawn to him, and I find myself moving toward him against my will.

"You're not weak, Ievis," I say softly.

He offers me a smile, but it's forced and sad around the edges. "I wish I could believe you. I *want* to believe you. I want your voice to drown out all the voices in my head that are screaming at me that this is wrong—that *I* am wrong. I want it more than anything."

He reaches out and takes my hands in his, tugging me closer, as close as we were yesterday before . . . I take a deep breath, leaning into him, lost in the swirling gold of his eyes. My stomach grumbles, snapping us back to reality before I can make the mistake. Ievis releases my hands, stepping back and running his hand through his hair with a chuckle.

"We should get you fed." He gives me a sly smile. "You humans are quite weak and require constant nourishment."

A surprised grin spreads across my face. "Oh, as if you Fae don't also require constant food intake. I saw you eating plenty the other night at dinner!"

Ievis matches my grin as he sinks back down onto the ground. "Well, shall we eat?"

"We?" I ask, raising an eyebrow as I settle next to him.

"I was on my way to find food of my own when I ran into you earlier. I confess, I am quite hungry."

I laugh and gesture to the food. "That explains why there's so much."

Ievis shifts, reaching for a slice of bread and placing his other hand behind my back. I smile and lean casually against him as I select food for myself. As we eat, I enjoy the strange comfort his presence brings. He's not the Fae warrior I always dreamed of, but maybe, just maybe, he's something better.

CHAPTER THIRTY-SEVEN

ALAK

The pass through the mountain shows no signs of travel, but Luc and I remain ignorantly hopeful that we'll find survivors. As the sun begins its final descent, we're about to give up and stop for the night when I feel a slight tug of magic. I freeze, my attention fixed ahead of us.

"Do you sense something?" Luc asks, watching me carefully.

"It could be nothing," I mumble.

"But you do sense something?" Luc presses, leaning forward on his horse to peer at the dim path ahead. "What is it?"

I shake my head. "I don't know. It really could be nothing, but there's magic ahead." I turn and look over at Luc. "It could be a trap, bandits, or just a batch of magical plants or animals."

"So we proceed with caution," Luc says matter-of-factly before turning and giving a command to those behind us. When he looks back at me he's wearing a tight smile. "Let's find out."

As we ride on, the magic grows stronger, and I'm positive it's definitely more than naturally occurring magic. This magic was placed here by someone, but I can't quite distinguish what kind of magic it is. Luc seems to sense my wariness and keeps one hand on his sword and one on the reigns. When we get right upon the magic, I hold up a hand, signaling for Luc to stop. It's a barrier of some sort, and I can't sense what it's hiding on the other side.

"Let me go on ahead," I whisper, nerves swirling in my stomach. "There's a lot of magic here blocking me. Once I get on the other side of it, I'll know what we're dealing with."

"What if you find something bad?" Luc asks, his voice steady.

"If something happens to me, or if I disappear and don't return, leave."

"Alak—" Luc starts but I cut him off with a wave.

"I'm sure I'll be fine, but it would be better for me to go alone. If I run into trouble I can wisp away to safety."

Luc considers me for a moment before he concedes. "So be it. If you find a problem I can assist you with, please return for me."

"I can do that," I say with a nod. I turn my attention back to the road and take a deep, fortifying breath. "Here I go."

I urge Fawn forward and I pass through the tingling magic of a ward. At first I don't see anything worth warding, but I press onward, my breath trapped in my chest. I ride around a twist in the path and stop short. Stretched out in an open portion of the mountain are the survivors of the refugee camp. My relief quickly turns to sorrow when I take in the state of the camp. There are significantly fewer people than there should be, and the entire camp looks like it's on its last leg. They don't have the supplies they need and at least a third of the people scattered around appear wounded.

"Who are you?" a voice demands and look down to find a young pre-teen boy staring up at me defiantly, a makeshift weapon in his hand.

"I've come to help you," I say, lifting my eyes back to the rest of the camp. "Who's in charge?"

"Who sent you?" the boy demands instead of answering my question. His voice carries this time and several other heads turn our way. The reactions to my presence immediately flicker between fear and defense.

"Prince Ehren sent me, and I have aid waiting around the corner from Prince Luc of Ascaria," I reply.

The boy's eyes widen at my reply as whispers skitter throughout the camp. "Prince Ehren?"

"Yes. Now, who is in charge?"

The boy relaxes. "Same person as before. Mara Smythe."

"Good. Can you get her?"

No sooner have the words left my mouth than I see Mara already picking her way across the camp toward me. When she gets close enough to really see me, she rushes up to me, blinking like she's staring at a ghost.

"Alak?" she says, her voice hoarse and her eyes tired.

"Are these all the survivors?"

Her expression sinks. "Unfortunately." She glances over her shoulder toward a small cluster of people who are clearly not doing well. "And if something doesn't change soon we'll lose even more." She looks back at me. "Have you brought Prince Ehren with you?"

"Not Ehren, but I do have help waiting around the corner."

She perks up. "Really?"

I nod, already working to turn Fawn around. "Yes, I'll go get them."

Mara watches me with hope in her eyes and I rush back to Luc. When I pass through the magical barrier Luc sags with relief.

"I was starting to worry," he says. "What did you find?"

"The refugees are just ahead, around a bend," I reply. "They're not doing great, and they need more resources, especially medicine and Healers."

Luc takes in my words and nods slowly. "So it's safe for us to approach?"

"Yes, I didn't see anything that would harm us."

"Good," Luc says assertively. "I will meet with whoever is in charge, and we can figure out what resources are needed. Once morning comes, I will send another messenger back to the army to get more supplies or whatever these people need."

I nod in agreement. "Follow me."

I lead the way through the warding, though there's really no need as there's only one path to follow. Mara waits at the edge of the camp, hands clasped in front of her. Her shoulders lift and her eyes light up when we approach. I dismount next to her and Luc follows suit.

"Hello, *Mademoiselle*," Luc says, bowing to Mara. "I am Prince Luc of Ascaria, and I have come to give you aid."

A blush rises on Mara's cheeks as she takes in the prince with wide eyes. "P-Prince?"

Luc straightens and offers Mara a charming smile that would make Ehren proud. "*Oui, Mademoiselle.*"

Mara blinks rapidly as a smile twists on her lips. I try to bite back my own smile.

"Now, please, how may I assist you?"

Something about Luc's request seems to bring Mara back

to the present, and she sobers a bit, the joy in her eyes snuffed out.

"Why don't you walk with me and I'll show you? You can have your horses taken to the center of the camp with the few we managed to save, if you'd like. I'm afraid our setup isn't very fancy given our circumstances but—"

"We do not expect anything formal," Luc assures her.

Mara offers him a gentle smile, which he returns before turning to the men behind us and speaking to them in Ascarian. One of the soldiers replies and steps forward to take our horses to be led away.

"Come with me, and I'll give you the details you're probably seeking," Mara says, gesturing for us to follow her. She leads us through the camp to a fire in a small crevice in the mountain that provides some shelter from the biting wind. We take seats around the fire, getting as comfortable as we can.

"I'm not even sure where to start," Mara says, staring into the flames with a dazed expression.

"Can you share how you managed to escape?" I prompt.

Mara nods absentmindedly. "You know how we had magical warding and trails leading to the camp?" I nod. "Well, those wards would detect when magical people were approaching and could often alert us if the magic seemed like it was seeking to cause harm. After you left and we heard of more and more towns being attacked, we extended the edges out a lot further."

"So when the army came to attack you had a heads up?" I ask.

Mara shrugs. "A bit. It wasn't much time—ten, fifteen minutes at most—but it allowed some of us to escape."

She swallows and fights back her emotions before continuing.

"Not everyone could escape and others chose to stay and fight." Tears well in her eyes. "We knew if everyone escaped, Kato would find it suspicious and potentially seek out the survivors. By leaving some to stay behind, it made it look like a victory for him."

She chokes on a sob and Luc scoots closer to her, taking one of her hands in his. He whispers something gentle in Ascarian, and though I doubt Mara knows what he says, it seems to rally her.

"After the battle, some of us went back and found survivors. Most died within a few hours, but some we were able to save. Most of our hunters stayed behind to fight and were killed or seriously wounded, and without them we don't have much food. We had to leave so quickly without warning we lack almost all essentials. We lack the strength and rations to go much further into the mountains, so we've been stuck here in the same spot, hidden behind our ward, waiting for death to find us."

"We are here to help you now," Luc says, his voice firm but comforting. "I have one messenger that should be seeking us out soon with some supplies, and I will send out a messenger first thing in the morning to get more. I will get you out of these mountains and to safety. In the meantime, my soldiers will hunt and find you food."

Mara looks up at Luc through glistening tears. "Thank you. You came to save us just in time. I don't think we could've lasted much longer. You're a hero, Prince Luc."

Luc's cheeks redden and he dips his head. "It is my pleasure. I only wish my heroics were not necessary."

"Still, I'm grateful for you." Mara smiles softly and presses a quick kiss to Luc's cheek. He flushes a deep crimson as his eyes widen. He attempts a sputtering reply, and I duck my head to hide my grin.

"I'm going to go check on the horses and grab our bags," I say, willing to give Luc a little time alone with Mara.

"I can show Prince Luc where you can all set up for the night while you grab your things," Mara offers, standing. She turns to Luc, who's stumbling to his feet. "If that's all right with you, Your Majesty."

I didn't think it was possible for Luc to get any redder, but he does, flushing up to the tips of his ears.

"There is no need for such formality," he mumbles, waving his hand. "But to answer your question, yes, that is quite all right."

Mara grins and motions for Luc to follow her. He shoots me a somewhat panicked look, and I attempt what I hope is an encouraging smile before heading off toward the horses. I find them easily enough along with Luc's soldiers. They eye me suspiciously as I remove Luc's bag as well as my own, but when I offer to show them the way to Luc, they relax a bit, clearly understanding enough Callenian to know what I'm saying.

In order to give Luc a few more moments with Mara, I make sure we walk slowly under the guise of checking out the camp and our surroundings—which I do want to do, so it's believable. When we find Luc, he's a significantly lighter shade of pink than the last time I saw him, and he's regained a good bit of his casual confidence. When his eyes land on us, he straightens and nods.

"I was just telling Luc we don't have much to offer, but if you need anything, please let me know," Mara says as we approach.

"I'm sure we'll be fine," I say, stepping to Luc's side.

Mara nods, glancing between us. "I'll let you be then." She turns her full attention to Luc. "We can chat more in the morning once you've had a chance to rest."

Luc inclines his head, not bothering to hide his smile. "I look forward to it."

Mara shoots him once last smile before disappearing among the clutter of the camp. Luc clears his throat and says something to the others in Ascarian. They immediately start setting up a makeshift campsite of our own. I follow Luc to a little nook against the rocky slope of the mountain, passing him his bag.

"Thank you," he says, accepting the bag and sinking down on the ground to sort through his things.

For a few minutes we work in silence as we set up our bed rolls. Once we've got them laid out and everything situated, Luc turns to me.

"You know Mara from before?"

I shrug. "A bit. I've really only met her once before tonight when we found the camp the first time, but she's very close with Astra. They were childhood friends."

Luc nods, mulling over my words. I can tell he has something more to say, but he can't seem to bring himself to speak up.

"She's a really good person," I add, hoping to encourage him to say what's on his mind.

Luc lifts his eyes to mine and smiles, but there's something sad about it. "She does seem that way. After all, look at what she has done here." He motions to the camp around us. "This is not something just anybody would do. She appears truly amazing."

I furrow my brow. "Then why do you seem upset?"

Luc sighs, pulling his knees up to his chest and wrapping

his arms around his legs. For the first time since meeting him, he seems unsure and small. He seems vulnerable.

"She is lovely, and I really want to get to know her better," he whispers.

"I don't think that's a problem, Luc. She seemed to like you."

Luc shrugs, avoiding my eyes. "Probably only because I am a prince, and she was only being polite."

"Maybe, but I think it was more than that. From what Astra and Ehren have said, she's a decent person. I think she's being sincere in wanting to get to know you."

Luc pulls his legs closer, tucking his chin between his knees. "Perhaps, but even then, I am not here to find a relationship. I have to return to Ascaria when the war is over, and hopefully it will be over soon. I have responsibilities."

"Are you engaged?" I ask.

Luc raises his head, giving me a curious look. "Why do you ask?"

"I only wonder if your responsibilities include an arranged marriage."

"Ah," Luc says, shaking his head, resting his chin back on his knees. "No, I am not engaged. I am only eighteen, and barely that. I am in new footing with being a ruler. One thing both Nicolette and I agreed upon was that neither of us would marry for political gain alone."

Luc pauses, stretching out across his cot and leaning back on his palms. "No, the responsibilities of which I speak are more directly linked to ruling a kingdom. It is a lot, even with the help of my sister. Courting a beautiful young woman from a foreign kingdom that we have only just made a firm ally may be a very bad decision."

"But it could also be a good decision." I scoot a little closer to Luc while still giving him plenty of space. "Look, Ehren told me that your encouragement was partially why he and Cal finally got together. According to him, you said something about love making him a stronger ruler."

Luc nods. "That is true, but what does that have to do with this situation?"

"I think, maybe, the same idea can be applied here. Sure, Mara may not be the best decision, and maybe nothing will come of pursuing a relationship with her, but you can't know that unless you give it serious consideration."

Luc sighs, picking at a random loose thread on his bedroll. "She has not known me long enough to consider such a thing. She does not know me, my history. There are many who do not approve of the choices I have made, even though they were mine alone to make."

His voice sounds hurt, and I have the urge to find anyone who ever made him feel less and drag them to . . . Well, to do something. Apologize and beg for forgiveness on their knees at the very least.

"You could be right, but you share obvious attraction to each other, even if it's not something that will last. Maybe Fate thought you could use a bright spot in the middle of a war. Maybe you need to see the stars in the middle of the storm, and maybe that's Mara."

Luc sits up, carefully considering my words. "You think so?"

"Definitely. I know without Astra my world would be much darker. She's my guiding light, and I can't imagine going through all this without her. Maybe Mara won't be that for you, but at the very least she could be another friend."

For the first time since Mara left Luc smiles, some of his previous confidence returning. "I could use another friend."

I match his smile. "We can all use more friends." I reach for my pack and pull it into my lap. "Now, how about we eat some of our rations? Then you can talk to your messenger and figure out what they need to do. I'll write to Astra as well and update her and Ehren on what we found."

Luc nods, his grin holding as he reaches for his own pack. "Sounds like a plan."

CHAPTER THIRTY-EIGHT

EHREN

My injuries already ache as we pack up the camp and start our slow return toward the Summer Palace. It doesn't take long before I'm shifting atop my horse, trying to find a way to keep the pain at bay. Cal is the first to notice, shooting me worried glances, Astra noticing shortly after. I try to downplay my discomfort with forced smiles that fool no one. When we pause for lunch, I expect a lecture from Astra, but thankfully she seems distracted by the small black book she fetched from her unplanned excursion back to Timberborn. Cal doesn't say anything, but I can tell by the way he's set his jaw he knows something is wrong. He's proven correct when it's time to get back on the road and I can't even get on my horse.

"Ehren," he whispers, placing a gentle but firm hand on the small of my back.

I shake my head, attempting to mount again, but it's another frustrating failed attempt thanks not only to the aching stiffness from my injuries but also to the fact I'm missing a hand.

"Let me help you," he says, his voice pained. "Please."

I sigh and manage a nod, fighting back tears. Cal's strong arms support me as I climb atop Dauntless, gripping the reigns tightly in my hand as my cheeks burn with shame. I'm the rightful king of Callenia and I can't even mount my horse without help. How am I supposed to lead a kingdom?

As we ride, the pain gets worse, and I grit my teeth to keep in any sounds that would alert anyone to the truth of my condition. I seriously consider approaching one of the Healers and asking for something, anything to help with the pain, but I can't bring myself to do it. Every time the thought crosses my mind, I'm jerked back to my time in captivity. I associate the warmth of Healing magic with the torture Kato inflicted and the bitter taste of medicine with waking up disoriented in a dark room where I feared for my life.

My heart races with each memory, and it takes every ounce of willpower I have to control my breathing and not fall into a full-blown panic attack. If mere thoughts of treatment make me feel this way, how much worse would the actual Healing be? No, I can't go to the Healers. I can't let anyone know how broken I am.

When we stop for the night to make camp, I fall off my horse when I attempt to dismount, hitting the frozen ground with a sharp hiss. Cal is by my side in seconds helping me sit up. The world spins and dips around me as pain radiates through my entire body. I squeeze my eyes shut as a I involuntarily shudder, biting back a pathetic whimper.

"Ehren," Cal whispers, his voice trembling as he clutches me against his chest. "Should I get the Healers?"

"No!" I cry out, my eyes shooting open.

I've drawn the eyes of several people, but they all graciously glance away when they realize they've been caught gawking. I swallow hard and push Cal away. I stumble to my feet while doing my best to ignore the throbbing in my limbs.

"I'm fine. I was just a little . . . dizzy from riding all day." I stagger back a step, glancing away from Cal's furrowed brow. "I'm fine. Let's set up the camp." I look back at Cal who is clearly less than convinced. "I'm *fine.*"

Cal sighs, rubbing the back of his neck and he shakes his head. I know he wants to protest, but he won't argue with me publicly. No, he'll wait until we're alone in our tent before he brings it up. Which is exactly why I have to avoid our tent as long as possible. I make rounds throughout the camp as the tents are put up and fires are built. It's a struggle to remain upright at times, but I manage well enough. By the time the darkness has fully encompassed the camp, my empty stomach has me finally limping my way toward my tent.

I pull aside the tent flap with a shaking hand, preparing myself for a lecture. I freeze in the entry when I'm met by an empty tent. Cal has taken the time to lay out our things, bedrolls included, but he's nowhere to be seen. I can't tell if the swirl of emotions in my chest is disappointment or relief or a mix of both. Whatever they are, I shove them aside and sink onto my bedroll. I honesty didn't think the pain could get any worse, but that simple movement has tears burning my eyes again. I take a shuddering breath and try to focus on anything but the agony of my current state, but it seems pointless. The pain consumes every thought to the point that the rest of the world fades away. I'm only brought back to the present by a frantic voice yelling my name as hands grip and shake my shoulders.

"Ehren! Please, be okay. Don't be dead."

I crack open my eyes and a blurry vision of Cal slides into focus. His brown eyes glisten with tears.

"Hey," I croak, my voice coming out far more hoarse than I'm expecting.

"Oh, gods Ehren," he gasps, falling back on his heels. "I thought you were dead. Or dying."

I attempt a smile, but for some reason even that hurts. Instead I sigh and close my eyes.

"I'm fi—"

"Don't you dare tell me you're fine," Cal snaps, his tone harsh enough it makes me wince. "You are *not* fine. You need a Healer."

"I can't. I can't go to a Healer," I whisper.

"Why not?" Cal challenges. "Is it because you can't stand? I'll bring one to you. Hell, I'll bring them all to you."

"Cal," I murmur, forcing my eyes open.

Something about the way I say his name has even more worry crossing his face than before. I swallow and reach my hand to take his. He immediately intertwines his fingers with mine, squeezing hard as if I might slip away from him and disappear if he can't hold on tightly enough.

"Ehren, please let me help you," he pleads, his voice cracking. "I don't know what's wrong, and I don't understand why you won't let me help you."

I sigh, trying to find a way to describe what I'm feeling without making him think less of me. Nothing comes.

"Do you remember all that time ago when Makin and I had that falling out?" Cal asks. I nod and he continues. "You knew something was wrong with me, and you begged me to let you help. You told me that seeing me hurt caused you pain."

I crack a small smile. "You remember that?"

Cal scoffs, shaking his head. "Of course I do. Every moment we've ever shared is etched in my brain. I love you, Ehren. I loved you even then, and those words meant everything to me in that moment. And now you need to hear them from me."

He pauses, collecting himself as he meets my eyes. "You are hurting, possibly killing yourself, and I'm hurting and dying along with you."

In the midst of my misery, I feel a sharp new pain, though this injury is more emotional than physical. I squeeze his hand in answer as I try to find the words. Cal waits patiently.

I lift my right wrist. "There is no fixing this, along with the majority of the wounds I have left. They can't be fixed. They were inflicted with dark magic."

"We may not have the means to heal them, but surely something can be done to manage the pain," Cal insists. "Ways to help you cope."

I swallow, glancing away from Cal's tender, frightened gaze. "It's just . . . I can't explain it. Kato had Healers healing me between torture sessions. It's difficult for me to think of being healed, by magical means or otherwise, without those memories rearing fresh in my mind. When I lost my hand, a Healer gave me medicine that knocked me out so I could deal with the pain. I woke feeling like I was stuck in a nightmare. I don't know if I could take any sort of pain medication without going back there in my mind." I look back at Cal, my eyes swimming with tears. "Do you understand?"

"Oh, Ehren," he whispers, leaning forward to press a tender kiss on my forehead. "I wish you would have told me."

"I didn't know how. I know it's all in my head. I know that this situation is different, that these Healers only want to help me. I *know* that. But there's a piece of my mind that puts up a block every time I consider it."

"I think, given what you went through, this reaction is normal."

I shake my head. "No, Astra and Alak both underwent torture and they came back fine."

"Not everyone reacts to trauma in the same way. It's not fair of you to compare your reactions to theirs and vice versa. If you need to heal inside your mind in order to heal your physical body, that's understandable, but we need to find some sort of solution."

"I know. I don't mean to worry you."

A small hint of a smile plays on the corner of Cal's lips. "Ehren, I have known you most of my life. You're reckless and careless, and I'll always worry about you." His smile falls away. "But right now you're putting yourself in a position where you're killing yourself. You can't continue like this."

"I know. I'm sorry." I cock my head, giving Cal a half smile. "Forgive me?"

Cal answers by leaning forward and pressing a quick kiss to my lips. "Always." He hesitates before adding, "Will you please let me fetch a Healer? I'll stay by your side the entire time they work, holding your hand. I wasn't there for you before, but I'm here now. I'll keep you grounded."

Cal's words echo through my mind. He wasn't there before and simply having him here, being able to touch him, might be enough to keep my mind from wandering too far into itself.

"I'll see the Healer, but I want to go to their tent."

Cal frowns. "Can you manage that?"

I offer him a weak smile. "I think with you by my side I can do anything."

Cal rolls his eyes, but I catch the smile he's trying to hide.

"Fine," he concedes. "But if you collapse on the way there, I'm bringing them to you."

"Deal. Help me up?"

It takes a few tries and a lot of effort, but I manage to get to my feet. Every muscle and bone in my body screams at me. I have to lean heavily on Cal, but we make it to the Healing tent. Healer Heora is inside with Hanna and a boy with red hair who I realize after a moment is Saran.

"I was wondering when you would come to me," Healer Heora admonishes. "You should have come far sooner."

I duck my head, shame coloring my cheeks as Cal helps lower me to the ground since I can barely stay upright. "I'm sorry."

"No matter," she says, waving her hand. "You are here now. Let me assess your injuries so I can figure out what needs to be done."

Cal supports me from behind so I can stay upright. I suck in a breath as she kneels, extending her hands toward me. Cal wraps his arms around my waist, his hold firm yet gentle. I don't breathe the entire time her magic trickles over me. I practically gulp in air the moment she stops, a frown on her face.

"How bad is it?" I ask, terrified of the answer. "Am I . . . am I going to die?"

She offers me a tight smile. "No. Not today. Not from these injuries. However"—Cal's grip around me tightens—"most of these injuries were inflicted by dark magic and cannot be fully healed. They're quite similar to the scars Alak bears."

I nod, my heart sinking. Even though I knew this would be her answer, I was holding onto a small sliver of hope she might be able to help.

"They were inflicted by the same person," I mumble and she nods.

"I assumed as much."

"So there's nothing you can do?" Cal asks, a hint of desperation in his voice.

"Now, I didn't say that," Healer Heora says with a smile as

she pushes up from the floor and walks over to the corner of her tent where most of her medical ingredients are stored. "I may not be able to cure the source of the problems, but I can help with the pain the injuries cause and how they affect your body."

Jars clink together as she sorts through her supplies, muttering to herself.

"I, uh, I don't want anything that will knock me out, make me sleep."

She turns and looks at me over her shoulder, her eyebrows raised. "Are you sure? The strongest, most effective medicines cause a fair amount of drowsiness. Sleep will help your body heal faster."

"I'm sure."

"All right then." She turns back to sorting. "I may have to mix up something new." She lifts a couple packets and nods. "Yes, give me a moment and I'll make something that should help. Hanna, can you assist me?"

"Of course!" Hanna chirps, leaping up from where she's been sitting with Alak's cousin.

Saran watches her join her grandmother, his eyes widening with something close to fear. His attention snaps to me, and he scoots back so he's pressed against the corner of the tent. His chest moves rapidly with jerking breaths. Is he frightened of me? The longer I look at him the more he shrinks into himself.

"So, Hanna," Cal says, cutting some of the growing tension in the tent, "is Pip doing all right?"

"Oh, yes," Hanna says, her head bobbing up and down as she hands ingredients to her grandmother. "He's with his grandfather right now. I think Pip's really happy he found us. They seem to be bonding well. His grandfather knows a lot about Sight and his knowledge is going a long way to help Pip accept certain aspects of his magic."

"That's good," I manage, trying hard not to look back at Saran.

"It really is. I know Pip has had me and Grandmother, but he was lonely. Now he has someone else watching out for him." She shoots us a smile. "It's nice to have people looking out for you."

I smile, leaning back against Cal who presses a kiss to my temple. "Yeah, it is."

"All right," Healer Heora says, walking our way. "This"— she holds out a small jar which Cal accepts—"goes directly on your wounds. It will numb the area and help to heal the injury with the least amount of scarring possible. And this"—she holds out a second jar—"will help you manage the pain. I made it as strong as I could without adding too much of the ingredient that would make you drowsy. Take a pinch of it as needed, but try to go at least a couple hours between doses or your body will build up a resistance to it."

I nod as I take the second jar. "How long will I have to take it?"

Healer Heora's expression grows heavy. "It is likely you will be dealing with the pain the rest of your life." Cal inhales sharply behind me and she hurries to add, "I pray to the gods I am wrong, but the extent of the dark magic behind the creation of these injuries is extreme. You should still be able to have a relatively normal life, but there will likely be bad days."

I take a deep breath and manage a nod. "Thank you."

Cal helps me stand and we slowly make our way back to our tent in silence. Once we're alone, I ease down onto my bedroll while Cal lights the lantern and sets the medicine between us. I carefully remove my shirt, ignoring the pain the best I can. When I meet Cal's eyes, they're swimming with tears as he takes in my scarred and bruised torso.

"Hey," I say, cupping my hand to his cheek. "I'm going to be okay."

"You heard what the Healer said," he whispers, his voice hoarse.

"Yeah, I did. She said I'd be able to have a relatively normal life." I pause, my heart picking up its pace. "I still want to spend that life with you, if you can accept and be okay with the fact I'll have bad days."

"Ehren," Cal says softly, placing his hand over mine, "I want to spend every moment with you—never question that. I only hate that you'll be suffering, especially since this should've been me."

"No, we're not going there again," I say, my voice firm. "I don't regret trading myself for you, and I don't want you regretting it either." I force a weak smile. "Now, can you help me with this salve?"

Cal nods and grabs up the salve. He's very gentle as he rubs the medicine over each wound, his long fingers working into my skin in a warm, comforting way. By the time that last one has been treated, I'm already feeling some relief, the medicine working to numb the pain at its source. Cal helps me change into a new set of clothes before I take a pinch of the other medicine. It's mostly composed of crushed leaves and herbs with an almost minty taste. It starts working quickly and for the first time all day I feel like I can breathe.

"Better?" Cal asks, watching me warily.

I smile a real, genuine smile. "Much better."

"Really?"

"I won't lie to you, Cal. Do I feel completely healed? No, I still feel discomfort, but I do feel significantly better than I did a few minutes ago." I glance to where our bedrolls lie side-by-side. "Let's go to bed."

A smile drifts onto Cal's lips as he nods. "Let's go to bed."

I start to make myself comfortable on the floor, and Cal practically pulls me on top of him. I smile and settle closer, resting my head on his chest. I take a few deep breaths and slowly fall asleep to the steady sound of his heart beating as one with my own.

CHAPTER THIRTY-NINE

ASTRA

Part of me wishes I had never gone back to get Kato's journal. It's a heavy reminder, constantly weighing down every thought. I'm almost ashamed how long it takes me to notice that Ehren is clearly in pain from his injuries created at my brother's hand. Thankfully, Cal is on it, watching over Ehren. And me. The first night we stop to make camp, I immediately find a quiet corner to myself. I would have stayed lost in the pages of the journal if Cal hadn't pulled me out and made me eat. When I asked why he wasn't with Ehren, he brushed me off, saying I was the one who needed him, but the moment I was a done eating I know he went off in search of Ehren.

On our second day of travel, Ehren noticeably feels better and whatever had been tense between him and Cal seems to be smoothed over. I feel guilty at the relief that washes over me when I realize I can focus on the journal and worry a little less about Ehren. I tell myself that if I can find something in Kato's words that will help me reach him—the real him—then every-body will benefit. It takes a bit of practice, but by the time we've stopped for lunch I'm reading on horseback without falling off.

By the fourth day, I've lost track of how many times I've read the journal from front to back. I decide to turn in a little earlier than normal, hoping that maybe some rest will clear my head and allow me to find some sort of solution. Unfortunately, even when I close my eyes, the words swirl against my eyelids, mocking me. I toss and turn, trying my hardest to force my thoughts to something calmer, something hopeful. When Felixe appears at my feet with a sharp bark, I'm relieved.

"Hey, buddy," I mutter, sitting up and scratching him behind his ears.

He yips and drops a small scroll. I smile and scoop it up, but the smile quickly fades as I read Alak's words. I've barely finished the letter before I'm leaping to my feet, Felixe popping up onto my shoulder to come with me. I race toward Ehren's tent and throw open the tent flap. Ehren and Cal sit in the middle of the tent facing each other, their knees touching. They both jump and stare up at me.

"Ash?" Ehren says, immediately rising, albeit a little slower than normal. "What's wrong?" He glances briefly at Felixe then back to me. "Is Alak okay? Is Luc?"

"Yes, they're both fine. They found the refugees, or at least what's left of them. It's . . . it's not good."

With a trembling hand, I pass Ehren the note. Cal steps up behind him and reads over his shoulder. The further down the paper Ehren gets, the deeper the crease between his brows. When he finishes, he hands the letter back.

"At least they're alive," he offers. "We need to send help, though. I'm not sure what they need. Food? Should we send some of our rations?"

I nod. "If we can spare anything, it might help tide them

over until Luc's army can send more food and supplies. It sounds like what these refugees need the most are Healers. Luc's army isn't overly magical, I'm assuming."

"From what he's told me, those that are magical haven't had much training, so even if he has Healers in his ranks, they may not be able to do everything needed to save these people," Ehren says.

"I can help some," I say, "but I may need to take at least one other Healer with me. Maybe two, if you think we could spare them."

"We should be able to," Ehren replies. "My bigger concern is whether you and the Healers will be able to wisp back to us if you have to stay more than tonight. I don't think it's wise for us to stay in one spot for too long, considering Kato has to be furious we stole Saran. We can slow our pace so we don't get too far ahead, but I don't know that anything beyond that would be safe."

I bite my lip as I think. "You're right. I feel like I could probably find my way back to you, but it's trickier the more people I have with me. I could use the connection Kai has with his shifters, but I don't know how it will work at this distance. Plus, I think I should focus on taking people with me who can actually help with the healing. If my magic wasn't needed to bring the Healers back over the extended distance, I'd consider staying with Alak."

Someone outside the tent clears their throat. Cal steps forward and opens the tent flap to reveal Hanna. She ducks inside the tent with a grin.

"Pip said you needed to talk to me."

I frown. Why would Pip . . . ? My eyes widen.

"We might need your grandmother more than you," Ehren says, offering the girl a smile.

"No, Hanna is exactly who I need."

Ehren shoots me a curious look. "Why?"

"Hanna and Pip have a special connection." I look at the girl. "Don't you?"

Hanna pauses before nodding hesitantly. "We do, but I don't think I'm supposed to know that. Pip knows and his grandfather knows. I heard them talking about it the other night, and it all makes sense."

"Wait," Cal cuts in, glancing between me and Hanna. "What kind of connection?"

I raise my eyebrows to Hanna in a silent question and she nods. I turn to Cal. "Hanna and Pip are bondmates."

Cal's eyes widen as his mouth drops open.

"Like you and Alak?" Ehren asks with a small gasp.

"More or less. Obviously, they haven't been through the bonding ceremony, but even before Alak and I completed the bond, we could still find each other. If I take Hanna with me, she can help Heal and care for the refugees and lead us back here, following the bond she has with Pip."

Ehren studies Hanna for a moment before nodding. "All right. Cal and I will go through the camp and gather up what supplies we can spare if you want to go to the Healers and make arrangements with them. As we make our rounds, I'll fill Kai in on the plan."

I nod. "Sounds perfect. Meet me in the Healing tent when you're ready."

I take a quick moment to write Alak a note so he knows I'm coming, and I head to the Healing tent. Healer Heora isn't present, but the palace Healer is. She immediately starts sorting through their supplies so Hanna and I can pack them up. Saran watches curiously from the corner of the tent, slinking closer as we load up a bag. By the time Healer Heora returns, we have everything ready to go. Once she checks over our packed bag and confirms we should have everything we should need, we wait for Ehren to arrive with the rations. When the tent flap opens, however, it's Kai who enters, a large bag on his shoulder.

"Here's some of the food Ehren and Cal gathered," Kai says, lowering the bag to the floor. "Cal and Ehren took the rest to their tent. Apparently Ehren had an idea and needed to check something."

"Does he want us to wait here or head to the tent?"

"Tent, I believe."

Hanna, Healer Heora, and I follow Kai to the tent, but since the tent is small, I'm the only one to head inside. Ehren sits in the middle of the space, a map spread out in front of him while Cal stands behind him.

"Kai said you had an idea?" I say, squatting down next to Ehren.

"So, according to Alak, the camp would have been in this area," Ehren says, jumping right in as he motions to a spot on the map near the mountains. "That means their most likely escape would've been through here." He traces his finger along a mountain pass. "They're probably planning on following the pass all the way until it comes out closer to where the fortress lies, but"—Ehren shifts, tracing the first path to another section of the mountains—"they could cut through here and avoid traveling the treacherous mountain passes in winter. There's even a small village near the mountain base that could help them replenish any supplies before they head on, or even provide some housing for those that need it."

"Is that village safe?" I ask.

Ehren looks over at me. "Last I heard, it was. I believe Luc has some of his people stationed nearby as a precaution."

"That could work." I smile at Ehren. "Good thinking."

Ehren huffs and it sounds awfully close to a pleased laugh as he rolls up the map and passes it to me. "Take this and show Luc. See what he thinks."

I nod, accepting the map. "I'm sure he'll agree, but I'll pass on the information either way."

I push up from the ground and turn to Cal.

"Here are the rest of the supplies," he says before I can ask, lifting a bag from where it sits on the floor next to him. "It's not much, but it should help."

I shoulder the bag, shooting Cal a grateful smile. "I should probably get going."

"Wait," Ehren calls, reaching up for Cal to help him stand. Cal hoists Ehren to his feet and he takes a step toward me. "Be careful."

I open my mouth to remind Ehren that I'm not only going to be with Alak and Luc but also going to a place reasonably far from the current warfront when he pulls me into a tight hug. I return the embrace and press a quick kiss to his cheek before pulling away.

"Don't worry, I'll be back soon. In fact, the sooner I leave, the sooner I can return."

I give Ehren one last peck before I join the others outside.

"So you have a plan?" Kai asks, his jaw tight.

"I think so."

He hesitates before asking slowly, "Do you want me to come with you?"

I meet Kai's eyes and offer what I hope is a reassuring smile. "If you feel the need to come along, I won't stop you, but I think we both know you're needed here."

Kai studies me a moment before sighing. "I'll see you soon."

He hands over the pack of supplies to Healer Heora and gives us one last nod before he disappears back into the camp. I turn to Hanna and Healer Heora.

"Ready?"

They both nod and I curl my magic around us all and dive into a wisp. The warmth of the camp disappears, replaced by the cold of the mountains. It takes my eyes a moment to adjust to the sudden dimness, but when they do I find a grinning Alak in front of me, Luc blinking at his side.

"Hello, love," Alak says.

"Hey," I say, stepping forward for a kiss. I lift the bag from my shoulder and gesture for the others to step forward with their supplies. "Ehren pulled together some rations that should hold the camp over until you get more."

"I can take them to Mara," Luc says, flushing as he rushes to add, "That way you and Alak can take a moment to catch up."

A smirk plays on Alak's lips as he takes the bag from me and passes it to Luc. "Go ahead. Astra and I won't be far behind."

Luc motions to Hanna and Healer Heora and they follow him into the dark camp.

"It doesn't look good," I mutter as I watch them go.

"It's not ideal, but thanks to your help, I think they'll be okay." Alak draws me into his arms, and I look up at him. "I've missed you, love."

I smile and kiss him. "I missed you, too."

We only take a couple minutes to ourselves before we decide it's best to join the others. After a brief reunion with Mara that involves a lot of tears and hugging, I jump in and help Hanna and her grandmother with the Healing while Alak and Luc make the rounds distributing the rations. Alak rejoins me after a bit, and I can tell he's paying close attention to my magic levels to make sure I'm not overexerting myself. It's not much later when Alak lets out a small gasp.

"What?" I ask, looking up at him from the little girl's leg I've finished bandaging.

Alak stares off past me, his eyes wide. I follow his gaze to a girl who can't be more than fourteen or fifteen years old. She looks exhausted and is likely only standing thanks to her friend who's holding her up.

"Who is she?"

Alak shakes his head like he's clearing his thoughts. "This warding was impressive, but I thought it was like before—a bunch of different people weaving their magic together. I was wrong. It's all her."

My attention darts between Alak and the girl. "You're sure?"

He nods. "Positive. I couldn't tell before, but now that she's this close, I have no doubt."

"No wonder she looks so exhausted. I wonder if she's taken a break at all."

"Her magic is very low," Alak replies. "She'll need to take a break soon or . . ."

He trails off, but I know what he's implying. The girl will kill herself, or at the very least, fall into a comatose state. I quickly cross the camp to the girl, Alak a step behind. When I stop in front of her, she blinks up at me, seemingly surprised by my attention.

"Hello," I say gently. "Is it true this warding is all you?" I motion vaguely to the air and the girl nods. "It's very impressive."

"Th-thank you," she says, dipping her head.

"You should take a break," Alak says, matching my tone. "Your magic is very low and can't last long like this."

The girl shakes her head. "I can't. If I stop, the Dragkonians can find us. We almost died before. I can't lose anyone else."

The girl's words stir a pit in my stomach. I know exactly how she feels.

"We can take over the warding for a bit," Alak offers, motioning between us.

The girl looks skeptical.

"We've kept an entire palace warded," I add, giving the girl what I hope is a reassuring smile. "Compared to that, this camp will be a piece of cake."

"But you've already used a lot of magic healing people. I've seen you," the girl argues.

"That's true, but I still have enough left for this, especially with Alak's help. We're soul-bonded."

The girl's forehead scrunches with confusion.

"It means we can share our magic," Alak explains. "Which is helpful since I have illusion magic that is perfect for creating protective wards."

That seems to be enough for the girl, and she sags in her friend's arms. "Okay. If you're sure."

Even though I don't have Alak's Syphon powers, I still sense the warding as it starts to fade. Alak and I quickly weave our magic together, throwing a new barrier up in its place. Alak's brow furrows with concentration before he nods and smiles.

"It's just as strong as before," he assures the girl. "Now rest and let your magic refill."

The girl's smile is weak as she nods.

"Come on, Millie," her friend says, steering her away. "Let's find you a place to sleep."

As much as I want to follow the girl and make sure she does get the rest she needs, I head back to help the Healers instead. With my magic tied up in the new warding, I'm relegated to simple bandaging and handing out medicine, but it's all that's needed from me. By the time we're done, the sun is rising and I'm too exhausted and drained to even think about wisping back to rejoin Ehren. Instead, I curl up with Alak in a quiet corner and sleep while we wait for word from Luc's messengers.

When I awaken, Alak is gone, but Luc is situated not far away. I sit up and he glances at me with a gentle smile.

"Did you rest well?"

I shrug, rolling my neck. "As well as one can given our condition."

Luc hums, nodding knowingly as he turns his attention to papers spread on the ground in front of him.

"What are you looking at?" I ask, scooting closer.

"Ah, I am looking over the maps." Luc shuffles them, spreading everything out so I can see them. Two are of Callenia —one looks to be the map Ehren sent—and another is of Ascaria. He's used coal from the fire to mark certain places on each map, leaving his fingers covered in black ash.

"You're planning a battle?"

"Not exactly." He shifts to the side so I can move closer. "Alak mentioned to me this morning that your prince suggested we cut through the mountains here." He taps the mountain pass already circled.

"Yes," I say with a nod. "Ehren said there's a village at the mouth of the pass that could give more aid."

"My records show the same." Luc lifts his eyes from the maps to meet mine. "I sent instructions with my messenger to have some of my nearby troops sent to the village for additional protection. Now that we have snatched the boy from Kato's grasp, I expect his attacks may become more sporadic and dangerous, like a cornered animal."

I suck in a breath, not wanting to think of the harm my brother is causing, though I can't disagree. I remind myself that this Kato—the one destroying villages and going after our friends—is not the Kato I know. He's a darker version that's been manipulated by an evil entity. My thoughts must show on my face because Luc places his hand over mine.

"I am sorry," Luc says softly. "I should not speak of your brother in such a manner."

I fail at a smile as I shake my head. "No, you're right. Kato will become more dangerous. We should prepare."

Luc gives my hand a comforting squeeze before pulling his hand back and focusing on the maps.

"If we can move out today, I believe we can reach the village in about a day. Hopefully we will not fall far behind Ehren. It would be best for us to be together when your Fae companions figure out the missing elements to taking down those evil beasts."

I nod, but I'm not sure what else to say. Like Ehren, Luc has a clear, clever mind and a talent for coming up with workable plans. Perhaps it's a prince thing.

"I only wonder . . ." Luc trails off, shaking his head. "Ah, no. She would be safer . . ."

Luc sighs and I furrow my brow. "Who?"

Luc's attention jerks up as if he hadn't meant to say his thoughts aloud. He meets my eyes for only a moment before he glances off, his cheeks growing bright red.

"No one. It was a foolish passing thought," he mumbles, his words jumbled together.

I smile softly. "If you don't want to tell me, of course you don't have to. It's your business."

Luc glances up at me sheepishly. "It truly is nothing. Only . . ." He sighs again and his shoulders drop in something close to resignation. "Your friend is lovely, and I wish I had more of a chance to chat with her." He quickly shakes his head and starts gathering up the maps. "It is no matter."

"Luc," I say gently, placing a hand on his arm. He stills and looks up at me. "If you mean Mara, I can guarantee she would love to get to know you better as well."

His cheeks grow a darker shade of red, and he draws a shaky breath. "Do you truly believe so?"

I nod and offer him a sincere smile. "Definitely. Mara is the friendliest person I know, and she is always open to making more close friends."

Luc attempts to hide his smile, but it slips onto his lips anyway. He clears his throat, cheating away as he resumes arranging the maps into a neat stack.

"Then, perhaps, I will attempt to be her friend." He shoves the maps into his bag and turns back to me. "Thank you."

"It's no problem." I glance out over the camp. "I actually need to go check in with Mara before I head back to Ehren. Would you like to come with me?"

Luc considers me for a moment before he nods slowly. "If you are sure I would not be in the way."

"Of course you wouldn't be." I push up from the ground and offer Luc my hand. "Coming?"

He smiles and accepts. I pull him up and we head through the camp. It doesn't take us long to find Mara. She greets us with a tired smile that grows brighter when she sees Luc. It only takes me a moment to confirm that my efforts are much appreciated and that the camp is already in much better shape. When Mara points me toward where Alak should be, I leave Luc in her care. I find Alak checking in with the girl we met the night before.

"So I can put the warding back up?" she's asking.

Alak nods almost reluctantly. "But be careful. You magic is replenished but not full."

The girl nods but it's her friend who speaks up. "I'll keep an eye on her."

The girl frowns at her friend. "I'll be fine, Viv." The girl looks back at Alak. "Right? If I use a little magic, just enough to keep us hidden, I'll be fine?"

Alak hesitates a moment, so I step forward and answer for him. "It's always best to err on the side of caution." I stop at Alak's side and he slips his arm around my waist. "Use your magic when necessary in small amounts and make sure you take breaks so your magic can refresh."

"She is correct," Alak says to the girl before planting a kiss on my cheek.

The girl glances between us with a scowl. I think she might protest, but in the end she loosens her shoulders and nods.

"Fine. I'll be careful." She pauses before adding, "But I won't hesitate to put myself at risk if it means saving everyone else."

"Millie," her friend admonishes, but the girl shakes her head, cutting her off.

"No. I have magic for a reason, and I'm going to use it for good." She meets my eyes and takes a step closer. "You know the prince well, right? You're his sorceress?"

I swallow, managing a nod. "Yes, I am."

"Is there any way the prince would let me help him?"

"I—" I glance at Alak but he only shrugs. I turn back to the girl. "I'm sure if you're willing, he would accept your help."

Millie perks up while her friend scowls. "Tell him I'm willing." Her friend opens her mouth to say something, but Millie speaks first. "It's my magic and my kingdom. If I can help in any way, if I can save lives, I will."

I nod. I can tell there's no point in fighting against her determination. "I will let Ehren know."

The girl smiles. "Thank you."

"Now, before you replace your warding and I take ours down, you should probably get some breakfast," Alak jumps in.

The girl nods and allows her friend to lead her off. Once they're gone Alak turns to me.

"Morning, love." He gives me a proper kiss before pulling back with a sigh. "You're leaving me now, aren't you?"

I give him a quick kiss. "I'll leave soon. I want to make sure I'm not needed here for anything else first, but I do need to get back to Ehren."

Alak nods, but the light in his eyes dims. "I understand." He pauses as a grin creeps onto his lips. "We should make the most of our time then."

He pulls me in for another kiss, this one far more heated. I surrender to him completely and for a moment, forget we're in the middle of camp. Something nearby crashes, and I jerk back, gasping to catch my breath. Alak looks down at me through lidded eyes as he places a gentle hand to my cheek.

"I love you, Astra," he whispers, tracing his thumb along my cheekbone.

I smile softly and lean into his touch. "I love you, too."

He lowers his hand and laces his fingers with mine. "Let's go make our rounds around the camp so you can leave with your mind at ease."

I nod and allow him to lead me through the camp. A couple minutes later, Felixe appears, perching on Alak's shoulder. I manage to prolong my departure for an hour, but the camp needs to get on the move, and there's no reason for me to linger. Before I leave, Alak pulls me into a tight hug.

"I can't wait until this war is over, so you and I never have to be parted," he whispers in my ear before pressing a kiss to my cheek.

I pull back and offer him what I hope is an optimistic smile. "Soon."

After one last kiss, I step back, turning to Hanna and her grandmother.

"Ready?"

Hanna nods. "What do I need to do?"

"Just think of Pip. Concentrate on your connection," I reply. She closes her eyes and small smile flits on her lips. "Can you sense him?" She nods, keeping her eyes closed. "Good. Now hold onto that feeling."

I wrap us in my magic and connect with Hanna's, allowing her thoughts to direct our wisp. The camp around us fades, and we reappear in a different setting surrounded by Ehren's army, already on the move. It takes me a moment to orient myself, but I quickly find Ehren, riding on Dauntless with Pip and his grandfather only a horse away. Kai is behind me, Luna walking alongside his horse. Ehren catches my eye and smiles, bringing his horse to a halt. It only takes a couple minutes before we're situated and ready to resume our journey. Ehren rides next to me so I can fill him in. His shoulders noticeably relax once he hears that the survivors will be okay, though we know that relief is likely only short lived. We both know we're reaching the beginning of the end.

CHAPTER FORTY

RONAN

Ievis's fingers tap an unsteady rhythm on the desk as he glares down at the text in front of him. I do my best to ignore him as I lie stretched out on his bed, propped up on a pile of pillows while I thumb through a copy of faerie stories he calls "inaccurate trash." I turn the page, taking in the beautiful, foiled artwork as Ievis swears—at least I assume it's swearing since he's speaking his language, but the words don't sound kind—and throws his book across the room.

"Research going great, huh?"

Ievis growls, twisting in his chair to face me. "I do not need your cheek."

I grin, tilting my head. "Perhaps you could use a . . . distraction?"

Color rises quickly across Ievis's pale cheeks as his eyes widen, flicking momentarily to my mouth. I lazily drag my tongue across my lips, Ievis tracking the movement. He swallows hard before turning back around in his chair, hunching over the book.

"I do not have time for your games. Maybe you should leave."

My heart drops along with my smile. While he's been careful and cautious, we've made progress the last few days. We haven't kissed again, but we also haven't fought. Not really. Nothing more than playful banter. There have also been casual touches and real effort on his part not to push me away.

I ease off the bed, the mattress creaking slightly as I push to my feet. "I do apologize," I mutter, my voice coming out far more strained and formal than I like. "I will let you work."

Ievis sighs, straightening in his chair but not quite turning to look at me. "I did not mean that. You can stay." He glances at me over his shoulder, his golden eyes meeting mine. "I like having you here."

I shake my head. "No, I really don't want to be a distraction. I feel like I've played my part in helping you solve the puzzle, and now I'm lingering where I'm not needed."

Ievis rises from the chair with the fluid grace that belongs only to the Fae and crosses to me in three smooth strides. A small gasp escapes me when he loops an arm around my waist and tugs me closer, barely any space between us. My breath hitches and my eyes shutter closed as he leans forward, the warmth of his cheek pressing against mine.

"Stay," he whispers, his lips brushing my ear, sending a pleasant shiver down my spine. "I want you to stay." He pulls back and my eyes flutter open to look into his. "Please?"

I swallow, struggling to get my racing heart in check. "I really don't want to distract you from your work. This is important."

A smile curves on his lips and my heart melts. "I would be more distracted wondering what you were doing if you left. Stay?"

I manage a nod and his smile grows. Gods, he's beautiful.

"Good." He releases me and steps back, his hands falling awkwardly to his sides as if he's not sure what to do with them now.

"What, uh, what are you working on, exactly?" I ask, walking toward the desk, my hand gripping the head of my cane tighter than usual in a desperate attempt to ground myself in some way.

"I am working on tying the magic together," he replies, sinking back into the chair and glaring down at the book. "I have found a way to use my magic to create two spells: one to create the warding we need and one to bind the Dragkonians' life-force to the isle." He turns a page. "I'm struggling to find a way to tie them together to make one spell."

I furrow my brow. "Do they have to be one spell? Can't they work as two?"

"Technically, yes, but they would not be as strong." Ievis looks up at me. "I want to ensure that no one else can break one of the spells again in the future. By binding them together, it would be impossible to break; the spell would be too strong, too solid. It also would ensure that no beast would escape the spell. Even one survivor would be too many."

I find myself nodding, though I don't fully understand how his magic building works. "You have no leads?"

Ievis hesitates before shaking his head. "Not one that would be ideal."

"Not ideal, but there is a possible solution?"

Ievis glances away. "Perhaps." He hurries to add, "I do not want to hastily use a solution simply because it exists, not if a better option could be found."

I hum in agreement. "Is there anything I can do to help combine the spells? Some research I could dig up?"

Ievis shrugs with a heavy sigh. "I doubt it. This is the whole point of my magic. Anyone with the right bloodline can wield magic, but only a select few, like myself, can actually craft something new from practically nothing. Anyone can wield a spell, but very few can create one."

"How exactly does that work?" I ask, my curiosity getting the better of me. "Creating a new spell? How is it different than regular magic?"

Ievis furrows his brow. "It is difficult to explain." He shifts in his chair. "Magic exists essentially everywhere in the world. If someone is born with magic, it usually has a specific focus— earth, air, water, fire, and so on. Many Fae are born with more than one expertise and humans, from what I understand, usually have one. To be able to use any sort of magic beyond that with which one is born usually requires the assistance of spellwork or a magical object."

Ievis pauses, looking up at me to see if I'm following.

"Like my warding magic," I offer. "I was born with it and therefore I can easily use it, but if wanted to create fire I would need to use something such as a Syphon stone."

Ievis licks his lips, nodding. "Precisely. Some magical traits, such as wisping and basic spellwork, can typically be accomplished no matter the type of magic since they do not require a focus, but most things are tied directly to the type of magic a person is born with."

"How does your magic differ?"

Ievis twists in his chair and stares down at the book spread open before him. "I was born without a true focus. I can pull magic directly from the air, more or less, and craft it into any sort of magic I desire."

He lifts his hand and startled gasp escapes my lips as a small, dancing flame comes to life in his palm before twisting in a delicate rose as real and beautiful as those in my gardens at home. He sighs and closes his hand into a fist, the magic snuffing out.

"Of course," he continues, still looking away, "I can't really maintain concentrated magic for long, but what I can do is twist it into a spell and make it wieldable by others. I essentially take magic and make it into something new, something that couldn't otherwise exist on its own. Like taking flour and making bread or combining herbs to make a salve. I can create spells of great power and magnitude that can be wielded by others with magic that they couldn't create themselves. It is not exactly creating something from nothing, but it is as close to the power of the gods as it is possible to have."

I blink down at Ievis. I knew he was powerful—there was a reason he came here in the first place—but now that I have a better understanding of how his magic works, I'm blown away. I can tell by the way his shoulders sink, however, that it's a power that has weighed heavily on him his entire life. I place a hand on his shoulder. He startles slightly but does nothing to evade my touch.

"Is there any way I can help?" I ask, my voice barely above a whisper.

He looks back up at me, his expression strained. "Would you be willing to stay nearby? Your presence is comforting, though, given all my instruction and training, it shouldn't be."

I offer Ievis a soft smile. "Of course."

I settle on the floor next to the desk. I only remain there for a handful of minutes before Ievis insists we'd be more comfortable on the bed. He takes a stack of books to flip through while I lie next to him, my head resting on his shoulder. I don't even realize I've drifted off until I'm awoken by a knock on the door.

Ievis stiffens under me as I blink, trying to clear the sleep from my mind.

"Yes?" Ievis calls out.

The door is flung open and Iefyr waltzes inside. When their eyes fall on the two of us in the bed, they grin. I feel more than hear Ievis's low growl. I immediately struggle into a sitting position, fully intending to flee the bed, but before I can get far, Ievis's arm snakes around me, keeping me pressed against his side.

"What is it, Iefyr?" Ievis demands, his tone threatening.

Iefyr's grin only widens. "No need to be so snippy. I have only come to inform you that Prince Ehren has returned."

Ievis straightens. "Are we needed?"

Iefyr shakes their head. "*You* are not yet needed. The prince has requested a meeting in an hour, during which you can let him know the progress you've had with your spell creation." Ievis nods and his sibling turns their attention to me. "You, however, may be needed now."

I arch an eyebrow. "Me?"

Iefyr nods. "Indeed. It seems a young boy has been brought back with the prince, and he is being . . . surly."

My heart leaps with this information. "So they were successful in getting Saran?"

"It would appear so."

I frown. "But how can I help?"

"Ah, well, the boy refuses to speak a language anyone else can understand."

I bite back a laugh. I know very well what it's like to be able to speak Yallik when no one else around you can.

"Where is he?"

"I believe he has been taken to a room in the northeast wing."

"I will be there shortly."

Iefyr nods, shooting their brother one last knowing look before they back out of the room, shutting the door behind them. I go to scoot off the bed, but Ievis still has me firmly in his grip.

"If I'm going to go check on the boy, you'll need to release me," I tease, tilting my head as I look over at Ievis.

He tenses a moment before relaxing his grasp and slowly withdrawing his arm. "Will you be in the meeting with the prince?"

I shrug as I ease off the bed. "If I'm needed." I grab my cane and turn to face Ievis, who's watching me carefully, his face betraying nothing. "Do you want me there?"

He turns his attention back to the book in his lap, very purposefully not looking at me as he mumbles, "I would not mind your presence."

I grin. "You can admit you'd like me there, Ievis."

He raises his eyes to mine and something in me stills at the intensity of his gaze.

"I want you there," he says, his voice low and rough.

I struggle to hold my smile as something very warm and very welcoming rushes over me. It takes very ounce of self-control I possess not to jump back on the bed and kiss the Fae male senseless. I clear my throat and straighten, my face warming.

"Then I'll be there." I glance toward the door. "I should go find the boy."

"Right. Right. Go on." He gestures toward the door. "I will see you later."

I hesitate a moment, resisting the urge to brush a quick kiss on Ievis's cheek. In the end I manage to restrain myself and leave the room with a sigh. I'm halfway down the hallway before I realize I'm not entirely sure I'm headed in the right direction. Fortunately, it doesn't take much wandering before I catch the exasperated tones of a maid pleading with a young voice jabbering away in Yallik. I approach the room the conversation is coming from and peek inside through the open door. I'm guessing this room used to be a nursery or a study of some sort. A very tired looking maid stands in the center of the room, while a young boy with red hair scowls up at her.

"I can't understand what you're saying," the maid says, weariness lining every word.

"*I don't want to be trapped in this bloody room,*" the boy replies, his Yallik thick and rich.

The maid groans and I suppress a chuckle, stepping into the room. "*It's rude to converse in a language no one else can understand.*"

The boy's eyes widen as he startles back a step while the maid turns her frown to me.

"Hello," I say, inclining my head to her. "I'm Lord McDullun. I heard that I could be of assistance?"

She seems surprised by my sudden appearance, but she blinks, recovering quickly. "I . . . If you could, perhaps, tell me what he's saying, I would greatly appreciate it."

"It appears he would rather be elsewhere," I reply.

The maid sighs. "There's nowhere else to take him."

"*I'm not a child! She keeps treating me like a child,*" Saran mumbles in Yallik. He gestures to the room. "*Only a toddler would be happy in here.*"

I bite back a laugh. "If you would speak Callenian, which I am positive you know very well, your chances of being allowed to do something more interesting would likely increase."

The boy glares at me. "Fine." He crosses his arms and turns to the maid. "Take me somewhere more interesting."

"Please," I tack on, giving the boy what I hope is an admonishing look.

He rolls his eyes. "Please?"

The maid glances between us, her expression worried. "Prince Ehren asked that I watch over him somewhere out of the way. I don't know—"

"Perhaps I can offer a solution?" I say, cutting her off. "I need to go outside and check the warding. If Saran would like to accompany me, he is welcome to come along."

"Oh, I don't know," the maid hedges, though I can tell by the way her shoulders loosen she would love nothing more than to pass the lad off to me. "You're too important to take over babysitting duties. I'm sure you have other things to do. Prince Ehren did instruct me to care for the boy."

I chuckle. "I can assure you I have nothing more pressing at the moment, and I doubt the prince would mind if the lad came with me. If anything is said to you about the boy disappearing from your care, send them my way."

The maid hesitates a moment while she considers my offer before nodding. "Very well. Thank you, Lord McDullun."

She sweeps from the room quickly, almost as if she's afraid I'll change my mind. I turn to the boy to find him staring up at me, his brow crinkled as he studies me.

"Are ya really a Clan Lord?" he asks.

"Ah, so you do speak Callenian quite well."

The boy blushes and glances away, shoving his hands in his pockets. "Aye. I just wanted to have some fun."

"I understand, but when something becomes aggravating for the other person, it's best not to draw it out. Understand?" The boy nods, refusing to meet my eye. "Good. Now, to answer your question, I am indeed a Clan Lord."

The boy's expression brightens as he looks back up at me. "Really?"

I smile down at him. "Really. And I do need to check on the warding if you want to join me."

The boy tilts his head in consideration for a moment before he nods. "Aye. I'd like that."

It takes a few minutes to locate a cloak for the boy, but then we head outside. He remains quiet until we're nearly out to the first warding stone, but I can tell he's thinking hard about something.

"If you're an Athiedor Lord, why were ya so keen to join Prince Ehren? Didn't ya want Athiedor to be free?"

The question bursts out of him like he simply can't contain it a moment longer. As soon as the words escape his lips, his face turns bright red with embarrassment and regret, and he glances off.

"That's a fair question, I suppose. I take it your family sided against the prince?" The boy nods. "Why do you think that was?"

Saran shrugs but when I don't offer any explanation of my own he sighs. "My Da always said Athiedor was meant to be free, that the Callenian royalty were only good fer nothin' bastards. When Master Kato promised him protection and a free Athiedor, he didn't even hesitate to join his side. When the Clan Lords signed a treaty with the prince, he was furious."

There's a certain heaviness in the boy's voice that makes my heart sink.

"Where's your Da now, Saran?"

The boy looks up at me with cold eyes, and I know what he's going to say even before the words leave his mouth.

"He's dead, along with my Ma and my brother. My sister is the only one still alive, and from I've heard, she's gone mad."

Even though he manages to keep his voice steady, grief weighs down each word.

"You know," I say softly as we come to a stop at the warding stone, "my father is also dead."

The boy's eyes widen as he looks up at me. "Yeah? Did he die in the war?"

I shake my head. "He died a few years ago, but it doesn't necessarily make it easier. Some days I miss him a lot."

Saran nods, looking down at his feet. "I wanted to make my Da proud," he whispers. "And he was so proud when Kato chose me. *I* was proud Kato chose me." He blinks up at me through tear-filled eyes. "I thought I was working to help Athiedor be free, like Da always wanted, but then Kato started to hurt lots of people. I didn't want to help him anymore. I lied about what the shadows told me, and my Da—" He breaks off as his voice wavers, but he raises his chin and continues. "My Da died in the battle because of bad information. Niall, my brother, blamed me."

"Hey," I say, easing down to kneel in front of the boy so I'm more or less eye level with him. I keep one hand on my cane and place a hand on the boy's shoulder. He meets my eyes, his chin quivering. "It wasn't your fault."

"But it was!" he yells, tears breaking free. "If I'd been honest, he'd be alive!"

I hesitate, trying to find the right words, though I suspect there are no right words when it comes to telling a child that sacrificing their own father may have been the right choice.

"Did you save more people than you hurt?"

Saran sniffs. "What?"

"By not telling the truth, did you save people? Innocent people?"

Saran considers me for a moment before nodding slowly. "I saved a whole village."

I give his shoulder a gentle squeeze. "Then you did good. I am sorry you lost your father and your brother, but it wasn't your fault. They made a choice to follow Kato, and they made choices to go into battle. Whatever happened were consequences of their own actions."

Saran sniffs again, dragging his arm across his face to wipe his nose. "But what do I do now that I'm alone?"

I sigh and focus on refreshing the warding magic so I have a moment to think. When I finish, I look over at the boy to find him watching me expectantly.

"Do you know the plans for your sister?" I ask, pushing up and resuming our path toward the next stone.

Saran shrugs, scuffing his toe in the dirt as we walk. "I think someone said something about sending her away. I don't know. She's gone mad, though, so I don't think she could take care of me even she wanted to be around me. I'm an unwanted orphan."

"You don't think she wants to be around you?"

Saran refuses to look up at me. "I wouldn't want to be around the brother that killed—helped kill—my Da."

I hum and look ahead. "I suppose I could understand why you think that, but from what I've seen of your sister, she loves you very much. She was quite adamant that you be rescued and protected."

I glance down at the boy to find him staring up at me with wide eyes.

"Really?"

"Aye. She cares for you and your safety very much. You two are all each other has right now. I doubt she would turn you away."

Saran looks back down at his feet. "Yeah. Maybe." He sighs, kicking a small stone that goes skirting across our path. "But even if she does want to keep me around, she probably won't be allowed to stay as close as Athiedor."

"You want to stay in Athiedor?"

The boy scowls up at me. "Of course I do. It's my home. I'm proud to be from Athiedor."

A thought rises and I try to push it away, but something about the determination in the boy's voice has me seriously considering it.

"What if you could have a home in Athiedor, but it was with a different Clan?" I ask carefully.

"You mean somewhere other than Clan Dughlas?" I nod and the boy tilts his head in thought. After a moment he shrugs. "That'd be okay, I guess. Better than being dragged off somewhere new or forced to stay in Callenia." He looks up at me. "Why?"

I swallow and slow to a stop as we approach the next stone. I turn to face the boy and take a steadying breath.

"If, when the war is over, you need a home in Athiedor, you are welcome to join me at my estate in Clan McDullun."

The boy's eyes widen and his mouth drops open. "You mean I could stay with you? But you're a lord!"

I smile softly and incline my head. "Aye, I am. And I'm a lonely lord." I mean to keep my voice light, but more emotion and heaviness creep in than I intend. "There are not many children running around my estate, and it's far too quiet for my taste. You, and your sister if permitted and willing, are welcome."

Saran holds my gaze, his jaw set. "What happens when you have a child of your own?"

A small huff escapes before I can stop it. "I doubt you'll

ever have to worry about that, but even if it does somehow manage to happen—which, once again, I see no possibility of it occurring—you will still be a welcome resident."

Saran considers me and I catch a small smile twisting at the corner of his mouth. After a moment he nods sharply. "All right."

I grin. "Good." I turn and gesture down at the stone. "Now, why don't we finish up this warding spell, and then we'll head inside and find a snack to tide us through the meeting with the prince? Sound like a plan?"

Saran gives me a truly genuine smile as he nods. "That sounds good."

I return the smile and feel like maybe for the first time in a while things might actually turn out okay.

CHAPTER FORTY-ONE

EHREN

My nerves remain unsettled the entire time Astra is away with Alak and Luc. I expect things to return to normal once she returns, however, I still feel anxious, like something will inevitably go wrong at any moment. To put my mind at ease and hopefully subvert Kato's likely expectations, Cal suggests taking a small detour. I'm not sure if it works or if we're just lucky, but we manage to make it back to the Summer Palace without any major incidents.

It's mid-afternoon when we arrive, but I almost wish night had already fallen so I could have an excuse to hide away in my chambers and avoid everyone's expectations for a little while longer. Cal seems to sense my hesitation to jump directly into business, and immediately tells one of servants who's come out to greet us that we'll meet with everyone in an hour. I shoot him a grateful smile before making arrangements for someone to watch over Saran so we can head to my room in peace.

Once the bedroom door closes behind us, I draw Cal into

429

my arms and kiss him. When I pull back, I lean my forehead against his.

"Thank you," I whisper, brushing a ghost of a kiss on his nose.

"We can wait until morning if you need more time," he says, linking his fingers behind my neck.

I shake my head. "No, let's get it over with."

I sigh heavily and release Cal. He drops his hands but remains by my side as I cross my room and throw open my wardrobe. The small movement should be simple, but it makes me wince, traces of ever-present pain shooting down my back.

"Would you like me to run you a bath?" Cal asks, glancing toward my washroom. "You can wash up and soak your sore limbs a bit."

I scowl at him over my shoulder as I toe off my boots. "You're not a servant, Cal."

He laughs softly and steps up behind me, wrapping his arms around my waist as he leans in to kiss my neck.

"No," he whispers, his lips brushing my ear, "but I'm willing to help you with whatever you need, especially if it gets you out of your clothes."

My cheeks warm. I'm still not entirely used to Cal's bold, flirtatious side and love when he shows it.

"Besides," he continues, his voice low as he pulls away, his long fingers already working to undo the buttons of his shirt, "I would be more than happy to join you."

Longing pools in my gut, and I suddenly have the overwhelming desire to push off any meetings for the rest of the night and spend the time with Cal. In my bath. Then my bed. Then anywhere else I can have him. I close my eyes and shake the thoughts from my head.

"No, if we get in the bath now, I'm not sure we'll make it

out." I turn and meet Cal's eyes with a smile. "Maybe that can be my reward for making it through the afternoon?"

A devious grin twitches on Cal's lips as he shrugs out of his shirt. "I'll make sure you're rewarded well then." His expression sobers, as he notices I haven't started to undress. "Do you need help changing?"

I swallow and glance away. Even though it's been a few days since my injury, even things as simple as changing clothes can be difficult. Things should be getting easier, but they aren't. They likely never will. Cal must sense the dip in my mood because barely a moment later he's turning me to face him, his hands settling on my waist as his eyes search my face.

"I didn't mean to upset you," he says, his voice tight like he's trying to hold back his emotions.

I shake my head, glancing to the side. "You didn't."

"Ehren . . ."

I look back into his eyes and offer him a weak smile. "Really, Cal. It's fine. And yes, if you could help, I would appreciate it."

"Whatever you need, my prince," he says, pressing a kiss to my cheek.

We take our time changing out of our travel clothes, pausing to rinse a little of the road from our skin using the washbowl. Cal helps me with tenderness, pausing occasionally to press a kiss to one of my many scars. We finish quickly enough we have a little time to ourselves. We curl up together on my bed, foreheads pressed together as we hold each other. When the time comes to head to the Meeting Hall, I reluctantly allow Cal to pull me from the room.

When we arrive, I find a few members of my Guard loitering about with Jess, Kaeya, Winnie, and Nyco huddled in one corner. When Jess sees me, she stomps my way.

"Now that you're back, you can be responsible again."

A smile quirks on my lips. "Done with ruling already?"

Jess groans but I don't miss the sparkle in her eyes. "It's exhausting."

"Well, from what I've heard, you handled everything very well."

She shrugs. "I did what needed to be done." She glances down to my missing hand, but nothing more than basic interest shows on her face when she looks back up. "How are you doing?"

"As fine as can be, I expect." I pause, licking my lips, trying to find the words to ask what I need, to voice what I've been thinking over for the past several days.

Jess narrows her eyes at me. "You're acting suspicious."

A small laugh escapes me. "Nothing suspicious, but I have proposition for you. It's something I've been thinking about more and more lately."

"A proposition?"

"Yes, and I hope you'll consider it carefully."

She glances over her shoulder at Kaeya, who's listening carefully to every word we say. "Fine," she says, turning her attention back to me. "What's your proposition?"

I meet her eyes with a steady calm I haven't felt in months. "I want you to rule Callenia."

She stumbles back a step, her eyes wide. "What?"

"I want you to rule Callenia," I repeat. "You've proven your-self twenty times over since you arrived. You're what our kingdom needs, Jess."

"But . . . No. You're the rightful king," she sputters, shaking her head.

"I'll rule with you," I continue quickly. "Prince Luc and

Princesse Nicolette are ruling together, and I think we'd be good together, too."

"What makes you think that?" she demands, a challenge in her voice. "You and I are almost as opposite as can be."

"Exactly. We balance each other. Besides, you were born first. You should be the queen, but because of stupid rules and regulations, you're not. Father may have cast you from this kingdom, but I'm asking you to come back. Rule with me, and one day, I will step down and let you have the kingdom all to yourself. It's your birthright."

Her mouth gapes open as she stares at me.

"I struggle sometimes to even get out of bed," I confess, keeping my voice quiet so no one else besides those in our little corner can overhear. "My kingdom needs someone who can stay strong. You're that person, Jess. Please, rule with me."

"Do it, Jess," Winnie says softly, placing a hand on Jess's arm. "It's your destiny."

She laughs, shaking her head. "You're all crazy."

"They're not, *Jaanu*," Kaeya says, taking her hand. "I always knew you were meant for something greater than leading the Valley."

Jess blinks at her paramour in shock. "I need to think it over," Jess mumbles, shaking her head in what I assume is disbelief.

I nod. "That's all I ask. We'll be fighting our final battle soon and knowing that my kingdom—our kingdom—is in your hands will be a comfort in and of itself."

Before I can say anything more, I'm distracted by Astra and Kai entering the room. Astra catches my eye and offers me a reassuring smile as she crosses my way. I meet her halfway.

"Ready for this?"

I swallow. "I hope so."

Astra takes my hand. "You can do it." She gives my hand a squeeze before letting go. "I have faith in you, Ehren."

She leads the way to the throne-like chairs at the head of the table. I take my usual seat to her left, while Kai situates himself in Alak's usual chair, and Cal settles in the chair to my left. A small rumble carries over the room when three of the Fae—Hycis, Rynia, and Iefyr—enter the room. I figured everyone would be used to their presence by now, but I suppose they've stayed mostly hidden away. Hycis shoots Astra a toothy grin that seems equal parts amusement and threat. I tense up, but when Astra returns the smile accompanied by a small wave of greeting, I relax.

A few more soldiers trickle in—a mix of mine, Luc's, Jess's, and Kai's taking up various positions around the edges of the room. Ievis appears a couple minutes later, but he hovers in the doorway with a scowl. When he realizes Iefyr is watching him, he huffs and slinks into the room and takes up a position leaning against the wall behind where his sibling sits, his arms crossed. When Ronan enters a moment later, Saran skipping along behind him, something very close to a smile crosses Ievis's lips for a brief moment as he pushes away from the wall, shoving his hands in his pockets. Ronan smiles affectionately toward the grumpy Fae and takes one of the few remaining seats next to Iefyr. Interesting.

I wait a few more minutes to make sure everyone I need is present before starting the meeting. When I stand, silence cascades across the room as all eyes turn to me. I swallow and take a deep breath. I can do this. I turn my attention to the Fae first.

"What can you report? How are the poisoned weapons coming along? And the spell?"

"Well, we don't have any way to stop Kato and his

magical army, but we can at least take care of the Dragkoni-ans." Hycis grins. "We have vast amounts of the poison ready to go. Many weapons have already been well-coated, and we have enough extra to cover additional weapons from the other armies."

My heart picks up pace in my chest. "So you're saying we actually have a chance to end this once and for all?"

"Correct," Hycis says, her eyes shining. "You only need to figure out how to take out that false king who's leading the army."

Kato. She means Kato. I turn my attention Astra. Her face is more somber than I've seen it in a while.

"Speaking of my brother," she says, her voice barely above a whisper as she meets my eyes, "I think you might have to be the one to kill him."

I glance over at Cal before looking back at Astra. "Why me?"

She drops her eyes to the table, forcing a smile I don't believe. "Because I'm not the one who received the sword blessed by the gods." Her smile falters as tears fill her eyes. "I'm not sure I could do it anyway."

The sudden weight of the task presses down on me, and I squeeze my eyes shut for a moment. When I open them, I manage a nod.

"I'll do it so you don't have to, but I won't relish it. Not real-ly," I manage, my voice barely above a whisper. "But if you need me to do it, I will. If we can't find a way to save him, that is. You still have the journal."

She nods, pulling the small book from her pocket and flip-ping to a random page. "I do, but think it's a fruitless endeavor."

I place a hand on her shoulder, not sure how to continue or

comfort her in the middle of this crowded room. Thankfully, Hycis speaks up, breaking the tension and drawing attention.

"If the spell Ievis is putting together works, we may need Astra with us to seal the Isle. She won't be at your battle for the kingdom," Hycis adds.

I nod, looking to Ievis. "How close are you to completing the spell?"

"Days," Ievis answers, crossing his arms as he shifts, clearly uncomfortable having the attention on him. "I have the two spells required to complete the task. I am currently searching for the best way to use my magic to tie them together."

I lick my lips and nod absentmindedly. "So, we should start moving our armies into place?"

Iefyr nods. "It would likely be best. I don't know much about human armies, but I imagine the strategy is much the same—you want to strike when they're weakest."

I glance over at Astra. "Do you know when Luc and Alak are set to arrive?"

Astra nods. "I received word from Alak this morning that confirmed they should arrive in two days, weather permitting."

Kai clears his throat, drawing my attention. "Should we send word to all the armies to gather at Embervein?"

"Is that wise?" Jess cuts in. "Surely Kato would react poorly if he sees armies gathering outside the palace."

"I may have a solution to that, actually," Astra says quickly. "There's a girl coming here with Alak and Luc who has incredible masking and warding magic. She could easily hide all of our armies. It wouldn't be a long-term solution, as it would drain her magic, but if we timed it well enough, she could give us an advantage."

Jess nods, considering Astra's words. "You're sure she'd be willing to do this?"

Astra nods. "Yes."

"Even then," Jess cuts in, "we should probably leave the armies in place that are protecting specific cities."

I nod. "Of course. We'll only move armies whose movement won't put innocents at risk. Even without them, we should be able to mobilize a good many soldiers to Embervein." I let my gaze travel across the table. "Any other concerns?"

"Not a concern, necessarily, but I may be able to add some assistance for the battle," Ronan says calmly. When I nod for him to continue, he straightens in his seat and places a box on the table. When he flips it open, I vaguely recognize the stones lying on the velvet.

"Are those portal stones?"

"Aye," he says with a sharp nod. "I've worked with Master Arcanis to create escape routes of a sort. We can set up these portals around the edges of the battle to allow the wounded access to more Healers and magic than we could otherwise offer. It would also allow innocents to escape and seek refuge among our allies."

I blink. Ronan's offer is unexpected but welcome. It's well thought out. Having our way in but as well as a way out has my heart racing. It has me realizing that this is really happening.

"How will you get to Atroxmorte once the spell is ready?" I ask, focusing my attention back on Ievis as I struggle to keep my breathing steady. "I'm assuming you'll need to be on location for the spell to work?"

"My portal magic can get us to the edge of Paravlia," Iefyr

answers for their brother, offering me a gentle smile. "From there we will take a ship to get closer to the Isle."

"How many days will you be on the ship?" I press, my heart pounding so hard I can barely hear anything over it. Everything is happening so fast. I should have been prepared. I should have been more ready.

"Four, maybe five days. By design, Atroxmorte is far from the land," Iefyr replies.

Panic rises in my chest, and I look over at Astra. In a handful of days, she'll be far away, risking everything. She offers me a weak smile and takes my hand in hers.

"We'll be done and together soon, the war nothing but a memory," she whispers, squeezing my hand in a way that tells me she's as frightened as I am. "We can do it, Ehren."

I take a shaky breath and release it slowly. "We can do it."

Everything is falling into place. Soon the war will be at an end. Or we'll fail miserably and all be dead. My chest contracts at the thought and I struggle to breathe. In a matter of days everyone in this room could be dead.

"So, we gather our available armies in Embervein," Cal cuts in, his steady voice drawing me out of my spiral.

"I can send some of my shifters with the message," Kai offers. "They will be able to travel faster and more efficiently than a normal messenger, and that way we can make sure everyone receives the message in time."

I nod, fighting to stay in the moment. "That would be appreciated." I let my eyes trail over everyone in attendance. "Anything else we should discuss?"

"I think we should have a ball," Winnie declares with a clap of her hands.

Her suggestion startles me, causing all my panic to immediately flee as I blink at her in confusion.

"A ball?" Kai frowns, voicing what most of us must be thinking.

"Yes," Winnie says, holding her chin high. "In a few days, once Luc has returned with his army but before everyone goes off to fight. Obviously we can't have a full ball, but we can dance and spend the night together having fun. It's a custom."

"I like it," Astra agrees with a wide smile. "A ball." She turns to me. "And she's right—it is a Callenian tradition to have a ball before sending an army out. It's meant to be good fortune." Her foot nudges mine under the table. "What do you think?"

I laugh. I can't help it. The idea of planning a ball when the world is about to end is ridiculous. And yet . . .

"I think it sounds amazing," I say, the grin still on my lips as I meet my sister's bright eyes. "Let's have a ball."

Part Three: Downpour

CHAPTER FORTY-TWO

The next few days stretch endlessly, a shadow hanging over us all. As agreed in the meeting, Kai sends shifters out as messengers to all the available armies, instructing them to gather near Embervein. I reach out to Naskein and confirm that the portals will be ready to go. Saran insists on helping and constantly asks the shadows questions, relaying that Kato's attention is elsewhere and, for now, we are safe. He also manages to confirm the locations of the various armies. When I relay the information to Ehren, he seems apprehensive to use information from the boy—not from lack of trust but out of care and concern for the boy himself. Once he hears the determination in Saran's voice, however, he accepts the information without protest, though I can tell he's still slightly uncomfortable using the boy.

Luc and Alak arrive a couple days after our meeting, as expected. They're a bit surprised to hear about the ball in a few days' time, but neither argue. I find myself spending all my spare time with an increasingly grumpy Ievis, Saran often by my side. By the time the day of the ball arrives, tensions are high. I try to keep myself distracted by reading stretched out on Ievis's bed while Saran reads one of my books of faerie stories in an armchair in the corner of Ievis's room.

"There's no other way," Ievis grumbles before slamming his book shut.

I sit up and send Ievis a concerned look. "Are you okay?"

Ievis growls and shakes his head, refusing to meet my eyes. "We are out of time and there is no other solution."

He looks over at me and something about his expression is . . . apologetic?

"Ievis," I say, sliding off the bed and crossing to him without grabbing my cane. "What's wrong?"

"Nothing and everything. I—" He sighs and shakes his head. "Never mind. I have a solution, and we leave in the morning."

I offer him a tight smile. "At least you have a solution that will work the way you need?"

He nods. "It is not the best solution, but it is a valid solution." He glances to the small clock on the bedside table. "Should we get ready for the ball?"

I cock my head, looking down at the handsome Fae. "I thought you were dreading the ball."

Ievis mumbles under his breath, and I lean closer.

"I'm sorry, I didn't quite catch that."

He makes a sound somewhere between a growl and sigh.

"I said," he grits out, a blush rising on his cheeks, "I do not mind a ball if it means getting to dance with you."

I grin and drape my hands over his shoulders as I bend down and kiss his cheek.

"I look forward to dancing with you, too," I whisper in his ear before kissing his cheek one last time and standing straight.

"*You two are gross,*" Saran complains in Yallik from his corner of the room as he makes a face. "*Caitlyn and Niall were always that way, too. It's too much. Find a room.*"

I laugh heartily while Ievis scowls. So far he hasn't been able to translate the Yallik, and he hasn't bothered to hide his frustration when it's in use.

"*We are in a room—Ievis's room.*" I switch to Callenian before Ievis combusts. "And what did I tell you about speaking Yallik when others can't understand it? It's rude."

Saran shrugs, clearly not giving a damn. I sigh and stand straighter, reaching for my cane.

"We need to get you ready for the ball." I gesture for Saran. "Come on."

He groans, sinking down into the chair. "Do I *have* to go?"

"You don't have to, but I think you'll have fun." He groans again and I bite back a smile. "When I was your age I never got to attend any of the formal balls, and I always missed out on the cake."

Saran brightens, sitting up in the chair. "There's cake?"

"Lots of cake, as well as other treats."

Saran tilts his head before dramatically sighing and setting the book aside so he can rise from the chair. "I suppose a ball wouldn't be the worst thing to do."

I chuckle. "I'm sure there are many worse things." I place my free hand on Saran's shoulders and direct him toward the door. I pause in the doorway, glancing back at Ievis. "I'll see you in a bit?"

Ievis grunts and nods, waving us off.

Saran trails along with me to my room, and we get ready together. Despite his earlier protests, he practically preens in his new emerald green tunic. Even though the tailor who put together his outfit was swamped with work, he had no issue putting both the Fae Fox crest of Clan Dughlas and the rose crest of Clan McDullun on the boy's breast pocket. I dress in a tunic I fetched from my home. It's a similar green, stitched with golden thread and bearing my rose crest.

Despite his earlier protests, Saran is practically bouncing as we make our way to the ballroom. We're close enough to hear string music playing when we run into Hanna dragging Pip toward us as his grandfather follows behind at a slower pace. Hanna is dressed in a sweeping dress made of layered pink tulle while Pip is dressed in a sharp black tunic. They come to a halt in front of us, and Hanna grins at Saran.

"This is my very first ball!" she says, her eyes bright. "Pip's too. Have you been to a ball before?"

Saran straightens his shoulders, making himself as tall as possible. "I've been to many dances before, but nothing this formal in a palace."

"Well, then, let's get in there!" Hanna cries, lunging forward to grab Saran's wrist.

Saran shoots me a slightly panicked look over his shoulder as Hanna drags him and Pip toward the ballroom. I chuckle to myself and give the boy a thumbs up before he disappears inside.

"Oh, to be young again," Pip's grandfather—Gavin, if I recall correctly—says, stepping up to my side. He glances over at me. "Though, I expect you're much closer to their age than you are to mine."

I offer him a polite smile. "Perhaps, though there are many days where I feel much older than my years suggest."

He nods knowingly. "I suppose that is part of the territory of coming into a leadership at a younger age."

Not sure how to respond, I merely hum in agreement. Gavin motions for us to head to the ball and I nod, falling into step beside him. When he pauses just outside the door and looks up at me, fear swells in my chest as I turn to him.

"Keep the boy with you, follow your gut, and all will be well," he says, his voice weighted.

"Saran?" I ask. "Is this a prophecy? Did you See something?"

He lifts a shoulder in a half-shrug. "As much as I ever See anything, but yes. The boy holds more power than he knows, and if you listen to him, if you trust him and yourself, despite your reservations, all will turn out well."

"For me or for us all?"

Gavin offers me a sad smile. "Ah, of that I cannot be sure."

A few other guests—Ascarian soldiers judging by their uniforms—push past us to join the ball, but I'm frozen in my spot.

"You can't tell me more?" I press.

"Only that you're on the right path. Beyond that, I have nothing more I can share." He sighs and forces a smile. "We should probably head inside and keep an eye on our wards, don't you think?"

Without another word, Gavin moves into the ballroom. It takes me a bit longer to collect myself, but I follow suit a moment later, a man at the door announcing my presence and title.

According to Astra, the ballroom at the main palace is far larger and grander than the one here at the Summer Palace, but I can tell immediately that this far outdoes any ballroom I've been in before. The walls themselves shine and shimmer with gilded columns running along the outer edges of a glorious marble dance floor. As I weave into the crowd, I spot Saran off to the side with Hanna and Pip, all three of their eyes fixed on the ceiling above. When I look up to see what caught their attention, I gasp. The domed ceiling is filled with what appears to be an exact rendition of the night sky, the stars shining bright enough to light the room.

"Isn't it marvelous?" A cheerful voice says behind me. I turn to find Princess Cadewynn.

"It is quite lovely. I assume this is Astra's doing?"

Cadewynn's head bobs as her eyes shine. "Yes. There was one time, back in Embervein when she was practicing to dance, where she lit our practice room with stars. She promised that one day after my father—"

The girl stops abruptly, her eyes dimming for a moment before she rallies herself, but even then some of her previous joy has diminished. She shakes her head.

"No matter. Astra promised to one day fill a real ballroom with stars."

I smile gently at the princess. "And Astra made good on that promise."

"Very much. I— Oh, thank you, Nyco!" She breaks off, turning her attention to her handsome young Guard handing her a cup of sparkling cider.

"You're more than welcome, Winnie," Nyco says, pressing a quick kiss to her cheek that has her blushing with delight as she accepts the cup.

"I can hold your drinks if you two wish to dance," Sama says, stepping up next to Nyco.

Nyco glances between the two and asks, "You don't mind?"

Sama smiles softly. "Of course not."

Nyco winks at the girl. "I'll dance with you next."

"And I'll hold the drinks!" Cadewynn insists almost too brightly.

I offer the trio a polite departing nod before making my way to a quiet corner to watch the festivities, taking in the sea of familiar faces. Astra and Alak are the easiest to find, already in the center of the dance floor. Astra wears a sweeping amethyst gown that clearly displays her beauty and power, while Alak wears a stunningly crafted deep gray tunic. Kai is also present with a gorgeous woman in a deep red dress who insists on dragging him onto the dance floor despite his obvious protests. When Ehren and Cal arrive, everyone pauses briefly to acknowledge their presence, Cal's ears turning a deep crimson when he's introduced as "Captain Callon Browen, Future Prince Consort," before the music and dancing resume.

I make my way over to the food table to sample the selection that was wrangled up for the occasion and indulge in some wine. I'm midway through my second glass when the Fae arrive with Jessalynn and her crew. My heart picks up, but immediately drops when I notice Ievis isn't among them. Rynia and Hycis head directly to the dance floor as Iefyr heads my direction. They pretend they came for the food, selecting a small teacake before making their way to my side.

"He will be here," they say, nibbling the cake. "Oh, this is quite good."

I straighten, knowing it would be pointless to deny that I know who Iefyr is referring to.

"It's fine if he's otherwise engaged," I say, hoping my voice doesn't betray my lie. "I suspect a ball isn't quite his style."

Iefyr chuckles. "Most definitely not—especially not a human ball—but he will be here nonetheless." They look up at me with a sly grin. "After all, Ievis has never been very good at denying himself when he truly wants something."

Before I can ask exactly what Iefyr means, they're shoving the last bit of cake into their mouth and moving toward Astra and Alak, who are leaving the dance floor several feet away. I sigh and move further into the corner to watch the revelry, wishing I had brought a book with me. I'm debating if I want to abandon the event altogether when I'm vaguely aware of someone stepping up behind me.

"May I have this dance?" a low voice says in my ear, making me jump.

I spin around and come face to face with a smirking Ievis. "Gods! You need to stop sneaking up on me!"

Ievis grins. "But it is so fun." He takes a step back and bows from the waist, giving me a full view of his beautiful fitted golden tunic as he extends his hand. "So, may I have this dance?"

My heart leaps into my throat as I consider his offer. "I-I'm not a very good dancer," I hedge, glancing off as my face warms.

The truth is, my leg has always made dancing difficult. I'm typically paired with lovely young women and expected to lead when I could barely manage to guide myself with any sense of grace. Dances often end poorly, with both myself and my dance partner stumbling into each other constantly before I'm allowed to bow and make a quick exit. No amount of dance lessons ever seemed to alleviate my issues, either.

Ievis shakes his head. "I was promised a dance."

I open my mouth to protest and he silences me by placing a warm finger on my lips.

"One dance, then if you do not desire another, I will not insist on more."

I swallow and Ievis drops his finger from my mouth. "And if I do? Insist on more, I mean."

Ievis smiles, making him breathtakingly beautiful. "Then, my sweet little human mistake, I will dance with you as long as the gods will allow."

My heart swoops and when Ievis extends his hand again, I

accept. We're halfway to the dance floor when Iefyr material-izes at my side, offering to look after my cane for me. Ievis instantly takes the lead the moment we step onto the dance floor. At first I stumble as usual, tripping over my own feet, but Ievis never releases his grip.

"Relax," he whispers, pulling me closer as he guides me, his steady hand gripping my waist. "I have you, and I am not going to let you go."

My brain stutters, as does my heart, but I do as he says, relaxing into his hold. After that everything goes smoothly, and we remain on the dance floor until I've lost count of how many dances have passed. I start to take more notice of those around us, and when Astra shoots me a knowing smile, I feel my cheeks heat. When I look back up at Ievis, his brow is furrowed.

"Are you okay?" I ask as the music slows, the current dance coming to an end.

He nods, but glances away. "Would you mind taking a break with me?"

"Of course not. Should we grab some more food or head outside?" I ask, nodding to a garden exit not far away.

"Outside," Ievis says quickly. "We can discuss things more privately."

I nod and allow him to lead me from the dance floor, his hand resting at the small of my back. Since Iefyr still has my cane, I lean a little heavier than usual on Ievis, but he supports me without complaint. The cold wind snaps around us as we step out, but it doesn't fully assault us until we're several yards from the ballroom and away from the cover and protection of the palace walls. I shiver as we come to a stop, and Ievis doesn't hesitate to wrap me in his arms and draw me tightly against him.

"I am sorry it is so cold out here."

"It's fine," I say, pressing into his warmth. I tilt my head to look up at him. "What did you want to talk about?"

Ievis doesn't answer right away, taking a moment to shift our positions slightly so he's blocking the wind and can release his hold on me a little.

"Do you think they will all hate me if one of them did not come back?"

I pull back from Ievis, putting a little space between us so I can look him properly in the eye. "What? Who do you mean?"

He sighs, looking away to avoid my eyes. "What do you know of bonded magic?"

"Only what I've read in books or seen between Alak and Astra." I pause as I connect his words. "Wait, are you saying one of them may not make it back from the Isle?"

"Bonded magic is very powerful, especially when one of the wielders has raw magic," he answers carefully, avoiding my question. "There are some spells that require such strong magic to work properly. Sometimes they even require more than one bonded pair. It cannot be avoided."

"Ievis," I say slowly, "will either Alak or Astra have to sacrifice themselves to cast the spell?"

Ievis looks back at me, something akin to sorrow in his eyes as he nods once. "I have looked for another way, and I will not stop trying to find another solution."

"But time is running out," I whisper, echoing his words from earlier.

He nods, taking my hands in his. "Could you forgive me if I cannot find another way?"

"Will you tell them beforehand?"

"Of course. Before they cast, they will know the price."

"And if they choose not to cast?" I ask, already knowing the answer.

"Then we will fail to seal the Isle unless I can, by some miracle, find another way."

My heart sinks faster than lead, and I close my eyes, taking a deep breath to steady myself. Ievis runs his thumbs overs my knuckles, and I find comfort in the simple motion.

"I swear to you, Ronan, I will do whatever I can to bring them both back, but if I cannot . . ."

He trails off and I nod, looking back up at him. "I know them well enough to know they'll choose to sacrifice themselves to save us all. If one or both of them do not return, I'll know that you did all you could and that they made the choice freely."

Ievis nods, shifting closer to me. "If we succeed, then the war will end." He offers me a weak smile. "At least we would have that."

"True. Though hopefully it will come without too much more sacrifice."

"What will you do after the war?" he asks. "Will you stay in Callenia as an ambassador?"

I hesitate before shaking my head. "No. I will return home to Clan McDullun. I'll continue to be a liaison between Athiedor and Callenia if needed, but I'd prefer to do it from my own home. I have duties there as a Clan Lord, and I love my people dearly."

"You are a good man," Ievis says, his voice calm. Too calm. My heart sinks as I anticipate where the conversation is heading.

I swallow, glancing away. "I expect you'll return to your realm?"

"I will."

Even though in my gut I knew what the answer would be, hearing it confirmed fills me with crushing disappointment. I can't believe I was foolish enough to fall for a Fae who hates humans. There's no way he would stay. There's no way we could have made anything work. It's all been foolish lust and —

"But I may not stay away if I am welcome here."

My thoughts screech to a halt as my gaze focuses on him. "What?"

"Do you know how Faerie rings came to be?"

I shake my head and he chuckles.

"I am not surprised. I always told you your human records are lacking."

He gives me a teasing glance, and despite my current state of disappoint, I almost smile.

"Faerie rings, my little human," he murmurs affectionately, brushing his hand along my cheek, "were originally made so that Fae could sneak off to visit their human lovers without the use of a formal portal."

I still, my heart beating in my throat as I put his words together. "You mean—"

"They are simple to make if you have enough magic," he continues, allowing his hand to trace slowly down my neck until his fingers come to rest on my pulse point. "If you wanted, I could easily help you grow a Faerie ring on your land."

"So you can visit?" I ask, my voice coming out hoarse as my heart flutters beneath his fingertips.

"Yes." He drops his hand to my waist. "I would, of course, need to visit and check in on Iefyr from time to time."

My mind reels. "Check in on . . . Iefyr?"

"They are my sibling after all."

"Ievis," I say, struggling to keep my voice even and steady. "Are you suggesting what I think you are? Do you really mean to visit the human realm long-term? To stay longer than necessary? With . . . me?"

The corner of his mouth tips up as his hand returns to cup my cheek, his thumb tracing along my jaw. "I am saying, my distracting little human, that I have found a reason to stay in your realm and that reason is you."

My breath catches in my throat as he closes the distance between us, his lips crashing against mine with an eagerness I've never been on the receiving end of before. I make a desperate sound and press into the kiss, my hands twisting the fabric of his tunic as I clutch him closer as if my life hinges on this kiss. Despite the fierceness of the kiss and the way he nips at my lip, Ievis cradles my face gently with one hand, the other tenderly placed on the back of my neck, guiding the kiss. I can barely stand it. I press closer to him and he stumbles back, the hand on my neck dropping to my back to steady me. I'm forced to draw back a moment, practically gasping for air like a fish on dry land. I look up into Ievis's eyes and find his pupils blown wide, surrounded only by a thin ring of molten gold.

"Perhaps we should go back to dancing?" he says, his voice rough.

I take a moment to answer, struggling to get my thundering heart under control.

"Do you want to dance?" I ask, slightly embarrassed by how out of breath I sound.

I'm pressed so tightly against him I can feel the vibrations of his chest as he hums in reply. Desire thrums through me and I say a silent prayer to the gods that Ievis doesn't want to go back into the dance and can be convinced to go somewhere more private.

"I like the idea of holding you close," he says, leaning forward to nip my ear. "I can hold you close when we dance."

A shiver runs down my spine as he traces my jaw with a series of kisses.

"There are other places you can hold m— Oh!"

I break off with a small moan as Ievis nibbles a sensitive place on my neck. I release his name in a soft gasp and he chuckles.

"My room or yours?"

"M-mine," I stutter, trying very hard to control myself as he works his way down my newly exposed collarbone. "If you don't stop, I'm not sure I'll make it there."

He presses one last kiss to my skin before he pulls back with a roguish grin. "Very well. Shall we wisp there directly to ensure you make it?"

I manage a nod and the next thing I know we're in my bedroom. Ievis kisses me again in earnest as I stumble backwards toward the bed. When my legs hit the side, I fall onto the mattress with a short gasp. Ievis leans over me, hands braced on either side of my head.

"We forgot to fetch my cane," I mumble, surprised that I can think of anything other than the handsome man looming over me.

"I am sure Iefyr will take care of it," he says, lowering to kiss my neck.

"And Saran. Someone needs to make sure—"

Ievis chuckles, pulling back. I stumble into silence as he presses a finger to my lips.

"Do not worry, my darling. I asked Iefyr if they would watch after the boy should you and I mysteriously disappear."

I blink up at Ievis. "You planned for this?"

He shrugs. "Planned? Perhaps a little. Hoped? Most definitely."

Heat returns to his gaze and he straightens and begins to undo the buttons of his shirt. I prop myself up on my elbows to get a better look at him. Every single thought flees my mind as inch after inch of Ievis's muscled chest is exposed. I'm delighted to find that the swirling black ink I'd spotted previously on his forearms also curls across the expanse of his chest, adding to his beauty.

"Like what you see?" he asks with a smirk.

I manage a nod, unable to find the words, and he smirks.

"Good," he purrs, tossing his shirt to the side. "Because unless there are more things on your mind you feel we must discuss first, I'm ready to commence. I have to leave early in the morning, and I do not plan to waste another minute talking."

He pauses, looking down at me and I swallow.

"Do you need help disrobing?" he asks, his long fingers deftly unfastening my pants.

"I—" I start, but my words are swallowed by a sharp gasp as Ievis jerks my pants down my legs.

"Better," he purrs, his eyes raking over me before his sultry gaze meets my wide eyes. "If you want to stop, we can, but I can promise I will make it very pleasant for you."

"You've had a lot of lovers?" I manage, my voice coming out a bit squeaky and breathless.

He smirks. "Enough to know I am very good, but I can promise you I enjoyed none of them as much as I will enjoy you tonight," he says, radiating confidence that has me fumbling for my tunic buttons without another moment of hesitation.

I shimmy out of my clothes faster than I ever have before. When I'm finally laid completely bare before him, he assesses a moment before leaning down and kneeling and taking me in his mouth. I choke on a gasp and grip the sheets in my fists. It takes a shamefully short time before I'm gone, Ievis working me thoroughly. When he steps back and looks down at me, he runs his tongue across his lips.

"I thought you were beautiful before, but that was nothing compared to how you look right now," he says, looking down at me with nothing short of adoration.

"And here I was thinking you despised humans," I mumble, my voice rough.

His expression darkens for a brief moment before he leans down to press a kiss on my hipbone. "I can admit I was wrong about your kind." He kisses a little lower and I choke on a strangled gasp. "Thankfully I had a very compelling human to help me move past my prejudices."

He straightens and looks down at me, and I decide I've never seen a more beautiful sight.

"There may be times when those old thoughts creep in, and I will need you to bear with me and help me work through them."

"Of course," I say, pushing myself up on my elbows. "Whatever I need to do to keep you."

I reach for him, and he allows me to pull him down onto the bed into a heated kiss that's equal parts emotion and lust. We shift so we're lying side by side. I try to sit up, but he draws me against his chest.

"It's your turn," I protest.

He presses a kiss to my temple. "Do not worry about me. We have all night. I promise there is more to come."

Thank the gods Ievis is a Fae who keeps his promises.

CHAPTER FORTY-THREE

One of the advantages of having the ball is not only getting to keep my promise to Winnie by covering the ceiling with stars, but also getting a chance to get ready with Mara. Even though most of the refugees chose to stay in one of the two villages they passed through, Mara agreed to accompany Luc all the way to the Summer Palace. The last few days, the two of them have been together every available opportunity, but I still manage to steal moments with my friend. Tonight she's almost back to her bubbly self as we dress and prepare for the ball.

Alak disappears to some other corner of the castle while we get ready. We have a lot to catch up on, though much of what we share isn't exactly light. When Alak reappears, Mara insists on giving us some time to ourselves, but given the content of our conversations, I have a very good feeling she has plans to meet Luc before the ball. Her deep blush when I mention my suspicions is more than enough confirmation.

Even though I swing by Ievis's room on the way to the ballroom to discuss an important matter with him, Alak and I are among the first in the ballroom, Cadewynn, Sama, and Nyco joining us not much later. When Cadewynn sees the stars she wraps me in a warm hug, pressing a kiss to my cheek.

"Your magic is always so beautiful," she whispers, her head tilted up as she marvels at the stars.

Bloody battlefields flash through my mind, and I shake my head. "Not always."

Cadewynn frowns, pulling her attention from the stars to look at me. "It may not always appear as beautiful as this"—she gestures to my handiwork—"but it always accomplishes something good."

I open my mouth to protest but she holds up a hand, hushing me.

"No, all the lives you've saved while being willing to sacrifice yourself is beautiful, and I won't hear another word." She lowers her hand and smiles. "Now, this is a ball, so we should dance! Oh, or maybe we should check out the food first? Or mingle more?"

Cadewynn flounces away with her partners at her side, and Alak takes the opportunity to slide his arm around my waist and pull me closer.

"She's right, you know," he murmurs pressing a quick kiss to my cheek. "Your magic is beautiful."

"Alak—"

He silences me with a quick kiss. "Not tonight, love." He pulls me toward the dance floor. "It's time to enjoy ourselves."

I smile and allow Alak to sweep away my worries. I didn't think that was possible at this point, but somehow he manages to provide a decent distraction. It's easy to get lost in the beauty of the ball, but I make sure to dance with everybody I can, knowing full well this could be the last time I see some of them alive. The only person I miss is Ronan, who spends his entire night dancing with Ievis before disappearing.

I drink and eat and dance until reality catches up with me. I look around the ballroom and spot Luc and Mara tucked into a cozy corner, chatting away as they share a glass of sparkling wine. Alak stands near a garden exit engaged in conversation with Cal, but I don't see Ehren anywhere. Kai leans on a wall near the exit, watching me affectionately. I make my way over to him and he smiles down at me.

"Are you done dancing?"

I glance over my shoulder at the revelers and nod. "I think so." I look back at Kai. "After all, I do have a journey tomorrow. I should rest."

Kai hums in agreement. "I was thinking of heading in myself. Perhaps I can accompany you?"

I offer him a tired smile. "Of course, though I would like to find Ehren if I can. There's something I want to give him."

My hand goes almost instinctively to my pocket where I've hidden the small secret Ievis helped prepare.

Kai offers me his arm. "Let's see if we can find him together."

I accept and allow Kai to escort me from the ballroom. As we leave the joyful cacophony behind us, I turn to look up at him.

"Kai, if we make it out of this alive, will you stay?"

Kai sighs, staring straight ahead and refusing to meet my eyes. "A part of me wants to."

"But a part of you needs to go?"

He smiles down at me sadly and nods. "There is a piece of my heart that is not in Callenia, and I find I no longer can live without them at my side."

My lips part as I blink up at him. "You have a special someone?"

Kai scoffs, but there's something gentle and tender about the sound. "They're not to me quite what Alak is to you or what Cal is to Ehren. I'm not made for that type of . . . desire."

"That doesn't mean that you can't hold someone dear, that you can't have that one special person who means more to you than anyone else in all the world, someone who you would move heaven and earth to find, protect, and cherish." I stop and look up at Kai. "I want you to have that, and if you've found someone that completes you in a way no one else can, you should be with them."

He tucks a stray strand of hair behind my ear. "Even if that means leaving you and Callenia behind?"

I manage a small smile, though my heart breaks a little. "Even then."

We resume our walk but part ways when we reach the corridors leading to our rooms. I have an idea of where Ehren might be. I bid Kai goodnight, and he leaves after pressing one last kiss to my cheek.

I find Ehren much where I expect, staring out a window overlooking a frost-covered training field set off to the side of the palace.

"Are you okay?" I ask, walking up behind Ehren.

He leans against the window, his gaze unfocused as he stares out into the night. "I don't even know how to process how I feel right now."

I step to his side and link my arm through his, leaning against his shoulder. "I know what you mean. On one hand I want this all to be over and done, but on the other, at what cost will victory come?"

He sighs, shaking his head. "I just pray it's a price we can pay."

"I have something that might help," I say, reaching into my dress pocket and withdrawing a small silver pearl.

He accepts it, scowling down in confusion as he turns it over in his palm. "What is it?"

"Ievis helped me make it," I explain. "It's a concentrated bit of my magic mixed with a little Fae magic. Kato will be hard to bring down without it." I glance away as Ehren nods, slipping it in his pocket. "I'm well aware of what you may have to do, Ehren. When the time comes, do not hesitate to kill Kato. I've lost too many people due to hesitation. Do what needs to be done."

"So you've found nothing new in the journal?"

My shoulders drop, and I resist the urge to pull it from my pocket. "I've found a lot in the journal," I confess. "But I'm not sure any of it will help."

"Tell me anything that might," he insists, taking my hand.

I sigh. "Kato was always so proud of me," I say quietly, my voice almost a whisper. "Sometimes I think he may have been prouder of my accomplishments than he was his own. If there's any way to reach him—the real him deep inside—it might work to remind him of that pride."

Ehren nods, seriously considering my words. "I can try to reach that part of him, remind him what he lost, what's at stake."

Tears burn my eyes as I meet Ehren's gaze. "Even so, you must promise me that if that doesn't work, or if Kato doesn't give you a chance to try, you have to follow through. We've already lost too much, and I won't lose anyone else. Promise me, Ehren. Promise."

He hesitates only a moment before lifting his chin. "I promise."

We stand for several minutes, just staring out the window, relishing the quiet moments we have together before the chaos of war invades once again.

"I should probably go to bed," he finally mutters, pulling away from the window. "I march into battle tomorrow. Well, toward battle tomorrow." He looks down at me. "You should probably get some rest, too. I don't know what the Fae have planned, but it'd be best to be fully rested."

I nod, biting my lip as I glance off.

"What is it, Ash? You know you can tell me anything."

I blink up at him, debating my next request and deciding to ask anyway. "Would you mind if I came with you? At least until Alak is done with the ball? I don't want to be alone."

"Of course. You're always welcome in my bed." He pauses, his eyes shining with mischief as I laugh. "Gods, that sounded inappropriate, didn't it? Don't tell Cal I said that."

I giggle. "Oh, I'm telling him."

We wind through the palace corridors up to his room. He kicks off his boots and collapses on the bed while I wiggle out of my own shoes. I settle next to him, resting my head on his chest and snuggling into the comfort he provides. For a while we talk about everything and nothing. Little by little exhaustion takes hold and our words spread further and further apart until we both drift off.

When I wake it takes me a moment to remember where I am. The memory of last night floats to the surface as I carefully shift into a sitting position so as not disturb Ehren or Alak— who apparently ended up in bed with us last night. It also seems that Cal made it to bed, Ehren currently nestled against him. My movement wakes Cal, and he turns his head to me, blinking in confusion before a slow smile spreads across his face.

Good morning, he mouths. I grin and mouth it back.

Cal motions to the balcony with a questioning nod. I reply with an agreeing nod of my own. Cal slides out from under Ehren and slips from the bed. I sit up a bit straighter, scowling at Ehren as I try to figure out how to leave without waking him. I glance up at Cal for help, and he grins, leaning forward and practically plucking me from the bed. I nearly squeal with surprise but manage to muffle the sound into a soft gasp.

"Sorry," Cal whispers as he sets me on my feet.

"It's fine," I whisper, grateful for his help.

Cal offers me his arm and I accept. He leads me onto the balcony, closing the door behind us as I lean against the balustrade. It's a clear morning, frost covering the landscape like a silver blanket, perfectly peaceful in the early morning light. It's hard to reconcile the peaceful scene with the battles and bloodshed we set out for today.

"Did you sleep well?" Cal asks, drawing me from my thoughts as he steps to my side, his hands clasped behind his back.

I smile sheepishly, ducking my head as pink rises on my cheeks. "I'm sorry to take up space in your bed. I didn't mean to stay all night."

Cal laughs softly as he shakes his head. "It's fine. Really. I'm glad you're there for Ehren."

I look up and meet Cal's eyes. His love for Ehren shines like a beacon.

"I'm glad he has you," I reply. "You make him really happy, you know?"

Cal smiles, his eyes shining as he steps forward, placing his hands on the balustrade. "He makes *me* happy." He looks down at me and his smile grows. "Some days I still can't believe that I get to be with him. For so long, I thought I was destined to always be on the sidelines, alone and waiting."

I nod with a slight chuckle. "I know that feeling all too well. Being a one-of-a-kind twin might sound appealing, but in reality I was always treated like an oddity. I was sure I would never find someone to see me for who I truly was."

"But you did," Cal says, his voice barely above a whisper. "You found Bram and then Alak."

A familiar pain stabs my chest at Bram's name, but I don't let it take me down.

"I'm sorry. I shouldn't have mentioned—I'm sorry."

"No, it's fine."

Cal places his hand over mine, covering it completely. I look up and meet his eyes to find tears shimmering there.

"Astra, I know you have a job to do," he says, his voice steady, "but I need you to come back. Ehren has lost so much, and if you don't return, I'm not sure if I can bring him out of the shadows."

Tears sting my own eyes as I nod once. "I'll come back. I swear it."

Cal nods and shifts his gaze to the frost-covered landscape. "I know you have enough pressure, and I don't mean to add to it. I just can't lose him."

I place my other hand on top of his and give it a small squeeze.

"I promise, Cal, I will do everything in my power, and," I add with a grin as I nudge his arm, "I'm told I have a considerable amount of power."

Cal laughs, a rich full sound. "And that's why you and Ehren get along so well. Neither of you can stay serious for too long."

Before I can respond, the door behind us opens, and a sleepy Ehren steps out.

"Talking about me?" He grins, crossing his arms and leaning against the doorframe.

I roll my eyes. "Not everything is about you, you know."

Cal grins and shakes his head.

"That answer confirms it. You *were* talking about me. I can't say I blame you. I'd talk about me every chance I got, too."

Cal laughs and crosses to Ehren, drawing him closer for a kiss.

"You're insufferable," Cal murmurs as he steps back.

Ehren's eyes shine as he replies, "That's one of the reasons you love me."

Ehren snakes his arm around Cal's waist and pulls him into a deeper kiss. I clear my throat. Ehren draws back and looks at me over Cal's shoulder, arching an eyebrow.

"It's cold out here and you're blocking the door," I reply, wrapping my arms around myself for dramatic effect.

Ehren sighs and drops his arm, taking Cal's hand instead. "Fine. We'll take this inside."

Ehren waggles his eyebrows at Cal, whose ears turn pink. I follow behind, closing the door against the bite of the morning air. I hear a groan and glance over at Alak as he rolls over in the bed, his eyes finding me.

"Shite," he mumbles. "Is it morning already?"

"Unfortunately," I sigh, collapsing onto the bed next to him.

"Why don't we," Alak purrs, wrapping an arm around me and pulling me closer, "just stay in bed"—he kisses the corner of my lips—"and pretend there aren't Fae waiting to drag us to our deaths."

I smile and press my lips to Alak's. He receives my kisses eagerly, pulling me closer.

"Hey now," Ehren calls out. "If Cal and I can't have our moment, neither can you. Especially since you're in *my* bed!"

I turn my head and stick my tongue out at Ehren. His eyes widen for a moment before he throws his head back and laughs. Before either of us can say more, we're interrupted by a knock on the door.

"I'll get it," Cal says, striding across the room.

Cal opens the door to reveal Kai. I leap from the bed and dash to him, wrapping him in a hug. Kai stumbles back, a tight grin slipping onto his lips.

"Morning." I grin up at him as I step back.

"Morning," he grumbles, his gray eyes shining. He lifts his gaze to Ehren then back to me. "Everything is ready."

The happiness leaves the room in a whoosh, leaving depressing reality in its wake. I take a deep breath and turn to Ehren.

"I guess I should head back to my own room and get ready. The Fae aren't exactly patient people."

Ehren clenches his jaw as his eyes meet mine. He takes a step toward me, then pauses before rushing forward and pulling me into his arms, clutching me against his chest with a small wince.

"Be careful," he whispers in my ear. "I know you need to do this, but come back to me."

I wrap my arms around him, hugging him close. "I will. I promise."

Ehren draws back, placing his hand on my arm as he studies me. A smile plays on his lips, contradictory to the tears shining in his eyes.

"Who knew that my mission to save the twins from their

own destruction would lead to me meeting you? And that the fiery scholar from Timberborn would go on to be not only a powerful sorceress but also one of the most important people in my life?"

Tears well in my eyes as I lunge forward, pulling Ehren back into a hug. He places his chin on top of my head as he gives me a squeeze.

"I love you, Ash. I'm proud of you."

This time when I draw back, both of us have tears on our cheeks. How am I supposed to leave him? I let my gaze drift to Cal and find him crying silently as well. Even Alak looks on the verge of a full breakdown.

"All right," I laugh, wiping my tears away with the back of my hand. "Enough of this. This isn't a goodbye. It's a 'see you later' because all of us, every single person in this room, will be back together again soon."

"Right. Of course," Ehren says, clearing his throat as he straightens. "No goodbyes."

"No goodbyes," Cal echoes with a nod.

"Well," Alak drawls, sliding from the bed. "No goodbyes, but we still have places to be."

Ehren nods as Alak crosses the room and takes my hand. I turn to Kai.

"Let's do this."

CHAPTER FORTY-FOUR

ASTRA

As expected, we arrive in the main courtyard to find Ievis, Iefyr, Hycis, and Rynia already waiting. I'm only slightly surprised to find Ronan lingering at Ievis's side. The bags I prepared last night rest on the ground next to theirs. This is really happening.

"Ready for an adventure?" Hycis grins as we approach, though there's something heavier in her voice than usual.

I force a smile. "Ready as I'll ever be."

I turn and look at Ehren. He's standing too straight, his hand gripping Cal's a little too tightly, but otherwise he's the perfect picture of a prince on the verge of war. I step toward him and press one last kiss to his cheek.

"I'll see you again soon," I promise. "I'll see you after we win this war."

I glance at Cal who smiles and nods his goodbye before I turn to Kai. He stands off to the side, watching. I can tell he doesn't like the idea of me going off without him, but he's the leader of the shifters. His place is on the battlefield.

Ronan's jaw is set as he offers me a tight lipped smile and a parting nod. "Be careful." He shifts his attention to Ievis. "You too."

Ievis offers Ronan a smile that might be considered cocky if it wasn't soft around the edges. "I will not need to be careful, but I promise to return."

Ronan takes a deep breath and releases it slowly. "You promise?"

"Yes."

Ronan surges forward, startling me, and presses a quick kiss to Ievis's mouth. I half-expect Ievis to shove him away and am even more surprised when Ievis catches Ronan as he steps back, pulling him in for a deeper kiss.

"Well, *that* was unexpected," Hycis mumbles, watching the two as Ievis finally releases his hold on Ronan.

"Was it?" Iefyr asks, a small smile playing on their lips. "I find it rather expected."

Ievis grunts, shooting his sibling a quick glare. "We need to stop lingering. We have places to be."

"Yes," I say straightening. I look at Iefyr. "How do we do this? How does your magic work?"

Iefyr grins in response, holding their hands in front of them, palms out. A thin line of blueish purple light appears, widening slowly as they pull their hands apart. They concentrate on the portal and nod to us once it's several feet wide. I swallow and exchange a wary glance with Alak, but Hycis is the first to go through, Rynia a step behind. Alak grabs my hand and leads me though, Ievis and Iefyr following.

We trade our frost-covered palace courtyard for a snowy landscape along a dock. The air here is far below freezing and bites through my cloak.

"That's our ship," Iefyr says, nodding to a boat bobbing in

the water nearby. "I portalled here a few days ago and made all the arrangements."

Ievis frowns. "Without me?"

Iefyr grins at him. "You were otherwise occupied."

"Do we have a captain or are we manning it ourselves?" I jump in before the siblings can argue much more.

"The captain was less than eager to head toward Atroxmorte, so we're sailing on our own," Iefyr replies.

Rynia steps forward with a small smile. "I'm actually not a forest Fae. I was born in the Southern Fae realm near the water, so when Iefyr asked if I could assist in sailing, I was happy to play my part."

"I drew her into the forest," Hycis grins, pulling Rynia close. "Once she realized she couldn't live without me, she obviously had to stay."

Rynia rolls her eyes but allows Hycis to draw her into a kiss.

"Enough of that ridiculous affection," Ievis growls. "We have a duty."

"This is going to be a pleasant trip," Alak whispers with a sigh as he watches Ievis stomp away.

I bite back a grin as we follow Ievis down the dock.

Sailing is dreadful. The only time I've been over the water was the ferry to Portia. This trip is different and much worse. I spend the first two days seasick below deck in a tiny, cramped room the size of a closet. Alak seems entirely unaffected, but he never leaves my side, caring for me the entire time. On the third day, I finally manage to find my sea legs enough to wander the deck, though the icy winds often have me retreating back inside.

Hycis seems equally disgruntled by the cold, often swearing under her breath. I busy myself practicing the words to the spell Ievis has created, so when the time comes, I'll be ready.

Toward the end of the fourth day, we catch our first glimpse of the Isle in the distance. My heart drops to my stomach as I stare at it. Even from miles away, I can feel the dark magic. Alak steps to my side and wraps his arms around me.

"It's worse than I thought," he whispers. "I knew I would feel the darkness, but this—it's beyond any evil I've ever felt."

I nod and press closer to him. "At least when we're done, this will all be over and all that evil will be trapped."

The Fae work together to put a shield over our boat to keep us more or less protected, but we have to approach the Isle incredibly slowly so we aren't detected and delayed. According to Ievis, we will need to be as close as possible to the Isle for his spell to work properly. It's the evening of the fifth day before he finally decides we're close enough, which is good considering the Dragkonians now sense our presence and swarm above us, the occasional beast swooping down to test our shield.

"What needs to be done?" I ask. "How do I seal it?"

"It cannot be sealed by you alone," Ievis says, meeting my eyes for the first time in days.

There's something he's not saying. I glance from Ievis to Iefyr. "What is it? What needs to be done?"

"In order to create a seal strong enough, the magic must be performed from both sides," Ievis says slowly, something close to sympathy shining in his eyes.

It takes a moment for his words to sink in but when they do, my eyes go wide. "You mean someone has to be on the Isle when it's sealed?" Ievis nods. "That's suicide!"

Ievis nods and exchanges a look with Iefyr before adding,

"It cannot be any two people casting the spell. They must share magic."

Share magic. The words settle over me like a flame. My legs go weak as I back away from him, shaking my head.

"No, you can't mean . . . No." I shake my head faster. "No. No. No."

I look over at Alak. He's come to the same realization. Tears brim in his eyes as he looks at me.

I shake my head firmly. "No. There has to be another way."

Alak takes a step toward me, "Astra—"

"No," I say. "We'll find another way."

Ievis looks at me, shaking his head. "There is not any other way. This was the only way to craft the spell. Believe me when I say I looked for any other option and none could be found."

"Fae have bonds," I say, talking quickly. "Why can't it be a Fae?"

"There will be a Fae," Hycis says, stepping forward, her face set like stone, but there's a glimmer of sadness in her eyes. "The spell requires two bonded Fae and two bonded humans."

Her eyes dart to Rynia and I follow her gaze. Rynia's eyes are rimmed with tears.

"You knew beforehand."

"We did," Rynia says softly. "Ievis told us the night of the ball."

When I look back at Hycis, I see something in her break just for a moment before she regains her composure. "It is what must be done."

I step closer to Ievis. "I volunteer to be on the Isle when the border is sealed."

"Astra," Alak says, stepping toward me and taking my hands in his. I don't want to look at him but I can't help it. His emerald eyes shine with sorrow as he whispers, "We both know you're not going to be the one on that island when the barrier closes."

Something in me shatters and I collapse against Alak.

"Alak, no. I can't live without you," I plead, tears breaking free. "I can't do it. I'd rather die than live without you."

He squeezes his eyes shut and when he opens them a tear slides down his cheek. "I was going to marry you when this was all done." He brushes his thumb across my cheek, wiping away a tear. "We were going to be so happy. I was going to make sure you found light in the darkness."

I choke out a sob. "Alak . . ."

"Astra—" His voice breaks off in a sob but he recovers quickly. "Love, I need you to live for me when I'm gone. Make new dreams and follow them to their fullest."

"No!" I scream, jerking away. "Don't you dare surrender like that! You fight, Alak Dunne. You fight! We'll find another way! I can't—No. No!"

He meets my eyes for a moment and then leans down and presses his lips to mine. This kiss is fire and ice. It's a stormy sea and a calm night. It surges through me. Alak pours more of himself into it than any other kiss. It's ultimate and earth shattering. It's not until he pulls away I realize that it's because it's meant to be our last.

"I love you, Astra," he whispers, brushing my hair from my face. "I'm so glad I met you and was able to spend the last few months by your side. You made life worth living. Loving you made up for everything bad in my life." His voice breaks as a tear slides down his cheek. "We were always meant to be, and this was always our purpose. Thank you for loving me."

He steps away from me to Hycis so quickly I barely resister his movement until he's by her side. I step forward but my legs go weak. He turns to Hycis and nods. Before I can stop them,

Hycis takes his hand, and with one last look toward her own bondmate, they disappear. I turn to Rynia with a panicked look to find her crying. She meets my gaze.

"We have to stop them!" I cry in desperation. "You can't want this any more than I do. Please, Rynia, do something. Do anything. Bring them back!"

She shakes her head, composing herself the best she can. "It is too late. The decision is made."

Ievis turns to us. "They are in place. We must begin, or the opportunity will be lost and their sacrifice will be in vain."

Sacrifice. The word echoes through my brain with a shattering agony. No. *No.*

"Now is not the time for human emotions," Rynia says, but her voice trembles with emotions of her own. "We—we must be strong."

How can they expect me to perform magic when the world around me is splintering into pieces? I reach through the bond and find Alak at the other end. He gives me a nudge and somehow, that gives me strength.

I take a deep breath and meet Ievis's eyes. "What do we do?"

Ievis guides us quickly while the Dragkonians scream overhead. I take Rynia's hand so her magic and mine combine. She begins speaking the Fae spell, and I feel the magic stirring. I attempt the spell, the Fae words tripping awkwardly over my tongue, but it's working. Our magic reaches through our bonds as we combine strength with Alak and Hycis on the Isle. I push my emotions aside and concentrate on the magic. It swells and surges with each word we speak, the power sparking in the air. I feel our wall weaving together.

The Dragkonians scream and fight against it, but the stronger the spell becomes, the weaker those outside the barrier grow. Dragkonians fall from the sky, crashing into the ocean with unholy screeches that send shivers across my skin. I close my eyes and focus harder on the spell, my voice growing louder with each word. Rynia's voice joins mine with powerful force. It's nearly done.

As we yell the last phrase into the sky, the barrier snaps shut. All the Dragkonians still in the air fall, their black bodies twisting and writhing. But I barely notice. I fall to the deck of the ship, gasping for air as I clutch my chest. I can't breathe. Every inch of my skin is on fire and pain fiercer than anything I've ever felt crushes me. I desperately reach out my magic, clutching for the bond, but it's not there. Not even a whisper remains. All that's left in its place is agony and aching loneliness.

My scream cleaves the air. Every emotion I've ever felt tumbles down on me. I'm suffocating. Death would be less painful. I manage to look over at Rynia and see the same intense anguish on her face as tears stream down her cheeks. Ievis and Iefyr watch us with sympathy, but she's the only one who understands. I stumble toward her, and we wrap our arms around each other, but there is no comfort here, only combined sorrow and mourning. We clutch each other tightly, knowing we will never be the same, knowing we will never be okay.

A small whimper pulls me from sorrow long enough for me to acknowledge the small Fae Fox nuzzling my arm. I look down at Felixe through my tears as he places a paw on my knee with a small whine.

"I'm sorry, boy," I whisper. "He's gone."

Felixe lets out a whine, and I gather him into my arms. I'm not sure Fae Foxes can actually cry, but the trembling creature in my arms is definitely mourning in whatever way he can, his keening mewls nothing short of sorrow.

I finally manage to rally, though I'm not sure how much time passes. Ievis has disappeared below deck, but Iefyr remains. I meet their eyes.

"I need to go home," I say, my voice raw and hoarse. "I—I can't stay here, so far away. I need to portal. Please."

Iefyr considers me a moment before nodding. "You sacrificed a piece of your very soul. Sending you home is the least I can do in exchange for your sacrifice. Where exactly do you desire to go?"

"Send me to Ehren."

Iefyr nods, bowing their head as they summon their magic. "It shall be done."

I take a deep breath and step forward into their swirling magic, cradling Felixe in my arms. I have no idea what will greet me on the other side, but it cannot be worse than what I'm leaving.

CHAPTER FORTY-FIVE

EHREN

There's an empty place in my heart as I watch Astra step into the Fae portal with the others, but I know it has to be done. Even after the portal fades away, I continue staring at the air until Cal's arms slip around my waist, bringing me back. I lean into his touch only for a moment before I clear my throat and turn to the others.

"I suppose we should be on our way as well. We have a war to win."

Cal smiles weakly as he takes my hand, squeezing gently with comfort and agreement.

Within the hour, our army is on the road to Embervein. We move swiftly, masked by magic, but my nerves still swirl inside me. I wonder how many of these soldiers will make it out alive. Maybe none of us will survive.

It takes five days to reach Embervein. Our other armies are already in place, thousands of our soldiers surrounding the area on every side. Though we can't see the full force of Kato's soldiers, many of them behind masking magic, what soldiers we can see has me wondering if our armies will be able to hold their own.

Millie, the teenage girl who arrived with the refugees, uses careful magic to keep us hidden while other soldiers with magic work together to maintain a spell that traps Kato and his forces in Embervein so they'll be forced to fight instead of fleeing to regroup. Hopefully we can maintain a little element of surprise and use it to our advantage.

After taking a quick dose of medicine to help ease the pain brought on by constant riding, I meet with Jess, Kai, Luc, Cal, Ronan, Pax, and any other leaders of significance I can so we can finalize our plan. We lay out our armies, mixing magic and non-magic users evenly throughout. It's a game and the pieces need to be in the right places. Only, unlike a game, if we lose, people die and the kingdom falls.

As agreed, Ronan will stay behind the lines of the active army with Saran and most of our Healers, including Princess Elaine, to assist the wounded and protect portals so those who need them can escape or receive additional aid. He takes a few of his portal stones to set up a little farther on the other side of our armies so they too can make it to the portals that can take them to safety and Healing. Healer Heora will wait near those portals with Pip, Hanna, Gavin, and a few other elected healers and soldiers and help those who need assistance before passing through. A few additional Healers trained in fighting will join the soldiers on the battlefield.

It's early evening when we all gather together, every general, captain, and soldier of standing. Every prince or leader. My nerves twist so violently in my gut it's all I can do to keep down my meager dinner of bread and soup. When their eyes turn to me, I rally, using some unknown power inside me. I suppose it's the power every good king has buried inside that he pulls out for times like this. I stand on a slightly raised platform and look over the crowd.

"I pray to the gods that when we walk away from the battle tomorrow, that everyone here will return to their homes, but we all know that is unlikely. Tomorrow, we march into a battle we may very well lose. We are outmatched when it comes to magic and Kato and his minions have no problem dwelling in darkness while we dwell in light. But we still must fight. If we do not, we have doomed not only ourselves but the world. So, together, we will push against the evil that threatens us and, should the gods bless us, we will walk away victors."

Several heads bob in agreement, but the air is thick with tension.

"Go back to your tents and rest tonight. We attack at dawn."

Murmurs flood throughout the crowd as I turn away and head into my tent. Cal follows behind.

"That was an excellent speech," Cal says, the corner of his mouth turned up in a slight smile, but his eyes are somber.

I sigh and run my hand through my hair, glancing to the side. "It's all true." I lift my eyes to meet Cal's. "We may very well lose. Especially if Astra and the Fae aren't in place yet."

Cal nods and looks down, fiddling with his sword in its sheath. I close the distance and take his hand in mine. He meets my gaze, but his eyes are lined with seriousness.

"Ehren," he says, drawing my name out in a way that stills me.

"Whatever you're about to say, don't."

He tilts his head and offers me a sad smile. "I need you to make me a promise."

I swallow, barely breathing as I reply, "Anything."

"I need you to promise that if I am lost in battle tomorrow
—"

"No. No. You'll make it out."

"—that you won't fall apart again."

I shake my head and try to pull away, but Cal tightens his grip on my hand so I can't move back more than a step.

"You can't . . . No . . . I can't . . ."

"Please, Ehren," Cal pleads, his voice breaking on my name. "I need to know that if I die you'll be okay."

Tears burn my eyes as I jerk my gaze to his.

"How can I be okay with you gone?" My chest feels tight and I struggle to breathe. "Cal, you are my reason for living. Without you, I . . ."

Cal squeezes my hand. "Ehren, I need you to live for me if I'm not here anymore. The thought of you suffering—"

"Then you have to live," I cut him him off, taking a step closer. "I can't promise you that I'll be okay if you are gone because I know I won't be. I need you."

A small sob escapes Cal's lips as he nods, looking down. "I wish I could protest, but to be honest, I feel the same way about losing you." He lifts his eyes to mine. "The mere thought that something might happen to you has me on the verge of madness. And to think you may even slightly feel the same . . ."

I close what little distance remains, wrapping my arm around his waist and drawing him closer. I pull my hand from his and trace a finger down his cheek. He sighs and leans into my touch.

"If something were to happen to me—"

"Ehren—"

"No, listen. If something were to happen to me, I would want you to live and find love again."

Cal laughs softly, pressing his forehead to mine. I take his hand, weaving our fingers together.

"Ehren, you are the love of my life. If I lost you, I could never love someone again. A heart that broken can't possibly heal enough."

My heart skips a beat and I close my eyes.

"And yet you asked the same of me?"

Cal draws back just enough to look at my face and my eyes flutter open to meet his. We hold the gaze for a moment before he leans in, brushing his lips across mine. When he starts to draw away, I pull him back into a deeper kiss. He reaches up, twisting his fingers in my hair as he presses against me. We lose ourselves to the kiss, pulling apart several moments later, gasping for air.

"Ehren, I—"

"We're under attack!"

I jerk back and throw open the tent flap, my eyes scanning to see who's yelling. The entire area is in chaos. On the horizon, Kato's army charges our way in full force, with even more soldiers than I anticipated. Cal steps up behind me, sword drawn. I look back at him and my heart plummets.

"Time for war."

Cal nods once and presses one last kiss to my lips before we charge into battle with the rest of our soldiers.

CHAPTER FORTY-SIX

RONAN

The battle begins before any of us are truly ready, not that war is ever something that you can truly be fully prepared for. The soldiers fall into their lines quickly, while I take up my position along the outskirts of the battle. Several Healers and a few helpers are stationed with me, including Princess Elaine and Kai's second in command, Eleni.

After a few carefully spoken words, my portals are buzzing and ready to go. Saran swallows hard and calls on his shadows. They lick the air around him as he whispers to them, too quiet and low for me to make out his questions.

"Our numbers would be equal without the Dragkonians," he says, looking up at me.

I nod, allowing my gaze to trail over the clashing armies. "And with the Dragkonians?"

Saran doesn't reply, but the grim look on his face is answer enough. We're outnumbered. Even with the poison provided by the Fae, we could very well lose this battle and the whole war if Ievis can't pull through in time. But, no. Ievis *will* pull through. I have faith in him.

I straighten and pull on my magic, surrounding us in a ward that will keep us and our portals protected. It doesn't take long before the wounded start coming in. Some of the soldiers wisp directly outside the warding and are helped inside. Others are wisped by others or brought in on stretchers or in the arms of their comrades. The Healers work quickly to assess each injury before either tending to the wounds or sending the injured on through one of the portals. I help where I can, bandaging wounds and passing out ointments, but I keep glancing at Saran as he stands off to the side whispering to his shadows. When he gasps, turning wide eyes to me, I rush to his side.

"What is it?" I ask, placing a hand on his shoulder as I kneel in front of him. I scan his face. "What's wrong?"

"There are a bunch of people trapped at the northwest corner. They're badly burned and have no way out," he replies, his voice shaking slightly.

"They can't wisp?"

Saran shakes his head. "None of them have magic."

I stand, running a hand through my hair. We have to get them.

"I'll go," a man behind me says.

I turn and face him. He has a fresh bandage on his arm, but he otherwise seems okay.

"This won't keep me down," he says, nodding to his wound. "I have plenty of magic left. I can go fetch them."

"And I'll help," a young woman says, stepping to his side. Her clothes are covered in blood but whatever injury she had must already be healed or it's minor enough not to be an issue.

"Can you direct us to them?" the man says, looking to Saran.

Saran glances at me, then nods. "The shadows can."

If his reply confuses the soldiers, they don't show it. A moment later, shadows snake toward them and they disappear, retuning a couple minutes later with two people each. They blink away as I rush to the people they brought. They're burned badly and hacking something awful. The Healers are only a step behind me, their magic swirling around us. The rescued soldiers are already on their way through a portal by the time the other soldiers return with more survivors.

This becomes on ongoing cycle. Saran finds a group of people that need saving and those that have been healed wisp out and return with wounded. Time blurs around us as the battle intensifies. The Healers are getting weary, sending more and more people through the portals as their magic wanes. Even Saran seems strained, beads of sweat pooling on his forehead despite the chill around us.

When Saran detects a group of people inside the castle who need rescuing there's a heated debate on whether or not they should be rescued.

"No," one soldier with a nasty Dragkonian scratch across his eye protests. "They could be the Fire King's people. We can't bring them in."

Saran shakes his head. "They're not. They're servants and innocents that were dragged into the war by others," he insists.

"Did your shadows tell you this?" the man scoffs.

Saran raises his chin. "Yes, and shadows can't lie."

"No, but the people could lie or deceive the shadows."

Saran opens his mouth to argue, but I cut him off with a sharp wave. "Enough." The man shoots me a glare, but I don't have time for his nonsense. "I'll go." I turn to Saran. "Lead me to them."

Saran hesitates only a moment before nodding and whispering to the shadows. Once I'm wrapped in their coolness, I close my eyes and pull into a wisp. When I open them, I'm in the castle. There are obvious signs of the battle raging outside. Cracks run up the walls of this corridor and debris shakes from the ceiling as a roar of magic blasts nearby. I scan the area and easily find a group of five people huddled in the corner. I race toward them, nearly stumbling over my cane in my hurry.

"Do any of you have magic?" I ask.

The oldest among them, a young woman in her twenties, looks up at me with wide terrified eyes.

"Aye," she says, her Athiedor accent evident. "I do."

"Can you wisp?"

She nods. "But I don't know the castle well enough to get out."

I take a deep breath. "I can lead you somewhere safe, but I'll need your magic to fuel the wisp. I can't take all of you on my own."

She hesitates a moment before whispering, "How do we know we can trust you?"

"I swear on the life of my father, an Athiedor Lord," I reply, hoping she can understand what that oath means, hear the weight in my words.

She studies me and I almost think she's on the verge of declining again when she nods. I extend my hand and she accepts, taking the hand of one of the others while I grab the hand of a young boy who can't be much older than Saran. Once we're all connected, I guide our wisp back to the portals.

"Caitlyn!" Saran cries out, lunging forward to wrap his arms around the woman.

She stumbles back, clearly startled, but then a soft, tired smile curls on her lips as she returns the boy's embrace.

"Saran," she whispers, pressing a quick kiss to the top of his head. She pulls back and frowns down at the boy. "What are you doing so close to the battle?" She turns a sharp, judging gaze to me as she adds, "I thought you were to be kept safe."

I bristle at her accusation and straighten. "He *is* being kept safe."

"No, Cait," Saran says. "It's not what you think. I want to be here. I'm helping, but I'm on the right side this time."

Caitlyn smiles down at him affectionately as she brushes a lock of hair from his face. "That you are, brave boy." She straightens and looks to me. "And how can we help the right side?"

Her question throws me for a moment, but it doesn't take long for the newcomers to be put to work helping with the others. With Saran's shadows now crawling over the castle grounds, we're finding more and more innocents who need rescuing. Some are in immediate danger and we send people to fetch them right away. Others are in secure locations for now, so we leave them until we have more resources.

Even with the additional help we're receiving, it feels like we're losing the battle. More and more wounded pour in, the injuries growing worse by the minute. My energy is seeping as Dragkonians and magic users attack my warding. I pour in more magic to keep them away, but I can't last long like this. When the wounded suddenly stop appearing, it's almost welcome until I realize something is very wrong. I turn to Saran, whose face is set in a deep frown.

"What—"

He shakes his head before I can even get the words out. "I don't know." He mutters under his breath, I assume to the shadows. He shakes his head again, mumbling something else. This time his eyes widen.

"Wh—"

He holds up a hand silencing me, whispering again.

"They've put up a barrier," he finally says, looking up at me. "A strong warding between us and the battle to stop anyone else from seeking aid or escaping."

"How many?"

Saran pauses, looking down at the shadows curling around his waist as his lips move soundlessly. He looks back up at me. "Three, well, four. Three with warding specific magic and a fourth that has some sort of magic that strengthens the others."

"Where are they?"

Saran nods behind me. "That way, not far past our own wards."

I turn to the soldiers nearest who are receiving treatment from a Healer. "Do any of you have a weapon I can borrow? Preferably a bow?"

"I have a dagger," one says, lifting his weapon in a trembling, bloody hand.

"I have one, too," another says, offering me his as well.

I accept the daggers with a nod—they're better than nothing—and turn to leave.

"You can't go past the barrier," Saran says, grabbing my arm. "They'll kill you!"

"Someone has to and all the other soldiers here are in no shape to go."

"You can't!"

"Saran—"

"If you die, our wards will fail," he says, desperation clinging to his voice.

I take a deep breath and kneel before him, forcing him to meet my eyes.

"If I die or am seriously injured, you'll know first from your shadows, aye?"

He nods, tears welling in his eyes.

"If something happens and I can't make it back, I need you to let everyone know. Get them through the portals. If I fall, I will send out as much magic as I can to keep the warding in place so you'll have time." I reach out and brush a rouge tear from the boy's cheek. "You can do that, right?"

He sniffs, his chin trembling as another tear falls, but he manages a single nod.

"Good," I say, doing my best to control my own emotions as I push up with my cane. "You've been very brave, Saran, and I need you to be brave a little longer."

He nods once more, and I turn and follow a trail of curling shadows. I pass through my own ward and crash into magic that is cruel and bitter. Crafting a newer, smaller ward around myself, I push through, fighting their magic. It's strong, but I'm determined. The enemy soldiers clearly weren't expecting me to break through their barrier as quickly as I did, and I have a brief moment of surprise to attack them.

My father never dragged me to weapons training like some of the other Clan Lords did with their sons. Living in the peaceful corner of Athiedor that we did, there wasn't much need, but he taught me some basics for our various hunting trips. That training comes in handy, and I flick one of the daggers their way. I hit my mark in the stomach, and while it's not a killing blow, it's enough to startle him. The warding around me weakens as his concentration fades with his pain before he wisps away.

Now that they know I'm a threat, they're ready to attack. One of the others sends a surge of concentrated warding magic at me. I block it well enough, but it causes me to stumble back a step. I know there's no point in throwing the second dagger; they could block it too quickly. Instead, I charge forward with as much force as I can, keeping myself warded behind a shield. I crash into them and slash at them with my dagger, but they're far from weaponless. I realize exactly how lacking my training is when I find myself in hand-to-hand combat. My attacker has a dagger of his own and manages to catch my side. The gash stings, and my cane falls away to the side as I stumble, crashing down. One of the soldiers lunges at me, and I twist out of his way. As quickly as I can gather my wits, I spin back around and stab blindly. I get lucky and strike his throat. His eyes widen as I pull back the blade. I stagger to my feet as he chokes on his own blood, hands clutching at his throat.

One of the two remaining soldiers, a middle-aged woman, hits me with the full force of her magic. It literally takes my breath away and I bend over, gasping desperately. She laughs and strikes again, stepping closer. She traps me in a bubble made of her magic. I try to draw a breath but find she's somehow managed to remove all the air. My head spins as I struggle to breathe. The world twists and blurs as the woman laughs. I force myself to focus, barely holding my pain at bay, and call on my magic. One blast. Two. Three. I manage to put a crack in the shell of the bubble. I suck in air desperately as I strike again, dissolving the warding.

The woman's smile fades into a snarl as she lunges toward me like a feral animal. I dodge her blow and stumble to the side. I spot my cane lying a few inches away and snatch it up, grabbing the tip. She's charging at me again before I'm fully upright, so I swing wildly at her. I hit her stomach and wind her enough to halt her attack. The grip of my cane smashes into her head with my second blow and she falls. I don't know if she's dead, but she's very, very still, and I sense the warding dissolve behind me.

Breath heavy, I turn to face the last survivor. The man

swallows and raises his hands in surrender before wisping away. I take a shuddering breath and blink back the tears burning my eyes. I stare down in horror at my cane, blood dripping from the bronze rose grip and sliding down the wooden shaft.

My breathing turns choppy and I gasp for air. I killed someone. My eyes flick to the other body strewn across the ground. Two people. I suck in a breath and nearly faint from the sharp pain in my side. I press my hand to waist and my fingers come away covered in crimson.

"Oh, that's right," I mumble to myself as I stagger back a step. "I'm dying."

I chuckle and it quickly morphs into a delirious laugh. I turn and move unsteadily toward the portals. I know I should use my cane, especially given the gash in my side, but I can't bring myself to place my hand over the bloody grip.

The world twists around me, everything fading out of focus. I'm vaguely aware of my body hitting the ground. The world goes dark for a moment, but a cry tears through, bringing me back. I take a shuttering breath and push up into a sitting position. I can feel the darkness tugging on me, and I'm quite ready to give in.

I hear a cheer rise up and I turn and blink toward where I can just make out the glowing portals. I stagger to my feet and realize that everyone behind my warding is looking up. I follow their gaze in time to see the Dragkonians careening from the sky.

"He did it," I mutter to myself, dropping to my knees, my face lifted toward the sky. "He bloody did it."

I feel something wet on my face and realize with a start I'm crying. I'm not entirely sure why. Maybe it's relief that Ievis's spell succeeded. Maybe it's general hysteria due to my loss of blood. Or, perhaps the most likely, it's knowing that I'm dying, and I won't get to see Ievis again to tell him how amazing he is.

I drop forward, my palms slamming against the cold earth as the tears trail down my cheeks. If only I could make it back to the Healers. I struggle to move forward, crawling toward them, but I can't do it. I collapse, allowing my aching eyes to close. I hope my Clan will forgive me for not announcing an heir before my death. I hope they remember I fought with honor. I hope...

CHAPTER FORTY-SEVEN

EHREN

"Form your lines!" I scream, racing toward the front lines. "Form your lines!"

Whether by instinct or some bit of magic I don't understand, we manage to pull ourselves together, fighting back our attackers. The soldiers are easy enough, even with magic they're still human, but the Dragkonians are another story. They swoop from the sky, breathing black fire. Those lucky enough to have magical armor or good magical shielding can survive the blasts, but most fall, never to rise.

Jess and her army are trained well in magic and can hold their own better than most. Kaeya uses her water magic to move the poison through the air, taking down dozens of Dragkonians on her own.

My body aches with every movement, but the medicine I took earlier seems to be holding the worst of it at bay. Cal fights at my side and we move almost as one. No one can stand against us. Our weapons are coated with poison, so we even bring down every Dragkonian that dares to fight against us.

But most aren't so lucky. As every second passes, more soldiers fall. We're losing, I realize, and if we truly lose this battle, there will be no fighting another day. We lose today, we lose the war.

"Hold the line!" I yell as the enemy soldiers surge around us. "Hold the line!"

A burst of magic explodes from my right, followed by screams. I'm not sure if it's our side or theirs. I look around wildly. There are too many fronts. We can't continue like this much longer. We can't fight attacks from the air and the land. We can't hold out against the magic of the Dragkonians.

"Ehren," Cal breathes.

I pull my blade from the body of a soldier and look over at him.

He's looking up, eyes wide. Terrified, I follow his gaze and my heart stops. They're falling from the sky. The Dragkonians are falling. Astra did it. Something between a sob and a laugh breaks from my lips as I look back at Cal. He grins, his face easing into relief.

I turn my attention back to the battlefield. It's not over yet. Those on the side of the Dragkonians are looking around in wide-eyed fear, unsure of what to do. Another burst of magic draws my attention and I finally see Kato. He lands on the top of the hill and looks over his soldiers.

"We can still win!" he roars. "Magic will vanquish!"

His words seem to rally his soldiers, and they rush back in. Without their Dragkonian counterparts, however, they're weaker.

"Take back our land!" I yell in response, and we surge forward.

I turn toward Cal but before I can speak he says, "Let's kill him. Together."

Side-by-side we race across the battlefield, the sounds of swords and magic bursting around us. A few enemy soldiers get in our way, but we strike them down. Justice is finally within reach, and there's no way we're backing down now. Kato sees us coming and grins. He wants this showdown as much as I do. When we're finally face-to-face, he looks down at us and grins.

"So, this is what it comes down to? My sister's human pets versus me," Kato purrs, cocking his head.

"Draw your sword," I spit, raising my own, Cal mimicking my actions.

Kato laughs with a careless shrug. "Fine. Foreplay be damned."

Twin blades of fire appear in his hands and he charges. He hasn't been fighting like I have, and his body isn't in constant pain. He has more energy, more power. But vengeance is on my side. No matter how he strikes, I block it. He wisps to strike from behind, but I spin too quickly for him to succeed. He scowls in frustration and tries again.

"Your sister taught me a thing or two," I say with a grin.

He growls and charges forward, his swings wide and fueled by emotion. This time Cal jumps in, blocking one sword, but the other manages to catch my leg just enough I can feel the sting of the fire. I stumble back with a hiss, and Kato glares in triumph. Cal catches me before I can fall.

"You okay?" he whispers, his eyes trained on Kato.

I nod and lick my lips, pushing away from his arms. "I'm fine."

My leg screams, but I use the pain to fuel my next attack. And the next. And the next. Cal and I move like one, our motions echoing off each other in perfect sequence. Kato retaliates with fury. He's so focused on our bladework he doesn't see me drop my sword and reach in my pocket as Cal strikes hard and fast. He doesn't notice the tiny pearl of his sister's raw magic mixed with Fae magic contained in a single orb. He doesn't notice, that is, until I unleash it.

"Close your eyes," I hiss to Cal as I shut my own eyes against the flash of blinding silver light.

When I open my eyes, I see Kato stumbling back, his swords gone. I whisper ancient words under my breath, drawing on the magic I stored in my rings and his magic stills. His eyes go wide as my spells take effect.

"What have you done?" he roars, eyes flashing. "What did you do to my magic?"

I grin, scooping up my sword. "I figured I'd even the playing field."

He lunges toward me, weaponless, hands extended. I dodge, but even without his magic, he's a trained soldier with lethal skill. He spins and lands a blow to my cheek. He swings again and I dodge to the side, but he kicks my knees, sending me to the ground. Cal exhales sharply, stepping toward me but I shake my head. Kato is focused on me, seemingly having forgotten Cal exists. He towers above me, eyes gleaming with hate. Cal meets my eyes for the briefest second and my message is clear.

Kill him. Stab him in the back.

Like he did to my father.

Like he did to Bram.

In one smooth motion, Cal plunges his sword through Kato. As his blade strikes flesh, it glows with the power of the gods. Kato gasps and chokes, his eyes wide as he glances down at the sword tip sticking from his chest. Cal yanks his sword out and Kato's body falls to the ground. Sputtering blood, Kato rolls over and looks up at me.

"You think you've won?" He chokes on his own blood. "You haven't won. Killing me, locking up the Dragkonians, it won't stop magic from rising."

"I never wanted to stop magic," I say, raising my sword, preparing for one last killing blow. "I only wanted to stop you. Your sister wanted to stop you. You would be so proud of the woman she's become. She's so strong and valiant. She's come close to breaking so many times, but somehow she holds it together. I think that has something to do with you."

Something flickers in Kato's eyes, so I continue.

"The girl you grew up with is still there at her core. She's gentle and loving and kind. Even until the end she looked for a way to save you. She loves you Kato, and you'd be proud of the woman she is now."

Right as I'm ready to give up, to stab my blade into his heart, something in his face shifts. His eyes seem less dark, turning to a familiar amethyst. He gasps and squeezes his eyes shut before looking back up at me. The shock in his face is alarming and I stumble back.

"Kato?" I whisper, my voice hoarse.

"Tell her I'm sorry," he manages. "Tell Astra I never meant . . . Tell her I love her, that I . . ."

He opens his mouth to say more but the words never come. He stills, his eyes shuttering closed, but his breathing doesn't stop entirely. He's still alive, albeit barely. I raise my eyes to Cal and find he's already watching me. His mouth drops open, and I can see the conflict.

"Damn it," he mutters, kneeling next to Kato to put pressure on the wound. "Get a Healer."

"Cal are you sure? I promised I wouldn't make you—"

"Healer! We need a Healer!" he yells, his voice echoing over the battlefield as he presses his hands over Kato's wound.

I kneel on the other side of Kato and place my hand over Cal's. "Thank you."

Cal shakes his head. "If this bastard so much as looks at you wrong . . ."

"I know. I know."

"And we're either keeping him locked up until his dying breath or exiling him as far away as possible."

I laugh at Cal's determined proclamation and press a kiss to his lips. A Healer stumbles to my side and halts, staring down at us.

"Your Majesty?" he asks with a puzzled scowl.

I stand and clear my throat. "Heal Kato as best as possible and make sure he's held captive for questioning."

The Healer blinks rapidly for a moment before nodding. "Of course, Your Majesty."

He quickly kneels next to Kato, warm healing magic flowing over the wound. Kato moans but doesn't wake.

"You may want to take measures to ensure that he remains unconscious," Cal suggests, stepping to my side. The Healer nods, continuing his work as Cal turns to me. "Let's bring this war to a close. Shall we?"

He extends his hand, still covered in Kato's blood, but I grasp it anyway, drawing him closer to press a kiss to his cheek.

"Let's finish the war."

I pluck up my sword, and we rush back into the battle. Most of the soldiers that witnessed their leader fall are scrambling from the battlefield while others fall to their knees, surrendering. Many still fight, but without the Dragkonians or Kato, we finally have a clear advantage. When a few soldiers arrive and drag Kato from the battlefield, everyone takes notice, Jessalynn most of all.

From across the field of bodies and magic, her eyes find me. She glances toward Kato then back to me. I nod and a wild grin spreads across her face.

"The Fire King has fallen!" she cries, raising her sword over her head. "Long live King Ehren!"

Several eyes turn toward me as they echo her cheer. I stand straighter. All around the battlefield, soldiers drop their weapons. Magic ceases as Kato's allies drop to their knees. My people, my soldiers take the field, our allies marching by their side.

Long live King Ehren.

The chanting continues.

Long live King Ehren.

Long live King Ehren.

Long live King Ehren.

We didn't lose.

Long live King Ehren.

We have won.

The realization crashes over with a wave of relief. I turn and look at Cal. He meets my eyes and we stand there for a moment, lost in what has happened. Slowly, Cal's lips turn up into a smile and he drops his sword, dashing forward to pull me into his arms.

"We did it, Ehren. We did it."

I pull back and stare into his eyes. "You did it."

"No, it was both of us together."

I grin and look around at the cheering soldiers. No matter how battered, how bloody, they still celebrate, smiles of relief on their faces. I'm so caught up in the celebration, I don't notice the soldier creeping up behind me until it's too late. Cal screams my name and I spin only to find a sword aimed at my throat. I don't have time to react more than to squeeze my eyes shut. But nothing happens. I open my eyes to find my attacker frozen. His sword clatters to the ground as he falls forward, revealing a wide-eyed Pip. I look down and see a black handled dagger sticking from the mans's back.

"You saved me," I marvel, staring at Pip.

He still looks horrified, but he nods.

Cal pulls me into his arms as he looks to Pip. "You saved your king. Thank you."

Pip nods again, shrugging as he glances down at the body between us. I know this will haunt him for the rest of his life, and I make a note to help him heal as much possible. Before I can say another word of thanks, however, he's scampering away. I huff a laugh, shaking my head.

I lift my eyes and scan the battlefield, still filled with celebration and cheering, my heart pounding. I'm swarmed by the masses in the throes of victory. But I don't care about them. Once I'm sure no more desperate assassins are coming after me, I turn back to Cal, my lips finding his with crushing power which he reciprocates willingly. Fire pours through me as the kiss heightens. I don't care about the crowd around me. I want him here and now. As my hand fumbles with his shirt, sliding up to touch his skin, he laughs and pulls back.

"Later," he mumbles, his voice rough and eyes shining. "I swear to you, my prince—my *king*—I will have you, and we will celebrate this victory to the fullest."

His words rush over me, and I press my lips to his before allowing myself to be led through the cheering crowd. Jess finds me and slaps my back between my shoulder blades. I wince but she only grins.

"Well, brother, we did it." Her eyes drift over the celebrating forces. "Despite the odds, we did it. We saved our kingdom."

I nod, licking my lips. "The work has only just begun. We have to decide what to do with those still against us and count the dead. We also have to hunt down and take care of Kato's other supporters who—"

Jess cuts me off with a wave of her hand. "My people are gathering up the prisoners. We can sort the dead later. The wounded are already making their way to Healers if they haven't already received aid, and we can arrange to send scouts out later to find the remaining traitors." Of course she's already put thoughts into action. She turns to me and her grin grows. "But right now we celebrate. We deserve it."

I match her grin. "So be it."

We make our way to the camp. Cal and I walk hand-in-hand. I'm eager to get to my tent and finish what the kiss started. I feel a pulse of magic and turn to see Astra stepping out of a portal a few yards away. I grin, but that grin quickly fades. Her cheeks are stained with tears and everything about her is broken. Is it because she thinks I killed Kato? No. She sanctioned that. My eyes fall to the small Fae Fox in her arms. I've never seen Felixe so sullen. That must mean . . . I look around. My heart stops. No. It can't be.

I release Cal's hand and find myself rushing to her. She lunges toward me, collapsing into my arms. Her tears soak my shirt and I hold her tightly.

"He's gone," she sobs. "H-he's gone." She pulls her head back and looks up at me. "I can't feel him at all. He's gone, Ehren. He sacrificed himself." She shakes her head. "He's gone."

I release a sound that isn't human as I fall to the ground, Astra in my arms. Tears rack my body as I hold her. I know I should be strong for her, but her sorrow is my sorrow. All joy from victory is gone. The cost was too high.

A hand grips my shoulder and I look up at Cal, his cheeks wet with tears. I search his face, trying to find some semblance of comfort, but he feels the loss nearly as keenly as I do. I lean back into Astra and we allow our tears to consume us.

Part Four: Aftermath

CHAPTER FORTY-EIGHT

RONAN

I wake with a start, completely disoriented. I'm in a dimly lit room on a . . . cot? I blink and glance around, realizing I'm in a makeshift Healing room of sorts. Dozens of cots are spread all around, occupied by soldiers in various stages of the Healing process. Memories of the battle crash in so hard, I wince, placing a hand to my pounding head. I take a deep breath and look down at my clothes and find that my blood-soaked shirt from the battle has been replaced by a new, crisp white shirt that's roughly a size too big. With a confused scowl, I lift the edge and peer down at my side. Even though there's not much light, I can tell that whatever gash was there before has been Healed into a thin, pink scar. I take a shuddering breath and carefully trace a shaking finger along the faint line.

"Unfortunately that will always be there," a soft voice says, making me jump.

I quickly drop the hem of the shirt and twist to find the speaker. A young woman with long black hair and gentle smile stands near the foot of my bed, a jar of something in her hand.

"Oh, I . . ." I clear my throat. "Do I have you to thank?"

She shakes her head. "No, that was not my handiwork. I believe you were initially saved by a potion delivered to you by Eleni, one of the shifters, and then healed further by someone else. I have merely taken over Healing duties for the time."

"Ah, I see. Well, thank you, nonetheless." I glance around. "May I inquire as to my location?"

The young woman laughs. "I suppose you would be curious, given you were near the portals when you fell. You're at the castle in Embervein."

Embervein. And I'm clearly not a prisoner. My heart starts racing.

"So, the war? We won?"

The woman's soft smile grows into a full-fledged grin. "Yes. The Dragkonians have been slain and the Fire King has been taken prisoner."

I sit up straighter, frowning. "Kato lives?"

The woman's smile fades a bit as she nods. "He's locked in the dungeon, his magic gone. The king promises that he will no longer be a threat."

My heart skips a beat at her words. "King? Ehren is king?"

A slight blush rises on the girl's cheeks as she dips her head. "Well, his official coronation isn't for another couple weeks as he wanted to give the kingdom a few weeks to mourn and recover, but I suppose he's king all the same."

My heart comes to a full stop, my breath stolen. "How long have I been asleep?" I ask desperately, swinging my legs over the edge of the bed as I stare down the girl. "When did the battle end?"

The woman hesitates a moment before replying slowly, "The battle ended nearly seven days ago."

"I've been sleeping for seven days?"

She nods. "Between the low levels of your magic and the

severity of the wound, it was a miracle you lived. Your body needed time to heal."

Something beyond my own will propels me from the bed, and I find myself searching for an exit. "I need to see the prince —the king." I turn and look at the woman. "Do you know where he is?"

She blinks rapidly at me, seemingly startled by my sudden movement. "It's barely past dawn. I imagine he is sleeping."

Of course. Just because I'm finally up and ready to go doesn't mean that the rest of the world isn't still recovering from everything they've been doing while I've been sleeping.

"Besides," the woman says cautiously, "don't you need that?" She motions to something leaning against the edge of my cot.

My eyes zero in on my cane, my heartbeat catching in my throat. Someone has taken the courtesy to clean it for me, and yet, all the blood might as well still be there. I can see it as clearly now as I did on the battlefield. I clench my hands into fists at my sides. Logically, I know I need a cane, but I also know that I'll never be able to use this exact cane again.

I back away from the woman, shaking my head. "I'll be fine."

She frowns but doesn't protest. "All right, then. When the prince does rise, he'll likely take breakfast in the dining hall."

I thank her and stumble from the room. I'm not used to walking without an aid, and I'm sure I look like a staggering mess to anyone I pass. I'll need to find another cane soon, but I'm sure it will be low on the list of important things in the wake of the recent war.

It doesn't take long of wandering down endless corridors to figure out how exactly out of my element I am. I thought the Summer Palace was something to behold, but it has nothing on the main castle in Embervein. This place is huge, and I'm incredibly lost. I finally stumble upon a doorway leading outside to what I assume is one of many gardens. The early morning air is cold and bracing, but even after my extremities begin to numb, I can't seem to make myself go back inside. I wander further into the garden and sink down onto a stone bench surrounded by bare bushes.

I almost died. The realization crashes in on me hard and I struggle to catch my breath. I almost died. I wonder how many did die. I wonder if Ievis was successful in rescuing both Alak and Astra or if one of them is suffering now. I wonder how many of the people I know and love were lost to the war. I wonder what my father, the gentle man of peace that he was, would think of me now. I wonder what he would say when he found out that his only son was a killer. Oh, my kills were justified and had I not done what I did, many others may have died, but I took life all the same.

I don't know how long I sit with morbid thoughts turning over in my head, but in the time I sit, the sky above turns from a muted gray-blue to brilliant splashes of pinks and oranges ending in a soft, brilliant blue. Only then, when the traces of sunrise are fading, do I rise and head back inside.

As I make my way down the hall, following the sounds of castle life, my limbs tingle as heat returns feeling to them. It's almost painful but I find myself embracing how it makes me feel alive. It reminds me that I have a purpose. I follow a trail of people to the dining hall. I stop dead in the doorway, taking in the vastness of the room. Tables are scattered all around, several bearing trays of food for those already seated. Most look like the table in the dining hall at the Summer Palace, but others, like the longer tables set up along the far end of the room, are clearly made for royalty and the like. My stomach sinks as I realize I have even less of a place here.

I'm ready to run back to my garden when someone calls my name. I turn around and come face to face with Ehren. He's smiling, but he looks tired around the eyes. Cal, who's only a step behind, looks equally weary as he offers me a smile of his own.

"You're up!" Ehren says, clapping his hand to my shoulder.

I manage a small smile. "Aye, I am."

"Excellent." Ehren looks past me into the hall. "Would you like to join me for breakfast? There are a few things I'd like your input on, assuming you're still willing to be my Athiedor Ambassador."

I swallow, nodding. "I am happy to assist in whatever way I can."

I follow Ehren up to the head table. Cal takes a seat on his right, and I settle to his left. I glance around for Astra, but the Court Sorceress is nowhere in sight. I swallow my questions, however, as a servant steps up with offerings of food. I fill my plate with sausages, eggs, and toast.

"Several of the castle suppliers nearby were more than happy to help us restock supplies once we locked Kato up," Ehren explains, nodding to the food on my plate.

"So Kato is locked up and not dead?" I ask carefully, spreading a bit of berry jam on my toast.

Ehren nods, chewing a bite of food before answering. "He lost his magic in the process, so he's less of a threat. I haven't quite decided what to do with him. I'm waiting . . ."

He trails off and Cal places his hand on Ehren's knee.

"Who didn't return?" I ask, deciding there's no point in hiding the fact I know something is wrong. "Astra or Alak?"

Ehren looks at me, deep sadness in his eyes. "Alak. Hycis

didn't return either. Apparently the spell required pairs of bondmates and only one of each pair came back."

Dread pools in my stomach as my next question weighs heavily on my tongue. "And the other Fae? Did they return?"

Ehren nods, taking another bite of food. "Iefyr brought Ievis and Rynia back through a portal a couple days ago once they returned their borrowed boat."

My heart rate picks up. "Are they still here?"

This time Ehren shakes his head. "They stayed only long enough to confirm that we were fine, or at least as fine as could be expected, and then they returned to their world." Ehren looks up at me and offers me a weak smile. "Ievis checked in on you before he left."

"Did he—" I clear my throat. "Did he leave a message for me?"

Ehren's smile falters. "No. Should he have?"

I shake my head, looking down at my plate, my appetite vanishing. "No." I force my attention back to Ehren. "What did you want to discuss?"

"Oh, well, as you can imagine a fair number of Kato's followers were from Athiedor. There's been some debate over what to do with the prisoners. Some of them committed crimes minor enough that they can easily be forgiven, but others . . . Well, their crimes are more severe. Should they be returned to the Clan Lords for punishments to be doled out or should we keep them as prisoners of war?"

I mull over his question a moment, taking a few bites of food to buy myself some time to think. "Is Athiedor truly meant to be free?"

Ehren nods quickly. "Yes. The paperwork has already been drawn up. As soon as I am officially crowned king, the decree will go into effect and Athiedor will be free."

"Then it is my recommendation that you return any pris-oners to their Clans unless they have committed extremely dangerous or treasonous crimes. Those closest in league with Kato should be kept here, but anyone of lower rank should be sent home to serve their sentences."

Ehren nods and Cal shoots him a small smile before leaning forward to look down at me.

"That was his instinct," Cal explains. "But he wanted to make sure."

"Your instincts are good," I say to Ehren. "I appreciate you asking, though."

"Of course." He pauses before adding, "Would you mind writing to the Clan Lords in an official capacity as ambassador with the prisoners' information and crimes? I can do it if needed, but—"

I wave my hand, cutting him short. "I'm happy to help. I'm sure you have a million other things on your plate right now."

He makes a sound that's somewhere between a chuckle and a scoff. "To say the least."

We fall into easy conversation as Ehren details all the things that go into helping a kingdom recover after a civil war. When he confesses he can't wait for Jess to return, I frown.

"You're giving up your crown to your sister?"

"More like sharing it with her," he replies with a shrug. "We're going to rule Callenia together. She just had to go back to the Valley first and tighten some loose ends."

"Does everyone know?"

Ehren gives me a sheepish grin. "Not yet. I plan to announce it at my coronation."

A laugh escapes my lips, and I find myself shaking my head. Ehren isn't going to be a very orthodox king, but I already feel refreshed by his energy.

When we're done with breakfast, Ehren leads me to an alcove in the library where I can work in peace. When he takes note of my missing cane, he promises to have another made for me without even questioning why I don't want to use my old one. I have a feeling he not only knows but understands.

I'm more than happy to busy myself with the work, allowing the hours to pass by in a flurry of scribbles and stacks of paper. I'm over halfway done when footsteps approach my alcove. I don't even bother glancing up from my current letter, assuming it's Ehren or Cal coming to check on my progress.

"It figures you would be in the library."

I jerk my head up, my heart leaping into my throat. Ievis stands in the doorway, leaning casually against the frame, his arms crossed. I stumble to my feet, pressing a trembling hand on the table to steady myself as I stare at him. He's just as beautiful as I remember, perhaps even more so.

"I thought you went home."

The corner of his lips twitch as he restrains a smile. "I did. I had some things to take care of."

"But you came back?"

He pushes off the door and tilts his head as he meets my eyes. "I did." He takes a step closer. "I promised I would return."

"How? Can Iefyr now breach the worlds?"

He shakes his head, a small smile curving on the corner of his mouth as he steps closer. "Though I did combine a bit of their magic with mine to create a one-time spell to connect me to you so I could follow a trail of magic back."

I swallow, my mouth suddenly dry. "And how long will you stay?"

Another step closer. "How long will you let me?"

"I won't push you away."

"Good."

He closes the distance between us in two smooth strides. Or perhaps I close the distance. I can't be sure. All I know is that a breath later I'm wrapped in the strength of his arms, our lips pressed together. I lose myself in rapid kisses, only remembering where we are when he presses me back against the table. I jerk away with a gasp.

"Wait," I mutter, placing a hand on his chest to keep him at bay. "This is foolish."

Ievis frowns and steps back, releasing me. "Why?"

I shake my head. "You're a Fae and I'm a human. There's no way this can last. You have your own life to live."

"Do not worry about me living my life. I have made the necessary arrangements, and when you return home, I can create a Faerie ring so I can come and go between our worlds as needed."

"But I'm *human*! I'm going to die! I almost did die." I add the last part in a whisper so quiet I wonder if Ievis heard me.

"I know." He sets his jaw. "When I saw you lying there, unconscious, I wanted nothing more than to hunt down those that hurt you and kill them. Imagine my surprise and pride when I learned you already took care of them for me."

He reaches out a hand and cups my cheek, drawing a startled gasp from me. I lean into the warmth of his touch for a moment before forcing myself to pull away.

"I'll still live a short life. A human life."

Ievis nods, glancing to the side. "I have considered this which is why"—he turns his attention back to me—"I sought out a spell when I went home. One that would bind our life forces together."

"What do you mean?"

"My life is unusually long, long enough that you humans

call Fae 'immortal,' but if I bind my life-force to a human, that long life is split between us. My life would be shorter than the average Fae lifespan and the human's would be longer."

My heart races in my chest so fast I'm afraid it's going to fly free. "You can't possibly want that."

He growls, moving so close the tip of his nose brushes my own. "You do not get to tell me what I do or do not want." He steps back and sucks in a breath. "Besides, it is not a choice we have to make today. We are both still relatively young for our species. We can spend years enjoying one another and getting to know each other better. If in a few years we decide that forever is what we want, I will cast the spell."

He reaches out a hand and traces a finger down my cheek. I shiver as my eyes shutter closed, a tear escaping. He brushes it away gently and takes my hands in his.

"Ronan," he whispers. I open my eyes and look up at him. "Will you let me stay?"

I stare into his searching golden eyes and nod. "Yes."

The word is barely out of my mouth before his lips are on mine again. He kisses me breathless for a moment before he draws back enough to look down at me.

"I have something else for you."

"More than the possible promise of forever?" I tease, smiling up at him. "I'll need to find a gift to give you in return."

His eyes darken as he grins, pressing a quick but fierce kiss to my lips before stepping away. "I'm sure you can find a way to make it up to me."

Heat pools in my stomach at the low, rough tone in his voice. I'm ready to pull him in for another kiss that I hope leads somewhere else—preferably a bedroom, if I even have one of those here—when he walks toward the door. I scrunch my brow in curious confusion as he leans down and plucks up something hidden out of sight.

"I thought you might need this."

He holds up the most beautiful cane I've ever seen. My breath catches in my throat as he passes it to me. I turn it over in my hand, staring down in awe. The grip looks to be made of a real rose, but when I touch the red petals they're as firm as any gold would be. Below the rose is a bright green vine twisting tightly down a light brown wood shaft that's been polished so that it shines. Upon closer inspection, I discover that the vine is not only as sturdy as the wood and the rose, but it also has tiny red buds nestled in its leaves. The tip of the cane looks to be made of a diamond, but I imagine it's actually a far more precious gem known only to the Fae.

"Ievis this is . . ." I trail off, knowing there are truly no words to describe this gift.

"Not enough, I know," Ievis finishes for me.

I blink up at him in confusion. "No, it's perfect." I look back down at the cane, eager to avoid his eyes as I ask, "How did you know I would need a new cane?"

"I heard what happened with your old cane, and I knew you would not likely want to use it again."

I look up at him, my heart sinking. "Because I'm weak."

Ievis smiles gently. "Because you are my kind, gentle, and tender human, and I would not have you any other way."

A small sob escapes and I collapse against Ievis. He wraps his arms around me and holds me close.

"I have never been in a war before and therefore I have never had to heal from one, but I am here for you, Ronan."

I press closer into him as he presses a kiss to the side of my head. "Thank you."

He holds me for a moment before I regain my composure and pull back.

"Now, do you need to finish this up or should we go find some lunch?"

I manage a small smile. "I can finish this later. Let's get some lunch and then maybe we can catch up?"

Ievis grins. "I like that plan."

He presses one last kiss to my cheek before we head out into the new world that's been created, walking hand-in-hand.

CHAPTER FORTY-NINE

ASTRA

I can't make myself get out of bed. It's been weeks, and I just can't do it. Sometimes I can make it as far as my washroom, but I can't make myself bathe. Other times I can barely sit up to get down a bite or two of food.

Felixe comes and goes. Sometimes I wish he would stay longer—we're all each other has left—but he's also a painful reminder of what I've had and lost.

Ehren visits a couple times a day. Perhaps more. Honestly, I'm not sure how much time has passed. Everything blurs together. All I know for sure is that I'm back in my old suite of rooms in Embervein, and I can't imagine anything more painful than losing Alak.

I'm drifting back into my near endless state of sleep when I'm drawn out by a soft knock on my door.

"Ash?" Ehren calls through the door. "I'm coming in."

The door creaks open, bringing with it a beam of light that has me wincing until it clicks shut.

"I brought coffee," Ehren says, his shadowy figure holding

up what I assume is a mug, the gentle aroma of roasted coffee beans floating my way.

I sink further into my mattress, pulling the blanket tighter around me. "I don't want any."

Ehren sighs, setting the mug on my bedside table before walking toward my balcony and throwing open the curtain. Sunlight floods my room and I squeeze my eyes shut against the assault of light. Ehren's boots click on the floor as he comes back around the bed. My mattress dips with his weight as he crawls in behind me, his arms wrapping around my waist, holding me close.

"So, I came up with a plan," he says, placing his chin on my shoulder.

"Ehren—" I start, but he cuts me off before I can get another word out.

"No, no, no. I made a plan and as we both know, I'm excellent at making plans. So hear me out."

I sigh but don't protest, even managing a small nod.

"Good," he says, placing a quick kiss to my cheek. "So, I came up with a plan. We are going to lie here for ten minutes and wallow in complete misery. Then, when those ten minutes are over, we are going to get up and face the world. I'm going to run you a bath while you drink your coffee, and then you're going to get as ready as you can."

My mind flits back to a similar circumstance not all that long ago. Only I was the one begging him to get out of bed.

"It's not that easy," I mutter, my words muffled by my blanket.

"I know, Ash. I know." His hold on me tightens. "You lost the person who means the most to you in the entire world, the person who completes you. If I ever lost Cal, I know I wouldn't be able to get out of bed. He's my everything. And we aren't even magically combined. When you lost Alak"—a small sob escapes me at his name and Ehren pulls me closer—"you literally lost a piece of your soul. I don't think you can heal from that. But I need you to try."

I know Ehren is right. I *know* he is. He's right about everything.

"Please, Ash. I need you to try because I keep waiting for you to step to my side, but you're not even in the room. I keep turning to you for your advice, and you're not there. I know I have Cal, but it's not the same. I need you in a different way than I need him. I need my Court Sorceress. I need *you*. I'm getting crowned king in a little over a week and I really want you there. I need you there. So, I know it's entirely selfish on my part, but can you try again for me? Please?"

His voice trembles with a desperation I haven't heard from him in a long time. Tears burn my eyes. Can I do this? I should be able to.

Ehren's hold on me loosens, but he doesn't release me. I can sense there's something else he's not saying. I take a deep breath and turn over so I'm facing him.

"There's something else," I whisper.

He nods, hesitating before he speaks, so quietly I barely hear his words. "Bram comes home soon."

A new, fresh ache clenches in my chest. Ehren blinks back a tear and sniffs. He opens his mouth once, twice, before he finally finds his words. "I really need you there, and I think you need to be there for you as well. Bram would want you there."

I struggle to contain the multitude of emotions. I swallow, keeping them at bay. Finally, I manage a nod.

"Yeah?" Ehren asks, his eyes widening as hope floods his voice.

"I'll try," I promise.

"Good. Thank you." He kisses my forehead before shuffling off the bed. "I'll go run you a bath and you can take it from here?"

I manage to get into a sitting position. "Yeah."

Ehren's shoulders sag with relief. "Okay. Now you drink that coffee while I get the bath ready." He nods to the mug on my bedside table. "You need the strength."

He disappears into my washroom and I grab the mug with a sigh. The coffee has gone a bit cold. I could pull on my magic to warm it, but ever since I used my magic to seal Alak away on an island of enemies, I haven't quite found the strength to use it. I still manage to get down half the mug by the time Ehren returns.

"Bath is ready to go. I'll lay you out something while you wash, but if you don't like it, feel free to pick something else. I'll wait out in the main room while you get ready."

"You don't have to wait."

"I know I don't have to. I'm basically king now. I have people who will do things like waiting for me." He winks and I feel a small smile tug at my lips. "I *want* to wait and make sure you're okay."

He offers me his hand, and I accept so he can help me to my feet. After weeks lying mostly in bed, I'm unsteady, but Ehren helps me to the washroom, only leaving when I assure him I can undress myself. It takes a me a moment, but I finally find the strength and will to remove my clothes and get into the water.

Ehren has filled the tub with scented oils and bubbles. I use some of the rose soap he's laid out on the edge of the tub with a washcloth, and I manage to wash away days of sweat and grime. I'm tempted to sink beneath the surface of the water and never leave the tub, but once the water has gone cold, I climb out. I use a towel set off to the side to dry myself before heading back into my bedroom. As promised, there's a dress lying on my bed. When I walk out into the main room, I find Ehren draped across one of my armchairs, a book in his hand.

"Feeling better?" Ehren asks, lowering his book.

I nod. "Better enough."

"Excellent." Ehren snaps the book shut and bounces to his feet. He crosses to me and offers his arm. "Shall we go?"

I manage a small smile and accept. He leads me from my room with a flourish. As we make our way down the hall, I catch a few servants exchanging wide-eyed glances at my presence, but they quickly shift their attention when I look their way. When we stop outside the large doors of the library, relief washes over me.

"I thought you might like to remain hidden," Ehren says, dropping my arm.

"Thank you." I look up at him. "Where will you be?"

Ehren lifts in shoulder in a half-shrug and glances down the hall. "Here and there." He sighs, running his hand through his hair as he turns his attention back to me. "There's so much to put into place. I can't wait for Jess to get back. I could really use her input."

"When does she get back?"

"Hopefully tomorrow, assuming she didn't get held up."

I nod. When I make no move to open the library doors, Ehren leans down and presses a quick kiss to my cheek.

"I'll come by and check in with you in a bit." He pulls the door open just wide enough for me to fit through. "I promise."

I swallow and step inside, immediately comforted by the presence of books. I glance over my shoulder and catch one last encouraging smile from Ehren before the door closes. Taking a rallying breath I step further into the library, glancing around for the librarian or even Cadewynn. I hear voices drifting from the alcoves, one more familiar than the other, though both are in another language. I follow the sound and stop in the doorway of an alcove. Kai stands off to the side, arms crossed as he smiles down at a table littered with maps. Next to him stands a tall, thin figure, talking rapidly with a pair of silver spectacles slipping down their nose and their dark, shoulder length hair tied back. They say something that has Kai smiling at them affectionately. I start to back away, suddenly feeling like I'm intruding. I bump the doorway on the way out, and Kai's attention snaps to me, his whole body tensing.

"Astra?" he says, relaxing slightly as he frowns at me.

"I didn't mean to interrupt," I mumble, stumbling back a step.

"You're not interrupting," he insists, crossing to me. He reaches out like he wants to gather me in his arms, but he hesitates, shoving his hands in his pockets instead. "You're out of bed."

"Ehren," I say, and I know by the way Kai nods his head it's explanation enough. I glance past Kai into the room. "What are you doing?"

"Oh." Kai looks over his shoulder at the person behind him then back at me, his expression soft. "We're looking at maps."

"I rather like them," Kai's companion says in a rich accent, stepping forward. "Kai has been showing me some of the royal collection, and I must say, the whole thing is fascinating."

I can practically feel the excitement vibrating off of them and a true smile curves the corner of my mouth.

"Do you make maps?"

They nod, their spectacles slipping further down their nose. "Yes, but most of my maps are merely copies. I haven't had much opportunity to travel and see things firsthand until more recently." They shoot Kai a look before taking a step closer. "My name is Nova, by the way."

"Ah, yes," Kai mumbles, clearing his throat, his cheeks flushing. "Nova came from Paravlia with news from the rest of my pack once they heard the final battle had been fought and won. They are . . ." He trails off, searching for the word.

"Your someone," I finish for him, grief clutching my heart.

Kai's expression clouds as he nods. "Nova is my someone."

Something in me cracks and Kai must sense it immediately because the next thing I know I'm encased in a hug so fierce it steadies my world. I bury my face in his chest as a small sob escapes. Kai holds me closer as I cry. After a few minutes, I manage to collect myself and I pull away from Kai, wiping my eyes with the back of my hand.

"I'm sorry," I whisper to Nova. "I just—"

They wave their hand. "No need to explain. I will never judge anyone for their grief. Gods know I've struggled to make sense of life in the wake of tragedy in the past. Sometimes it takes a while to find what you need to move on past the grief so you can live again. That may take you days or it may be years." They exchange a look with Kai. "If you need Kai to yourself, I am happy to make myself scarce."

I shake my head. "No, I don't need that."

"What do you need?" Kai asks.

I take a deep breath and look around the room, hoping an answer will present itself. When my eyes land on the table, I take a step closer, focusing on a map on the edge of the table. It's different from the others. The lines are more precise in a way and show more artistic style.

"Did you do this?" I ask, tracing the lines of a river.

Nova nods, their cheeks reddening. "I did."

I look up at them. "This is really good."

Nova ducks their head. "Thank you."

"They're really quite talented," Kai says, stepping to their side.

The pride pouring from his voice warms me. When Nova looks up at Kai, their expression is so tender. Kai looks so happy. I want that again. I had that, and it was stolen from me.

Suddenly I know what I need to do to move on, or at least I know where I need to start. A dark shadow passes over me like ice, and I take a step back.

"Astra, are you okay?" Kai asks, studying me with concern.

"No, I'm not okay," I answer honestly. "There's something I need to do." I offer Kai what I hope is a reassuring smile, but I'm sure I fail. "I'll catch up with you later. It was nice meeting you, Nova."

Nova nods, their brow furrowed with concern, but I sweep from the alcove before they can ask any questions. I practically race from the library through the castle, ignoring all the curious glances. Even though I've never been to this section of the palace before, I know where I'm going. I'm sure it's my imagination, but the further into the belly I go, the colder it gets. When I reach the final staircase that leads down into the dungeons, I freeze. I don't know why I thought I could do this. I can't face him. I can't, I—

"I haven't been able to go in, either," a voice says, startling me.

I spin around as Pax steps from the shadows to the left of the doorway. His hands hang limply by his sides and dark circles line his eyes.

"We can go together, if you'd like," he offers, his voice heavy. "Maybe we can face him together, yeah?"

My head feels like it's filled with lead as I nod. Pax offers his arm and I accept it. As we step into the darkness of the dungeon, it's more than just the winding stone staircase that's spiraling. I clutch Pax's arm so hard I'm sure I'm leaving behind bruises, but he's holding onto me like I'm the only thing keeping him from sinking. Step by step we descend the stairs, keeping each other upright. When we reach the bottom, we find two guards. They straighten but must recognize at least one of us, offering nods of acknowledgment as we walk by.

Most of the cells are occupied by prisoners of war. A few call out to us, but their voices are drowned out by my pounding heart. I think Pax stops and addresses a couple guards, possibly asking for directions, but I can't even focus on that. He guides me through the dark, twisting aisles until we reach a cell all by itself at the far end. Inside is a lone figure, crouched in the corner, his head in his hands. I don't know why I thought I could do this. I stumble back a step, but Pax is holding me firmly, frozen himself, his breaths coming out sharp and shallow.

"Kato?" he whispers.

The figure's head jerks up and sure enough, my twin is before me, but he's different. The swagger and confidence I always associated with him has vanished entirely. His eyes are wide and desperate as they dart from Pax to me. He eases to his feet, approaching the bars of his cage with caution. Metal scrapes the floor and my eyes dart down to the shackles around his ankle. When I look back up, Kato is gripping the bars so tightly his knuckles are white.

"Ash?" His voice is hoarse and rough, likely from disuse. "You're alive." He sounds relieved and something about his relief angers me. "No one would tell me if you were okay."

Fury rises in me like a dark beast and I launch forward, yanking my arm from Pax's hold.

"No," I say, my voice quiet but far from calm. "No, you don't get to care about whether or not I'm okay. Not when it's your fault my world has fallen apart. Because I might be alive, but I am far from okay and it's all your fault."

Kato's expression shifts to something akin to anguish. "Ash —"

"No!" I scream, my voice echoing through the dungeon as starlight pours out from me, filling the dark space. "You don't get to call me that. That nickname is reserved for people who I love, who love me."

"I do love you," Kato insists, his eyes filling with tears. "You have to believe me, Ash—tra. I never meant to hurt you. I swear to all the gods I didn't. I love you with all I have, and I only wanted us to be safe. You get that, don't you? People were trying to hurt us because of our magic and when the me in my dreams promised a way to protect you, I followed him. I didn't realize until it was too late that I was being influenced by something dark. I tried to get back to you. I swear I did. But I was stuck. I was trapped inside myself under the control of someone else. Please, believe me."

I didn't think my heart could crack into any more pieces, but somehow it does. What's left shatters and tears pour down my cheeks. My magic settles and dims around me as I try to figure out exactly what I'm feeling. A little part of me wants to tell Kato I forgive him. I know he was under the influence of Caedios. I asked Ehren to save him. I want my brother back, and I could have him. He's right here in front of me.

But there's another part of me that knows Kato had a choice, and that he chose wrong. He's the reason my soul was torn in two. It's because of him I couldn't get out of bed for days. It's because of him my world has gone dark. I can't forgive him. Not yet. Maybe one day, but not today.

"No, Kato," I whisper. "There is so much blood on my hands that I can never wash away. You turned me into a villain. I have become the thing of nightmares."

"No, that was the king," Kato argues, his voice hard. "I took care of him to protect you."

I shake my head. "If that were all, maybe I could find a way to move on and mend this broken thing between us, but I lost Alak because of you."

Kato inhales sharply. "What?"

A humorless laugh escapes. "So no one told you?"

Kato shakes his head. "No, no, no. I didn't kill Alak. I managed to hold him back enough to save Alak. He—I killed Bram. But you didn't love Bram anymore."

"Of course I still loved Bram!" I yell. I take a deep breath and squeeze my eyes shut. "I loved Bram and Makin and Alak." I open my eyes and meet his directly. "I loved them all and you stole them from me."

"I never stole Alak, and I didn't kill Makin."

"Alak died sealing the Isle that you opened, and Makin died at the claw of a Dragkonian. I almost lost Ehren to grief, as well, and that was before you hurt him beyond repair and cut off his hand. You destroyed almost everything in my life that was good."

Kato hangs his head. "I'm so sorry, Ash."

"No, you don't get to say you're sorry like that fixes anything."

He raises his head and meets my eyes. "I know." He sucks in a breath. "Will you ever forgive me?"

I shake my head. "I honestly don't know."

"What about you?" Kato shifts his attention over my shoulder and only then do I remember Pax.

I turn and look at Pax, who's staring at Kato.

"I want to," Pax whispers, his voice trembling. "Gods help me but I want to." He glances at me quickly before stepping closer to Kato. "I loved you—maybe I still love you—but this you isn't the you I fell in love with."

Kato nods. "That's fair." His hands fall from the bars and hang limply at his sides. "If I were in your places I doubt I could forgive me." He meets my eyes, and something close to sympathy stirs inside me. "I know I've said it and I know it's worthless, but I really am sorry."

He steps back into the shadows of his cell and sinks to the ground. He lifts his head.

"I still love you," he says, his voice so quiet I barely hear him. "Both of you."

When he doesn't say anything else, Pax loops an arm around my waist and tugs me against him.

"Let's go," he whispers.

I nod numbly and allow him to lead me from the dungeon. The world around me is a haze. I only recognize that he's brought me to the kitchens when a warm mug is pressed into my hands. I take a sip of something rich and sweet as Pax steers me to a stool off to the side. I take another sip and another, slowly coming back to myself. I can make it through this. By the time I've reached the bottom of my mug, I feel stronger. Somehow, I've survived this long and I will not let this loss define me. I will not let the darkness win. It might be hard some days—most days, even—but I will survive this somehow.

Now the war is over and it's time to heal, though that healing may be painful. For some of us, it may take a lifetime.

But we have no choice but to move forward. I rise from my stool and manage to offer Pax a smile. Together, we will heal and start again.

We are strong.

We are powerful.

We are the stars amid the storm, and we will not let the darkness keep us down.

EPILOGUE

ASTRA

Immortality. It sounds good but it's hard. I've lived a long time. I've seen many beautiful things and experienced many sorrows.

I saw Ehren reign for fifteen years before he stepped aside in favor of giving the kingdom to Jessalynn to rule alone. He heralded in the most prosperous times for Callenia, freeing Athiedor and strengthening relations and allies. He was good and fair and most loved of any king. His people didn't understand why he stepped down, but I did. And I was proud of him for ruling as long as he did. He and Cal lived out their remaining days in solitude, blissfully hidden away in the Summer Palace, which they enchanted and warded to keep most everyone away. They both died naturally of old age within days of each other.

When word got out of Ehren's death, the world mourned. We had visitors from every corner of the continent. He was buried with a grand ceremony and many honors, Cal by his side. In the courtyard of the Summer Palace I had a marble statue erected of Ehren and Cal holding the magical blades together. I'm half surprised Ehren didn't rise from the dead to make me take it down, but I imagine that Cal held him back, telling him that he deserved it and many more.

Jessalynn led Callenia through the next several years with ease, building on what Ehren started. She had four children of her own, and every single one of them called me "Auntie." She offered me the position of Court Sorceress, but I stepped down when Ehren did. My heart just wasn't in it anymore. When she died, her oldest child became king. He also offered me a court position, but by that time, too many ghosts haunted the castle.

Cadewynn outlived her brother by ten years. After going on an expedition across the continent researching and cataloging magical creatures with Sama and Nyco, she spent her last years buried deep in the libraries of Naskein. Her research and histories changed the world and the way people viewed magic. She made a huge difference, but remained quiet and humble until she drew her last breath.

Kai is buried in the mountains of the Hundan Valley in an unmarked grave next to where he buried his sister. It was what he wanted. After the war, he spent many years leading the pack in Paravlia with Nova at his side. They even went exploring together so Nova could add to their collection of maps. In his later years after Nova died, he sought me out. He was old and gray, but otherwise unchanged. I treasured the last few years we spent together until he went peacefully in his sleep.

Ievis spent a decade or so with Ronan in Athiedor as Ronan fulfilled his duty as Clan Lord. One day Ronan named Saran his heir and followed Ievis into the realm of the Fae. Since he combined his life force with Ievis's, he still lives. We visit each other occasionally, but not nearly often enough.

Prince Luc formally courted Mara and eventually made her

a queen over Ascaria. Her and Nicolette became fast friends, though Mara assured me no one would ever take my place in her heart. She made an amazing queen.

I grow weary now. Almost everyone I knew in life has gone, passed on. But I am still young to look at and have ages to go before I fade. I've met many people in my decades of life but none have impacted me as much as these few. Being in Embervein was too difficult after Ehren passed. There are too many memories in those walls. Too many ghosts. I am happy in my mountain home, secluded and alone.

Some days, I think of Kato and what he could have been had he not let darkness consume him. I miss him. Every single day. But I don't let my thoughts dwell on what-ifs. I can't. Even after all this time, his betrayal and mortal death still weigh on me. The immortal part of him died when Cal slew Caedios with the sword from the gods, so even though we did finally make peace before he and Pax left to carve out a little corner for themselves to serve out his banishment, he wouldn't have lived long enough to be by my side now. We should have lived forever, together, but that possibility has been long gone.

Today is a day like any other. I brew my tea and sit and watch the sun rise. I'm lost in the melody of morning when I hear a familiar but long-forgotten voice.

"You really make yourself hard to find these days, love."

I still, turning slowly as tears well in my eyes at the familiar face. His eyes hold the same weight as mine. Like mine, they're old eyes on a young face.

"Alak?" I say softly, my voice breaking.

"Hello, love," he says, smiling. "Are you practicing your magic? Every day?"

I laugh and nod, standing to my feet. "Of course. My first

instructor told me it's extraordinarily important, not only to keep my skills sharp, but also to keep my burden low."

"He sounds like a smart man, that instructor," Alak grins, that familiar light twinkling in his eyes.

"He had his moments. That's for sure." I shake my head and take him in, tears welling in my eyes. "How are you here? Am I dead?"

He smiles, tears glistening in his own eyes. "No, love. You're very much alive."

"Am I dreaming?"

He laughs and shakes his head. "Not this time, love."

He takes a tentative step toward me, and I close the distance between us. I reach out, placing my hand against his cheek. He's warm. He's flesh and blood.

"How?" I choke out, a tear sliding down my cheek.

"I was taken away a while, but I'm back now. When the barrier went up, my sword started to glow as the Dragkonians closed in. I used it to cleave a passage into the in-between, and Hycis used her Fae magic to seal it behind us." He pauses and glances away, shadows haunting his eyes. "We could see you and Rynia on this side, but we couldn't reach you. My sword wouldn't let me bridge the worlds again. For the last hundred years I've been forced to watch you through the fog."

He raises his eyes back to mine, smiling gently. "Hycis never gave up. She found a way back for us."

I nod, a tear sliding down my cheek. "And now you're back to stay?"

"Yes, love, and according to Hycis, my time in the in-between has made me immortal, so I will never leave your side again."

For a moment, we stand there, just staring at each other. And then, it's like no time has passed. We're young again.

Truly young. I'm in his arms and his lips are on mine. It's been too long. Decades of waiting and finally, the time has come. Fate has come to call.

Suddenly, the weight of the world doesn't seem so heavy, and eternity doesn't seem so long.

The End♥

ACKNOWLEDGMENTS

Loud screaming and crying noises

Wow . . . Just, wow. I can't believe my little ADHD brain finished not only this book but also an entire series. AN ENTIRE SERIES. In total, the Fire and Starlight Saga came to over 700,000 words. If I'm going to be entirely honest, there is absolutely no way I could have gotten to this point without the help and support of so many people.

To my family and friends who have cheered me on from the start and believed in me, thank you. I know half of you expected me to give up at some point, but HA! I did it anyways. So . . . Yeah . . .

I would be remiss if I didn't start with the love of my life, my partner, my spouse, Ben. You had to listen to me ramble on and on about these characters and this plot for three years now, and you put up with it. You also made me amazing artwork for the covers and other promotional things and let me pay you in snuggle bucks.

Lana, your input throughout this series has been invaluable. This book and this series wouldn't have been even halfway decent without you, so thank you, thank you, thank you, thank you.

I also have to give a HUGE shoutout to my Beta readers, Karin, Shanti, Megan, and Mandy. Your reactions gave me LIFE and your input really helped to make this book work. I don't know if you can spot all the changes, but I can promise you, this version of the book is a million times better than the version you read because of y'all. Like, seriously, you helped me make a dumpster fire into a much nicer trash can that someone would actually keep in their kitchen.

But the real MVP award has to go to Andi, my editor. At least 75% of the changes you make may be commas and general punctuation mistakes, but you take my writing to the next level. With your skills and eye for detail, my books went from good to great.

To Bob Jones University, the super conservative liberal arts university that gave me my degree in Publishing, I used the skills you taught me to write this fantasy series filled to the brim with queer characters, and you have no idea how much joy that brings me. I have my diploma displayed in my office over artwork of Cal and Makin.

And, of course, I have to say THANK YOU to all of my readers. I'm like a sad little flower that needs to bask in sunlight to grow. You were my sunlight, and you helped me grow a whole garden. Okay, that sounded incredibly cheesy, but you know what? I'm going to leave that in there, because your support really did mean everything to me, and without you, I probably would have given up on this project a long time ago. Thanks for coming back again and again. I love you all.

Exit, pursued by a bear.

EXTENDED AUTHOR NOTE

Mentions of Suicide/Self Harm

No suicide attempts are performed on the page, but a story is told in Chapter Thirty-One of a character's past suicide attempts. This character also experiences some self-harm, but no details are given. Another character struggling with depression struggles with brief suicidal thoughts and purposely clutches something tightly in his hand until it cuts his skin (Chapter Twenty).

Amputation, Decapitation

This book has several battle scenes that are bloody and violent. In one scene an enemy's hand is cut off in battle. In Chapter Twenty-Eight, a character undergoes off-page torture that leads to a battle ending in the loss of a hand as well as two decapitations. The descriptions are not overtly graphic and are over quickly. The following chapters in this character's POV occasionally show this character struggling to come to terms with the amputation.

PTSD & Past Trauma

This is a reoccurring thing throughout the book as Astra struggles with the guilt of having to kill off attacking enemies to survive and Alak battles with his past. Ehren also struggles to accept the losses he experienced previously as well as learning to cope with new injuries and his escalating duties in the war. Chapter Thirty-Eight shows a character struggling to accept help and treatment based on previous traumatic experiences.

Grief

Several characters grieve throughout the book as they relive previous traumas and experience new ones. This grief is especially strong Chapters Five, Six, Ten, Twenty, Forty-Four, and Forty-Nine, but there are glimpses of grief on and off throughout the book.

Depression, Anxiety

One character struggles with heavy depression throughout the book but it is especially heavy in Chapters Ten and Twenty. A character also has a brief panic attack in Chapter Ten and another slight panic attack in Chapter Twenty.

If you feel I have missed any content warnings, feel free to reach out to me: amberdlewisauthor@gmail.com

ABOUT THE AUTHOR

Amber D. Lewis is a highly combustible combination of caffeine, mismatched coffee mugs, and shiny things. In her spare time (and, quite frankly, when she's supposed to be doing other things) she writes fantasy and other stories.

The Fire and Starlight Saga is Amber's first series, though she has more books in the works.

facebook.com/amberdlewisofficialauthorpage

instagram.com/mugshots_n_bookthoughts

bookbub.com/profile/amber-d-lewis

goodreads.com/crymeariversong11

tiktok.com/@thewriteamber

patreon.com/amberdlewis